"No fast

...the officer said, his voice a growl in her ear, his breath hot on the back of her neck. "Or I'll remove you from the premises bodily."

Bodily. Which meant, his hands on her body. The idea crackled across her skin.

"Going for another cheap thrill?" she rasped.

"What?"

She lowered her voice to a near whisper and turned to look at him. "You grabbed my boob on our last tussle."

"That was an accident, and you know it. Come on, you think I need to cop a feel on a suspect to get off?"

No, she supposed not when he looked like that. Arrogant son of a bitch.

In her peripheral vision, she sensed other officers at the ready, but Kade's body heat enveloped her, overwhelmed her senses—and had her Dragon panting. Were they... flirting? No. Not possible. Why did her body tingle then? Why was her Dragon shivering with a lust she hadn't felt in forever?

ACCLAIM FOR JAMIE RUSH'S
THE HIDDEN SERIES

Dragon Mine

"Awesome...not to be missed...a quick, sexy read!"
—MyBookAddictionReviews.com

"It's just a quick taste of what's to come with the series but it was fun, satisfying, and has me ready for more...This one is worth the read if you love paranormal romance and just want a quick dragon fix."
—HerdingCats-BurningSoup.com

"The lighthearted approach to the dark paranormal world won me over...I liked the humor, I liked the love rediscovered story line, and I just plain liked the story!"
—TheWindowSeat13.com

"A great novella to begin things...I cannot wait for the rest of this series...Full of vivid imagination, emotional growth, and challenging battles both physical and magical, *Dragon Mine* is a must read."
—RomanceWitchReviews.blogspot.com

Dragon Rising

"A fast-paced paranormal romance, full of danger, mystery, and smoking hot romance...I'm completely hooked on this series and I'm looking forward to the first full length novel."
—ReadinginPajamas.wordpress.com

Also by Jaime Rush

MAGIC
POSSESSED

A Hidden Novel

JAIME RUSH

FOREVER

NEW YORK   BOSTON

Copyright © 2014 by Tina Wainscott
Excerpt from *Angel Seduced* Copyright © 2014 by Tina Wainscott

Forever
Hachette Book Group
237 Park Avenue
New York, NY 10017

www.HachetteBookGroup.com

Printed in the United States of America

First Edition: January 2014
10 9 8 7 6 5 4 3 2 1

OPM

Forever is an imprint of Grand Central Publishing.
The Forever name and logo are trademarks of Hachette Book Group, Inc.

The Hachette Speakers Bureau provides a wide range of authors for speaking events. To find out more, go to www.hachettespeakersbureau.com or call (866) 376-6591.

The publisher is not responsible for websites (or their content) that are not owned by the publisher.

ATTENTION CORPORATIONS AND ORGANIZATIONS:

Most Hachette Book Group books are available at quantity discounts with bulk purchase for educational, business, or sales promotional use. For information, please call or write:

Special Markets Department, Hachette Book Group
237 Park Avenue, New York, NY 10017
Telephone: 1-800-222-6747 Fax: 1-800-477-5925

This book is dedicated to everyone who has a dream and works like hell to make it come true.

Chapter 1

The scream tore through the cypress trees and gripped Violet Castanega's heart like a strangler fig's roots. She dropped the amethyst and silver necklace on her worktable and ran out the open doorway of her workshop. Chumley, her tan hound, ran up beside her, his brow wrinkled as she stared in the direction of the sound.

It wasn't good when a man screamed like that. That was not the sound of horseplay or a foot being run over by a swamp buggy, but of life being torn from a body. Her brothers and cousins flashed through her mind as she ran barefoot across the muddy ground. She'd spent thirty years roaming the acres of her family's land, most of them without shoes. Rocks and roots dug in, but she knew instinctively how to shift her weight to soften the impact. Chumley ran beside her, his paws slapping the ground.

Another sound, lower and more guttural, squeezed her heart, and damn it, she was already having a hard time breathing. She thought it came from the southern edge of their land. The stitch she usually felt when running pinched her side like two sharp claws.

She emerged from the thicket of pine trees into the more open area of the palm farm, running between the low rows of bushy sago palms and through the outer edge of thicker areca palms. Her pace slowed as she searched for whoever had screamed. She heard shouting. Others were coming, too. She tried to pick out the identity of the voices that were filled with the same fear she felt, but they were too far away.

Her foot hit something. Grabbing on to a feathery palm frond didn't stop her momentum. She pitched forward, her hands sinking into the soft ground. Before she'd even scrambled to her feet, she found him, bloody and motionless on the muddy ground. Gods, not mud—blood. It soaked the ground around the naked body. Her gaze zeroed in on the source, a gash on a man's chest. Then it moved to his face.

"No, no, no." She dropped down beside him, clamping her hands on his cheeks. "Arlo!"

He was warm. Not cold, not stiff. But he didn't respond. She searched for a pulse point at his throat, but her finger slid in his blood. His clothing lay shredded nearby. That meant he'd Catalyzed, turning Dragon so quickly that he didn't have time to disrobe. Which meant he'd been attacked. Her Dragon tingled with awareness, the threat of danger rolling through her cells like a wave of energy.

Two people ran closer, smashing through palm fronds. She opened her mouth to call for help but stopped. Maybe those footsteps belonged to her family and maybe not.

"I thought I heard Vee," a man said.

"But that scream...it wasn't her."

"I'm here!" she called, hearing her voice falter.

Her brothers burst into view, their wide-eyed gazes taking her in as they rushed forward.

Ryan and Jessup took in the blood, and Arlo, and both went into defense mode, spinning around, their bodies rigid and ready to fight.

"Are you all right, Vee?" Jessup asked, sliding his wary gaze toward her.

"I...yes. But Arlo..."

"Keep watch," Jessup told Ryan, dropping down beside her. He assessed her with light green eyes that usually sparkled with mischief or flared with ire. Crescent Dragons had flames in their eyes, visible only to other Crescents, and Jessup's blazed with anger and shock. "What happened?"

"I...don't know. I heard the scream and came running, probably like you did. He was already...dead."

Jessup felt for his pulse, too, with a hand much steadier than hers. He spit out an expletive, his mouth tightening. His voice was a growl as he again surveyed their surroundings. "Someone came onto our land and killed him. Ambushed him, no doubt. How the hell did they sneak up on Arlo?"

Arlo was the oldest of her siblings and had seen the most action during the centuries-old feuds between the Dragon clans.

"He was drinking," she said. "I smell booze on him."

He'd struggled with alcohol and drugs the last few decades, a dangerous combination when you were a Crescent. You couldn't afford to be out of control when your DNA held the essence of a god, especially when you were a Crescent Dragon. The Dragon part took advantage of weakness, eager to manifest and play. Or kill. Arlo's very human addictions gave control to a magick beast that lived by its baser instincts.

Jessup lifted Arlo's body slightly. "Someone killed him for his power."

Violet sucked in a breath. The blue Dragon tattoo sprawled across his chest was gone. "He's been Breathed." Her Amethyst Dragon, wrapped all the way around her like a belt, vibrated in fear and anger.

Every adult Dragon wore their Dragon's essence on their body, a magnificent image that manifested during their Awakening ceremony when they turned thirteen. The fact that it moved and kept watch over its person was hidden from Mundane humans, who saw only a regular tattoo. When one Dragon Breathed in the power of another, their Dragon disappeared.

Ryan stepped closer, still watching but taking in his brother's still form. "It's got to be one of the Fringe clans."

The Fringe consisted of the marshy land along the outskirts of Florida City and Homestead, where several Dragon clans had settled.

Violet came slowly to her feet. "It doesn't make sense. We haven't had any clashes or encroachments lately."

"The Murphys started an alligator farm, damned copycats. That's an encroachment. And the Augusts copied our tourist show."

"Both were years ago. And *they* copied *us*, so why would they come onto our land and attack?"

The fire in her brothers' eyes scared her. There had been relative peace—okay, more like the Cold War kind—for the last ten years. Nothing more than a few broken bones and torn flesh. She craved that peace, being able to wander their land without fear of being attacked.

Jessup laid Arlo back down. "We need to kill someone." Heat radiated off him as his Dragon pushed to Catalyze.

"We don't even know who did it," she said. "Let me do some snooping, find out who's behind this."

Ryan shook his head. "No, I think we need to kill someone."

"Stop." Her own impulsive nature, along with her Dragon, pushed hard to join in. "Give me some time to figure this out. If someone's got a vendetta against us, I can find out who it is. No doubt, he's been talking, bragging, or bitching down at Ernie's."

Jessup's eyes flared in his bossy, big-brother way. "You're not going to Ernie's by yourself. I—"

She pressed her finger to his collarbone. "You are not coming with me." She shifted her gaze to Ryan. "You'll both barge in, banging heads together. And then you'll end up in the Conference Room, and it won't even be with Arlo's murderer. I can take care of myself. Haven't I had the best teachers?"

"Yeah, but—"

"Let me approach this logically. Once I get a lead, I'll let you know. Then—"

"We kill someone," Jessup said.

"Yes, we kill them." Violet met Ryan's gaze. "We'll scrape out his or her eyeballs and feed them to the gators." The old Violet reared her head and bared her fangs. The one who jumped into a fight without thinking, who'd attacked an officer of the Hidden to defend Arlo, even when he was in the wrong. The Violet who used to be as hotheaded as the rest of her family. She took a breath. "But if you go off half-cocked and kill the wrong person, it'll start a war again. Dad died because of this damned feud business. So did Grandpa and Great-Uncle Hank and . . . the list goes on. I don't want to lose you two. I'll find out who's behind this. I promise."

Ryan looked at Jessup. "She is good at ferreting out information. She figured out which of the cousins was stealing our oranges. And the idjits who were digging up the royal palms at the nursery."

Jessup was still taking in the desperation in her eyes. She let him see all the hurt, just for a second. Any longer and he'd chide her for it. Castanegas didn't cry; they got revenge. That was their motto. But that motto would get them killed.

Jessup made a grunting sound. "All right, cupcake. You've got a day."

"Give me two."

He shook his head but said, "Then we start digging around ourselves."

Violet knew exactly what kind of digging he meant.

The sign on the roof of the ramshackle building read THE FRINGE. Couldn't get clearer than that who belonged, at least to the Crescent community. Ernie couldn't hang a MUNDANES NOT WELCOME sign, because regular humans didn't know they were called Mundanes by Crescents. They didn't even know there *were* Crescents, or a facet of their world called the Hidden that contained people who turned to Dragons, sorcerers called Deuces, and descendants of fallen angels called Caidos. Not to mention demons, Elementals, and other creatures from which nightmares were made.

The bar sat on the outer edge of Florida City, tucked in a grove of oaks dripping with Spanish moss. Only four other vehicles were in the lot, as she'd expect at midday.

Ernie had owned the place for a hundred and eighty years. He belonged to none of the Fringe clans, which made him neutral—a status he held on to with calloused hands.

Her boots crunched on peanut shells as she walked into the gloomy interior. The large space was divided up into separate areas to accommodate clutches of clan groups. Ernie demanded civility in the public space, banishing those who participated in fights.

"Violet, a surprise to see you in here." Ernie, with a face that looked as though he'd been crunched in a vise from top to bottom, set a bowl of peanuts on the bar as she approached. "None of your people are here."

She'd had to drag home a drunk brother and even her father a time or two. Sometimes they needed assistance, not because they'd had too much to drink but due to the activities in the Conference Room, where disagreements were settled in a way that required no civility. All of her brothers had fought in there at one time or another, coming out broken and bloody. And that's when they'd won.

She glanced at the four men playing darts over in the corner and fought not to roll her eyes. Augusts. She clenched her fists at the sight of Bren, who was already giving her a lascivious smile. As he always did, he made a V with his fingers and waggled his tongue suggestively in the crotch.

She stuffed her disgust, refusing to give him the satisfaction, and turned back to Ernie. "I'm here to see you."

His wiry eyebrows bobbed in surprise. "You know you're a bit young for me."

"You're hundreds of years too old for me. So stop flirting and give me an AmberBock draft."

"You break my heart, you do." But he wore a smile as he pulled the draft.

Because of their god essence, Crescents lived longer than Mundanes—and aged very slowly. Ernie looked to be in his sixties. At thirty-four, she was a mere babe in Crescent terms. She idly cracked a shell and lined up the peanuts side by side on the bar.

He set the frosty mug on the shellacked bar top. "What're you after then, if not my buff, brawny body or rapier wit?"

So not in the mood for humor, such as it was, she swallowed back the grief that wanted to bubble out. "Arlo's been murdered."

Ernie digested that, his wide mouth flattening even more. "Damn. What happened?" After she told him, he shook his head but didn't look shocked.

"There's been talk, hasn't there? If something's going on, it usually starts here. Nothing gets past you."

He soaked in her ego strokes, his shoulders widening. "I pick up tidbits here and there." Then he caught on to her, and his proud expression hardened. "But I stay out of it. Switzerland and all."

"Ernie, I'm not asking you to take sides. Just pass on the gossip."

His gaze flicked to the men. "Fringers have been edgy lately. Restless and downright ornery. I heard there's a big solar storm erupting, and we're already getting the effects of the flares."

"We've felt the effects of solar storms before, and it didn't make people kill."

He hesitated, then relented. "There's been murmurings, but not about your clan."

She took a draw of her ice-cold beer, feeling it tingle across her tongue and down her throat. Damn. Clan problems again. "What about then?"

"Defensive, not offensive." He leaned across the bar, as casual as could be, and flicked off the peanuts. "Arlo's not the first Fringer to be whacked lately."

This was getting worse. "Who?"

Ernie held out his squat fist and flipped out one finger. "Liam Peregrine, killed a week or so ago." Another finger straightened. "They found something at the scene that pointed to the Wolfrums. So no surprise that Peter Wolfrum was Breathed two days later."

She pulled out her phone and put in the names. She had a photographic memory, but hearing information didn't imprint worth a damn.

He shifted his gaze to the men by the dartboard, and his voice lowered. "Larry's grandmother, Shirley, six days ago. I don't know what they found, if anything, but two days later, Bobby Spears turns up dead."

No, she didn't want to be in this place again of tension, hatred, and constant fear. "Bobby is—was—a kid!" she hissed. "What, seventeen?"

Ernie nodded, his expression somber. "Good kid, too, for a Fringer, anyway."

She fought not to look at the Augusts and clue them in that they were talking about them. Another blunt finger on Ernie's hand flicked out. Gods, no more.

"Dan Murphy, killed two days ago."

"Breathed?"

"Every one of 'em."

Her stomach cramped, like a demon had reached right into her insides and twisted it.

"With the history between your clans, could be they thought you did it. Arlo's death was probably an act of revenge, like some of the others."

"Did they find evidence?" She would not believe someone in her family was involved.

Ernie shrugged. "Haven't heard one way or the other."

She was cold all over but tried to reveal nothing of what she felt. "We wouldn't attack another clan unprovoked." Fringers always had a reason, or at least they believed they had one. "Six murders in ten days. That's crazy. And scary as hell." She finished half her beer and set a twenty on the bar.

As she strode over to the Augusts, they snapped to attention. The oldest son scanned her, clearly trying to assess her intent. *Come on, like I'm dumb enough to confront four of you?*

She kept a table between them and gave Larry, the oldest member present, her attention. "I heard about your grandma. I'm sorry to hear that."

Larry narrowed his eyes. "How'd you know?"

The second oldest stepped forward. "Ernie told you, didn't he?"

"I heard it through the grapevine and was trying to get him to confirm it before I approached you. The way that he tried to pretend ignorance told me it was true."

Larry stuck a wad of chew between his teeth and gum. "You wouldn't happen to know anything about it, would you?"

"I know we didn't do it. And that she's not the only one." The Fringers didn't go around advertising when they'd lost one of their own. It revealed that your family was now a little weaker. "Sounds like trouble's brewing again." She curled her hands over the back of a chair. "*You* wouldn't happen to know anything about Bobby Spears's death, would you?"

Dragon energy crackled off them. Bren, the youngest and, unfortunately, the one she knew best, stepped forward. "Not a thing, sweetheart. Kid was a jerk. Probably into something or other." He came around the table and stopped too close for her comfort.

She didn't back away. "Why would someone kill Shirley?" The August matriarch was one of the few of their clan who didn't cause trouble. "I'm not being nosy," she said when no one spoke up. "We've had peace in the Fringe for years now. Six murders in ten days... someone's trying to stir things up. I want to find out who."

That got her a chorus of low chuckles. Bren placed his hands on her shoulders, angling his hips closer. "Aw, Vee, you gonna make things right for all us Fringers? Get justice?"

She pushed him back. "You don't get to touch me."

He gave her a contrite look. "You liked when I touched you before. You used to sigh..."

She slugged him, which slammed his head to the side. The others stepped closer, their fists tightening as Bren caught his balance.

He laughed it off, even as his eyes still swam. "Damn, Vee, you still got a hard-on for me, don't you?"

"Stop calling me Vee, and I couldn't care less about you." She narrowed her eyes. "You do know women don't get hard-ons, right? Or are you getting the genders of your lovers confused?"

She wouldn't admit how much she wanted to cut off his balls and feed them to the raccoons, because that would reveal how much he'd affected her. He'd wooed her, saying all the right things. Not how beautiful or clever or sexy she was, but how their getting together would heal the rift between their families. She'd let down her defenses and bought it.

Eventually all his questions about their alligator operation, cleverly coated in mild curiosity, burrowed down to her cynical self. He was using her to get information about their farm and shows. Not long after, they opened up their own alligator wrestling tourist attraction. She'd been so mad at herself, but not because her heart had been broken. She hadn't given it to him. Her pride had taken a big hit, even to this day, and that was nine years ago.

She turned to the oldest brother. "Did the Spearses kill Shirley?"

He hesitated, then said, "Yeah."

"How do you know?" She'd seen enough retaliatory murders based on nothing more than speculation.

Bren's expression changed to fierce. "We found that stupid skull handkerchief Bobby wears all the time about twenty yards from her body."

None of this felt right to her. Not that Fringe justice ever felt right. The Spearses would rear up and strike back. And the wars would start once more.

Chapter 2

She was either making a huge mistake or saving her family. Too damned bad she didn't know in advance which it was going to be. Violet stood on the steps of the Guard's headquarters. She'd heard that it was fashioned after the government buildings on the Crescents' ancestral island of Lucifera, and that this building had been here since the beginnings of Miami.

There was no written history of Lucifera, only legends handed down orally over many generations. As in many ancient cultures, Luciferians worshipped gods specific to the island. A fluke of nature allowed several gods to become physical on the Earth plane, where they fell to sensual temptations. Eventually, two disgruntled gods and one overly righteous angel decided procreation was a bad idea and instigated a war between their progeny. The war caused a violent schism that not only reversed the gods' physicality but also broke the island apart, forcing the inhabitants to flee to Florida.

Etched symbols like hieroglyphics adorned the two-story columns along the front of the otherwise nondescript building. Violet recognized several symbols, mostly the Dragon gods with which she was familiar. Some of her Crescent jewelry store customers requested pieces with the symbols for various gods. No one ever requested a necklace depicting the Tryah, the trio who started the war.

And we're on the verge of war now.

Maybe rage and violence were in the blood, the vengeful tendencies just a throwback to the flawed beings that sired them so many generations ago.

The imposing dark blue doors did not invite the curious. Crescents knew the "financial services firm" was a front for the Hidden's police force. One couldn't go to the Miami police complaining that your neighbor's magick was disrupting your satellite signal. Or that your brother was murdered by a Dragon. The Guard's main focus was enforcing Rule Number One: Crescents must never expose their magick to the Mundanes. Then there were Crescents who'd gone Red, their term for magick psychosis.

Violet betrayed her clan with every step she took toward those ultra-tall double doors. As much as she hated the idea of going to the Guard for help, she had no choice. There was going to be a lot more bloodshed if she couldn't convince them to intercede. She took a deep breath as she clutched the steel handle. *Act like none of your family has ever been on the wrong side of the law.*

Compared to the bright Miami sunshine, the lobby was dim and cool, dominated by shades of blue. Even the woman behind the reception desk wore a dark blue blouse.

"I need to speak to someone about a murder." That last word caught in Violet's throat. When the receptionist asked her name, "Castanega" came out even hoarser. She had to repeat it, and the woman's eyebrows rose.

Yes, I'm one of those *Castanegas.*

The woman's previously placid expression soured. "Did you commit murder or are you reporting on behalf of the victim?"

"The victim."

She opened a drawer, pulled out four pieces of paper, and clipped them to a board with a practiced hand. "You'll need to fill these out."

Violet could only stare at the words DEATH REPORT at the top. Her fingers trembled as she reached for the clipboard. The woman jabbed a pen in her direction and walked into the back room.

Crescents in general had their prejudices against Fringers, viewing them with the jaundiced disdain bestowed on hillbillies. Since Fringers didn't want outsiders poking into their business, they happily perpetuated the stereotype. Mostly it worked, and the Guard stepped in only when illegal activities might draw the attention of the Mundane police.

The joke was on the Crescent population, really. Fringe families had taken land no one else wanted long ago and cultivated it. The marshes and swamp areas were the most beautiful, rich, and private of all the inhabitable land in the area. To Violet, the busy, loud city was the unwanted area.

The receptionist returned a few moments later. "Someone will be with you shortly."

I bet.

She bet right. Once all the papers were filled out, with the cold facts of her brother's life and death crammed into lines not nearly long enough, she spent the time checking emails on her phone and confirming a couple of appointments with jewelry stores. Finally she played a couple rounds of Angry Birds before a voice penetrated. "Miss Castanega."

A young man stood in the open doorway with that same sour look. He'd drawn the short straw, evidently. She was so sick of being judged by her name, her family.

She swallowed the weariness and plastered a professional expression on her face. He took the clipboard and said nothing more, just walked into a large room filled with desks. Expecting her to follow, she assumed. The Guard's officers wore business attire, not uniforms. She didn't need to see his magick tattoo identifying him as the lowest officer, an Argus. The fact that he led her to one of the desks crammed into the center of the room said as much. There were only two levels of officers in the Guard. Vegas handled higher-level issues, and Arguses handled everyday Crescent matters.

Several other officers sat at their desks, engaged with complainants. She heard snippets of conversations about the crazy neighbor releasing orbs from his roof and Aunt Betty running naked down the street. Those officers not busy watched her openly, as though they were ready to be amused. Someone whistled the banjo theme from *Deliverance*.

Idjit. That movie was set in Georgia, not southern Florida.

She gripped her alligator purse handle tighter. The skin came from their farm, the purse from the company that fashioned them into four-hundred-dollar bags and belts. She wanted to tell these people that their operation used every part of the gator so nothing went to waste. That the income from their various enterprises provided well for the families it supported, far better than the Guard probably paid their employees. They also ensured that the alligator population thrived, that the nests in the wild were protected.

Violet met a few curious gazes, most giving her a dose of a sneer. Her Dragon rolled over her senses, bringing everything into hyperfocus. She felt its heat as it pressed close to the surface.

Back. Not a good place to show yourself. You'll—we'll—be pounced, blasted, and incinerated before we can blink.

She pushed it back deep inside her and found the more tolerable sight of paintings situated between doors, done in various mediums, styles, and probably eras. Depictions of the gods, even the ones who fell. For younger generations, the gods were mythical, part of distant history. Her clan descended from Mora, Dragon goddess of creativity and beauty. Here she was illustrated as a gorgeous green Dragon surrounded by flowers and butterflies. She was about to snap her fangs around the neck of a bird with bright plumage.

The man led her to a female officer's desk. "Here, K, this one's all yours." He shoved the clipboard at her. "I've got better things to do."

Mia Kavanaugh, according to her nameplate, gave him an acidic look but turned to Violet. "Please sit." Her gaze skimmed the top of the report, and Violet could tell the moment her last name registered.

Mia's moss green eyes took her in, swirling with trademark Deuce mist that, like Dragon's flames, could only been seen by Crescents. Mia set the clipboard down and met her gaze. "Ms. Castanega, please tell me your family hasn't killed the Mundane who is screaming to the world that there's a gator ape in the swamp. The supposed huge alligator that walks upright at times."

Dragonfire, that's where she was going? "Even though Smitty's always sneaking around on our private land with his video cameras, we have refrained from harming him. This has nothing to do with him."

"You piqued his interest. One of your family members obviously revealed your magick. Which makes you a reckless element—"

"This has nothing to do with that idjit, and we are not reckless." Well, most of the time. Wild, daring, and a little bit crazy, yes, but all aware of the punishment for breaking Rule Number One: death. "The murder I'm here to report is my brother's."

"Details?"

Don't cry. You're good at holding back tears after years of being teased by three brothers. Now two...

She held back the rest of her thoughts and the sob that threatened to erupt. "My brother Arlo was murdered yesterday by a Dragon who Breathed his power. He was attacked on our property without provocation. But—"

"You know the Guard doesn't interfere with the swamp clans' feuds." Mia lifted the clipboard, her face relaxing as she thought her job here was done. "We will, of course, file the proper paperwork."

So his death would be filed with the government but not the suspicious nature of it. No need to involve the Muds—the Mundane police force.

"I'm not just here because of my brother's murder." Violet pulled out a piece of paper and laid it on the desk. It contained the names of the other deceased Fringers. "Swamp trash," she knew they were called more often than the Fringer moniker they'd given themselves long ago. "As I was about to say, there have been five similar murders in the last ten days. All Breathed. Someone's inciting the feuding clans."

Mia barely glanced at the list. "The feuding clans are inciting the feuding clans. That's what you do down there."

"We've been at peace for the last ten years. But it won't last. My family is ready for blood. I'm sure these other families are, too. That's how it works: someone's killed for 'good reason' and there's a retaliation murder, and then another." She thought of one family in particular that had been completely wiped out twenty years ago. It pained Violet to know her family was responsible, even if the Garzas deserved it.

Violet pointed to the list of names. "I bought time by doing this research to show a pattern. But my family is only going to hold out so long before they start looking for justice." She met her gaze. "You can prevent bloodshed by finding out who's behind this. A teenage *boy* died."

Movement beyond the woman caught her eye. One of the office doors opened, and a man walked out. Her Dragon snarled at the sight of the Deuce Vega who had tangled with her family on several occasions in the name of the Guard, Kade something or another. The one she'd attacked. *But let's just forget about that, shall we?* His green-eyed gaze homed right in on her. Something fiery sparked between them, surprising her because she didn't know what it was exactly. *Sure as hell wasn't* that. She turned back to the Argus. "Will you investigate?"

Mia shook her head. "I'm sorry, but this looks like typical Fringe infighting, and we are way too busy to deal with that particular kind of crazy right now. Maybe it's the effect of living on the edge of the Field. Who knows what the lack of full *Deus Vis* does to you after a while—"

"We get plenty of *Deus Vis*."

Latin for "god force," it was the essential energy that sustained Crescents' god essence. The supernatural energy emanated from the crystals that composed the island of Lucifera. The energy was still present. Ships and planes in the Bermuda Triangle found that out firsthand when their instruments malfunctioned. The Field of *Deus Vis* extended in a crescent shape into the Miami/Fort Lauderdale area, fading at the edges. The Fringe lay at the southern curve of that edge.

"But how would you know? I don't mean to sound derogatory, but to give you an example, if you grow up crazy, that's your norm."

If Violet cared to consider it, maybe it made sense. The Fringers *were* on the edge, in more ways than one. But she didn't care to consider it. This Deuce had a lot of nerve to write off her concerns, to dismiss the death of her brother and five other Fringers as the by-product of a *Deus Vis* deficiency.

Violet stood, snatching up her paper. Her cheeks burned when she saw those who had been listening, smirks on their faces. Kade's expression, as he paused outside the door, held curiosity, as though he were trying to figure out who she was. The last time he'd seen her she was grimy with mud, having just come from feeding the alligators.

Kade stood near a brass plate that read LT. ALEC FERRO. Maybe the lieutenant would be more open-minded. She aimed for Kade, pasting on a docile expression. The jerk was a waste of honey-colored hair and a mouth made for sin. Too bad a scar marred his gorgeous face, though the waves of his hair partially hid it. She remembered when the wound was fresh, bleeding like a bitch down the side of his cheek.

"Can I help you?" he asked, his shoulders stiffening as he obviously realized she shouldn't be wandering around in here on her own.

She feinted left at the last second, pushing open the door and approaching a middle-aged man at his desk whose fire in his eyes indicated he was Dragon like her. Good. He came to his feet.

"I'm sorry to barge in on you, but your officer isn't taking me seriously. My name is Violet Castanega."

A hand clamped onto her arm, followed by the scent of sandalwood. Kade took her in with a surprised expression. "You're *Violet Castanega*?"

Yeah, the one who jumped on you. She tried to yank her arm away and focused on Ferro. "I need to talk to someone reasonable."

"I'll escort her out, sir."

Kade started to pull her away, inciting her Dragon. Getting into an altercation with a Vega at the station— or Catalyzing to Dragon—was only going to prove how uncivilized Fringers were. Or crazy, as the Argus had implied. She would not prove them right.

"Dragons are being murdered." She kept her gaze on Ferro as Kade pulled her toward the door. "Someone is targeting the Fringer families, starting a war..."

Ferro held up his hand. "Wait, Kavanaugh."

She'd been out the door, but Kade stopped at his commanding officer's order. Ferro crooked his elegant finger, indicating that Kade close the door. Several officers, including Mia, hovered, ready to tackle her.

Mia Kavanaugh. Ah, the two green-eyed jerks were related. Even though Kade looked to be in his late twenties or early thirties, he *felt* older. Mia was probably younger than Violet.

She focused on Ferro, who felt much older. He was distinguished and poised, the benefit of having lived a long life filled with privilege and pride. Behind him, a large, gilt-framed portrait showed a Dragon incinerating a village. The plate mounted on the bottom of the frame read DRAKOS. Dragon god of war, and one of the Tryah. This man apparently idolized him. Maybe not so good.

Ferro said, "Finish what you were going to say."

Her control had paid off. She pulled free of Kade's grip, handing Ferro the paper on which she'd outlined the timeline of deaths. "Someone is killing and Breathing Dragons, and they've chosen the Fringe clans because they know the Guard will figure it's us misbehaving. One of the most vengeful families was targeted first. An unprovoked attack on the Peregrines guarantees backlash, so who in their right mind would do it? Then the Peregrines killed one of the Wolfrums, their biggest and closest foe."

Ferro leaned back in his chair, perusing the list. "Sounds like the typical barbarian activity we've seen before."

"But the initial attacks weren't provoked. You hear things in the Fringe, at the least, rumors. Three people were killed, so the victims' families felt they had reason to take revenge. We don't kill without reason. Someone wants war. I'm asking you to find out why."

"What would one hope to gain by inciting the clans?" Ferro rubbed the gold pendant he wore, a symbol for Drakos.

"That's what I'm hoping you can find out. Being the authority, and outsiders, maybe you could ferret out more information than I can."

"Fringers aren't exactly cooperative where the Guard is concerned. Which, frankly, is why I'm surprised that you've come to us. Does your family know you're here?"

She almost snorted. Thankfully she held it in. "No. We don't have a cordial relationship with the Guard."

Kade did snort. "If only you would stop breaking the law…"

She flashed him a flame-eyed look, even if he was right. The Fringers, her clan included, had a long history of flouting authority. When they claimed the land at the edge of the Field more than three hundred years ago, they'd decided they also lived on the edge of the law. "If the Guard intercedes and conducts an investigation, the clans would back off." She hoped.

Ferro glanced at her list, then at her. "I know it's upsetting to lose one of your family members, but these feuds have been going on for… well, since Lucifera. I remember the warnings about wandering into the pirate clan territories."

"You were there? On Lucifera?" The island had been destroyed *ages* ago.

He gave a curt nod. "Even then, the Castanegas and other clans had a reputation. The island's *Deus Vis* drew ships to it like a magnet, trapping the inhabitants the way we are trapped here. Some were pirate ships, crewed by barbarians. Those clans were already enemies, and their hatred for each other erupted into battles. They were banished to the far side of the island and carved out territories adjacent to one another. Just as they did here."

She craved more information about the island and the legends. None of her living clan members had been on the island. "So you remember the war?" She nodded to the painting.

"I was only eight at the time. I remember the fighting, but the Tryah were scapegoats." He gave her a tight smile. "At least that's my opinion. But you're not here to discuss Lucifera."

No, she wasn't. "This isn't about the feuds." She pressed her hand to her solar plexus. "I feel it here. Something isn't right."

"I think it's probably a combination of the temperament down there, plus the unusually strong fluctuations we've been seeing from the impending solar storm."

"We've felt the effects before, and they've never incited anyone to murder."

"I would suggest you weather the storm and stay out of trouble."

He was dismissing her.

Violet's gaze went to a map of Miami on the wall behind him. Went, in fact, to a red pin at the western edge of her clan's territory where Arlo had died. She took several steps forward, Kade shadowing her.

"You know about the murders." She tapped her photographic memory and pictured where the other Fringers had been killed. This map pinpointed each gruesome location with a red pin. "What are the yellow pins for?"

Ferro moved to block her view of the map with his compact muscular body. "We are investigating, Ms. Castanega.

As you can see." His words grated out. "But I cannot discuss the details of the case at this time." This didn't make sense. He was dismissing her, yet he knew about the murders. "Thank you for your concern," he said. "I'm sure it took a lot of courage for you to come here." He looked beyond her. "Escort her out."

Okay, *that* was a dismissal. Kade put his hand on her back to guide her out the door. The prickles that zinged through her at his touch were as odd as what she'd felt when their eyes had met. She involuntarily jerked away from that electric touch. He grabbed her arms and shoved her face-first to the wall, pinning her wrists with his iron grip.

"No more fast moves," he said, his voice a growl in her ear, his breath hot on the back of her neck. "Or I'll remove you from the premises bodily."

Bodily. Which meant, his hands on her body, carrying her right out of there. The idea crackled across her skin like the heat flush she got when she had to go into the alligator pens. Except Kade smelled a hell of a lot better. And she knew that firsthand, since all of his hard, muscular body was plastered against hers. Which should piss her off, not make her want to spin in his arms and test him on that bodily thing. Fortunately, she couldn't budge an inch, squashing that insane temptation.

"Going for another cheap thrill?" she rasped, her cheek mashed against the wall.

"What?"

She lowered her voice to a near whisper and turned to look at him. "You grabbed my boob on our last tussle."

"That was an accident, and you know it. Come on, you think I need to cop a feel on a suspect to get off?"

No, she supposed not when he looked like that. Arrogant son of a bitch. "It wasn't just an accidental brush. You lingered. And spread your hand to cover more area." In her peripheral vision, she sensed other officers at the ready, but Kade's body heat enveloped her, overwhelmed her senses—and had her Dragon panting.

He kept his voice low, too, his mouth close to her ear. "Interesting how you remember every nuance of it. You must have enjoyed it."

She bucked, anger pulsing through her. "I should have reported you, for all the good that would have done." Wait a minute. She could swear a hard ridge pressed against her back. Ignoring the odd sense of triumph, she said, "Mmm, seems like you're enjoying this."

"It's just an adrenaline reaction from a potential altercation with a troublesome Dragon."

"If you say so. I was only moving away from you. I don't like being touched. If I promise to be a good girl, will you let me go?"

The mist in his eyes swirled provocatively. "*Can* you be a good girl? Is that even possible?"

"Try me." She shifted her eyes to the group of officers behind him. "After all, you have plenty of backup."

A spark of playful challenge lit his eyes. "Oh, baby, I don't need backup."

What were they talking about? Oh, Heathe, Dragon goddess of sensuality, were they *flirting*? No. Not possible. Why was heat throbbing through her body then? Why was her Dragon shivering with a lust she hadn't felt in forever?

Enemy! I know it's been a while, and then only with boring ole Mundanes, but really. Have some self-respect, beast!

"I'll be a good girl," she said, hearing the contriteness in her voice.

"Mmm. We'll see about that." Kade released her, and she rubbed her shoulders where he'd held them. "I can find my own way out."

"Sorry, policy." His fingers settled on her mid-back again as he guided her toward the door. "I have to escort you."

She heard someone whisper, "Wouldn't want her to go bat-shit crazy in here."

Her mouth tightened in response, the only one she would show.

Another man murmured, "Kade said she's as nuts as the rest of the Fringers. I wouldn't mind her going nuts on me."

Several men chuckled, the thick sound of innuendo charging their laughter.

Kade lifted his hands, not looking the least bit contrite. "You did go crazy. Jumped me, tore a chunk of my hair out."

"You were beating my brother to a pulp."

"He deserved it. I came to arrest him. He should have gone peacefully. Instead he Catalyzed and went all scales and fangs on me."

She swallowed back the angry things she wanted to say as the memory of that terrible day returned. She eyed the fine line that lanced Kade's right eyebrow and across his temple. "Nice scar."

He paused at the door that led out to the reception area, drawing his finger across it. "Yes, it is. Scars are a badge of honor in the Guard. Arlo did me a favor." He arched that eyebrow. "Gives me a dangerous look."

"How'd that shiner work for you? Did that make you look mad, bad, and dangerous, too?"

A black guy who reminded her of Wesley Snipes hovered nearby, amusement on his face. "Kavanaugh, you didn't tell us this little girl gave you that shiner." He eyed her up and down, the kind of survey that made her feel marginalized. His taunting gaze remained in place as it shifted to Kade. "You must be getting soft."

Now it was Kade's mouth that tightened into a line. This was not friendly camaraderie, especially since the black guy was jabbing Kade in front of her.

Why the hell she had the insane urge to defend him, to say that he'd fought...well, like a tiger, she had no idea. No, take satisfaction at humbling him in front of his colleagues. And umbrage at the Wesley guy calling her "little." Not at five-foot-seven.

Get me out of here. She turned the door handle.

It wouldn't move. Damn. She wanted to leave. Now.

Kade leaned close, pressing a series of buttons and pushing the door open for her. "Allow me."

She gave him a look that, while it may not kill, hopefully would singe him. Except, no...he gave her a bemused half smile. She stalked out. Behind her, she heard the muffled laughter of the people who had no doubt heard every word of their exchange.

Chapter 3

Kade watched Violet Castanega's sassy little ass sashay through the lobby to the entrance. He could tell she wanted to look back at him; she started to but snapped her head straight, pushed the door open, and slammed it shut behind her. Wow, did she look different from the last time he'd seen her.

When he'd arrested Arlo six years ago, someone jumped on his back, wrapping her long legs around his waist and arms over his shoulders. He'd known instantly it was a woman—her breasts crushed against his back had been the first clue. Her shrill voice blasting his ear with "Let him go!" the second.

He'd reached back to dislodge her and accidentally grabbed her boob. Okay, maybe he had lingered on that firm and soft and luscious mound of flesh...for maybe two seconds. She'd nailed him in the eye with her elbow. It was only after he'd thrown her off that he realized it was Violet,

the once-lanky, scrappy teenager he'd seen during an earlier investigation into Arlo's activities.

Before she could launch another attack, he reminded her
that assaulting an officer would result in arrest, and she
backed off. She'd been wearing tattered jeans, a muddy
tank top, and boots, and she smelled of earth. A red scarf
covered her dark brown hair, but her braid had hung down
her back and tendrils of hair had escaped. To his surprise,
her untamed self had tugged at the rebellious, wild side
he'd had to stuff deep inside. And it still did, apparently.

The spark between them was bizarre. Never would he
nail a Fringer, doubly so, since they were all Dragons. Not
even one with silky hair falling over her shoulders and a
long, lean body. He returned to the pit, where several pairs
of eyes were on him.

"Did you spank her for giving you that shiner, Kavanaugh?" Treach called out, followed by a chorus of guf-
faws.

"I think you were a little too distracted and let her get
the best of you," Baker said. "You *wanted* to spank her."

Kade shook his head, learning long ago that to respond
was the weaker action. He headed to his office, a tantalizing image of Violet sprawled across his lap while he
spanked that lush behind flashing into his mind. That was
not helping his hard-on.

His sister, Mia, sidled up next to him. "What was *that*
about?"

"The shiner?" He waved it off. "She was fast, nailed me
while I was dealing with her brothers." He wasn't getting
into the boob part.

"No wonder you never mentioned who'd given you that
black eye. These chauvinistic bastards will never let you

live that down." She shot them a derisive glance and lowered her voice. "But that's not what I was talking about. There was an erotic vibe in the way you dealt with her, and ooh, the way the mist in your eyes is swirling now."

He kept all expression from his face, including annoyance at her observation. "I was making sure she didn't cause a scene. Nothing more."

She gave him a skeptical look, which he deserved because he knew exactly what she was talking about. He didn't have an answer for it either, because no way was he attracted to a Castanega. Even a sexy, sassy one. "Take note, little sister. With people like her, you've got to establish dominance immediately. The moment they think they've got the upper hand, they do."

The usual light of admiration returned to her eyes, the way it did whenever he imparted his wisdom to her. "I see that. You didn't let her get away with anything, while she completely got away from me. That's why you're one of the best Vegas in the department."

He loved her admiration, and he didn't. He knew too well how betrayed one felt when the object of your admiration fell and shattered to pieces. She was too young to remember when all the years of their father's sterling service to the Guard exploded in scandal. A woman had made wild accusations about a member of the Concilium, the government entity that oversaw the Hidden and instituted the rules. Somehow their father had gotten involved, emotionally, maybe romantically. Stewart Kavanaugh had helped the woman escape, and both were killed.

Everyone had kept the ugly details from Mia, then age seven. As far as she knew, a crazy woman attacked their father. Weeks later, their mother had taken her life, unable to deal with the betrayal and scandal. She was a selfish, weak woman who cared more about her reputation than her young daughter.

On top of that, Kade had been demoted to Argus. Some people complained that he'd been fast-tracked to Vega because of his father's influence and that he didn't deserve his position because his reckless behavior made the Guard look bad. Maybe that was true, but they conveniently forgot the thirty years that he was a Vega who closed almost every case. Five years of toeing the line, exemplary work, and living by the rules had earned him Vega again—humiliating, belittling years that changed him from cavalier and edgy to a model officer.

"Kavanaugh," Ferro called out, leaning out of his office. He saw Mia and added, "Kade." Ferro remained standing once Kade closed the door behind him. "Take the Castanega woman out."

The words hit Kade like a cold slap, so out of the blue he had to clarify in case he'd misheard. "'Take her out'? You mean kill her?"

"I thought you were beyond needing the terms explained."

Kade bristled. "For barging into your office?"

The corner of Ferro's mouth twitched. "You're questioning the order?"

"It seems extreme, sir, if that's what you're basing it on."

"It has nothing to do with her conduct here." Ferro gestured to the map. "We've been watching the Fringe for a while now. These killings are connected to her, and her act about being concerned is just that."

That assertion was nearly as surprising as Ferro's order. Kade saw Violet as many things, but murderously devious?

"Why do you think she came here asking for our help to stop the murders? Like you said, it took a lot of courage for her to step into this building."

"Not courage; a psychopathic mentality that runs in her bloodline. Remember, her family massacred a whole Fringe clan some years back. Our sources say the Castanegas are behind the recent murders, and Violet is right in the thick of it." Ferro lifted the paper she'd brought in. "Her coming here was undoubtedly part of some bigger plan. Drag us in and kill off our officers, maybe. Or get us to take out some of their enemies under false pretenses. Whatever her motive, it's part of some sick game. Eliminating her will serve as a warning when they see that the murder was not committed by one of their own. And hopefully put an end to this."

He let the paper drift down to his desk. "I don't care if they kill each other off in principle. Worthless pieces of trash, all of them. A blight on Crescent society. Their skirmishes have always acted as population control, but in the age of the Internet and instant news, they threaten to expose what we are."

The insults prickled across Kade's skin. He'd heard them spoken about his father after the debacle. He didn't like the Fringers, but he wasn't going to agree with Ferro's assessment.

Ferro leaned on the desk with both hands. "Make this your priority." Which meant drop everything and do it now.

Vegas were akin to Special Ops, called in when the mission was dangerous or required a special skill. He had to trust his superior. "I'll take care of it, sir."

"I don't appreciate having to explain myself to my officers."

Kade had to hold back his sneer. "Understood, sir."

The Guard didn't have people killed for less than a good reason. Kade wasn't always privy to the reasons, and, frankly, he'd never been concerned about it. Orders were orders. Still, the prospect of whacking Violet sank his stomach.

Because you felt her body against yours? And got a hard-on? Think with the right head, Kavanaugh.

He would carry out his task as ordered.

Kade drove south, through the city and toward the marshlands known as the Fringe. Normally, adrenaline would be shooting through his veins like a thousand Red Bulls on his way to a kill. This time he was having a hard time working up the excitement to do his job.

As he reached the edge of the Fringe, he felt a tightening in his gut. Finally. Except it wasn't eagerness or adrenaline. It was…dread? Because he didn't want to kill her. There it was.

Keep your focus. It's a job.

Each clan had a large parcel of land that was divvied up between the various subfamilies. Many had different businesses, nice legal ones like vineyards and farms. But sometimes their farms consisted of marijuana plants, one of Arlo's transgressions. The Guard cared more about the possibility of attracting the Muds' attention than the illegality of the farms.

Centuries of living as they saw fit gave the Fringers the impression that they were outside the bounds of the law. Centuries of living with the threat of being extinguished by your nearest neighbor made them skilled at fighting.

Violet was no delicate flower. She'd held back at Head-quarters. He knew her ferocity well enough. And yeah, he knew the feel of her breast, and her body wrapped around his...though not in the good way.

Not that you want her wrapped around you like that. Because that would make this assignment much more complicated.

His cock had different ideas, thickening at the memory. Hell, he wasn't even experiencing physical contact and there it was, waving to get his attention. He really needed to get laid.

Violet's faced flashed in front of him.

But not with her.

Earlier, he experienced that bizarre moment of spotting someone you knew but not recognizing them. She'd cleaned up nice, dressed in white pants that made her legs go on forever and a dark blue shirt that molded to her upper body. Though he would have definitely recognized her once she gave him the *go screw yourself* look.

Kade drove down a weed-overgrown gravel road and parked his car behind a stand of Brazilian pepper bushes. Between Arlo's drug running, some assault charges, and the old coot who'd seen a gator ape, Kade had been to Castanega property enough to know his way around. There was plenty of acreage for the family's enterprises; most centered around alligators. Demons were no big deal, but those scaly toothy creatures with perpetual grins gave him the creeps.

Kade walked the boundary between Castanega land and the long-vacant Garza land. This was not the cultivated, trimmed, and polished South Florida most people imagined. While the pepper bushes with the red berries took over open stretches of land, the tall feathery Australian pines created dense forests elsewhere. In places where the non-native plants hadn't invaded, slash pine trees with their long needles offered more sap than shade.

A wet summer left the ground muddy and created large marshes in some places. It was hard to walk quietly in muck. His black boots sucked free of the moist earth with every step. The smell of earth, mud, and decay filled his nostrils. Sweat trickled down his back. Even in the hot, muggy summers, Vega attire consisted of long sleeves. The black rayon allowed for movement and ventilation, but neither helped when trekking through the woods in September—a month that, in South Florida, typically was as steamy as the one before it.

Mosquitoes buzzed all around him, but none dared land on him. They seemed to sense the magick in Crescents, largely leaving them alone. But they *wanted* to suck his blood and hovered annoyingly all around. A startled hawk screeched and alighted from a branch. If he hadn't seen the hawk, he'd suspect it was the Fringe "language," whistles and nature sounds they used to communicate over distances. Like warning of an intruder.

Two things the uniform designer did allow for were quick-drying material and ease in extracting Deuce weapons. Kade ran his fingers from wrist to inner elbow, feeling the spark of magick. The dagger "tattoo" thrummed with magick, courtesy of a specially commissioned Guard tattoo artist.

He suspected Violet's home was a cabin in the western edge. Her face dominated his mind, the smell of her, the tingle he'd felt when her wrists were clamped in his hands, her body against the wall. A part of him had wanted her to dart off again, craving the chase. Because he knew he'd catch her.

He shook the thought away. Now he *would* catch her. And kill her. He didn't have to like or agree with the order; he simply had to carry it out. It wouldn't be the first time. Or the last.

He paralleled a gravel road, barely visible in the distance, until he spotted a burgundy Infiniti parked in the driveway. Synthetic pop music floated from somewhere beyond the house. He surveyed the area. The house was small but quaint, painted a soft yellow with white shutters and gingerbread trim. The recently mowed grass that surrounded the house in a tidy square was lush and green. Plants and flowers overran the planting beds, a wild mess. Except it wasn't, he realized, seeing a loose but deliberate arrangement of the various plants. Somehow the undisciplined aspect intrigued him more than the sculpted bushes and trimmed trees in his yard in Coral Gables.

He recognized the music now: Berlin, from the eighties. "The Metro." It fit Violet, tough and in your face. Odd, since Violet seemed too young to have been more than a child in the eighties.

Who cared what she liked to listen to? The knife tattoo came to life, filling his hand with the heavy feel of metal. He clutched the dagger as he rounded the rear corner of the house. Farther back sat a large workshop with several long tables in the center of the space and shelves that lined the walls. She was doing something at one of the tables.

He cut back into the woods and came up behind the metal building. As he sidled up along the side, he nearly gave himself away when his shoe bumped an alligator in the bushes. He slapped his hand over his mouth as he stumbled back. The alligator leered at him with glassy eyes. *Wait a minute.* Kade tapped the gator with his shoe. It was hard. Hell, the thing was stuffed. He crouched near the edge of the open bay and watched Violet.

Hopefully she was planning the next murder, doing something to prove her guilt. He tried to see inside the many clear boxes on the shelves. They looked like they were filled with colorful stones. She worked a pair of pliers on a leather strap with jerky movements, cursing when a string of beads fell and scattered all over. Damn. It wasn't destructive; it was jewelry. She bent and picked them up, her pants stretching tight over her ass. One bead bounced and landed within a few feet of him. She hadn't seen it, but a big, dopey-looking dog did. Then the dog saw him.

Uh-oh.

Its tail thumped on the floor, which was covered in outdoor carpet. Okay, not a guard dog but still problematic. He stepped out of view and heard Violet throw the beads and issue a guttural expletive.

She darted out of the workshop, her face buried in her hands, and passed within three feet of him. The dog followed, glancing back at him. Kade remained in place, watching her heaving shoulders as she reached the thicket of cypress and pine trees and fell to her knees.

The dog flopped down beside her and rested its head on her thighs. She buried her face in its fur, her fingers curling into the folds of skin. Her muffled sobs clawed right through him. These were not the cries of a woman putting on a show or upset over something that didn't go her way. This was grief, raw and keening. She said one word over and over, and finally he was able to make it out: Arlo.

She presented him with the perfect opportunity, too

grief-stricken to notice if her Dragon warned of a presence coming up behind her. He scanned the surroundings as he readied his dagger for a quick, merciful kill. His pulse throbbed at the side of his throat as it did in these situations, and his fingers tightened on the hilt.

Except his body wouldn't move. Every preconceived notion he had about Violet—unkempt, untamed, violent—fled his mind, replaced by vulnerable, fiery, and innocent.

Innocent.

Former fellow Vega Cyntag Valeron had just come to him that morning, out of the blue, to decipher a magick book. He'd been cryptic about both it and the woman with him but clear about the advice he'd imparted: "Trust your gut above all else. If it doesn't feel right, it's probably not."

Kade's gut screamed, *Don't kill her.*

The oaths he'd taken as a Vega to uphold the law at any cost fell away, replaced by a conviction that Violet was not guilty of some murderous conspiracy.

One moment he stood frozen in his inner turmoil, and the next, a Dragon's gaping mouth was lunging for his throat. He twisted but still got knocked on his ass twenty feet away. He landed in a marshy area, sending a wave of muddy water spraying. His breath escaped in a hard gasp, and he hardly had time to breathe before the Dragon moved into view.

Dappled sunlight shimmered off her maroon scales. She lunged down at him, fangs stopping half an inch from eviscerating him. Inside her open mouth, magick flares capable of inflicting any type of pain fired to life. Her catlike eyes shrank. "You!" The fierce flames in her eyes didn't soften one bit. "How dare you sneak up on me!"

Her voice as Dragon was low and rumbly, but every bit

of her anger projected through loud and clear. He rolled, coming to his feet in one swift movement. What to say? He knew she was embarrassed at being caught in such a vulnerable moment, and being Amethyst, she was all emotion, not to mention unpredictable and high-strung.

"Violet, I—"

"Idjit! People are killing each other by sneaking onto our land. So either you're here to arrest me or you've got a death wish. And if it's the latter, I'm more than happy to grant it." She charged at him again.

He pressed his hand to her forehead and "shot" her. She Catalyzed to human in the same instant that she flew backward. Her body hit with a hard thud, her arms out at her sides.

He ran toward her, calling his dagger, which had been thrown, too. It burned back into his skin as he reached her. "You okay?"

She was sprawled out, mud streaking her naked body, her eyes wide and stunned. She looked...good.

Good and mad. "What the hell was *that*?"

"Magick taser, a new Guard weapon. It sucks out your magick, which in a Dragon's case, makes you human again." He held out his hand to help her up.

She gripped it, jerking him forward and off-balance. He held on to her hand and took her with him. They landed together in the mud, a tangle of bodies. His fingers slid across her skin as he got to his feet. She slugged him, catching his jaw because he was a bit too distracted by the feel of her to be as quick as he should be. She still looked as though she'd kill him.

"Why can't I Catalyze? What'd you do to me?" she screamed, gripping his shirt and shaking him.

Damn, she was strong. She reared back to hit him again, and he caught her fist. Their hands collided with a loud *slap*. She slammed him in the chest with her other hand.

He shoved her into the puddle again, trying to immobilize her. "I'm not here to hurt you. Look, I have no weapon." He held out his hands, showing her his dagger tucked away.

She kicked him in the stomach and tried to crawl away. Which left her sweet, mud-slicked ass in full view. A groan started climbing his throat but he stifled it.

"Assaulting an officer," he muttered, grabbing her around the waist. "Again."

"So it is a death wish then?" She jerked her head around, pinning him with a glare as sharp as his dagger. "Since you have no reason to arrest me."

"Settle down now, darling."

She let out a growl worthy of her Dragon and jumped on top of him, her hands around his collarbone. "Don't you dare call me 'darling.'"

"It slipped out," he grunted as she ground him into the mud. "It doesn't mean anything." But damn, that word never slipped out while on duty. She was firing up his wild side big-time. Her thighs squeezed his hips; her hands pinned his shoulders. He tried to gain control but she wouldn't budge. "Damn, woman, you an alligator wrestler?"

"Champion in the local division four years running, umpteen years ago." Her smile reeked of pride and challenge. And he always accepted a challenge. With a heave, he rolled her so he was on top. She kept the roll going, besting him again.

"Will you listen?" he said.

She grabbed a handful of his hair and jerked his head back. "I would have listened if you'd called the number on all that damned paperwork they made me fill out. While you were all inside laughing at me, I'm sure."

How to gain control of the situation without grabbing her somewhere inappropriate—somewhere that wouldn't piss her off even more? Damned tricky when she was naked. And muddy. Plus the fact that he wanted to touch her somewhere inappropriate. "I wasn't laughing at you."

"Sure you were. Inside. Outside you were giving me that smug smile you probably think...is...gorgeous." She fought as he tried to wrap his arms around her upper arms. "While you looked down your nose at me."

"Actually, I was looking at your tight shirt."

She slugged him in the jaw again, not really hard enough to do any damage. He threw his weight toward her, pushing her backward and coming down on top of her. Now he straddled her thighs, leaning down to hover above her.

"I was kidding," he said, his mouth only an inch from hers. "I was taking all of you in. I couldn't believe you were the same Violet Castanega I saw in muddy clothes and a tangled braid." He couldn't help the smile as he let his gaze drift from her neck down to her chest that rose and fell with deep breaths. The mud didn't cover the curve of her breasts or the hardened nipples that made him wonder if she was enjoying this on some deep level, too. "Then again, you do look extraordinary in mud."

"Let me up!" She tried to buck him off, which drove her pelvis up and dangerously close to smashing his balls.

He lay all his weight on top of her. "Not until you promise to stop fighting."

"I can't promise that. How long do the effects of your magick stun gun last?"

"Up to thirty minutes."

She bucked again, but he finally had her under his control. And he liked it. His women were always willing. Something about the fight completely turned him on, especially the way her pelvis bumped against his.

Her eyes widened. "Holy dragonfire, are you...does fighting get you...hot?"

He supposed, with all of this writhing around, it was inevitable that she'd notice his erection. "Not usually, but then again, I've never fought a feisty, naked female in the mud before. I have to admit, it's doing strange things to me." At her surprised look, he added, "Well, you asked. I answered honestly."

She took a deep breath to calm herself. "Okay then, answer this honestly. Why are you here?"

That was a bit trickier, but he could stick to the true part. "I came to ask you more about your allegations."

She just stared at him for a moment, her brown eyes disbelieving. "Instead of catching me in the parking lot, or calling, you sneak onto my land and surprise me. Are you kidding? Are you friggin' kidding me?"

"No, I'm not. Why else would I be here?"

She let out something like a growl. "After I was summarily dismissed, why would the Guard suddenly take me seriously and send someone out? And for god's sake, why *you*?"

He had those kinds of *why* questions, too, none he could share with her. "I'm not here on behalf of the Guard."

She furrowed her eyebrows. Mud streaked her face, her toned body, and gods help him, she was tantalizing.

"What's that supposed to mean?" she asked.

"I came on my own, because what you said piqued my interest. There's no need for the senseless deaths that would come from clan wars." He'd seen that fear in her eyes when she'd appealed to Ferro. "I want to hear everything you know."

She seemed to weigh his words. He knew how to lie well when he had to. It was part of his training, though he rarely used it in his personal life. This situation blurred the line. Violet was blurring all kinds of lines, obliterating others.

She took advantage of his introspection, because he was suddenly spinning off of her, compliments of an impressive twist and kick of her long, long legs. He came to his feet, ready for another attack.

She was stalking over to where her clothes had shredded when she'd Catalyzed. She held the remains of the nice, tight shirt she'd been wearing to her chest. Suspicion drenched her expression. "You're serious?" Kade saw a mixture of hope and skepticism in her eyes. And that eradicated any last shred of doubt that she was behind this.

"Very." He pulled off his shirt and tossed it to her.

She snatched it out of the air and wriggled into it, giving him one last heavenly view of her full breasts and flat stomach as she pulled it on. She pushed her muddy hair from her face. "Why do you care? We're all marsh trash to the likes of you."

"The likes of me? Because I'm a Vega?"

"Everything about you." She swept her gaze over him. "You move like royalty, you act like you rule the world, and you look untouchable."

Which he found amusing since he was as muddy as she

was. She waited for his answer. He rubbed the mud, now itching, from his neck, buying time. Royalty, huh? He sure as hell didn't feel like any of that at the moment. At least she hadn't called him pretty. "My gut says there's something going on, just like you suspect. If the Guard won't listen, then I will."

"Why sneak up on me? You know what 'animals' we all are." She'd heard someone say it, obviously, as she mimicked it with a sneer. "We do act on instinct, at least our Dragon does. I didn't even know you were there; my Dragon did. I could have killed you."

He gave her a smile he was sure *was* smug. "No, you couldn't have."

She rolled her eyes. "This is a bet, isn't it? Can Kade Kavanaugh nail the marsh trash? You might as well go home. Ain't gonna happen. You're totally not my type."

Except those hardened nubs poking against his shirt told a different story. Of course, so did his cock, even as he said, "Neither are you, if that makes you feel any better. I'm a Deuce-gal kind of guy." Although this Dragon appealed to him more than any other Crescent—Deuce or Dragon— that he'd encountered before. And that was just . . . crazy. "I'd never try to nail a woman for a bet." He let his mouth curve into a smile. "Only for the mutual pleasure of both parties."

A sound escaped her throat, but she cleared it. "Are you sure you're not here to sniff out any more pot farms? Find something else to bust my brothers on?"

He didn't blame her for her distrust. She had good reason not to trust the Guard, as it turned out. "Arlo was the worst offender. He had problems, whether you want to admit it or not."

She gave a quick nod of her head. "He did."

"Now he's dead. Let's find out why." When her skepticism didn't waver, he added, "Violet, you went to the Guard for help. I'm here. Let me help."

The words broke down her resistance. The battle between distrusting him and needing him played over her expression. "You can't come in my house like that." She walked over to a faucet and turned the squeaky knob, using the hose to rinse her hair and face first. He watched, entranced, as water sluiced over her and plastered his shirt to her curves. After rinsing her legs, she headed toward him and held the stream over his head. He scrubbed his fingers through his hair, feeling the grit wash away. Then she stepped back and pressed her thumb over the end to pressurize the stream. She aimed it across his shoulders and arms first.

He swore she took vengeful pleasure in hosing him down. Or maybe it was just pleasure. Her eyes followed the mud as it slid down his bare chest. Hell, he could feel that gaze slide down his body, embers flickering in her eyes. The water was cool, the sun was hot, and he took the blast of water without giving away the war that raged through him.

Ferro's voice told him to take her out.

Cyn told him to trust his gut.

Berlin's female singer sang about flames reaching out for the sun.

Then she reached for his upper chest. "You've got a scratch. I must have done that." She gently brushed her fingers across it beneath the water's flow. A wake of sensation followed her caress.

"Violet," he said, cursing himself for the hitch in his voice.

That got her attention. "Am I hurting you?"

He took the hand at his chest and drew it down to the front of his wet pants. "This much." He thought she'd give him hell for being so brazen, slap him silly, and that would break them out of this moment of insanity. Because that was the only explanation, that the situation and adrenaline had tilted them right into crazy territory.

Instead, her eyes fired up, and he swore she actually *squeezed* his erection just a tiny bit. *Holy shit.* She angled one of her legs between his, her hands sliding to his hips. Her thigh moved up along his, and he bit back a curse. This *was* insanity. Not seconds before he'd proclaimed he was a Deuce-only kind of guy. But right now, he was feeling all of her Dragon heat. The directive from his superior officer, the insanity of this attraction, the danger he saw simmering in her eyes, not even the cool water that continued to bathe him did a damn thing to douse his ardor.

He took the hose from her hand and let the water wash over her. When his free hand traced her collarbone, she closed her eyes, her head lolling back. He suspected that surrender wasn't something Violet often did, which only made the gesture more profound. How the hell was he supposed to grasp for any last thread of sanity now?

"Violet," he whispered her name this time. He meant it to sound like a call to logic, but it came out as more of a plea. For more.

His shirt was plastered over her firm breasts, clinging to her hardened nipples. Damn, she was hot, all sleek skin and toned muscle. With her eyes on his, she peeled off the shirt.

Kade didn't stop to think; he just reacted. He dropped the hose, grasped her by the waist, and lifted her up. Her legs went around him, and their mouths collided. Her lips were soft against his, her tongue sliding in and tangling with his own. She made these little mewling sounds as she pressed closer, her legs tightening around his waist, her hands kneading the muscles of his shoulders and back. His hands slid from her hips to palm her perfect ass. Damn. Just *damn*.

She did some kind of sucking move with her mouth that traveled all the way down to his cock and made it twitch. His pants were the only thing separating them, and if she kept up this rodeo ride, it wouldn't take magick to bust through that barrier. His fingers tightened on her smooth, wet flesh, and he switched to hold her with one arm, moving his other hand to her firm, round breasts. Her small nipples were pink, beaded, and his mouth actually watered at the thought of sucking on them. Before he could claim one of those glistening peaks, she was kissing him again so he plucked at her nipples instead. Her moan of pleasure vibrated through him, clear to the soles of his feet.

She was fire in his arms, a breathing, writhing enchantress. The sun beat down on them, burning his back and heating her dark hair, fueling the already raging fire between them. She ground against him again, increasing the friction. If he didn't get inside her soon, he was going to lose it right there. With rough hands, he stilled her hips.

His mouth trailed kisses along her cheek and throat, and with a deep breath, he took in her scent, all nature and wild and free. His lips found her nipple, tugging on the bead. His free hand trailed under her firm ass. His fingers found her wet, hot center, making her hips buck against his cock and pushing him closer to the edge. Getting a woman hot and bothered was nothing new, but this was Violet. Wild. Forbidden. Somehow that made it astounding. He slid his finger all around her swollen nub, wringing a cry from her lips.

He had skills, magickal ones, too, but she flew apart before he had the chance to use them. He rode her through the tempest, touching and stroking in a way that maximized her pleasure. She arched and screamed, held him, no, *hugged* him close. Her head rested against his shoulder as she caught her breath.

Then her whole body tightened in a different way. "Oh, my gods, what are we *doing*?"

"Well, I just made you come and—"

She slid to her feet and stumbled back, grabbing up the shirt. "No, I mean, what are we doing? This is—"

"Crazy. Insane." He raked his fingers back through his hair. "And amazing." He still had a raging hard-on, and his body fairly thrummed with the need for release, but what...the...hell?

"No, let's stick to the crazy insane part." She pulled on the shirt, shock in her eyes. "If my brothers had come up on us..."

"That would have been awkward."

"Awkward? They would have killed you."

Chapter 4

Kade stood naked in Violet's laundry room while his clothes banged around in the dryer. She was taking a shower. She'd offered him the use of her other bathroom, but he'd declined. Now if she'd offered to let him share hers...

Enough of those thoughts. He'd barely talked himself out of releasing all of that pent-up tension the handheld way as it was. He went to throw away a leaf he'd found lodged in his hair when he stopped dead. *Whoa.* Nothing like bloodied clothing stuffed in the trash can to kill a guy's libido.

Ferro was convinced she was a killer. Maybe he was right, and this mission was warranted after all. Maybe it was simply libido that had him derailed. He'd certainly been derailed out in the yard. Not that a sexy woman had ever done that before. Using a hanger, he picked up a shirt. Yeah, lots of blood. He dropped it back into the can. Violet's possible guilt should have lifted a huge weight from Kade's chest. It didn't.

He pulled his clothes from the dryer and dressed. Violet emerged from her bedroom, just as he came out of the laundry room, in a white tank top and black pants, her clean hair slick and combed back. She hardly looked at him, shifting her gaze away. He couldn't decipher her expression, but he guessed a little wary, a lot guilty. A slight flush of embarrassment, and...heat. Damn, she'd been so *responsive*. So hungry for touch, for release.

And hell, you were the same way. Instead of stepping back, you had your tongue in her mouth and your fingers in her warm, wet—

Focus, Kavanaugh! "Care to explain the bloody clothes in the laundry room?"

Her face paled, but she did meet his gaze. "Arlo's blood. That's what I was wearing when I found him."

"Sorry. It's a habit to question signs of bloodshed." *Now* he felt relief. Oh, boy.

He had to stop this heat between them, here and now. He wasn't weak like his father. He wouldn't go down that foolhardy path, placing a woman above his duty and the greater good. They didn't even like each other. Well, parts of his body had liked her *very* much. His hands had enjoyed her, too, and his tongue...

He gave his head a small shake. But that wasn't the point. She reminded him that he was more than a robotic soldier. He'd done edgy things based on his gut, and he'd always succeeded. Sure, he'd caught hell for breaking the rules, but he'd never been wrong.

And killing Violet Castanega would be *very* wrong.

"You're thinking about what happened out there, aren't you?" she asked.

Yeah, let's go with that. "It was pretty—"

She put her finger over his mouth. "Don't say 'amazing.' That can never happen again. You know that, right?"

He nodded. But what he really wanted to do was suck that finger into his mouth. Fortunately she pulled it away before he could again give in to dangerous impulses.

She stepped back and waved for him to follow her. "I'll show you what I have."

I've already seen it, babe, and it is amazing. But she meant evidence. *Down, boy.* He didn't need for her to see his growing erection, one he shouldn't be having in the first place. *Evidence. Murders. Get on board.*

He cataloged her home, small, but clean and uncluttered. There was nothing overly feminine, but it had a softness to the colors, the comfy couch, and the paintings of flower-filled courtyards in what looked like Italy.

His gaze went to a chair at a small desk in her living room, and he made a beeline over to examine the envelope-flap-shaped back of it with his hands. "You have an Arne Jacobsen Series 7." He flipped it over and looked at the bottom. "Made by Fritz Hansen in the sixties."

She observed him with the nonplussed expression one might have if he'd opened her fridge and helped himself to a beer. "It's a chair. From a thrift sale."

He scoffed. "A *chair*. It's a classic. I have a 1966 Swan in my formal living room. That's a sofa to the uninitiated." She was clearly uninitiated in the realm of vintage furniture. He rose and waved his fingers in the direction she'd been going in. "Carry on."

She pushed the door open and passed a cluttered desk. Bins marked *Bills* and *Invoices* contained a few slips of paper; the *Processed, Now File* bin was nearly filled.

Sketches of what he thought were jewelry designs covered a drafting board. Beautiful designs, including a dragon with its tail wrapped around a gemstone.

He had a hard time reconciling all the aspects of Violet Castanega. Dragon. Entrepreneur. Vulnerable woman. Dismissed, yet proud enough to keep her chin up as she'd left Headquarters. No tail between her legs, this one. How many other sides did she possess?

Well, that sensual creature who'd gotten him totally hot was an interesting one.

She led him to a map of South Florida on the wall. On it she'd outlined the different clan territories in blue. Her wet hair hung to her mid-back, leaving a damp spot on her tank top. She had a long, lean torso, slim hips, and that nice ass that had felt so damned...amazing beneath his hands. He bet she'd look great in a bikini, sitting on the deck of his boat...

She pointed to the squares just south of Florida City and Homestead. Each square had a family name with which he was familiar. Her map also sported tacks, though not as many as Ferro's.

"Your commander knows about the murders," she said.

"Apparently. But this is the first I've heard about them." Was another Vega assigned to investigate? Then why was he dispatched to take out Violet? It didn't make sense. "I'm never privy to any case but the one I'm assigned to."

She contemplated that, maybe the kind of cases those might be. Like killing people. "So the Guard knows but isn't doing a damned thing about it."

"Historically, we've not been especially welcome here."

Her expression softened. "True. So they're sitting back and watching us wipe each other out. Nice."

Population control. He'd heard that term more than once, and now it seemed despicable.

She turned back to the map. "This was where the first murder occurred."

"Hence, the number one next to it. Clever."

She shot him an exasperated look. "I know I need to keep it simple for you Vegas."

He snorted, because that was usually the Crescent sentiment when discussing the Fringers. And while he'd seen plenty of them with nary a lick of sense, Violet had been well educated. She might have been an alligator wrestling champion—and he believed it—but she used words like *summarily dismissed.* She wasn't dumb marsh trash.

"As long as you don't go any higher than eleven, I'm fine." That earned him a smile, brief though it was. Holy hell, the sight of it, white, even teeth and faint dimples at her cheeks... He focused on the map again.

"How familiar are you with the Fringe clans?" she asked.

"Somewhat."

"There have been three murders, unprovoked as far as I can tell. And three retaliatory murders. So here's the thing: if I wanted to start a war in the Fringe, I would stir up trouble between the families who hate each other most. The Augusts found a handkerchief belonging to one of the Spearses' boys. Bobby wasn't the brightest bulb, but he was generally a good kid. So if he decided for whatever reason to sneak onto August property and kill the matriarch, why the hell would he leave evidence behind?"

"I could never pretend to understand how things work here. But yeah, it would make sense that he'd be very, very careful."

"Ferro's map had red pins roughly where each of the murders happened. It also had some yellow pins. What does yellow stand for?"

He had to be careful about giving away anything civilian Crescents shouldn't know. "Could be a number of things, including possible targets. Years ago, we worked a serial killer case, a Deuce who was targeting flimflam psychics. We mapped out the victims with red pins and every Mundane psychic in Miami who might be a potential victim with a yellow pin. Then we looked for a pattern."

She stared at the map, chewing the tip of her finger. "So if that's what your commander is doing, then he is on the case. Which should make me feel better." She turned to him. "But it doesn't. Granted, I'm not a commander of the Guard, but if I had someone in my office who could offer me more information—inside information—I wouldn't dismiss her. Or suggest, of all stupid things, that it's solar storm disruptions. I'd listen."

Yeah, that's what bugged him, too. Not to mention the seemingly impulsive command to take her out of the picture. "Agreed. But I've learned over the years that things aren't always what they seem. You have to trust the establishment."

She grunted and turned back to the map. "If that works for you. I didn't get to see his map long enough to imprint where the yellow pins were."

"Imprint?"

"Photographic memory." She tapped the upper right territory. "I think there was one in August land. Which makes sense, if he guesses that the Spearses would suspect the Augusts in Bobby's death. But here's the other strange thing. Okay, maybe there's trouble between the clans. But look how many clans are involved."

She narrowed her eyes, studying the map. "I think there was a yellow pin here, in Slade territory. Why would Ferro consider them a potential target? Though I think all the clans have had beefs with each other at one time or another, there's no reason for him to think the Slades will be targeted by any of the families already involved." She turned to Kade. "Unless he knows something."

Ferro knew something all right. "You're speculating that someone is purposely stirring up the clans. Inciting a war. Let's look at possible motives."

Kade saw something flicker in her eyes. Hope? Relief that someone was taking her seriously? The more she told him, the more he *was* taking it seriously. The details didn't add up. His gut didn't like the tidiness of "population control" and "Fringer" lawlessness. He didn't see how assassinating this woman would prevent additional murders.

It seemed to take some effort to pull her gaze from his and turn back to the map. "The victims are being Breathed," she said. "So it could be to gain power, plain and simple. But why target Fringe clans rather than the more anonymous Miami Crescent population? That would be stupid. And despite popular opinion, we're not stupid. Getting rid of the competition businesswise could be a motive. Or maybe it's a need for conflict. Some Fringers crave that. They grew up during a time of conflict, and some of them miss it—my brothers included. But they'd never incite war. They're all too aware of how many innocent people die in the crossfire. Children," she added with shadows in her eyes. "Do I have a case?"

"Definitely. I'm going back to find out what's going on."

"I don't want you to think that what happened outside was some kind of persuasion technique." She cleared her throat. "Just in case you wondered."

"You didn't need to persuade me," he said, letting her know with his steady gaze that he meant that both ways. "But it was very unprofessional of me to, uh, indulge in that kind of behavior. Which I have never done before. Just in case you wondered."

Her mouth started to curve into a smile, but she halted it. "Good to know. And we're clear that it cannot happen again."

"Perfectly." Hell, this was complicated enough without his raging libido. He turned and headed down her hallway, a plan formulating in his mind that would salvage his career and keep Violet alive. Kade would convince Ferro that this woman wasn't a psychopathic killer. Then, if he did have incriminating evidence to support his claim, he'd have to come clean.

"Vee!" A man's voice outside. "We're coming in."

Hands shoved Kade from behind into the room on the right. She closed the door on him just as the front door opened.

"What's up, brothers?" Violet asked, letting him know who was there.

If they knew he was in there, they'd go after him. Not that Kade could blame them. There were guys he would want to kill if he caught them in his sister's house. He rubbed his fingers together. He might have one more taser in him, but not two.

"That's what *we* came here to ask," one of the men said.

"You said you'd give me two days."

"I said one day," the same man said. "You said two days, and I didn't disagree. But knowing that son of a bitch who killed Arlo is out there burns my ass."

"Mine, too, but we don't know for sure who killed him. That's what I'm trying to find out. Someone's trying to incite the clan wars again. Come here."

Kade heard their footsteps going down the hall to the office. He pictured the layout of the house and hallway. If he slipped out, there was a chance he'd get caught. He peered out the window. A truck sat outside, someone inside it. Okay, he'd wait it out.

He looked around her bedroom, more feminine than the rest of the house. It reminded him of a margarita, crisp with light yellow walls and dark wood beam ceilings. Yeah, a margarita sounded real good right about now. While on his boat. Far away. With Violet in a bikini stretched out on the deck.

He took in the green spread adorning her bed, covered with an assortment of yellow pillows. Ah, this wasn't such a bad place to be. Other than the murderous Dragons down the hall. Chiding himself for being nosy—no, he was *investigating*—he continued to peruse her room.

She had an assortment of framed pictures on her long dresser, mostly her family. He picked up one of Violet with her parents. He knew her father had been killed, and it hit him that both their fathers had died under mysterious circumstances. Hers had been on Garza property, though he didn't appear to be poaching or doing anything wrong. Fringe-style, he'd been gunned down by a paranoid Garza. That was why the Castanegas had gone on a rampage, wiping out what was left of the clan.

He opened her drawers, finding one filled with panties

made of strings and bras of various colors. He felt beneath the lace and silk but found no incriminating evidence. He closed it, trying not to imagine her wearing them. On his boat. Or *not* wearing them. On his boat. He already knew what her body looked like, felt like. How her eyes flashed when she came apart. *Shit.*

Other drawers contained the work clothing he'd seen her in before: old, tattered jeans, practical T-shirts, and the baggy kind of sun-blocking shirt he wore when he took the boat out in the heat of day. Her closet was jammed with dress pants and other business attire, as well as some intriguing things tucked in the back: tight black pants, a deep red shirt cut low enough to reveal cleavage, and a few short dresses. Less intriguing but interesting all the same, a little girl's dress hung in the back, separated by several inches on either side.

Voices filled the hallway. He moved away from the closet into the center of the room, ready in case one of them had caught his scent. Some Dragons did that better in human form than others. His dagger tingled, ready to materialize.

"Give me one more day, Jessup," she said, and it sounded like it was through clenched teeth. "Don't you dare go off killing people based on speculation. There's been enough of that. In fact, someone's counting on it."

It did sound like a conspiracy theory. But who would benefit?

"You've got until the end of tomorrow. Then go do one of your booty call weekends in Naples. Keep out of it."

"Oh, please," she said, exasperation in her voice. "You think I'd run off and fool around while you're here getting yourselves killed?"

"Be a lot smarter." After a pause, Jessup asked, "Is someone here?"

"No, why?"

Kade stiffened. He leaned against the door, ready to put his weight behind it if they tried to open it. Unfortunately, he saw no way to lock it.

"I smell someone. I'd better check—"

"I was with someone. You smell him on me," Violet said.

"Just now? Here?"

"No, in Miami."

"Comfort sex. Got it," the other brother said. "That's why she's got that I-just-got-laid-and-it-was-good fire in her eyes."

The footsteps continued to the front door, and more speculation ensued. He listened as the doors slammed and the conversation continued outside.

He supposed it could've been comfort sex. Not that they'd gotten to the sex part—a fact his body wouldn't let him forget. Maybe that explained her need for touch, but it didn't do a damned thing to excuse his loss of control.

Kade stretched out on the bed, his arms behind his head. The linen bedspread was softer than he'd anticipated. He had to stop thinking about her in bed, on his boat, naked. Having a naked mud fight with a woman was one of his teenage fantasies. The girls he'd suggested it to went all squeamish on him.

The bedroom door opened, and Violet leaned against the frame, eyes narrowed and arms crossed over her chest. "You're enjoying that a little too much."

He arched one eyebrow. "Booty call weekend?"

"It's none of your business." She grabbed a small pillow and threw it at him. "Out of my bed."

"Hey, I was just passing the time." He ran his hand over the bedspread. "I guess it was a good thing we weren't closer to this earlier." Because he had no doubt they would have been tangling these sheets...oh, right about the time her brothers came barging in.

"That would not have happened. I came to my senses before—"

"I got off." He slid off the bed and came to his feet. She blushed. And there it was, the hesitation and hint of vulnerability that told him she wasn't nearly as unaffected as she pretended to be. He chuckled, running his finger down her nose. "Don't worry none about me. It's nothing a cold shower can't fix." Except he'd already gotten one of those, thanks to the hose. And it hadn't helped. "I'm going to talk to Ferro and find out what's going on. Tell him to get at least some Arguses out here to discourage any further trouble. If it's because of the solar storm fluctuations, it'll only be for a few more days. We're going to feel the brunt of it Thursday. We can forestall any more violence, investigate the murders that have already happened, and keep the peace you want so badly."

Her eyes flared. "I hope so."

They walked toward the front door.

She looked through the window first. "I want to make sure they're gone. If my family finds out I went to the Guard, it won't be pretty."

"Would they hurt you?" Yeah, considering his mission, it was damned strange to be worrying about her safety where her own family was concerned. But if he was tabling the directive to kill, he'd be damned if someone else caused her harm on his watch.

"They'd see it as a betrayal. We have a punishment

known as the wall of shame. The naughty are stripped to their underwear—the men, anyway—and cuffed to the outside wall of the barn." She shuddered. "Sometimes for days. And they play whatever music you can't stand."

Exposed to the elements, to the ridicule of peers. "Sounds barbaric."

"We have our own brand of punishment here in the Fringe." She shrugged. "I guess I'm used to it. And the threat of it works. Some of the cousins were stealing oranges from our two trees up at the house. Their punishment was being cuffed and having rotten oranges thrown at them. After a couple of days, believe me, they didn't want anything to do with oranges."

"You ever been put on the wall?"

"Once, when I was twelve. I borrowed my brothers' fishing gear and accidentally dumped it into the lake. They hung bait fish all around me and played the twangiest country music they could get their hands on. I don't want to suffer through that again."

His image of her being tied up, in her grown-up state, had a decidedly different picture—and outcome. One that hiked up his physical discomfort by another couple of degrees. He pulled out of those tantalizing thoughts and headed to the property line, knowing he'd be back. For Violet. For justice.

Chapter 5

Violet smoothed out the wrinkles Kade had made on her bedspread. Of all the nerve. Just because they'd had that weird moment outside didn't mean he could presume he was welcome in her bed. Her hand paused as she imagined him and his nerve lying on her bed, shirtless. Having a man in her own bed was a fantasy, rather than meeting them out of town. Gorgeous guy: check. Guy who totally turned her on: check. Kade Kavanaugh: no way in hell. Not going *there*.

But, oh, she'd nearly gone there, close enough to find sweet, mind-numbing release. Reeling from grief and frustration, along with the adrenaline high from their fight, she'd acted foolishly.

Foolish is wrestling with alligators. Tangling with a Vega—with Kade Kavanaugh—that's sheer insanity.

She huffed out a breath. She hadn't meant to touch him. Hadn't known that what began as an innocent rinse-off so he wouldn't track mud into her home would turn into a

seduction. Worst part was, she had started things by touching him and probably exuding some need to connect. She
could imagine it so clearly, the water sluicing over his
sculpted chest, his gaze on hers, and that need ... it all exploded inside her. He placed her hand over the hard length
of his erection and, instead of being horrified, she molded
her fingers over it and leaned into him. Suddenly, he was
hoisting her up and kissing her with a thoroughness she'd
never experienced before. Damn, the man could kiss. His
mouth did a number on her, and then when he'd touched
her, she'd been so ... *ready.*

Part of her felt sick, thinking that her reaction was a betrayal of her brother. But her family was in tune with their
primal Dragon urges: violence, pleasure, sex. They would
never judge her for drowning in sensuality; it was the facil-
itator that would have them going ballistic.

And to think minutes earlier you were about to kill him.
She still wasn't sure she could trust Kade as far as she
could throw him, which was, oh, about twenty feet if she
recalled correctly. Then again, if he was truly seeing her
side of things and willing to approach his boss about the
situation, it was probably a good thing she hadn't killed
him.

No, you couldn't have.

Argh, arrogant devil. She could so hear his confidence
in her inability to annihilate him. Damn, why did he get to
her? And in more ways than just being annoyed, which was
damned ... annoying.

She pushed the crazy tangle of feelings aside. She
needed to continue her investigation, even if Kade was
helping. She found Marshall Peregrine's number in the
phone directory. He was the patriarch of the family, and his

son, Liam, was the first victim of the spree. She dialed the number.

A boy answered, and Violet asked, "Hi, may I speak with Marshall, please? This is Violet Castanega."

Silence for a moment. Their clans weren't mortal enemies, but they'd had their share of skirmishes.

"Hold on a sec." The kid's heavy footfalls pounded in the background, and he told someone she was on the phone.

A man answered with, "Yeah?"

"I wanted to extend my condolences on behalf of the Castanegas," she said, meaning it.

"Uh...thanks."

"I'd like to meet with you at Ernie's. I think there's more to this than the Wolfrums acting up." Silence. "Please, before things get out of hand. Again. I've got some fresh alligator meat, if you'd like some."

Yeah, a bribe. Whatever she had to do.

"Two pounds?"

"Meet me in an hour?"

"You got it. But if this is some kind of trick—"

"It's no trick, Marshall. Somebody's playing us, all of us in the Fringe. I want to stop it before more people die."

Kade knocked on Ferro's door, then went in at his answer. He closed the door behind him.

"I trust it went smoothly?" Ferro asked.

"No, sir. I was in her house, waiting for her to return. She did, but she had her brothers in tow. Since my assignment did not include them, and complicated matters,

I remained in hiding. What I overheard made me question this assignment, because, quite frankly, she made some good points as she outlined her research to her brothers. Further, I found nothing to warrant her termination. I extracted myself, aborting the mission."

Ferro's expression hardened. "You did not kill her."

Well, he thought he'd made that clear. "No, sir." He walked over to the map. "It does appear that someone is trying to incite clan violence. She has a map like this—"

"Kavanaugh." Ferro waved his fingers for Kade to come back to the front of his desk. "There are things you don't know about this case."

"Bring me in then. Because from where I stand, taking her out seems an inappropriate course of action. I know the Guard considers every termination carefully, but Violet Castanega is innocent."

"Your job is to simply take her out. There's nothing else to be discussed. If you have a problem with the assignment, I can task someone else with it."

Dune came to mind. The son of a bitch enjoyed killing people. Kade straightened his shoulders. "We're trained to assess on the fly, to make decisions based on the specific situation."

"That pertains to the way you fight, evade, or escape. Not the overall mission. You do not get to decide to spare a target. Terminate her or remove yourself from the assignment."

Kade, meet wall. He shifted his gaze to the map and tried to discern where the yellow pins were.

Ferro stood, blocking his view. "As you know, all it takes is one turn of events—a woman, perhaps—to crash and burn a career. And others often pay the price." Was he inferring that Mia wouldn't get promoted if Kade screwed up? Ferro frowned. "I didn't want to demote you after your father's fall, but I couldn't ignore the complaints. After all, your father did use his position to protect you whenever you came under fire for not following the rules. You had a reckless edge, thinking you knew best about cases and suspects. And you see where that got you."

Dune had been the loudest objector, jealous bastard. While Kade used that edge to accomplish his goals, Dune had kept his nose to the line, cold and calculating. Yet Kade rose to Vega years before him, even though they both graduated from the Academy at the same time.

"Yes, it garnered me a ninety-seven percent completion rate."

Ferro's fiery eyes pinned him, and in that moment, he seemed very dragonish. "You got lucky that your antics didn't backfire. But if we let you carry on, other Vegas were bound to follow suit. They might not get so lucky."

Because they're not as good as I am. Luck, hell. He held that bit in. "I didn't know that Vegas were automatons with no authority to investigate or think."

He could feel Ferro bristle and saw the flames go all jaggy in his eyes. "There are times when those skills are required. The most important one, though, is to be reliable and do as you're told. I don't understand why you're so reluctant to do this. It's a simple kill order, something you've done many times without question."

"Before it felt right."

"And this doesn't?" Ferro put an edge into his words.

"No. My father taught me to trust my instincts." And Cyn had reminded him just recently. "That's what I did those times I was considered reckless."

"Your father's instincts were not always right, though, were they?"

That was a sore point. He didn't know what had possessed his father to defect. He still didn't understand, and despite all his digging, those answers continued to elude him. "I don't have all the facts in that case." Irritatingly so.

"Your father's instincts were clouded by his feelings for a woman. It happens, unfortunately. The human side of us is weak." Ferro gave him a dark look. "Is that what's happening here?"

Kade shook his head as he pushed the thought of his hands on Violet's ass far from his mind. "No woman would be worth throwing my career away for."

"You are not weak like your father. In fact, since his downfall, you completely changed and have been an exemplary officer."

Kade had become Dune, except for the liking-to-kill part. The thought shuddered through him. "Thank you, sir," he gritted out. Nothing was more important than regaining his position, his identity. For himself and for Mia.

"I know you're trying to do your job well, and I appreciate that. But I cannot have an officer in the field who doesn't trust his superior. Don't you trust my judgment?"

If Kade answered honestly, he'd be pulled this second. "I trust you, sir. Implicitly."

"Then do your job. And only your job."

Kade felt cold all over as his career pooled like water on his upturned palms, ready to pour through his fingers. Following orders was a lot easier than questioning them. "I'm on it."

Ferro waited until Kade left the building before making his call. He studied the map until she answered.

"It's Alec," he said. "I had a visit from Violet Castanega earlier. She's concerned about the recent rash of murders among the Fringers, thinks they'll start clan wars again. In fact, she suspects a conspiracy."

"A conspiracy. Really? Clever girl. I'd be more than happy to pay her a visit and *dissuade* her of the notion."

"No, she's being dissuaded by one of my Vegas."

"She'll be Breathed by someone else?" Her jealousy was clear in the sharpness of her voice.

"No, he's a Deuce. Someone who has no emotional ties to the family, other than previous arrests. Who will do his job in a cold and efficient way without letting the past ramp up his emotions." He hoped.

"You're saying my emotions will make me reckless?"

"I know how you can get when it comes to the Fringers."

She made a sniffing sound. "But it's a waste of Dragon power."

He pressed one of the red tacks in more fully. "Don't get greedy. Red Lust already breathes down your neck."

"Ridiculous."

He'd seen that edge of insanity simmering in her eyes ever since they'd taken on this mission. "We're so close, darling. Do you want to lose everything by going Red and being executed? I can't help you once our officials have you in custody. They have no consideration for personal relationships. In fact, if they find out I am your lover, I will be locked out of the proceedings completely." And reprimanded for not reporting the relationship.

Her silence reeked of fear. Her fear of death drove her.

She had witnessed her sister being murdered when she was very young and later she'd been orphaned. He had taken her in, protecting her from those who had killed her parents. He understood her need for security all too well, her need to gain power. No doubt, it had driven her to seduce him, despite his protests about their age difference.

"There's a reason we have a plan. Stick to it. Speaking of..." He pulled a yellow pin from the map and replaced it with a red one. "Go ahead and take out the next target. But I'm going to make one small adjustment that should really get things moving."

Chapter 6

Now that it was early evening, Ernie's was much busier. Vehicles crammed the lot, mostly trucks sprayed in mud and bits of grass. Violet's stomach tightened. She took a deep breath, grabbed the package of alligator meat, and got out. No sign of any of her family's vehicles. They were probably lying low, plotting.

A hand clamped over her arm, and she screamed. Her Dragon vibrated through her as she spun around, ready to whack her assailant with the package.

Kade met her motion with his upturned palm. "Whoa."

"Is that what they teach you in the Guard, to sneak up on people and grab them?"

"Yeah, pretty much."

He wasn't wearing the standard Vega clothing, dressed instead in blue jeans and a dark blue button-down shirt with long sleeves. And he didn't look the least bit apologetic.

She *hmphed*. "Don't touch me again, or I'll unleash my Dragon on you." Not that it had worked out so well last time. Wrestling in the mud with him—naked!—had been quite humiliating. And the aftermath...best not to go there. "What are you doing here? How'd you find me?"

"I was coming back and saw you pull in."

He'd come back. It hit her then, which hopefully meant the Guard was now going to cooperate.

"What did your boss say?" she asked.

The fog in his eyes darkened, like swirling smoke. "I'm here in an unofficial capacity."

She nodded. "So the Guard is willing to let war erupt here. Nice." She let her gaze draw down his unofficial self. "And you're here for...?"

She wasn't sure how she felt about him being here. Without the power of the Guard, what could he do? Part of her did appreciate his presence, but she was ignoring it.

"I want to get to the bottom of this." He nodded to the building. "You here for a drink?"

"Gods, no. The only time I come here is to help carry out one of my drunk family members. Or for information. You...can't go in there," she finished as he headed toward the entrance.

"Because I'm Deuce?" He kept walking, forcing her to catch up to him.

"And an outsider."

He linked his arm with hers. "But I have connections." His smile almost made her forget what a bad idea this was. Damn, it almost made her want a replay of the scene by the mud puddle.

She pulled him to a stop, untangling her arm from his. "If they recognize you as a Vega, there will be even more trouble. You're way outnumbered in there, and even as Dragon, I won't be able to protect you."

His smile grew even warmer, and he rubbed the back of his knuckles down her cheek. "You going to protect me, my fierce Dragon babe?"

She stumbled back. "Look, we had that…moment earlier, but I am not losing my head like that again. So no touching me, and no calling me 'babe.'"

He still had that smile on his face. "I know what that moment was about, so don't sweat it."

She blinked, surprised because she had no idea what it was about and *she* had participated in it. "What was it?"

"Comfort sex. Not that we got to the sex part, but you needed comfort. And I was handy."

And yummy and hot and… "Yeah, that was it. Sure, that explains a lot." But it didn't really, because she had been righteously aroused, which had nothing to do with wanting comfort.

"So you don't have to look at me like I'm going to eat you. Or kiss you again."

She arched an eyebrow. "Yeah, you did kiss me. And…a lot more. What's your excuse?"

That smile disappeared. Interesting. She thought he'd be all cocky or patronizing, like *I just wanted to make you feel better. What a great guy I am, huh?* But no, he looked unsettled. And she remembered that he'd seemed just as shocked by what had exploded between them. He rubbed the back of his neck. "I wish I knew. All I can tell you is that it won't happen again."

She felt some relief at the confident tone of his voice. "No, it won't."

"So let's focus on the matter at hand. I haven't had reason to deal with Fringers in recent years, so they may not recognize me. I can do a couple of things to help matters."

He scrubbed his fingers through his hair, moving his part to the side and mussing it in general. It made him look like he'd just gotten out of bed, which only complemented his bedroom eyes. Then he waved his fingers in front of his eyes and, amazingly, Dragon flames ignited in them. The sight tightened her throat and woke her Dragon.

"How'd you...illusion." She'd never seen a Deuce do that before, not that she was around many of them. "All right, since you have an answer for everything, how do I explain you?"

He arched one eyebrow. "Booty call weekend?"

She shoved him, not that he moved much. "You think I go around telling everyone I hook up with out-of-town guys?" She rubbed her finger across her mouth in thought. "But yeah, maybe you're someone I met in Naples while on business, my—"

"Lover. We haven't been able to keep our hands off each other since we met at the—"

"Landscape nursery where I was buying plants. You work there. And we're just friends."

He was watching her finger move across her lips. "We're more than friends if you're bringing me here."

We're more than friends, reverberated inside her. "Fine. But no hands all over. What happens in the Fringe stays in the Fringe. For-friggin'-ever. It's why I don't date Fringers. Usually things don't work out, and it's awkward every time you see the person."

"Is that where the booty call weekends come in?"

She let out an exasperated sound. "They're not *booty call* weekends. I don't go looking for a hookup. I travel all over Florida to find new accounts."

"Accounts for what?"

"My jewelry business. Running the books for the farm is my obligation, and I don't mind doing it, but my passion is designing and making jewelry. I started taking weekend trips to visit small galleries and jewelry shops to see if I could actually sell my products. I now have a dozen shops who carry my pieces, and I'm adding more all the time. Crescent-owned shops started requesting specific jewelry, like the gods' symbols."

Kade gave her a *that's cool* kind of nod. "Mia wears a piece with the symbol of Linnea, Deuce goddess of order and chaos. One of yours?"

"Maybe." She gave him a devilish smile. "Wouldn't that just kill her to know she was wearing something I, a lowly Castanega Fringer, made?" She touched the pendant at her throat. "These are my most popular, the symbol I created for Crescents."

Which invited him to lean close and take the pendant in his fingers to study the crescent moon with a diamond at the bottom point. Enough that she felt his body heat and the brush of his hair against her chin. His scent awakened her Dragon, awakened parts of her better left dormant.

All of his attention was on the pendant. "It's simple but elegant."

She cleared her throat. "Exactly what I was aiming for. Mundanes like them, too, even if they don't know the meaning. I call my business Luca, after the high god who oversaw Lucifera."

He rubbed his thumb across the gold, then met her gaze. "Your passion shows."

She couldn't breathe for a moment. There was something compelling about the word *passion* coming out of that made-for-sin mouth that was a fraction of an inch away from hers. The insane urge to trace her finger across his fine scar that did indeed make him look a bit dangerous assailed her. She stepped back, reclaiming the pendant. And her sanity.

"I want to hear more about the booty call part of these weekends," he said.

Damn Jessup for having to say that within earshot of Kade.

"While I'm traveling, I occasionally meet someone at the hotel who doesn't know about Castanegas or the Fringe."

"I get it. For a weekend, you're someone else. No one judges you."

"It's not that I'm ashamed of who I am. I just need a break from the judgment. And I don't meet a guy every time I'm out of town. I'm not desperate. It's got to be the right guy, the right situation." Though for the life of her, she couldn't remember any of them at the moment. She tilted her head. "You sound like you've been judged. But you're the top of the Crescent heap." And gorgeous, confident. Sexy as hell.

He nodded toward the building. "As a Vega, I'm judged here." He tugged his sleeve down to cover the tip of his dagger.

"True. I guess I never thought about that."

"You judged me the same way I judged you, isn't that right?"

"I guess it's a mutual disdain thing. We should go in now."

She headed to the door, and he fell in line beside her. "Is there one particular guy you hook up with during these weekends? Or a guy you've met up with more than once?"

"Now you're just getting nosy."

He shrugged but didn't look the least bit chagrined. "It's my nature." He gave her a few seconds to answer. When she didn't, he nodded toward her hand. "What's in the package?"

"Alligator meat. I threw it in as incentive for Marshall, the Peregrine patriarch, to meet me. I happen to know he's a big fan of it."

He wrinkled his nose, which made him look adorable. "I suppose it tastes like chicken?"

"Better than chicken." She started heading to the building again. "Marshall isn't going to talk with you there."

Kade slung his arm over her shoulders. "I'll be the distracted guy, just hanging around, not really paying attention. But I'll be paying careful attention, trust me."

He oozed lazy casualness, making her wonder what the real Kade Kavanaugh was like. Dedicated Vega, for sure. Totally sexy and extremely adept with his tongue. And fingers. And a little bit playful. Gods, a tantalizing combination of male. Dedicated enough to investigate the murders on his own time, and for that she was grateful. Now all she had to do was not let herself get too grateful. Because his arm across her shoulders and the proprietary way he pulled her close to his side as they entered the bar felt nice. Very nice.

Smoke and music assaulted them the moment Kade opened the door for her. Conversation and laughter from the back corner where the pool tables were, all the norm. Everyone in the place glanced at the door, also the norm whenever someone entered Ernie's. Several gazes remained on her, or, more precisely, Kade. She nodded at a few people but sought out Marshall, alone in the back near the dartboards. He sat slouched in the chair, legs apart, dusty cowboy boots flat on the wood floor.

She moved out of Kade's hold and wended her way through the maze of tables, pulling him along by the hand. Marshall's gaze narrowed on Kade behind her. She sat down and angled her thumb at him. "This is a friend of mine, Sebastian. We met at a plant nursery in Naples and became friends." She drew the word out to give him the idea. "I didn't know he was coming to see me, but he's here." She shrugged in a *What can I do?* way and turned to him. "Go play darts, Sebastian."

He gave her a look that seemed to say *Sebastian? Really?* But he took his cue with a "Sure thing, babe," and ambled over to an available dartboard. *Babe.* It should annoy her, but he was playing a role, after all. The only thing that did annoy her was the way the word echoed through her body. She'd never been anyone's babe before. He sorted through the house darts, the flights all pretty mangled, and then laid three in the palm of his hand.

Focus.

She handed the package to Marshall. "Thanks for meeting me. Arlo was killed this morning." Okay, she hadn't meant to blurt it out like that. But Marshall needed to know she also had something at stake.

"Sorry to hear that. Heard Shirley August bit it, too. Seems like things are heating up in the Fringe again."

"Someone's trying to heat things up. Liam was the first to get killed. Peter Wolfrum was next."

Marshall's upper lip twitched, enough to give away his part in that death.

"You had reason to believe Peter was the one who killed Liam," she said.

He hesitated, obviously not sure he wanted to admit it. His gaze shifted to Kade, who was completely immersed in trying to hit the bull's-eye. At least he seemed to be. She knew better. Between their soft words and the loud music, she wasn't sure how clearly he could hear their conversation.

"There's a code here," she said. "You kill one of ours, we kill one of yours. I don't think you attacked the Wolfrums unprovoked."

"No, but that's what they did," he said, banging his fist on the table.

Kade stiffened, ready to come to her rescue. She gave him a subtle shake of her head. Slowly, he resumed his game.

Marshall lowered his voice. "We didn't do nothing to them. Found my boy…" His chin trembled, which triggered her own grief.

Gods, please don't cry here.

She pushed down her tears. "How did you know it was the Wolfrums?"

"Footprints leading from the body to the border of their land. They snuck over and ambushed him. Now we're even. Unless they want more trouble." The flames in his eyes flared.

"Did you leave a calling card by Peter's body?"

"Oh, they'll know." When it was a revenge kill, they usually left a clue.

"What if they didn't kill Liam? And now they think your attack on Peter was unprovoked." They'd kill another Peregrine. And on and on. The Augusts and Spearses, the Murphys and her own family…Fear twisted her stomach.

"They did. Wouldn't make sense for someone to set them up."

"Any more than it makes sense for them to kill Liam in the first place?"

He got to his feet, tall and gangly. "How much of what goes on here makes sense anyway? What's your point?"

Damn, she'd never get them to stop the momentum without proof. Her gaze shifted to Kade. Maybe he could help with that. He released a dart, plowing it into the red center. She turned back to Marshall. "Somebody's behind all this, purposely inciting the clans to violence again."

"Why would anyone do that?"

"I don't know, but I'm going to find out."

"The Wolfrums are bored of peace," Marshall said, throwing a couple bills on the table. "Getting restless." He leaned close to her. "Sounds like you're warning me that they're going to retaliate. If they sent you, tell 'em to bring it on. We're ready."

"They didn't..." Marshall had already walked far enough away that he wouldn't hear her. She wasn't going to scream it out, not here.

It wasn't unusual to see the different clans mingling or playing a game of darts or pool. But she and Marshall's meeting wouldn't go unnoticed, especially since she'd brought in a stranger.

"That went well," the stranger murmured next to her ear. His warm breath washed down her neck, making her twitch and move back. He pulled a chair up next to hers, wrapping his hand over her shoulder.

She had to lean close to him to talk without the risk of being overheard. In a room full of Dragons, being overheard was possible. His hair tickled her nose and brushed her lips as she said, "He didn't go for the conspiracy theory, but I found out there were footprints leading from

Liam's body to the border between their land and the Wolfrums'. Again, obvious evidence. Sloppy." Her gaze was even with Kade's neck and collarbone. She kept it there and not on those faux Dragon eyes. "I need to talk to the Murphys, but that's not going to happen. We've got bad blood between us. That's what makes this so devious. Whoever is behind it is targeting the clans with blood history."

"Hey, Vee, who's your pretty friend?"

The slurred voice belonged to a drunk Bren, who parted from his brothers as they came in.

Kade muttered, "I am *not* pretty." He came to his feet just as Violet did.

"None of your business," she said. "Go away."

Kade stiffened beside her. "You heard the lady. Get lost."

Bren laughed. " 'Lady'? You're not from around here, are you?" He squinted his wobbly eyes as he studied Kade. "No, you're not. Let me help you out. I can tell you all the things Vee here likes. She likes loooong wet kisses—"

She slugged Bren, as she'd done earlier. He fell back against the table, barely grabbing on to it to keep from falling on his ass. Before he could say anything, she said, "Your kisses were awful. I had to wipe my mouth afterward. And during them I'd be thinking about my to-do list."

Kade chuckled. "You obviously weren't kissing her right."

"I did a lot right, didn't I, baby?" Bren made that stupid V and licked the crease. He'd actually thought it was provocative when they were dating despite the fact that she'd rolled her eyes and looked away every time he'd done it. Now that he knew it disgusted her, he did it every time he saw her.

This time Kade hit him, and he staggered back several steps. "You're disrespecting the lady. Knock it off or I will."

Violet threw her hand out when Bren's brothers rushed forward. "Stop! Your brother's being a jerk, as usual. I know you're not used to seeing men treat women with respect, but let it go." Of course, Kade was only playing a part.

Bren wiped his hand over his mouth, checking for blood. "We can take this into the Conference Room."

Violet shook her head. "No way." Ernie would kill her if she exposed the Conference Room to a Vega. She twined her arm through Kade's and tugged him toward the door. He went willingly, unlike anyone who lived in the Fringe who'd be spoiling for a fight. He watched his back, though, every muscle tight and ready for action. Kade wasn't spoiling for a fight, but he'd kick ass if he needed to. Bren watched with the same posture, though he looked ready to come after them.

"Pretty," Kade spit out, clearly disgusted.

"Well, you are pretty."

"I've got a scar, for hell's sake."

She paused at the door, lifting his hair and looking at it. "Sorry, but it's just not ugly enough. Maybe if it were all red and angry and came down to your mouth." She drew her finger down that imagined path, ran it across his lower lip. Then she slung her arms around his neck and planted her mouth on his. It was a *very* bad idea, an advance he might reject in surprise. But he fell right into it, tilting his head and opening his mouth against hers. His hand came up to cradle her cheek, and his tongue moved expertly against hers. Heat sparked between them as fierce and fast as it had outside her home.

"I thought we weren't going to kiss again," he murmured between kisses.

"We aren't. I mean, this isn't really kissing." Then, for a few moments, she fell into a mindless spin as he sucked on her tongue. She snapped back to reality. "We're pretending. For them."

"Ah." He slid his hands down to her behind and pulled her tighter against him. "Just as long as you don't mind that my reaction isn't pretend."

No, it wasn't. His hard ridge pressed against her stomach. "I guess I can't complain." She pulled back even when her body wanted to grind right into him, grabbed his hand, and shot Bren a look before walking out into the fresh air.

As soon as the door closed, she let out a scream. "That felt good!" She spun around.

He rubbed his fingers over his mouth. "Yes, it did. Now, want to explain what that was about?"

Her cheeks burned. "It was impulsive, which isn't like me anymore. Sorry for using you like that. Bren's such a jerk, and since we were already"—she didn't want to say *pretending* in case anyone was out there—"well, you know, something just came over me."

"Yeah, that seems to be happening a lot between us. So you were using me to get the ex jealous?"

"Gods, no." She continued to her car. "It was more of an eff-you kiss. Or really an eff-off kiss. Thanks for indulging me."

His gaze settled on her mouth for a moment. "My pleasure."

The words skittered down her spine because she was pretty sure he meant them. It was her pleasure, too, but she held back that sentiment. "So...now what do we do?"

He gave her a heart-stopping smile. "We could do it again."

Her Dragon jumped at his silky voice, and her pulse fluttered. "I meant about the investigation."

"Let's go to your place."

"You really are something, aren't you?" She laughed, feeling better now that she thought he was just a player. "This is a role, an illusion, something you Deuces are good at—"

"To look at your map. I had a chance to check out the one in Ferro's office. I want to compare."

Her cheeks burned again. "Oh. Of course."

He gave her a knowing smile. "Sometimes it's hard to tell the difference between illusion and reality. The lines blur. Boundaries disappear." The mist in his eyes swirled as his gaze held hers. Even though the Dragon flames had disappeared, it was still provocative.

She felt that fog swirling inside her, too. "We need to keep those boundaries solid, the lines clear." Her Dragon shimmered and sensually stretched. Damn beast should've been sated, not itching for more.

The door flew open, and Bren and his two brothers shot out.

"Parking lot fights are off-limits—" she started to say, but they ran to their truck, their faces pale and drawn.

"What's going on?" she asked them.

Bren paused, his fingers gripping the door's edge. "It's Butch. Someone killed him."

Chapter 7

Violet insisted on following the Augusts to find out what she could. She also insisted on going alone; it wasn't the time or place for Kade to accompany her. Kade jumped into his 'Stang and headed over to the Murphys. Violet was right; they had to keep those boundaries solid. He needed to recognize the illusion for what it was, because his body still vibrated from the chemistry of their kiss. He had been with beautiful, sensual women before, been entirely attracted to them, then said good-bye, it's been nice, and gone on with little more than a fond memory. Violet had him upside down in a way he'd never experienced, and that was dangerous for many reasons.

He shifted the car into high gear as he tore down the two-lane road and called Mia.

"Hey, do me a favor. Pull up Dan Murphy's records and see if his family has reported his death yet."

"Sure, hold on." A minute passed before she returned. "Nope."

Damn, that would make it harder if he couldn't visit under the guise of following up on the report. "All right, thanks."

He drove past a huge field of flowering shrubs, all in neat rows, ready to be dug up, potted, and sold to nurseries. He had to hand it to the Fringers; at least a handful of people in any given family worked hard to keep their businesses afloat. The troublemakers gave them all a bad rap. Unfortunately, there were plenty of them.

Kade hadn't had reason to come to the Fringe in years. The Murphys weren't a family he had any direct history with, though they still wouldn't welcome him.

As soon as he pulled up to the two-story main house, three people stepped out onto the front porch. Suspicion dripped from their expressions. Kade got out of the car and raised his arm, showing them the V symbol on his dagger. Their suspicion didn't lessen but their fighting stance did.

"My name's Kade Kavanaugh. I've got a couple of questions, and then I'll be on my way."

That softened their expressions a bit...the part about leaving shortly, anyway.

The older man approached after gesturing for what was probably his offspring to remain on the porch. "I'm Bob Murphy, head of this clan. What do you want to know?"

"There's been a lot of dying going on in the Fringe. I'm not here to accuse you," Kade added as the man's face shuttered. "The Guard keeps an eye on irregular activity, and six murders in ten days is damned irregular, even here. I understand you lost one of yours."

Bob glanced away, stroking his long, trimmed beard. "My son, Danny. Sons of bitches came right onto our property and killed him, sucked away his power. Ain't right."

"I'm sorry for your loss," Kade said, the trite and mostly meaningless phrase they were taught to say in these circumstances. Well, he was already tossing out the rules. "That ain't right at all," he said, pulling in the accent. "Trespassing, killing without cause. I'll bet you didn't put up with that for one second, did you? I sure as hell wouldn't have."

The man furrowed his brow in surprise.

Kade shook his head. "I know, I'm supposed to say how killing another Crescent is wrong, even out of revenge, but things work differently here. Frankly, I don't care about the revenge part. The Castanega bastard got what he deserved, you ask me. If he was the one who did it. And no, I'm not trying to get you to confess." He lifted his shirt to show he wasn't wired. "Someone's causing trouble down here. That's the person or family I want. I'd appreciate you sharing what evidence you found so I know who to go after."

The man considered Kade's request, then nodded. "The Castanegas are the ones you want. I found one of their alligator foot key rings they sell at their tourist trap. I know it came from their shop 'cause it has a little metal disk on the bottom with a *C* on it. Whoever done it left it right there, a few feet from Danny's body. Like he was showing off. Or taunting us."

Kade leaned against the car, effecting a casual pose, but he kept an eye on the man's sons. They appeared to be about to cause some trouble of their own . . . in his direction.

Bob followed Kade's gaze, and whatever look he gave them stopped their advance. To Kade he said, "They've been downright itchy to fight lately."

"You think it's the solar storm?"

"Could be, I suppose. My wife's been taking two naps a day, and that ain't like her. Seems to tire some out, and fire some up."

Kade nodded toward the key ring. "How do you know a Castanega left it? Anyone could have bought one."

"Fringers don't buy that kind of crap. And a tourist sure as hell isn't going to come onto my property. You saw all the signs warning people off."

Indeed he had. Only a foolhardy Mundane would continue down that road. "What about someone leaving it there as a setup?"

The old man shook his head. "That's not how it works 'round here. Usually it's a fight that grows into something bigger. I heard Jessup at Ernie's, oh, 'bout a month ago, saying how things are boring in the Fringe nowadays. That idjit is always spoiling for a fight."

Kade nodded. "Jessup's a pistol." He'd never had reason to arrest him, but Jessup was always eager to jump in and defend Arlo. "Would he be that arrogant, that desperate for action, to start a feud?"

"Maybe. And I expect he'll be coming for a visit now that Arlo's dead." He cracked his knuckles, and his eyes flared. "And we'll be ready."

Yeah, they were all spoiling for action. And now, blood. "What about Violet?"

"She used to be as feisty as the rest of 'em, but I haven't seen her much in recent years. She don't hang out at Ernie's, doesn't get into trouble. Hell, the last time I saw her in a skirmish was at the Swamp Festival, what, sixteen years ago. The Garza girl—Pilar—let out one of those ear-piercing whistles right in the middle of Violet's bout with a ten-foot gator, distracting her enough that the gator turned and nearly tore her arm off. Pilar done it on purpose 'cause she wanted the title and Violet had won four years running. Violet had control, I give her that. She went after Pilar, bloody arm and all, but she didn't Catalyze in front of the tourists who come for the festival. Pilar was banned from the competition forever."

That version of Violet was closer to the one who'd attacked him years ago, though he wouldn't have blamed her for going beastie on the Garza bitch.

"Violet's a good woman," Bob said. "Too bad she's a Castanega."

Violet was right about the prejudice she faced, even in the Fringe. "Why are they so bad?"

"They're troublemakers. Raucous."

"Sounds like everyone in the Fringe."

He gave an exaggerated shrug. "I think what makes them so reprehensible is they're the richest clan besides the Stramaglias."

Ah, now he was getting somewhere. Only it wasn't the place he needed to be. "During the violent times in the history of the Fringe, was it normal for someone to creep onto another family's land and kill the first person they come upon? And leave a calling card?"

The man scratched his beard. "Not really."

Kade pushed away from the car and held out his hand. The man eyed it for a moment before taking it. "Thank you," Kade said. "I meant what I said about being sorry. No one should have to die that way. I'm going to find out what the devil is going on around here and stop it."

Kade headed back to Ernie's, but there were people hanging out in the parking lot. He recognized a man he had arrested not too long ago, which meant the guy might rec-

ognize Kade, too. So he returned to Castanega land, hid his
car, and trekked back to Violet's house.

She wasn't back yet. Not wanting to be out in the open, he
went into her workshop. She kept everything clean and or-
ganized, bins of gems neatly labeled and stacked on shelves.
Several pieces sat on the worktable, mid-completion.
Amethysts and topazes adorned a necklace that reminded
him of a collar, big and bold. It sat next to a sketch she'd
drawn up with lots of flourishes. Another piece was delicate,
a spray of opal flower petals and emerald leaves. Off to the
side, a whole stack of sketches awaited.

There was too much... Violet in here. Her dreams and
passions, and even her dog, who got to his feet and ambled
over with wagging tail. Kade scratched the mutt's head, remembering how Violet had buried her face in the folds of
fur. Cats detested Dragons, something about their energy
being feline and yet not. It seemed to throw them off. Other
animals didn't mind, obviously.

"You're a good friend," he whispered, then checked the
window before stepping out into the muggy air. The presence of another being prickled through him. He froze,
searching. A Fire Elemental sat high in one of the cypress
trees like a dark red monkey. It watched with its big eyes,
making no move to alert anyone. The Fires often hung
around Dragons, and though they weren't pets, they sometimes had a loyalty to their Crescents.

Something hit him, sending him crashing to the ground.
He spun quickly, dislodging his assailant and leaping in the
opposite direction. His dagger filled his hand as he rolled
into the motion and landed on his feet, facing a Sapphire
Dragon. It unleashed a blue ice-cold plume. Kade deflected
the cloud with his magick and felt only the frigid outer

edge. The blue Dragon's black facial markings stretched along his temples and to the back of his smooth, sleek head. Male, by its energy, the only way to tell a Dragon's gender in most cases.

Kade held out his dagger in a way that showed his Guard designation. "Stand down."

"Yeah, it's that Vega son of a bitch, all right," the blue Dragon said. Ryan, Kade guessed.

But who was he talking to? Kade felt a bristling presence seconds before he jumped to the side and faced down a Carnelian Dragon.

"You got no right to be here. We have nothing illegal going on," the red Dragon snarled.

The Sapphire's vertical irises widened, and he seemed to smile. "He doesn't have his official un-ee-form on."

Red smiled. "Which makes you fair game. Especially since you're sneaking around our sister's place."

Jessup, then.

Just as Kade started to explain why he was there, a third Dragon burst from around the corner of the house. "Let's get 'em," the Citrine said, looking way too happy to do so as he whipped his deadly tail. "You did see the sign, didn't you? Trespassers will be fed to the gators. Or to the Dragons." He let out a long laugh.

Three on one. *Bring it on.* Two things hit Kade at once. He couldn't hurt them; they were Violet's kin, after all. And he couldn't tell these bozos that the reason he was investigating was because she'd gone to the Guard.

Hell.

They, on the other hand, would kill him in a flash. Two other things hit him—Dragons. His dagger flew from his hand as he dropped to the ground. He heard it hit the dirt a few yards away. All he could see were vividly colored scales and claws and fangs.

He threw his hands up, sending a flash of magick that kicked them back a few feet. Damn, but he wanted to pull out the fatal Lightning so bad his fingers tingled. Adrenaline throbbed through his body, narrowing his vision. Being attacked sent him into kill mode, and he had to fight to stop it. Wiping these morons wouldn't solve the case. More deaths sure wouldn't keep Violet safe.

He thrust out his hand, and the dagger flew into it. He readied the taser, rubbing his other fingers together. Was there enough juice to take out all of them? He had to touch their forehead, and that wasn't going to be easy with them out for his blood. They moved in on him, again forming a deadly circle.

"Violet knows I'm here," Kade said, slicing the blade through the air between them as he kept turning. Blue sparks arced off the tip, leaving a trail that acted like a barrier. Sparks crackled over his skin as he pulled the power from within.

Jessup snorted. "Yeah, right. 'Cause she's into Vegas. Especially Deuce Vegas."

"I *am* here on official business. You think six murders in ten days isn't going to snag the Guard's attention?"

Kade kept turning in a slow circle, but at any given moment, one of the three was in his blind spot. The Citrine, probably a cousin, jabbed his sinuous tail at Kade, who barely evaded the sharp point. The thing was like a yellow jacket stinger, painful when it touched, deadly when it sank in and injected poison.

While he was distracted, Jessup lunged at him fangs-first. Kade used his magick to Change one hand, extending his fingers and clamping them around Jessup's mouth. With the other, he managed to press the tips of his fingers to Jessup's temple. After a scream and a jerk, Jessup landed on the ground, naked and human. Kade was already facing the Citrine, who tried to grab him from behind. He sent a shard of Lightning at the Dragon's shoulder, singeing the scales.

Ryan grabbed at Kade, fangs scratching through his shirt and across his back. Though Kade managed to slip out of his grasp, the Citrine sandwiched him from the other side before he could fully extricate himself. The force crushed Kade between them, sending the air gushing from his lungs. As fangs came at him, he ducked, rolling out from between them. A foot stomped down on him, grinding his chest into the dirt.

"You all right, Jessup?" Ryan asked.

Jessup shook his head as he pushed up to his elbows. "Holy dragonfire, what the hell?" He aimed a murderous look at Kade. "Squash him like a cockroach."

"It's against Crescent law to assault an officer," Kade ground out, trying to get his hands free from where they were pinned beneath him. His dagger lay a few feet away, but without a hand to call it, it did him no good.

"The Guard don't care about what goes on in the Fringe," Ryan said from above him. "Lots of people die here, and the Guard is happy to file the paperwork and have fewer of us to deal with."

That was truer than Kade cared to admit. "They care when it threatens to expose the Hidden." He managed to free one hand and clamp it around the foot holding him down, sending a jolt of magick through his fingers.

The foot lifted, and a growl filled the air. Kade jumped

to his feet, his back stiff and sore. He swiped up his dagger and held them at bay.

"What are you doing at Vee's house?" Jessup was on his feet, looking no less dangerous in human form. "Sneaking around? Looking for evidence? Violet has never done anything illegal in her life." His upper lip lifted in a sneer. "Except for attacking you once."

"And giving him a black eye." The Citrine's tail flicked at Kade again, and he slashed at it with his dagger. Just close enough to shock it with the dagger's magick. The Citrine hissed and pulled it back.

"I'm here in an unofficial capacity." Kade's adrenaline-fired brain searched for an explanation. "The Guard *is* aware of the murder spree, but I'm here for... Vee. I need to look at her map." He'd have to call her Vee now.

That narrowed Jessup's eyes. "How'd you know about her map?"

"She asked me to look into the murders. Because we're... involved."

Jessup's upper lip lifted. "Involved how?"

"We met in Naples. She was there on business, and I was on vacation. We stayed at the same hotel."

He hated to commit her to that, but these guys were going to tear him apart otherwise. Or try. Then he'd have to do some damage, and things would get ugly all around.

"*Hell*, no." Jessup fairly vibrated with the need to Catalyze. He stared at his clenched hands. "What'd you do to me?"

"Taser. You'll be fine in about thirty minutes. Plenty of time for you to hear me out and see that killing me isn't in your best interests." He shot the other two a look, rubbing his fingers together. "I can give you guys some downtime, too, if necessary." They backed up a step. "Vee didn't want you to know about us yet, given the obvious. Believe me, we were surprised at the sparks between us, too." Very true. "But love knows no bounds, as they say." Something of which he knew little, but he'd heard the expression.

"*Love*?" Ryan ground out.

"No fucking way," Jessup said, backing away. That was a good sign, wasn't it, despite his obvious disgust? "I'm going to beat her butt something fierce."

"She's going on the wall of shame," the cousin added.

"Don't touch her." The words were out before Kade could even consider them.

"So now you're her great protector?" Ryan shot back, wrapping sarcasm around his last words.

"Yes." Kade held his dagger tight but lowered it to show that he wasn't a threat. He really didn't want to deal with these boneheads, but he was in it now. A lot of it, because Violet—Vee—wasn't going to be happy about his story. Then again, she'd passed him off as her lover at Ernie's. She'd kissed him. "Vee wanted to tell you in her own time and way, but now that the cat's out of the bag, let's work it out. For her sake. She wouldn't want you killing me, and she wouldn't be happy if I, say, cut your tail off." He aimed those words at the Citrine cousin. "Or your heads."

For those few seconds when he'd turned away, Jessup must have given a signal. Both Dragons threw themselves at Kade, claws digging into his skin as they pushed him into the dirt. He flexed his fingers, calling his dagger back, but one of the Dragons blocked its path. The handle thumped against his hard hide. Kade fought, pummeling them with blasts of magick. The tough bastards rode them out.

Time to shape-shift. Changing took a lot of his energy, so it was usually a last-ditch maneuver. Might as well go big.

A Dragon slammed into him as he drew in the magick and felt it race through his veins. It was illusion, not a flesh-and-bone transformation like the Dragons did. But the illusion seemed every bit as real. He felt the illusion, too, his body stretching and growing until he towered over the two Dragons.

They looked up at him, their eyes widening. "You picked a Dragon, you son of a bitch," the cousin said in his Dragon growl.

"A big-assed one," Ryan added.

That only made them fight harder, coming at him in a blur of claws and fangs. Kade fought back, trying not to inflict too much damage while protecting himself. Jessup was strangely absent from the melee, though Kade couldn't take his eyes off the other two to find out what he was doing.

Time to finish this. He reached out with his clawed hand and touched Ryan's forehead, hoping he had enough juice left to tase the both of them. He sent the magick through his fingers.

Ryan squeezed him in a bear hug. The taser's force pounded through Kade, powerful even secondhand. The punch of power sent them flying in opposite directions. A naked Ryan sprawled on the ground a short distance away. Kade searched for his dagger. It was on his arm, as inert as a regular tattoo.

Hell times two.

Dazed, and fatigued from the Change, he staggered to his feet. The cousin was staring at Kade. Smiling. Like he was about to see something really funny. Kade spun around in time to see Jessup swinging down on a rope from the tree, right at him.

A moment after his bare feet connected with Kade's head, the world went dark.

Chapter 8

As fast as the Augusts were driving, Violet caught up to them as they turned down their driveway. A group of them gathered near an outbuilding, and that's where the truck she followed parked. The early evening light cast a warm glow over a dark scene. Butch was a big, brawny jerk. Not someone easily overcome. He was on his side, blood staining the ground. So much like Arlo's death scene. Gods, was he really dead? Everything that had happened since that morning seemed surreal.

When she got out of her car, several people looked at her as though she'd Catalyzed into a chicken.

"What're you doing here?" Larry called out to her, his voice tight.

Bren turned to them, hitching his thumb at her. "Vee here is going to get justice for us. She's investigating the recent murders."

She heard various mumbling in response, mostly suspicion or skepticism. "You're not the only clan to lose a family member like this. Arlo... was murdered this morning." She listed some of the other names on her fingers like Ernie had done. "Think about it. Something's not right here. Why are Fringers suddenly killing each other in what looks like ambush murders? Somebody's targeting us, trying to incite us."

"I say we take out the whole Spears clan like you did with the Garzas," one August said.

"I didn't do that." She had nothing to do with it, being a kid at the time. She'd seen the bloody body of one of her cousins though, their only fatality in the skirmish. His mother had collapsed over it, sobbing so deeply that Violet had felt her own heart tear apart. "Let me figure this out before anyone goes on a rampage. Do we need to lose more of our people?"

Anger and the need for revenge sparked in their eyes, and yeah, she felt it, too. For Arlo. Revenge and rage were in their blood. She'd promised herself she would do everything she could to stamp that out of her psyche, to be the levelheaded one.

The Augusts were still grumbling, and she heard words like... *kill them.*

Time to use a different angle. "Kill the people or person behind this spree. Gut them, hang them from the tree. But kill the right person."

That got their heads nodding, a few murmurs of agreement. She was less hopeful about the mutterers.

"Who is the right person?" the patriarch asked, his grief and shock evident in his eyes.

"I'm working on finding out."

"Who was that guy you were with?" Bren asked. "Does he have anything to do with this?"

"He's a private detective." Close enough to the truth, though eventually someone was going to recognize him.

The patriarch arched his bushy eyebrows. "You involved an outsider in our business?"

"I involved him because he's objective. For the very fact that he is an outsider."

Bren said, "He wasn't an outsider when you stuck your tongue down his throat."

Well, I didn't know what his story was going to be at the time. "He's also a close friend."

Butch's wife collapsed in gut-wrenching wails. Several Augusts went to her side, while others drifted back to the death scene. Her grief brought Violet's to the surface, and she blinked back tears as she searched the ground. They didn't know the pattern of the murderer leaving a phony clue. She wanted to find the clue before they did.

"We already know it was those damned Spearses," someone said. "They retaliated on our retaliation. Not only is that against the unwritten rules, but it's also a declaration of war."

She sighted something hanging from a branch. The full import of the alligator foot key ring being there hit her hard. No one had seen it. Yet. She edged closer, pretending to get a better look at the body as the family discussed the wounds. Keeping her gaze on them, she snatched the key ring out of the bush. Seeing the *C* stamped into the base of the foot felt like a thunderclap in her heart. The murderer left it here to set up her clan as responsible for Butch's murder.

"Violet."

She spun, coming face-to-face with Bren's somber face. "Yes?"

"You should leave. You don't belong here at a time like this." Or ever, really, though he didn't say that. She clutched the key ring in her hand and held it next to her thigh. "I was only hoping to stop your family from going on a rampage."

"They're going to do what they're going to do." He reached for her hand. She kept it closed tight, her Dragon shuddering. If they knew this was here, and that she was hiding it, they'd take care of justice the easy way—by killing her immediately. She would have no chance against the group of them.

His hand wrapped around hers. "I appreciate what you're trying to do. I know how much having peace in the Fringe means to you, and yeah, I took advantage of that." He didn't look apologetic, but at least he acknowledged it. "But there are some of my kin who are hungry for blood, and your presence isn't helping."

She nodded, pulling her hand back. "I'll go now."

The keychain bit into her palm from holding it so hard. She grabbed for the door handle, and the gator foot fell to the ground. Bren was still watching, now a short distance away. She swiped it up, got into the vehicle, and took off.

Kade's shiny new Mustang wasn't in Ernie's lot. She searched for it all the way home. Had he given up the idea of investigating? She ignored the stab of disappointment.

Her mother waved her down as she passed the main house, two stories of plantation-style home. Kay Castanega was no Southern belle, though. The hard planes of her face, tanned and weathered, held no hint of makeup. Her work clothes, stained with old alligator blood, hung on her bony frame. Her ma hadn't dated since her husband's death.

Sometimes Violet was tempted to tell her it was all right by her, but she just couldn't get the words out.

The flames in her mother's light blue eyes barely flickered as she approached the car, grief etched as deeply as her facial lines. Violet rolled down her window as she slowed to a stop. "Everything all right, Ma?" It wasn't, of course.

"The funeral home called about Arlo's service. It's set for two days from now."

Violet had the urge to get out and hug her mom, but Castanegas didn't do things like that. They stood together, fought as one, but they didn't hold one another for comfort, didn't share any feelings but the angry ones. So Violet only nodded, her mouth turning down in a frown. "Did the boys tell you my theory?"

"Yeah, they said you were investigating. Be careful out there, Vee. You're putting yourself in the crossfire by nosing around."

Guess she wouldn't tell her that she had tread onto August land. "I'll be careful."

Ma nodded toward the back of the property. "Those boys are up to something. I heard fighting. When I went to check it out, Jessup met me in your front yard, said there was a coon in your workshop and for me not to worry about it. I knew he was lying, but I just didn't have the energy to find out what he was up to."

"I'll check it out."

Violet sped down the road. Her house, at least from the front, looked nice and normal. No sign of Chumley. She cut the engine, grabbed the keychain, and got out. Her senses were tuned in to her surroundings. Blue jays warbled in the pine trees, then let out loud squawks before taking off. The breeze ruffled the needles and bushes around her house. She walked around the back, finding signs of a skirmish where the dirt was messed up. But she and Kade may have done that. They'd gotten down and dirty, all right. Her workshop door was still open, no sign of a raccoon anywhere.

The sound of footsteps pulled her attention farther into the woods. Jessup and Ryan came into view, looking a bit too smug for guys who'd defeated a raccoon. Jessup had his trademark swagger, wearing only jeans. Ryan had a more deliberate gait and watchful nature. Both headed her way.

She hooked her thumbs in the front pockets of her jeans and waited for them.

Jessup spoke before she could. "Where have you been?" He had that post-fight glow in his eyes, vibrating with dangerous energy. Coupled with his five o'clock shadow, he looked downright predatory.

"Butch August is dead, too." She held out her hand, the keychain resting on her palm. "I found this near where he was killed and grabbed it before anyone saw it."

They both stared at it but neither looked guilty.

She said, "A handkerchief tied Shirley's death to the Spears boy. Footprints led from the Peregrine murder scene to the property next door. Now it looks as though you were responsible for Butch's death."

Jessup lifted his hands. "We're not stupid enough to leave something like that lying around, even if we did have a reason to kill Butch. Which we don't."

"I know that. It just goes to my theory that someone is setting us up so we'll kill each other." She dropped her hand, hooking the ring around her finger. "Ma says there was a raccoon in my workshop. What's going on? And don't bullshit me."

Jessup crossed his arms over his chest. "Vee, you need to come clean with us if you've been hiding something."

The underlying tension in his command prickled over her skin. "Hard to hide stuff if you're all living on one piece of land and working together every day." The good and bad about being close to her family.

"So there's nothing we need to know?" Jessup asked.

"Nope."

True enough. They didn't need to know about Kade.

Jessup nodded. "That's what I thought." He gave Ryan a look Violet couldn't decipher. "We'd better show her what we found."

They turned and walked back the way they'd just come, mock grave expressions on their faces. Mock because they were enjoying this. She followed, her curiosity winning out over her annoyance at their evasiveness. Whatever it was, it wasn't going to be good.

When she saw the lights up ahead, filtering through the pines and cypress, her footsteps faltered. Disco music poured from the speakers planted all around the grounds. "Don't tell me you tied the coon to the wall of shame."

They'd never done it to a critter. You couldn't blame an animal for being what it was; that's what Jessup said whenever one caused trouble. As they neared the barn, she recognized "The Hustle." She turned to her brothers. "You're playing Ma's disco music? Now that's just cruel."

Jessup chuckled. "We started out with Barry Manilow."

Now she stepped up her pace, passing the two. She was nearly running when she barreled around the corner and came to a heart-blistering stop.

It wasn't a raccoon clamped to the wall; it was Kade. As was customary, he'd been stripped down to his black boxer briefs and blindfolded, arms out at his sides. He was breathing; that was good. His dagger tattoo shimmered, fairly pulsed, so she was pretty sure he was conscious. There was something...erotic about the sight of him like that, the light glistening off the sweat on his chest and washboard abs, and it twined down through her stomach.

Jessup flung his hand at Kade, as though presenting him as a prize. "So I'm to understand you have nothing to do with him?"

Her mouth opened but no words came out. Too many things cascaded into her mind at once. First, that Kade had come back to her house alone. Why, *why* would he have done that? That he'd gotten himself caught by her brothers. That they hadn't killed him—yet. And mostly how totally inappropriate it was being turned on by the sight of him trussed up like that. What the heck was she supposed to say?

Ryan said, "Jessup and I were helping Patry find a stray hog when we saw a car hidden in the woods off the main road. We tracked him down to your workshop, where he was walking out like he owned the place. He claims he's doing you."

"I didn't say I was *doing* her," Kade spat out. "Have some respect."

Jessup stepped into her line of vision. "The only reason we didn't kill him was because he swore you two have a thing. I figured he was lying. Not my sister, dating a *Vega*." He said it the same way other Crescents said "Fringers." "Especially not this one. But I figured, what the hell, keep him here and find out for sure."

Violet leaned to the side, giving herself a moment to pull together a response. "If I Can't Have You" was playing now.

Kade was pushing subtly against the cuffs that held his wrists, fingers flexing. It was no use. He wouldn't be able to use his magick. "Sorry, babe, but I told them about us meeting in Naples, how we clicked, as crazy as that was."

He was calling her "babe" again. Gods.

Jessup rubbed his hands together. "So can we kill him for trespassing and because he's an asshole in general?"

They would kill Kade if she refuted his claim. He'd been in this position, too, outnumbered with no other recourse than to tell them that story. And he hadn't harmed them with his powerful magick. If Kade had been fighting in any other situation, he would have put a hurting on his attackers. Her brothers looked scraped and bruised, but she didn't see any serious injuries. As much as she hated the idea of betraying her family this way, she had no choice.

"We're...involved."

"String her up with him," Jessup said to Ryan, shaking his head in disgust.

Ryan made to grab her arm, but she shook him off. "No! You all may run my life, but you don't get to tell me who I fall for. *I* don't even have a say in that, apparently," she muttered under her breath.

"Vee, the last time you fell for some guy, it was that idjit Bren, who was only using you to find out our trade secrets. I warned you, but you had stars in your eyes." Jessup waggled his fingers in front of his eyes, his disdain clear.

"Stars for making peace between the families more than for him," Ryan added. "Remember, Jessup, she was only fourteen when Dad died. It hit her hard."

"And little Roddy died, too," Violet said, referring to the cousin who'd been killed during their retribution. "I didn't want anyone else killed."

"All I'm saying is, you don't have the best judgment where men are concerned." Jessup pointed at Kade. "Obviously. You shoulda just gone for one of the Murphy boys."

"Augh. Kade's far different than the Murphys."

"Like how? He's our enemy, so are they. Maybe he's better-looking." Jessup wrinkled his nose. "I'll give him that."

"He's got class. Prestige. Discipline."

Jessup waved his finger in a circle. "Whoop-de-doo. He's got his cause, we have ours. But his badge makes us a lot of trouble. So what's going on with you two exactly? He said the word *love*."

She had to keep her eyebrows from rising. *Oh, Kade. Really? Just bury me deeper.* "*In* love. You know, a nudge past infatuation. Oh, you wouldn't know, because you two never get to the 'in love' part. You wait. Wait 'til you fall in love and see if you have any choice in the matter. See if it makes sense."

Jessup looked at Ryan. "First she wants to go off and find fancy designers to buy our skins, then we let her start making *jewelry*, and now this." He nodded toward Kade. "She's gotten too full of herself."

Violet jabbed her collarbone. "I *am* full of myself. Finally. I put in my time slopping around in the mud checking water temps and slinging gator chow. I pitch in where I'm needed and do the books for the farm. But I'm a grown-up, and that means I get to make my own decisions."

"Mistakes, you mean," Jessup grumbled.

"Remember how you thought I was being silly contacting foreign designers? You stopped minding that our skins were being made into 'girly stuff' when our biggest checks started to come from them. Now I want to do the things I want to do."

"And you want to do him?" Jessup shifted his gaze to Kade, which made her look his way, too. "A Deuce?"

Her Dragon stirred. And purred!

Pretending! Big fat illusion, you dumb beast. He's not even Dragon.

Of course, each time they kissed, and that time he'd had his hands on her, she'd totally ignited. The memory now heated her blood and made her want things she shouldn't. In the midst of all this craziness, she had no business believing the charade she and Kade were putting on.

"Vee," Jessup pressed. "Do you want him?"

"Yes," she said, the word hoarse and scratchy. "Damn it, I get grief if I date a Fringer. I get grief if I date an outsider. Mundanes are out. There's nothing else!" Frustration stretched her words taut. No pretending there.

Jessup shook his head in his *I can't believe this* way. He approached Kade, whose body tightened in response, even if he couldn't see him. Jessup pointed his finger at him. "You pull anything or do anything to hurt my sister or my family, and I'll string you up here and cut off your appendages one by one. And I'll enjoy it."

He gestured for Ryan to go with him. She followed them, hating their disgust at her. She'd spent her life trying to live up to them, and after her dad had died, they'd stepped into the father figure role. Once they were out of Kade's earshot, she halted them.

"It's temporary, I swear, so stop looking at me like I've just wrecked the family name." Or their trust in her.

"Do you know what hell we'll suffer if word gets out that you've taken up with a Vega? And a Deuce, to boot?" Ryan asked. "We're not supposed to even like Deuces, much less date them."

"I'm not taking up with him." She glanced at the "him" in question, then forced her gaze back to her brothers. "We started talking, we laughed, and our eyes sort of locked onto each other's. Have you ever felt a zing with someone?"

"What's a *zing*?" Jessup asked.

She put herself back in that moment at Guard headquarters. "A sudden and surprising shock that feels really good. Your chest tightens and your throat goes dry and your body tingles. That's what we felt. I called him after Arlo's death, and he's helping me figure out what's going on. I know it'll never work but right now it's . . . nice," she finished on a soft breath. Too nice.

"You'll kick him to the curb eventually?" Jessup asked, his expression skeptical.

"Have I gotten involved long term with anyone?"

"Well, no."

"So there. And turn this music off."

She watched them wander off, both shaking their heads, and waited until they disappeared into the darkness. Then she turned to the specimen on the wall. Annoyingly, her stomach tightened. Her body tingled. Damn it, she was supposed to be mad at him.

She stalked to him. "You." She had to keep her voice down because she could feel her brothers' presence hovering just out of sight. Instinctively, they knew something wasn't right. She knew how to get rid of them. She grabbed a thick wooden block and set it in front of Kade, then stepped up on it so they were face-to-face.

"That you, Vee?" he asked. He inhaled, his mouth curving into a smile.

"Yes, *babe*," she said, a bite in her voice. "My brothers are still watching." To let him know that they still had to play the charade. She was inches from what she called a superhero chin, square with a deep cleft in it. She had the weirdest urge to run her finger down the groove. He smelled of sweat, aftershave, and mud, an alluring combination. Her Dragon was really purring now, which made her even madder.

She leaned close to his ear, which made his mussed hair tickle her cheek. "Why did you come back to my house? You were supposed to wait for me at Ernie's."

He seemed oddly calm, considering the circumstances. "There were Fringers loitering in the parking lot who might recognize me."

She trailed her finger down his chest, forcing a smile for her brothers. Just in case. "You had no right to go into my workshop."

He kept his head upright, shoulders taut, his Vega pride still intact despite his indignity. "You're right." He had a way of agreeing that wasn't quite genuine.

"And you got caught by my brothers," she hissed. "Putting me in a very bad situation."

His upper lip twitched. "I wasn't too thrilled about it myself. I thought you'd be displeased if I maimed them. Or told them how we really met," he added in a low voice.

Damn, he was right about that. He'd saved her a verbal spanking. "Thank you. You were in a tough situation, having to fight at a disadvantage. I didn't think about you telling them I'd gone to the Guard." When a bloom of affection and admiration filled her, she jabbed her finger into his hard chest. "You wouldn't have had to deal with any of that if you'd waited like we agreed."

"I didn't agree. And I don't take orders unless they're from my superior." His mouth tightened a bit. "And sometimes not even then."

Her finger was still pressed against his skin. "And of course, you see me as your inferior." That rankled, but she couldn't help grinning on her next words, especially since he couldn't see it. "But right now I *am* your superior. Given our current position."

"Indeed. I don't see you as my inferior, though. Just to be clear. Why can't I use my magick, by the way?" His question was casual, yet she sensed an underlying tension in his tone.

"Well, they didn't *tase* you."

"They sort of did, actually. Long story. There's something in these cuffs that's blocking my magick."

The cuffs were woven with various threads, one of which was a strand of Lucifer's Gold, a substance that annulled Crescent magick if it came in contact with the skin.

"Can't tell you. Family secret." She leaned so close her jaw brushed his and softened her voice. "Not until we're married." Her hand had automatically flattened on his chest when she'd moved forward. "Since we *lurve* each other."

His smile reminded her of the Cheshire cat's. "More than words can say."

Blondie sang about a heart of glass. Violet remembered dancing around the house as a kid when her ma played these old songs. The "pain in the ass" line was particularly apt right about then.

She felt, rather than saw, her brothers finally leave. They weren't voyeurs, and they certainly wouldn't want to witness anything sensual between her and Kade. She doubted Kade knew they'd left though. She liked having the upper hand with him. *Let's torture him some.* It was the least she could do after everything he'd done to her family.

She ran her hand down his chest, letting her thumb brush past his nipple, all the way to the hard ridges of his stomach. "Oh, but, Kade, say them, darling," she said in a louder voice. "You know how I love to hear you say them in that honey-dripping voice of yours."

He laughed, the kind of sound one makes when they're in a corner. Just when she thought he might stumble through some awkward words, he said, "Oh, baby, I love waking up next to you in the morning, with your hair all mussed and that dreamy light in your eyes. I love you in that red dress with the deep cut in the front, though you know I love you out of it even more. I love you when you're ready to fight, all full of piss and vinegar because no one's taking you seriously."

She was again at the station the moment their gazes met and that bizarre zing arced between them. Damn, the guy was smooth. And good at what he did. "Go on."

Despite his position, he seemed more than willing to indulge their charade. "Know what we did that really turned me on?"

She stroked his arm, her mouth only an inch in front of his. "Mmm, do tell."

"Wrestling in the puddle. The mud contrasting with your creamy skin, your nipples dusky and perky, and your fantastic ass, gods, the way it felt beneath my hands." He let out a sigh. "Can we do it again?"

His words twined through her stomach and down between her legs. She pressed her thighs together. Damn it, she wasn't supposed to be enjoying this so much. And he...he was playing the role way too well.

She dared glance down that muscular chest to the top edge of his boxer briefs, where the tip of his very hard erection pushed right up past the band. Could the guy be *that* good an actor? She'd heard that Vegas could play undercover well, but really...

She smacked his chest, nearly stumbling off the block. She had to grab his arms to keep herself from falling, and for the life of her, she couldn't will them to let go. "You're this all-powerful Vega, stripped down, blindfolded, and pinned to a barn wall. Being subjected to disco music! You should be pissed, humiliated. *And you... you're turned on.*"

"Well, I sure wasn't turned on when your brothers were flogging me. But now that it's you and me, and I'm pretty sure you're not going to kill me, I find it rather erotic. In fact, this is one of my fantasies, being under the control of a sexy woman."

He'd called her sexy. She blinked. Hadn't he? She shook her head, getting sidetracked once again. "You are depraved."

"I thought it would be with a woman I knew very well, but there's something edgy about it being you."

"Don't be too sure about that not-killing-you part."

His smile was all too real. "Oh, and naked mud wrestling is another fantasy of mine. So within one day, you've fulfilled two of my fantasies, Vee. You are quite the woman." He tilted his head. "Any fantasies I can take care of for you?"

"It's *Violet*," she bit out, trying to stanch the heat curling through her. She was no prude, but she'd never considered bondage arousing. A night of good sex with a handsome stranger in a hotel room, sure. Being tied up, having someone do whatever they wanted—she pushed the thought away. Was he still playing the part for her brothers' benefit? "I don't have any fantasies." But dragonfire, she had to admit having a Vega completely under her control could be one...

"Whoa, I can feel your heat, Vee. You're turned on, too."

"Am not."

"I felt this same heat coming off you when I had my hands on you, when you came apart in my arms." Even though she couldn't see his eyes, his smugness was clear. "Right now you have all the power. You can do anything you want to me. I'm at your mercy. You like that, don't you?"

She had to swallow the sigh that threatened to escape as she took in his body. She wanted to touch him, to run her hands down his biceps, across the rippling muscles of his chest and abdomen, and over his wide rib cage.

He was just playing the part. She reined in her lust. "We don't have to play this charade anymore. They're gone now."

"They've been gone for a while."

Damn, how had he known? Now her heat was due to her embarrassment. "I thought they might still be watching." She pulled off the handkerchief, revealing his moss green eyes and all that swirling mist deep inside them. "So how much of this was..."

"Real?"

"I was going to say acting. It was all supposed to be acting."

"Yeah, it was. So what happened?" His question threw her. He'd been as swept away as she had. "I'm going to guess the same thing that happened while we were hosing off."

Gods, *that*. She shook that thought from her mind. "Before I release you, I want to get one thing straight: we might be stuck in this pretend relationship, but we are not going *there*. Uh, again. I'll have a hard enough time living this down, and that's if I just chalk it up to a lust thing."

"Because you already fell for the wrong guy once. The cretin we met at Ernie's, right?"

She rolled her eyes. "I didn't *fall* for him. But yes, that was bad judgment. You would be even worse judgment."

"Me, worse than that guy?" He rocked his head back against the wood board. "Come on, you're killing me. What about my prestige? And class?"

"Not only are you my family's enemy, but you're also an outsider. And a Deuce. That makes you much worse." And most importantly, she felt the zing with Kade, something she'd never felt with Bren.

His expression sobered. "You're right. I am worse. The totally wrong person for you. This is a fling...theoretically speaking." He lowered his voice. "And we are only putting on a show. Let me down now." He'd banked the mist that reflected a Deuce's emotional state.

Did he mean she wasn't good enough for him? If he was, at least he'd put it a nicer way. She pressed the release buttons on the cuffs, and he winced as he pulled his hands together and rubbed his arms. She knelt to release his ankles, her eyes taking in that erection snug in his tight black boxer briefs and then his muscular thighs dusted with golden hairs.

In a flash, he had his dagger in his hand. While her Dragon wanted to Catalyze in response, she held it back. Kade held the knife at an angle, turning it back and forth, and then it morphed back into a tattoo at his arm.

He turned to study the cuffs. "Not a taser-like action that stifles the magick for a set time then. Only during contact." His fingers traced the threads; the golden thread was buried inside.

If it became known that they had threads of Lucifer's Gold, someone would steal them. Or confiscate them in the name of the Guard. Their government was the only entity allowed to legally hold the substance. It came from deep within the earth of Lucifera, and, even as the island was sinking, the inhabitants saved some of it when they escaped to Florida.

"If you guess, I'll have to kill you," she said, moving the wood block out of the way. "Let's get back to the mystery at hand. Which for me is what were you looking for in my workshop?"

"Can I get dressed first?" He grabbed up the jeans lying on the grass nearby.

She'd liked being in control of him. A lot. He'd submitted to her, and that still trickled through her bloodstream. Even though he was already pulling up his pants, she said, "I suppose."

"Sounds like you want me to stay naked."

"Do not."

He approached her, chest still bare, stopping inches from her. "If you *were* mad crazy in love with me, sounds like we wouldn't be able to have a relationship because of your family."

"I wouldn't be mad crazy in love with you."

"But *if* you were..."

"I'd catch hell. It wouldn't be worth the dissension."

"When I signed on to be a Vega, I knew a serious relationship was out of the question. But you didn't sign on for something like that. It's not right for your family to deny you a relationship or give you a hard time about who you choose to be with."

"I know it's not fair, but it's just how it is." She looked at the beauty of the marsh and the swamp beyond. "There are obligations that go with the good of being in a big family."

"Like keeping the books when what you really want to do is make jewelry. You're good at it. I saw your work while I was being nosy." When she shot him a look, he said, "Hey, I thought you'd rather me be in your workshop than in your bed."

She blinked at the memory of that.

He took her chin in his hand. "I know keeping peace is important, but every time you sacrifice what you want, you cut bits and pieces off your soul until there's nothing left."

She thought of the yellow dress hanging in her closet. "What do you know about sacrificing your soul?"

"My father worked his way up through the Guard ranks and then on to the Concilium with a stellar record. I was expected to be a certain way, to want certain things. Yeah, I grew up with prestige, money, high-class parties. No one thought it was clever when I flew down the banister to make my entrance. Or Changed to a wolf and ran across the buffet table.

"I wanted to be Guard on my own terms. For a while it worked, but life smacked me down. I had to make a choice: conform or lose what was most important to me. Being a Vega was all I ever wanted. I sacrificed my personal life for it, and my nature. I see you fighting that same struggle. Don't sell your soul, Vee. It strips everything away and leaves you empty and wanting something you can't even name. Something you've forgotten was inside you, but it's an ache that never goes away." He continued on toward the house, pulling his shirt down over his head.

She could only watch him while the heavy weight of his words sank into her chest. He'd shoved that playful, sexy guy deep inside him. Despite her words, she wanted him back. But what he'd said intrigued her in another way. Was he telling her to stand up to her family on her choice of boyfriend?

But he's not your boyfriend! You're pretending until you get to the bottom of this, or until he can convince his boss to have the Guard investigate. That's all. She killed the lights and caught up to him. He'd given up serious romantic relationships, which meant he'd probably never loved a woman. Yet, he'd sounded so convincing with all of that waking up next to her in the morning stuff he'd told her.

As they approached her porch, he reached into his pocket and pulled out his vibrating phone. She glimpsed the word *Ferro* on the screen before he stuffed it back in his pocket.

"I can give you privacy if you need to take that call—"

His expression shadowed. "I'll check in with him later."

Violet led him down the hall, turned on the light in her office, and walked to the map. Somberly, she pulled another red tack from her drawer and put it in the August property. How many more would die?

"I saw a yellow and a red tack in August territory on your boss's map." She turned to him. "Were you able to find out what the yellow pins meant?"

"He didn't want to discuss the case with me at all. But there were two red pins in August land. I thought you remembered it wrong."

"I'm sure they were different colors." She tapped her temple. "Photographic memory. Yellow changed to red. Red means dead. So yellow means a potential victim, like you said. There was also a yellow pin on Slade land. I want to know why he thinks a Slade might be a target. Their biggest enemy is the Stramaglia clan, and they haven't been involved in any of this. Yet."

Kade released a long breath. "Good questions, Vee—Violet." He slid her a quick glance. "We've never bothered with your Fringe wars unless they affected non-Fringers or appeared to be something that might get out of control. Your clan wiped out another clan entirely, and it didn't even warrant an investigation, as far as I know."

She stared past Kade, feeling the shadow of those dark days. "I was only fourteen then. My father, killed for no apparent reason, and everyone out for blood." She'd wanted to go, too, in a rage of grief and anger. Hearing her family's triumph, that they'd killed every Garza who was there, didn't give her the satisfaction it seemed to give them.

"I have another question, one you'll no doubt find uncomfortable," Kade said. "I talked to the head of the Murphy clan. He claims he found one of your alligator claw key rings near his son's body, proof that someone in your family was responsible. Is there any chance—"

"None." Her hand had gone to her chest though. She jerked the key ring out of her pocket. "Did it look like this?"

He backed up, a distasteful expression on his face. "That's what he described. With your *C* on the metal disk."

She squeezed the claw. "Someone left this at the Augusts', hanging from a bush near the body. Leaving evidence so blatantly at the scene of a murder, whether on purpose or accident, just doesn't happen. Especially twice." She fisted her hands at her sides, fury suffusing her. "I want to kill somebody, too. I want the Murphys to pay for what they did." She had to take a deep breath. "But I know they were only going by the code of the Fringe. It's the person behind this who has to pay. There's only one thing to do."

"Dare I ask?"

She jabbed her finger at the yellow tack. "I'm going to stake out the Slade land and wait for the murderer to show. And then I'm going to kill him."

"You mean *we're* going to stake out the property. Charade or not, we're in this together."

Chapter 9

What the hell was Violet doing to him?

Kade tried and failed to process his reaction to the enigmatic woman while she prepared dinner. If someone had told him at the onset of the day that he'd find himself in her kitchen, he would've called him ten kinds of crazy.

The scent of lemon cream sauce and sautéing chicken filled the dining area where Kade sat at the table. She had shooed him out of her kitchen, telling him she was a control freak when it came to cooking. Since they had to wait until it got dark before prowling the woods, she'd offered to make them a hearty dinner.

He stared at the text his boss had sent: STATUS.

It wasn't a question but a demand for an answer.

IN POSITION. WAITING.

A few seconds later: WHAT'S THE PROBLEM?

FAMILY TOGETHER IN MOURNING. NOT ALONE.

Kade knew he'd only be able to put off his boss for a

limited time before he was pulled from the assignment. He had to get to the bottom of this before that happened.

The family wasn't together, which was odd. Deuces weren't particularly close, but Dragon clans were. But then again, Violet had ostracized herself by taking up with him.

So to speak.

She was on the phone now, with the receiver tucked between her ear and shoulder as she cooked. "Ma, I'm okay...No, you don't have to come over right now. Unless you need some company—of course not...I didn't tell you about Kade because"—she shot him a look—"well, I think that's obvious." She turned back to her preparation. "Right now we're looking into what's going on around the Fringe. Kade's helping me on his own time...yes, because he thinks he loves me."

Her brown hair, pulled back in a ponytail, swished back and forth with her movements. She had a long waist with all the right proportions. But it wasn't her willowy figure that had him going against everything that was important to him. It wouldn't matter if she had the wrong proportions and frizzy hair. Killing her was wrong.

The words about sacrifice had rolled out of his mouth, but they'd come from a deep place within him. Violet was nothing like he'd assumed. Educated, classy, and more like him than he'd ever imagined. A kindred soul. He'd lost himself out there, falling into the charade of being her lover.

Which is the real charade? Look at yourself, working hard to be the stalwart Vega. He'd never told anyone how he felt, the ache of losing a part of his soul. Why the hell had he told *her*?

Thankfully she'd said how wrong he was for her, bringing him back to his senses. He was wrong in so many ways.

The dog lay sprawled on the tile floor looking at him with a curious and slightly suspicious expression. He'd given up having pets, too. He loved dogs, their loyalty and affection, the way they greeted their master as though he were the most important person in the world. But he never knew when he'd be gone for days or even weeks at a time, and that wasn't fair to a dog.

"Gotta go, Ma," Violet said, breaking him out of his thoughts. "The fettuccine's ready...chicken François... no, it doesn't mean anything. I make it for myself all the time. Bye." She hung up, pulling the colander out of the big cooking pot, letting the water drain, and pouring it into a bowl. He watched her arrange piles of fettuccine on two plates with tongs, place the pieces of chicken on top, and then pour the sauce over it all.

"This looks amazing," he said as she brought the plates to the table.

She sat down and waved off the compliment. "It's nothing. Ma makes these wonderful meals, and we're all too lazy after a long day to go home and cook when we can go to the main house and get fed. But I'm trying to become more independent."

He twirled several strands of pasta on his fork and took a bite. "Tastes as good as something I'd get at a nice restaurant." He nodded to the collection of cookbooks on a shelf in her island. "You like ethnic foods."

"Love them. It's one of my indulgences when I get out of the Fringe. I haven't had time to travel to all of those places, but I love Greek food, Italian, Indian, Cuban."

He didn't want to think about her other indulgence when she went out of town, and yet, the words "Tell me more about these *weekends* of yours" came rolling off his tongue. At her raised eyebrows, he added, "Since we met during one of them, I figure I should know. Do you usually meet the same person more than once?" She hadn't answered that question before.

"No, they're usually from out of town, outside the Crescent world. I take their number but never call."

He raised an eyebrow. "You hook up with *Mundanes*? You said out-of-town guys, but I didn't put that together with non-Crescents."

"It's less complicated. Okay, more boring, but there's no temptation to keep things going, romantic relationships with them being forbidden and all. I'm not looking for a soul mate. Sometimes I just need . . . a connection. I gave up on finding someone permanent a long time ago."

"After Bren?"

She started to say *no* but released a breath. "Yeah, pretty much. Marrying into my family, well, you see how welcome someone outside the Fringe would be. An outsider will always be an outsider. But dating a Fringer brings all kinds of history and family complications." She twirled a piece of pasta on her fork and stuck it in her mouth, regarding him while she chewed. "You said you sacrificed your personal life for your career."

"Having a loved one is a vulnerability. If someone's after me, for revenge or whatever reason, he'll have a hard time getting me. Grab my wife or my kid, and I'm putty."

"You, putty? You seem all soldier to me."

"I'd do anything to protect someone I cared about."

She nodded and shivered. "Is it that much of a war out there? We're so insulated here, busy with our own problems."

"It can be. Magick corrupts some Crescents, and it's my job to take care of those who present a danger to society."

She ran the tines of her fork through the sauce on her plate, drawing lines through it, then sticking it in her mouth. "So we'd be a perfect weekend matchup." Her eyes widened. "In theory. For the charade."

He couldn't help but smile at her quick back steps. "In theory." He also couldn't help the stirring in his blood.

She dove into her meal, her cheeks a bit pinker than they were moments before. It wasn't just the thought of hooking up with her that tightened his chest . . . and his groin. Or the way she sucked in her last strand of pasta or even the way she dragged her finger through the sauce on her plate and stuck it in her mouth with a little sound of pleasure. The different sides of her intrigued him: the feisty side that had given him a black eye; the soft, vulnerable one that cried when she thought no one was looking; and the sexy one he witnessed when he'd been blindfolded. He *liked* this woman. Liked the feel of her skin, the glow of her smile. The shy way she avoided his gaze sometimes, and the hungry way she watched him other times.

"I'm afraid of whatever you're thinking about," she said, and he realized she was watching him ruminate. No doubt the mist in his eyes was swirling like crazy.

"You should be."

She stood and took her plate to the sink, walking faster than she normally did. "I never thought about how hard it was to be you. I mean, having to live up to the Guard's rep."

So she was going to change the subject, eh? "I thought it'd be easy to live down to a Fringe rep, but I can see how that might be hard. We both suffer from others' prejudices."

She made a snorting sound. "Yeah, but you've got it easier. People respect you as instantly and mindlessly as they denigrate me."

He leaned back in his chair, regarding her. "And they assume you're as uneducated and undisciplined as the rest of the Fringers. For example, I'll bet most of them don't use words like *denigrate*. Then again, Murphy used the word *reprehensible* right along with *ain't*."

For a moment she looked conflicted. "Society makes a lot of assumptions about us, and quite honestly, there are Fringers who perpetuate those prejudices. I simply choose not to. My mother homeschooled me and did a good job. I read a lot, and if I don't understand a word, I look it up."

How many people had denigrated Violet in her life? He hated the thought of it. He picked up his plate and joined her at the sink. She rinsed it, then put it in the dishwasher.

"Thanks for dinner. It was incredible."

She shrugged. "We had to eat."

They'd decided to stake out the Slade property given the pattern they'd seen in the red tacks: the inciting murders usually occurred near the property line. Unfortunately, they'd have to monitor the line between the Slades and the Stramaglias, the most vicious of the Fringe clans. Getting caught by either, with tensions already running high, would mean an attack first, questions later.

She looked down, then back at him. "What you said to me out there about sacrificing your nature for your career."

"Never mind that."

"And every time you did that, bits and pieces of your soul were cut away. So how much of your soul, your true nature, is left?"

"I didn't think there was much left. But I'm here, aren't

I?" The wild part of him tugged at the edges. "And I did tell you my fantasies, after all."

"Mmm, that you did."

"I've never told anyone my fantasies about being under a woman's control."

She looked surprised. "I'm sure you have women at your beck and call. Surely one would indulge you."

He had to quell his grin. Was she fishing? "Sure, but the thing is, if I tell a woman about it, I'm essentially asking her to indulge me. She's following my request."

"I can see your...I guess you'd call it a dilemma. I thought you were making those fantasies up, just to rile me."

He raised an eyebrow. "Did they?"

She met his look with one of her own. "I would never be riled by a Vega."

Oh, she wanted to play that game, did she? He stepped closer, giving in to his wild side, brushing his thigh against hers. He drew his hand down the side of her neck to her collarbone. She sucked in a breath, and her lower lip trembled.

"Just like I'd never be riled by a Castanega." He moved closer yet, his gaze on her mouth. "But here we are." His other hand rested at her waist. He saw the flames in her brown eyes, and they touched off a fire inside him.

"Indeed." She breathed deeply, her gaze dipping to his lips.

He touched his mouth to hers. She put her hands on his shoulders, instantly engaging him. Magick crackled over his skin the same way it did when he used it in combat.

Whoa, what was that?

She opened to him, and he plunged his tongue in, hungry for her. She let out a soft sound, snuggling her body into his. He squeezed her waist and then dragged his hands down her hips. He rubbed his knee up her inner thigh, drawing another deep breath from her. She pressed her pelvis against his thigh. She wanted him, too, was just as helpless as he when it came to this crazy chemistry between them. The realization electrified his kiss. She clutched at him, ravaging his mouth back.

"Okay," she said between kisses. "You proved your point."

"What point?"

"That we can't seem to resist each other."

"I don't care about any point." He pinned her against the counter with his legs, grinding his pelvis into her stomach. Which created a delicious pressure, since his cock was pressed between their bodies. She rocked back and forth, increasing the sweet agony.

"I wish I could chalk it up to being in a dangerous situation, but I felt this *zing* between us at the station," she said, kissing down the side of his neck, circling back to nibble on his earlobe. "Even when I didn't like you."

"I felt it, too, and thought it was just as bizarre. Now that I know you, I want you beyond belief. But taking this any further is a bad idea," he murmured, skimming her breasts. There were reasons, but he couldn't think of one at the moment. He let out a soft groan as her tongue trailed along the outer shell of his ear.

Because her mouth was so close, he could hear her breathing step up as he cupped her breasts and circled her nipples with his thumbs. What a beautiful sound, especially when her breath hitched. He knew plenty of ways to make it hitch even more, to make her gasp and pant and beg for him to take her over the edge.

Maybe it was because he'd already touched her, already knew how to make her arch, and moan, and respond, that made this feel deeper. But that simple explanation didn't float. No, it went beyond that. He didn't just want to fuck her. He wanted her. And that was the problem. Because once he'd buried his cock inside that luscious body of hers, and wrapped himself around her, he wasn't going to want to let go of her.

Whoa. Where did that come from? Remember how wrong you are for her.

"If this is a bad idea, why are you still kissing me?" she asked.

He had to force himself to stop, even with his own admonitions ringing through his brain. He settled his hands on her waist, because he couldn't seem to make himself step away any farther. "It's that point I was making, that we can't seem to resist each other." He had to calm his breathing.

She looked mussed and shell-shocked. "I can't imagine what your superiors would think if you took up with a Fringer." She smoothed her hair in quick strokes.

If only that were the problem.

Was this how his father had felt around the female prisoner? If he felt this way about her, yeah, Kade could understand why he'd thrown everything away to save her.

"I was thinking about you. Your brothers would never forgive you if this progressed."

"No, probably not. But what you said about not selling my soul..."

His hands tightened on her waist. "I didn't mean by seeing me." His life was going to change dramatically. He'd lost the *V* on his arm when he'd been demoted. Its removal was torturous, inside and out. When he lost it again, he would have to explain why. He would not lie to her, because she would mean something if things went any further. Hell, she already did. "Your family hates me. That's never going to change. I've arrested your brother, inflicted wounds on many of you. I know how losing family, identity, and pride tears away everything under your feet. I don't want you in that position because of me." There. It was a sound argument. "I'm not worth giving up the peace in your family. I know how important that is to you."

She clutched his shoulders, meeting his gaze with a steely one of her own. "I've never run away from trouble, Kade. I try for peace but not at the expense of my heart. Someone recently gave me some excellent advice about that."

She was killing him. The ache in his chest sharpened, and he forced himself to back away. "It's dark. We need to stop these attacks. I need to get back to my life. You need to return to yours."

"To the Guard."

"Yes." To his life, at least. Beyond that, his future loomed like a dark hole. His only salvation would be uncovering some plot that exonerated Violet and her clan. "And hopefully your family will forgive you for your lapse in judgment. Let's go."

Chapter 10

What the dragonfire was she thinking? That last thing Violet needed was to be putting her hands or her mouth on a Vega. *Again.* Even if he was gorgeous and looked at her like…she couldn't quite pinpoint what she'd seen in his eyes, but it wasn't lust. Or only lust, anyway. And that was even more worrisome.

Want.

Hush, she told her Dragon. *Can't have that one.*

She and Kade headed out the front door, and she closed it behind them. Immediately she sensed a presence that didn't belong there. She automatically put her hand out to hold Kade from stepping down the front steps. "Someone's out there."

His magick bristled. Gods, she'd never felt that before; she'd never been around Deuces other than in passing.

"It's a Mundane," she whispered, now sensing that kind of energy. "Smitty probably. Damned nuisance."

She spotted the telltale red light of his recording device

way up in the tree and nodded subtly in that direction. Yard lights gave off colored glows around her palm trees and foliage, but not enough to illuminate the man. On a nearby branch sat a fire Elemental, crouched and clearly wanting to dislodge the intruder. Of course, Smitty couldn't see him. Flit, as she'd dubbed him, jumped to a closer branch, its eyes narrowed on its prey. She gave it a shake of her head. *Don't freak out the human. It'll be us paying for it.*

Smitty had already caused them plenty of grief. If he captured a Dragon skirmish on video and sold it to the media, they'd be in a heap of trouble. Crescents who worked in various capacities in the industry might discredit the footage as a hoax, but it would be their death knell. Once it hit the Internet, thousands of people would be dissecting it. And even worse, coming here to spot the "gator ape" itself. Egads.

"Enough of this." She reached into the house and grabbed the shotgun she kept by the door. "I'd love to go Dragon and incinerate him." She shot Kade a look. "But I'd get into all kinds of trouble." She flew down the steps, found the spot she wanted, and aimed toward that light. The bullet hit the branch just above the son of a bitch. She saw the camera drop and heard it hit the ground. He lost his balance and fell, too, becoming a pile of ill-smelling, badly dressed old man.

"Off my property!" she hollered, stalking toward him with the shotgun pointed at the ground. She had no intention of harming the man, but she wanted him to get the message: no friggin' trespassing. "Now."

He scrambled to his feet and searched for his camera. "I'm jus' lookin' for the gator ape. I know it's here. I'm pretty sure it ate the skunk ape, 'cause I ain't seen that one since I saw the gator ape. I know you got it here. Maybe more than one. Jus' let me have a picture, and I'll be on my way."

Yeah, right. And umpteen thousand others would be sneaking around taking his place.

"There are no apes here. Or anywhere. And no skunk apes either." Before he'd caught sight of a Dragon, he'd been hunting Florida's equivalent of Bigfoot.

As he reached for the camera, she let off another shot, shattering it into pieces. "Leave."

With a stumbling gait, he took off into the dark. She tucked her pinky into her mouth and let out a series of whistles warning that Smitty was on the loose.

A second later, her phone rang. Jessup. "Was that why I just heard two shots?"

"Yeah."

"Please tell me you killed him."

"Not hardly." She slid a look to Kade. "Not with a member of the Guard standing next to me. No, I don't want to kill him, and neither do you."

"Yes, I do."

"Okay, you may want to but you can't. He's crazy, annoying, but he is a human being."

"A crazy old coot who's going to get us terminated," Jessup said. "I'll keep an eye out for him. He'll probably come this way. Did you at least maim him a little?"

"Nope, but his camera is dead."

"Well, that's something." His voice lowered. "How's your investigation with the pretty boy going?"

"We're onto something now, so don't do a thing. Promise me."

"I'm only going to hold out for so long, little sister. And if I see one of them on our property, he's dead."

That's what she was afraid of, that everyone now had that attitude. Especially with her and Kade trespassing tonight. "I'm going to find the one who did it, who started all of this. And they're going to die." She disconnected, swallowing her own rage.

Kade was watching her, looking sultry in the shadows and colored lights. "You're a damned good shot. Remind me not to piss you off."

Her laugh came out husky. "Too late for that. Remember, you were an intruder, too. You tasered me, fought me—"

"*You* fought *me*. I was trying to explain why I was here, and you went all alligator wrestler on me."

Her mouth twisted into a smile at the memory of slugging him and grinding him into the mud. "I've tussled with smaller gators that were a lot tougher than you."

"Why, thank you for that."

"Just saying." She jabbed a finger in his direction as they walked toward her car. "And you trespassed in my shop."

"Technically it wasn't trespassing; the door was open."

"Technically it was, because you weren't invited in."

"You're right. I'm a trespasser, a man who would sneak up on you while you're grieving and tase you to boot." He stared hard into the distance. "I'm a bad, bad man, Vee."

She thought he meant that; all trace of that playful tone was gone. The man was mercurial. He kept his gaze on everything but her as they got into her Infiniti.

"You're not so bad," she said. "You're helping me investigate. That means a lot to me."

"I need to find out what's going on for myself."

She liked the idea that he was here for her, probably a little too much, so it was good that he wasn't playing the white knight role. He sank into a dark silence as she drove toward the front of the property. When she passed the main house, her ma flagged her down.

She walked over to the driver's side as Violet opened the window, but her sharp gaze was on her passenger. "I heard shots, thought you might have run him off."

"No, Ma, that was Smitty."

"Lord, I hope you didn't off him in front of the Vega. I've heard they'll turn in their own grandmothers rather than go against the code." She leaned in and snapped on the interior light. "I just wanted a gander at the guy who's going to drag you through the mud and leave you broken on the other side. Yeah, I see the attraction. He's got that bruised, bad-boy look. Bedroom eyes, and the kind of mouth that makes a woman think of staying in bed 'til noon."

"Ma," Violet whined. Hmm, maybe her mother's libido wasn't dead after all.

Her ma shifted those discerning eyes to her. "You didn't listen to me about Bren, so I doubt you will on this one since he's a helluva lot more appealing. But remember how you felt after the fallout on that one. There will be no pity this time either. The best we'll do is not to say, 'Told you so.' Then again, I can't guarantee it."

"I understand. Now, if you're done, we've got a murderer to catch so we can avenge Arlo's death." Much more important than getting this embarrassing lecture.

Kade leaned forward. "Ma'am, I'm not going to hurt your daughter. We're friends, that's all."

She gave them a skeptical look. "Yeah, I can see just how *friendly* you two are." She jabbed her finger in his direction. "Know this: I *will* hurt you." She patted the window and stepped back, watching as Violet pulled away.

Violet shook her head. "Sorry, that's how my family operates. Threaten first, assume next, and listen later."

"They're protective of you. Nothing wrong with that."

"There is something wrong with it. When they thought Bren broke my heart, do you think they comforted me? Hugged me or even patted me on the back and said, 'Gee, that's a shame. Here, have a pint of Ben and Jerry's ice cream.' No, my brothers beat the hell out of Bren and sent me pictures on my phone. Cold comfort."

"And if I hurt you, they'd probably send you a picture every time they cut off an appendage." He gave her a wry smile.

"Yeah, exactly." She pulled onto the road.

"At least you have family. They may be dysfunctional, but they care about you. I have the Guard. Talk about cold comfort."

"And your sister. You have her, too."

He kept his gaze straight ahead. "I do have Mia. She's a good kid, but extremely emotional. Her way of comforting is to freak out."

"I have a lot of family while you have respect." She let out a sigh. "Don't get me wrong, I love my family. Arlo and I weren't close, not since his addictions took over. But losing him, especially like that…" She shot him a look, her grief reminding her of those minutes she let herself express her feelings. "Well, you know. Damn you for sneaking up on me during a private moment."

"I'm sorry." Those words settled into the silence, and then he said in a soft voice, "You were crying alone."

"No, I wasn't. *You* were there."

"I mean, you *thought* you were alone. Does cold comfort apply to grief as well?"

"Our family will kill if someone hurts one of our own, but we…don't know how to hold each other or cry together. My brothers give me a hard time, tell me to buck up and be angry, not cry like a baby."

"I can relate to that."

Great, something else they had in common. They were supposed to be vastly different; so different, in fact, that there shouldn't be one smidgen of chemistry between them. They should have anti-chemistry.

A few minutes later, they were passing the clearly delineated border between the Slades and the Stramaglias. The latter had a fancy concrete wall along the front, with a fence continuing between the two properties. She found a place to tuck the car out of sight from the road.

Thinking about hanging out in the dark with Kade, with only the moonlight filtering down between the trees, she said, "We should separate so we can cover more area."

"Definitely. But how will I let you know if I spot someone?"

"Whistle. You know how to do that, don't you, Kade?" she said in Lauren Bacall's sultry voice. "Just put your lips together and…blow."

Kade rocked his head back, an agonized expression on his face. "I've had two unresolved, raging hard-ons recently. If you can refrain from references to putting your lips together and blowing, especially in that blatantly sexy way, my blue balls would appreciate it."

"I suppose this hasn't been fair to you, has it? I'm sorry. In my defense, I didn't ask you to fondle me."

He shot her an arrogant smile. "Oh, yeah, you did. Not with those lips but with your hips pressing seductively against mine—"

She pressed her fingers over his mouth, horrified by the truth of that statement. "That was my Dragon, taking over. Let's just say it's been a while since it's been . . . fed."

He grinned at that. "How long?" His lips moved against her fingers, warm and soft.

"Let's go back to communicating."

"We are communicating, babe." He took her hand and rubbed it back and forth across his mouth.

She shivered and pulled back. "I meant, about what to do if we encounter a murderous Dragon."

"I can whistle just fine, but not the Fringe way. You have a language all your own. Like that one you did to let everyone know Smitty was on the loose."

"Every clan has their own codes. For instance, one long, high-pitched whistle followed by two short ones is a Smitty alert. Other clans would have their own signal, if Smitty were bothering them. Unfortunately, he seems to target us because our property is accessible to him. Anyway, if I shared our codes with you, I'd be cuffed to the barn wall big-time. But we can come up with another code, just for us." Boy, did that sound intimate. "I mean, for alerting each other."

She hooked her pinky between her lips. "Put your finger like this, and then blow." She demonstrated with a sound like a whip-poor-will. "If it sounds like a bird, it won't tip off the son of a bitch."

He mirrored her movement and blew out a mangled

whistle. "I've never done it like this before." He whistled normally, a soft catcall. "Yours sounded natural." He tried her way again.

She wrapped her fingers around his hand, positioning it, and finding herself too close for comfort. Her arm brushed against his. "Try again." She kept moving his hand to change the angle until he got the sound right. Damn, his mouth did make her think of staying in bed late. And what they'd be doing. "Whip-poor-wills call repeatedly." She mimicked the sound. "They're calling for a mate, so you'll hear one call and then a second one answering."

He raised an eyebrow. "So we're going to call to each other like horny birds."

She let out a breath, backing away because she *was* way too close. "Birds don't get *horny*. Finding a mate and procreating is their instinct, their life's mission aside from survival."

He took her in with an amused expression... for a few seconds too long. "Thank you for that nature lesson. Is that how your Dragons are?"

"No, they're just horny," she said on a sigh, then quickly added, "Try the whistle again." She did not want the word *horny* to be floating between them.

He tried again and nailed it.

"Excellent. If I were a female whip-poor-will, I'd go for you."

"Vee, you kill me. You really do."

She reran her words in her mind. "I meant it as a compliment, not a come-on."

"Honestly, if you recited a grocery list, especially in that sexy Lauren Bacall voice, it'd still be a turn-on."

"Focus, Kavanaugh." Violet pulled out her map, and

they picked two points along the property line to stake out. She grabbed a small cloth bag from behind her seat with a backup set of clothing. The killer was Dragon. She knew as soon as she saw him, she'd Catalyze. "If we catch this person, we kill, right?"

"Ideally, we want to incapacitate and then torture for information."

"Is that how Vegas work?"

"If we need information. Otherwise we just kill. But we want to know why he's doing this. And if anyone else is involved."

"You do the torturing, and I'll kill, because I really, really want to kill him." She looked into the darkness beyond the Slade's front line of trees. "He's responsible for a lot of deaths. And plans to be responsible for more."

"Once I find out what we need, he's all yours."

Her Dragon clawed, hungry to emerge and exact justice. Usually Crescents' humanity was strong enough to keep the beasts' lust and bloodlust in check. The real trouble began if they broke loose. She pushed open her door. "Then let's go."

Kade led the way, blending into the night with his dark clothes and silent stride. He'd done this before. Of course, he'd done it on her clan's property more than once, busting Arlo for his pot farms. The very ones she warned him about having.

Arlo. You were messed up, but you didn't deserve to die.

No stranger to prowling in the dark herself, she followed. Kade had showered at her house before dinner. Funny how her own soap and shampoo smelled different on him. Better.

As she followed his silhouette into the woods, it was exactly as she imagined with the moonlight sprinkling down onto their path, over Kade, and across his face when he paused and turned to her. He gave her a nod and continued on. She remained there as planned, watching him disappear into the shadows.

She settled on the ground against a tree, tuning in to the sounds around her: the rustle of a creature foraging for food and, far off in the distance, music. The Slades were having a party. Once in a while someone hollered. Death hadn't yet touched them.

An hour passed, and then another. The party continued, making her wish she were there having fun instead of flicking off ants or some other bug she couldn't see as it crawled over her. A raccoon approached, then skittered off when it spotted, or smelled, her.

Kade's call jerked her out of her lethargy. She rose, following it while keeping an eye out for sounds and shadows. She called back, two lonely whip-poor-wills in the night.

Horny, indeed.

That Kade was calling meant someone was near, or approaching. Her Dragon vibrated, ready to Catalyze. She put her hand to her waist as she walked, feeling its heat as it moved against her skin. Kade wasn't far, and within a few minutes, she came up beside him. At the same moment, she heard the *crack* of a twig nearby. Then a high-pitched whistle, clearly a Fringe call. She didn't know what it meant.

Kade wrapped his fingers around her wrist and pulled her close. Her backside bumped into him. In the near distance, a flashlight blinked through the trees. His hand tightened on her, but otherwise he gave away nothing.

The Violet she used to be clawed at her as insistently as

her Dragon did. Kade must have sensed it because he put
his cheek next to hers and shook his head.

The man—given his heavy footfalls—cut a zigzag path
toward the property line. He gave another whistle, and she
thought it might be a check-in signal: *All clear.*

Then he turned toward them, slashing the light back
and forth. In a brief illumination of his face, she thought
it might be Paul Slade. He was no doubt doing a security
check, having heard about the murders. If he found them,
he'd attack.

Kade held out his hand, palm up. What looked like an
orb formed on his palm and quickly grew larger. It wob-
bled, like one of those oversized bubbles that big wands
made when you put them in a dish of soapy water.

She could now see Paul's face in the glow of his flashlight. The orb was nearly as tall as they. Kade pulled her
close against the front of his body and brought the bubble
over and around them. His hand splayed across her collarbone.

He whispered very softly in her ear, "Stay still. Quiet.
He can't see us but he can hear us."

She wasn't familiar with Deuce magick and had never
seen an orb like this. The bubble felt cold, which was an
odd contrast to the warm, muggy night.

Paul slashed the light closer and closer to the edge of
the bubble and then finally across it. The light didn't pene-
trate, bouncing off the edge. He did pause, looking in their
direction for a moment. Then he released another whistle
and moved on.

She and Kade remained in their insulated cocoon that
muffled the sounds somewhat. When Paul's flashlight was
only a twinkle, Kade said, "I'm going to extinguish the orb."

"I've never heard of an orb like this."

"It's a mirror orb. From the outside, the person sees only a reflection of the surroundings. If they look close enough, they could figure it out, but it's not likely in the dark."

The orb shattered with a soft *zzzt*, like a popped bubble. Before she could even wonder if she should return to her post, they heard another sound: flesh hitting flesh. Hard.

They ran, Violet loosening her clothing as she did so. The sight of two Dragons fighting sent her into Catalyzation. Now her night vision was crisp, clear, and tinted wine-red. Paul Slade and a Carnelian Dragon she didn't recognize slashed at each other. She smelled blood. The Carnelian's eyes flared as she saw them. Violet felt feminine energy.

Paul's Dragon took advantage of her momentary distraction and started to limp away. The female pulled out one of her scales and, with her clawed hand, threw it at him. Even though he ducked, it followed his movement and hit him in the chest, exploding in a flash of white.

No way. No friggin' way could a Carnelian do that.

Paul hit the ground, and the Carnelian came at her. Kade intercepted, bringing his dagger down with its arc of magick electricity. It cut into the Carnelian's back but didn't slow her momentum. Her fangs grazed Violet's shoulder before the Carnelian let out a scream and jerked back.

A white light roughly the size of a bowling ball shot up to float above them, shedding light across the area for Kade, who couldn't see in the dark like a Dragon could.

The Carnelian's vertical irises widened on Violet as she took a defensive posture. "*You.*"

"Who are you?" Violet asked.

The Carnelian pulled another scale and sent it flying at her. Like a mini-missile, it changed its course when Violet ducked to the side. She'd never fought a Diamond Dragon, only knew the legend about their scales.

The legend was true. Hell of a way to find out.

Kade tried to deflect the scale, but the damned thing was too fast. He sent a cloud of magick at it, his arms outstretched as though to ward off the hit. Blue arcs of electricity shimmered over his body, incredibly beautiful and dangerous all at once.

With Kade's focus on the scale, the Carnelian came up behind him. Before Violet could warn him, he was body-slammed into a nearby tree. Then she came at Violet. She met her halfway, slamming her armor-plated body into the bitch, who wasn't expecting that. The Carnelian fell to the ground but was on her feet and coming at her again.

"Why are you doing this?" Violet screamed. "Why are you starting a war?"

The bitch smiled. Her narrow tongue darted out to lick her lips. "Oh, Violet, it's too late to play the little peace-maker now."

Yeah, the bitch knew her, all right.

"Papa!"

They all turned at the sound of a young girl's voice. She stood next to Paul's body, horror on her face. She was too young to know of the past violence of the Fringe, hadn't suffered loss. She turned to them, and fear gripped her.

The Carnelian smiled at the girl as though she were a tasty morsel.

"Run!" Violet shouted at her. "Get out of here!"

She froze for a moment, and Violet heard the Carnelian inhale, ready to singe her. The girl bolted, and Violet rammed the red Dragon before she could unleash her Breath. Most Fringers were quick on their feet, and this girl was no exception. Before long, she was out of sight. She'd be alerting her family, and they would come with a vengeance.

Kade stabbed the Carnelian in her rear flank, but she stifled her scream of pain. No, she didn't want others coming. Violet didn't either. The Slades would see them all as the enemy. She knew only one other thing about Diamonds: they were vulnerable where they'd removed their scale.

This Carnelian not only had the powers of a Diamond, but she was also one of the most powerful Dragons Violet had ever been around. This was how she killed those other Dragons—including Arlo—ambushing them and using powers beyond the norm.

Which meant she had killed a lot of Dragons and absorbed their power.

Violet engaged her while Kade climbed the tree behind her. He rubbed his fingers together in the way she well remembered—the taser. The Carnelian looked for him as she spit fire at Violet. Kade hooked his legs over the branch right over her head, swung down, and reached for her forehead.

She ducked away from his hand as though she knew exactly what he was trying to do. Then she reared up and struck him. He went with the momentum, spinning midair and landing on his feet.

Pure friggin' grace.

He'd only just landed when the Carnelian spun, whacking him with her tail. He kept his balance and swept his dagger in an arc, cutting a swath of lightning from the tip of the blade. A regular dagger wouldn't have made any difference, but Kade had his own magick. Like a welder's flame, it cut into the scales. She threw her weight back, landing on Kade and crushing him.

Violet barreled into her, stabbing a claw into the hole the missing scale left. The Carnelian hadn't taken a scale from anyplace crucial, but having something the size of a knife sunk into her flesh would hurt like hell.

"Bitch," the Carnelian hissed, swinging her head at Violet, who ducked just in time.

"I was thinking the same thing," Violet said, clamping her mouth around the Dragon's arm. The need to kill charged through her blood, tingling in her fangs.

Kade grunted as he got to his feet, the only indication that he'd been hurt. He lifted his dagger above his head, muscles rippling with his grip as blue sparks ran up the length of his arms to the dagger. It flashed with the same brilliant blue as he brought what looked like a bolt of lightning down at the Carnelian. The bolt hit the tree first, slicing it in half vertically. The Carnelian dodged the bolt but the half-trunk hit her, knocking her off-balance.

"The hell with interrogation," he muttered, charging up the dagger again.

The Carnelian gained her footing as Kade brought the bolt down again, slicing into the top of her head. Blood poured down her face, and several of her "feathers" fell to the ground.

The air around her shimmered with a magick that blocked the bolt as it came at her again. She gritted her teeth, forming a shield Violet had never seen a Dragon create. The veins in Kade's neck bulged with the effort to push through the shield. They were both going to burn their magick out, which would leave them weakened. Then Violet would swoop in and kill the Carnelian.

Kade's bolt crackled and fizzled at the same moment the shield evaporated. Violet charged the Carnelian, who blasted her with a powerful stream of fiery breath. Violet fell backward, the fire singeing right through her scales, the heat stealing her breath away.

She blinked through watery eyes as the bitch readied another blast of Breath. Magick shimmered over Kade's body as he leaped with unnatural speed and height and landed on her back, grabbing the spikes along her spine. Only one small puff of smoke came out before she thrashed in her effort to knock him off. He used the spikes to climb along her back.

Be careful! One wrong move and you'll have a spike right through you.

He knew what he was doing. He moved fast, got a grip around her bloody neck, where the scales were thinner and more flexible, and drew back his dagger. He obviously knew where their kill spot was, just beneath their chin. As the tip touched the spot, the Carnelian rammed him into a tree so hard she heard something crack in his body. Gods, she *felt* it. One of the spikes missed him by half an inch, spearing the bark. He fell on the other side of her, out of Violet's view.

The Carnelian turned and lifted her hand, ready to drive knife-like claws down on him. Violet Breathed a stream of darts at her. The darts hit her shoulder, her arm—and Kade, who'd leaped up in the form of a shimmering tiger with huge claws of his own.

The Carnelian blew out a firestorm, obliterating the sight of Kade and forcing Violet to close her eyes or be blinded. She opened them as soon as she felt the heat diminish. The Carnelian was gone. Kade lay on the ground. Violet Catalyzed back to human and raced over to him, kneeling by his side. The violet glow of her spike pulsed at the center of his chest where he'd been hit. She'd been named for that color.

"Where's the Dragon?" he asked in a tight voice.

"Gone. You injured her pretty bad. She retreated. Are you all right?"

"What the hell did you do to me?"

"That's my version of your taser, only it paralyzes you physically, not magickally."

"That's right. I don't fight many Amethyst Dragons." He probably knew a lot about the different Dragon types, which was unfair because Deuces weren't as cut-and-dried.

But this Carnelian wasn't cut-and-dried either.

He could barely turn his head. "Weren't you taught to always look behind your target when shooting?"

"Of course! I heard something in your body break." Her voice had risen higher at the memory of that sound. "How was I supposed to know you'd be leaping up in the friggin' air?"

"I think I cracked a rib or three, but that kind of thing isn't going to stop me. This"—he tried to move his arm but only his fingers twitched—"will." He gritted his teeth and sent sparks over his body. She watched in fascination as they shattered her magick and dispelled the glow. His hands moved first, then his arms.

She held out her hand to help him up. "I've never seen a Dragon do what she could do."

He grasped her hand but stood up under his own power. "And she knew about the magick taser."

Violet gathered up the tatters of her clothes. "She knew me. She said my name, that it was too late to be a peacemaker. But I don't know who she is."

The sound of a weak whistle drew their attention to Paul, still lying on the ground. He was calling for help; that long call was universal. Footsteps pounded in the near distance, along with angry shouts.

Violet ran to his side, ready to Catalyze and Breathe healing energy into him. She felt his energy die before she could even try. "We'd better get out of here. If they find us—"

Kade pointed. "Look, she left tracks from Stramaglia land."

"Another setup. We have to get rid of them."

He sent a wave of magick across the dirt. "It's easier to cover something like this than, say, a dead body." He pulled off his shirt and handed it to her. "You obviously didn't have time to strip first."

"Sometimes Catalyzing is more important. I brought my bag of clothes. I'll need to grab it on the way back to the car." She pulled on his shirt, surprised by the way it felt comforting somehow. The same way his hand felt as he led her back along the property line. Though part of her wanted to pull away, because she didn't *need* him to guide her, the other part liked the feel of his hand wrapped tightly around hers.

And that was not a good thing.

Chapter 11

Ferro was sound asleep when he heard a commotion. The front door slammed shut, echoing in the foyer. Loud footsteps plodded across the marble floor. Dragon footsteps. It was probably Onyx. He took no chances, Catalyzing and stalking down the wide hallways he'd designed so he could manage them in Dragon form.

"Ferro!" She limped toward him, wincing.

Like the time she'd come to him so many years ago, injured and in need of him. She was the first being who had touched his heart. The only one. Funny, in his whole long life he'd always suspected others of getting close to him because they wanted something from him. Onyx had wanted something, too—his protection. For some reason he had accommodated her, and they'd grown very close these past years. He wasn't sure if he loved her. Wasn't sure what love was. But the thought of her dying struck fear in his soul.

He held her upright. "What happened?"

He saw at least part of the problem, a line seared across the top of her head, as though a blowtorch had been used in an attempt to cut her in half. He eased her gently to the floor. "A Dragon didn't do this." It was too sharply defined for a Dragon's breath. "Let me Breathe into you."

Dragons could heal faster and better when in their beast form, but Onyx needed some help. He sent his healing Breath into her, as he'd done that day she'd come to him. It bothered him on another level, her getting hurt like this. She had amassed so much power. Too much, but she would be handing much of it off soon.

Her shallow panting breaths calmed. He was dying of curiosity, yet he waited patiently for her to heal.

After a while, she struggled to sit up. "I had Paul Slade right where I wanted him," she said in a weak voice. "I think I killed him but I didn't get to Breathe him. Violet Castanega ambushed me." She spewed the name as though she were spitting out poison. "And one of your Vegas. A Deuce."

Violet. He knew she'd be trouble. She shouldn't even be alive. If Kade had only— The rest of what she'd said hit him. "A Vega? Are you sure?"

"I saw the V on his arm. And he was skilled, tried to taser me."

His chest felt heavy. "They were fighting...together?"

"Yes, definitely. I couldn't believe it. First, that *she* was there and seemed to know I would be there. They were ready for me."

He thought back to when the chit had been in his office, looking at the map. Had she deduced what the pins meant? She'd figured out there was something going on beyond restless Fringers. And Kade, he'd been questioning the order to kill her right from the beginning. Putting Ferro off, making excuses. Still, he hoped. "Describe him."

"Six-two, very fit, dark blond hair. Square chin with a cleft in it."

"Kade Kavanaugh." The name grated off his tongue.

"Wasn't he the one whose father tried to break out a prisoner twenty years ago?"

"Yes. Can reckless infatuation be inherited?"

Stewart Kavanaugh had been anything but reckless though. Other than defending his son's rash actions and pushing his opinions in general, Stewart was the epitome of a stellar member of the Crescent government. Ferro didn't know much about the situation, only that the prisoner made serious allegations against a member of the Concilium. Shortly after, she succumbed to the mental illness from which she clearly suffered. Ferro suspected there was more to it, but it wasn't his concern.

"Rest, dear. I've got to go into Headquarters. I'll be back."

"I want to kill her." Venom saturated her voice. "I deserve to kill her."

"You need to recuperate. You're too invested in her death. That's probably what threw you off."

"Being ambushed is what threw me off."

"That may have been my fault. I didn't think anyone would bother with the map. I should have kept it here or hidden. I will remedy that tonight. And you will rest."

People obeyed his commands, even if they didn't want to. He'd worked long and hard to gain that kind of authority. So why hadn't Kade obeyed him? Ferro should have given this assignment to another Vega the moment Kade questioned the order. Questioned *him*, by damn. Kade was good, and it was his history with the Castanegas that should have ensured his quick and lethal follow-through. How had Violet Castanega weakened him? She was attractive, but surely that wouldn't sway a Vega like Kade. Any Vega, really.

Kade would have to die, too. But Ferro had one resource to try first.

Mia headed into the Guard's headquarters two hours before her shift. Her mouth felt like cotton, her heart like a tight little ball in her chest. Ferro had summoned her with nary an explanation, other than it had something to do with Kade. She was terrified at what he was going to tell her.

If Kade were injured, Ferro would have directed her to the Mundane hospital or the unit housed in Headquarters where magick could be used freely. She'd nixed that possibility. Which left...

He's not dead. No, don't even think it.

She walked through the main room, as busy as always. Crescents were more active—and troublesome—at night, when they thought they could get away with it. Those who were assigned to the night shift were more seasoned Arguses. They were the ones waiting for a Vega to retire...or die.

No, don't think that.

Ferro's door was closed as usual. The guy gave her the creeps. She wanted to think it wasn't because he was Dragon. Though they all had an inborn prejudice, you couldn't afford to indulge it when your life depended on a partner who might be a different type of Crescent than you.

"Come in," he said in a flat voice when she knocked on the door.

She took in his face, desperately searching for an expression of pity. "Is Kade all right?" she blurted out because she saw nothing and couldn't wait another second.

"That's what I want you to find out." He gestured for her to sit. "Do you know what happened to your father?"

She blinked at the totally unexpected question. "I know a woman escaped the psych ward and killed him." Even during her stint working there, none of the old-timers would talk about what happened.

Ferro picked up a silver pen, regarding her thoughtfully. "It didn't happen quite like that. I probably shouldn't be the one to enlighten you."

"No, tell me. I always knew there was more to the story." Kade had never elaborated, and Mia had to admit that she was afraid to ask. It had to be something horrible and bloody and gory, and her dear brother was protecting her from it. But she was an Argus now, grown up and tough. Well, mostly tough.

He nodded, flipping the pen with the fingers of one hand. "A woman came in making all kinds of crazy accusations against one of the Concilium members. She was clearly delusional, perhaps schizophrenic. We locked her in the psych ward for her own safety. Of course, we investigated her allegations, as we are obligated to do, but they were unfounded. We realized she was a danger to herself, possibly others, and restrained her with the hopes of helping her. Unfortunately, she got worse.

"Your father went to see her. We don't know why, as we could find no prior connection between them. He visited her several times, and then he tried to break her out. The woman didn't kill him; one of our Vegas did when your father wouldn't halt." He flipped the pen over and over, pinning her with his cold stare.

She buried her shock and disbelief. Her throat was so dry she could barely push out the words. "Are you saying he fell so terribly in love with this woman that he threw away his career, his marriage—and ultimately his life—for her?"

"We don't know what he was thinking, only the end result. They say love can blind us, can make us crazy. Perhaps this was the case. I'm sorry that I had to be the one to tell you."

Her father, in love with a crazy woman? It didn't make sense. She only had vague memories of her parents, stoic and serious people. Kade had told her how highly regarded her father was, how he'd risen from Argus to Vega to commander and then on to the Concilium. One of them was lying to her.

It hit her then that Ferro was telling her this awful story for a reason. One that was connected to Kade. She swallowed the knot in her throat. "Why *are* you telling me?"

"I think your brother has fallen into the same situation. He was sent to dispatch a woman named Violet Castanega."

"The one who came here yesterday reporting her brother's death?"

"Exactly the one. She, too, seems to be suffering from schizophrenia and is causing trouble beyond what I can discuss with you. I sent your brother on a mission, the type he has completed successfully many times."

Her brother was a killer. She knew that, but he never talked about his work as a Vega, and she never asked. "I saw him leaving."

"Not only has he been vague about why he hasn't completed the assignment, but apparently he has also taken up with his target. Before I send someone out to remedy the situation, I am giving you a chance to get hold of him and find out what is going on. He'll be more frank with you, I hope. And you will be frank with me."

This time denial did rush out. "No, Kade would never take up with a Castanega. He hates them, all of them." But she remembered the way he'd held Violet's shoulders and leaned close, real close, and the way the fog in his eyes swirled like she'd never seen before. "Being a Vega means everything to him."

"I thought so. He worked very hard to regain his status." He flipped the pen again. "He didn't tell you that either, I suppose, how I had to demote him because of allegations that he had been promoted due to nepotism. Kade was a different man then. Reckless, thinking he didn't have to abide by the rules. A good Vega, yes, but a wild card. He worked hard, under a cloud of humility, to become Vega again, and his behavior has been exemplary. Until now."

She was sad, shocked, and furious all at once. She surged to her feet, unable to sit for another second. "I'll find out what's going on."

If Ferro sent someone else, would Kade be killed like her father was? She willed the panic from her face. "Don't send someone else." Realizing she was giving a commander orders, she added, "Please."

As pissed as she was at Kade, she didn't want him dead.

Chapter 12

Kade ignored the stabbing burn in his chest as he tried to find a position in the passenger seat that wasn't as painful. He said nothing as Violet spewed word after word, pouring out her adrenaline and her questions.

"Whoever she is, she hates me. Did you see the way she looked at me, the way she said, 'You,' as though I were vermin? Or is that *a* vermin? Anyway, she wanted me dead. But then she looked at that girl, and you could see she wanted to kill her for no good reason at all. And she was going to enjoy it. What kind of Crescent does that? Would she be considered a Red?"

The car swerved a little with her hand movements, the headlights washing over the yellow line in the center.

"Red Lust makes you crazy," he managed to say. "I don't think she was crazy. In fact, it would be better if she were. It's a lot easier to take out someone in the throes of mindless bloodlust than the ones who just like to kill people."

He sank into his thoughts. The Carnelian knew about

the taser, and not many did. It was a fairly new weapon, conjured by one of the powerful old Deuces on staff after much experimentation. More disturbing, Ferro's map had a yellow pin where Paul Slade was killed. The yellow pin in the August territory had changed from yellow to red. Target to completion.

Nothing about this situation felt right to him. Ferro had not been willing to explain a damn thing to Kade. If he'd had evidence, a few words would have cleared it up.

Not only was Kade's career in ruins, but also everything that he was, everything he believed in, was sliding through his fingers like sand on a Miami beach. He glanced at the clock on the dash; it was nearly five in the morning. Soon Ferro was going to grow impatient, pull Kade, and send someone else to finish the assignment. He had to get to the bottom of this before that happened. He glanced over at Violet, who was still working it all through in her mind.

"Ferro had a yellow pin in Slade territory," she said, echoing what he'd just thought. "Do you have a Seer on staff?"

"There are very few true Seers, and, as far as I know, the Guard doesn't employ one. Be a lot easier if they did."

She turned to him. "So how does he— You're hurt!"

He was way beyond physically hurt. "I'm fine."

"No, you're not. You're wincing like this." She made a face that almost made him laugh, which would really hurt. She pulled over and turned on the car's interior light. "Let me see."

He shifted to reveal a gash on his stomach. "It's not deep."

She winced again in sympathetic pain. "Can you heal yourself? I know so little about Deuce magick."

The Guard knew everything he could do. Few others did.

"My magick can heal me, but it takes time."

"I can heal you faster, but I don't know if I can heal a non-Dragon. We…" She had also been trained not to share too much information, no doubt. Crescents, regardless of class, didn't go advertising their abilities.

"It's not mortal. I'll be fine, Violet."

The pain wracking his soul was much worse. He had deceived her, had at one time intended to kill her. He didn't deserve her healing. Or her trust. Or… well, anything else. He wasn't ready to divulge his suspicions yet. If she suspected Ferro was corrupt, she'd lose trust in the Guard, and in him. Right now he couldn't leave her to deal with this by herself. He didn't want to delve too deeply into his reasons.

They drove down the long road to her house, a nice change from hoofing it on the sly. They got out, but Violet paused and stared into the darkness of the property to the west.

"What is it?" he asked, instinctively going on alert. His dagger tingled, and his fingers flexed, ready to receive the weapon.

She shook her head. "Sometimes I see a shadow move. It's probably an animal, maybe a deer. No one's been over there in years. I wandered over once, just to see. It was creepy, with vines overtaking one of the houses and weeds growing up everywhere. And sad," she added on a sigh. "We did that to them, obliterated their whole family."

She rubbed her arms and headed to the house. Kade surveyed the area, uneasy with all the places someone could hide here. She opened the door and stepped in, flicked on the light, and left the door open for him. He remained on the porch, uncertain that he wanted to follow her in.

She returned to the door opening. "What are you doing out there? Come in. I want to heal that gash. You'll probably want another shower. I sure do."

He stepped inside. "Oh, but I really liked your hose down," he said, trying to work up a wry smile. Inside he felt heavy and cold, like his organs had turned into a block of frozen mud.

Her mouth quirked. "Apparently too much. We had better stick to a shower. Separate showers, just to be safe. There's something about being outside, with a stream of water, that apparently has a strange effect on us."

"You think that was it?" he challenged. He'd thought her reaction was out of grief, her need for comfort. But now, he wasn't so sure.

"Of course." A light shone in her eyes, one he hadn't seen before. It tugged at his numb shell. "We fought together. And well. I thought Dragons were the only beautiful fighters, that Deuce magick was boring. Though it was pretty cool when you changed into a tiger that one time. Even if you were using it against us."

Was she calling his magick beautiful? Another tug. "I have to admit, I've never considered a Dragon gorgeous before. But you are." She *had* been beautiful, maroon scales glistening in the orb's light. It had reminded him of the vivid colors of underwater sea life when he went scuba diving.

She bent down to look at his stomach. "I'm going to try to heal you."

"Let me get cleaned up first." He'd stopped bleeding at least.

She held his gaze for a moment, and he felt another pull on his emotions. More like a jerk this time, the kind that knocks you off your feet. "I'll get you a towel," she said. "You can crash here if you want. I don't have a guest bedroom, but you can sleep on the couch. It's late."

Too late. He felt lost in her eyes, her soft voice. *Get out! Go. Say you've got to check in at work and sleep in your car.* "All right."

"I'll get you some sheets and a pillow, too."

She turned and walked away from him, his shirt barely covering her ass. Her long legs were scraped up, her feet dirty from walking barefoot through the woods. Beautiful, every inch of her. She opened a door in the hallway and pulled out a towel and washcloth. He felt his body move toward her, his hands reach out to accept them. For the second time within the last few hours, he was showering in her house.

He remained in the shower a while, letting the hot water pound his body. His thoughts twisted inside his head, crushing his chest even more than that damned Dragon had. He had to check in with Ferro soon.

Kade finally emerged, wearing jeans and nothing else. His first glimpse of Violet was a silk-clad behind as she bent over to tuck the sheets over the couch. He watched her for a moment as she set the pillow at the end after fluffing it up.

She turned suddenly. The blue tank top she wore, the same silky material as her shorts, tightened across her chest. "Lie down. You're still hurt, Kade. I'm going to heal you. No arguing."

He couldn't really tell her that the pain suited his mood, that he didn't deserve her healing, so he submitted. That she was ordering him . . . flashes of being pinned to the barn wall, under her control, tightened his groin.

Forget that. You're a mess.

She assessed his injuries. "Between my brothers and the Carnelian bitch, you're beat to hell."

He fingered the edges of his wound. Add the gash on his back and several broken ribs, and she'd have her work cut out for her.

She pushed the coffee table several feet away. "I'll need to Catalyze." She sat next to him, her hip brushing his thigh. He saw vulnerability in her rich, brown eyes. In the way her long fingers trembled as they tucked her damp hair behind her ear.

"You okay?" he asked.

She nodded too quickly, dislodging that lock of hair again. "It's just hitting me now. No one's ever tried to kill me." Little did she know. And she wouldn't know, if he had any say in the matter. She continued. "Not me as Violet, for personal reasons. Our family has had attacks where everyone's fair game. But she wanted to kill *me.*"

He shouldn't reach for that hand, shouldn't rub his thumb along the back of it. He was a cold killing machine. A man who didn't know how to connect emotionally to a woman, which was all the better.

"I'm all right," she said, staring at his thumb as though she'd never had anyone touch her like that.

Maybe she hadn't. No one to hold her while she grieved or processed what had happened. He didn't think, just pulled her down so that her cheek rested on his upper chest. Pain rocketed through him as she pressed against his broken ribs, but he held in the hiss.

He'd seen female Vegas deal with adrenaline after an altercation. They processed it differently. Rather than being immersed in it right away, like men did, women held it together in the moment and fell apart later. Most hid it, swallowing back the tears or letting them loose only in the restroom or in their car out in the parking lot. They would never reveal it to their comrades, who wouldn't offer more than cold comfort anyway. The men showed no emotion. For most of the senior Vegas, any empathy had been conditioned out of them.

Violet's shoulders shook, and he stroked her back, over the silk and the lace edge to the warmth of her skin. His fingers brushed against the strands of her damp hair.

"I'm supposed to be healing you," she said, the tears she was holding back thick in her voice.

"Let me comfort you first."

She shook her head, her mouth brushing against his bare skin. "Castanegas are tough. We don't cry."

"I've already seen you cry, Vee. I don't think any less of you for it. You lost your brother. You were almost killed." Twice. "I'll never tell."

A cry gasped out of her, one last attempt to hold it back failing. "Why are you doing this?"

"Because no one comforted me when my father died." They looked at him askance or whispered. Some gave him a sympathetic look while others acted as though he had the plague. "And I didn't cry either. Because Vegas are tough. We don't cry."

She laughed, mixed with a sob, and lifted her face to his. Her eyes were glossy with tears. "Then you can cry, too."

He shook his head. "I don't need to cry. But you can." He brushed a tear from her cheek.

"What do you need, Kade?"

He let his thumb linger against her cheek. *You. In my arms, my life.* Thank the gods he pulled the words back before they rolled out. "Right now, nothing."

She buried her face again and cried, but nothing like she'd done earlier when her sobs had ripped out his heart. Her hand lay on his stomach, fingers flexing, nails scraping softly against his skin.

Something he'd never felt before opened inside him, an overwhelming need to protect her, take care of her. Give her warm comfort, hot love…everything.

He would have killed her. The robot he was the day before would have come here, killed her when she was grieving, and then left. He would have gotten a "well done" at work and gone on to the next assignment. The obedient killing machine. And this beautiful, caring woman would be dead.

She sat up. "I'm hurting you, aren't I? I can hear your breathing coming in short puffs."

The release of pressure was as painful as when she'd first leaned against him. "It's okay," he said, though his voice gave away his pain. "It's just a broken rib or two."

"Kade! Why didn't you say something? Men! 'It's fine,'" she mimicked. "'I'm just wonderful, but don't mind my gasping in pain.'" With a growl, she stood and swiped at her tears. "Close your eyes."

He did, and heard the swish of her clothing hit the floor. The Catalyzation process was silent, but her heavy footfalls weren't. He opened his eyes, looking into her face. The lines of her head were like a fine horse, regal and elegant; her scales glistened in the dim light. Her wings, black with maroon highlights, were tucked against her back. Her eyes were catlike, as were her graceful movements when she planted her hands on the edge of the couch and leaned down.

"I'm going to send my Breath into you," she said, her voice low and gravelly. "It's the opposite of when a Dragon Breathes another's power. Instead of taking your essence, I'm going to send my essence into you. It'll feel hot, and maybe weird, but shouldn't hurt. I don't know if it'll work, but it's worth trying."

He was staring at her, unable to do more than nod.

"Don't worry, it won't bond us like it does Dragon to Dragon. At least I don't think so."

Hell, he was already bonded to her in a way he couldn't understand. "I didn't know you could bond that way."

"It's not a romantic bond,' but the healed Dragon will carry the healer's essence inside them for a while. Close your eyes. Open to me and relax."

Open to her.

He did, and felt the heat of her breath as she neared him. Her lips were softer than he imagined, though he felt the graze of her fangs. He opened his mouth, and her Breath flowed into him. Not down his throat, but *into* him. It felt exquisitely exotic. Her magick rushed like water pooling around each injury. He inhaled sharply at the sensation, breathing in the scent of her: like incense, musky and sweet all at once.

He heard her back away, and the magick continued to work its way through him until the heat subsided. When he finally opened his eyes, she was human again in her silky pajamas. She was sitting back, her hands on her thighs, watching him.

"It worked?" she asked, looking hopeful.

He patted his ribs, feeling nothing but a slight bruise.

"Yeah. Amazing. We have healing Deuces on the Guard staff. This felt different." Because Violet cared. Being treated by someone who cared...the feeling of it tumbled through him. More sensual, definitely hotter. He sat up. "Thank you."

"It's the least I could do, after all you've done for me."

For a moment he thought she knew everything, and she was all right with the fact that he'd once been about to kill her. But no, she'd never be all right with that.

Their gazes lingered, and he felt that *flash* that had hit him at the station. She abruptly stood, running her hands down her pajamas as though to smooth them. "I should get to bed. Let you sleep and continue healing."

He stood, too. "Yeah, that's probably a good idea."

They both stood motionless, neither making any move to leave. Then he stepped forward and kissed her. She fell into him, her mouth engaging his. Her hands slid down the sides of his body, around to his back, her fingers digging into him. He rubbed the back of her neck, then moved down the length of her spine. She shifted closer, making a sweet sound deep in her throat.

Crash. The rest of that numb shield fell away. Along with his convictions.

There wasn't a damn thing he could do about it. He was as lost as she seemed to be. He needed to feel her all over, sliding his hand underneath the back of her top. The action pulled it up in front, too, and he felt the bottom swell of her breasts brush his chest. Holy hell but he wanted to feel every inch of her naked body against his. From that first contact, the smell and taste of her had been burned into his memory.

She pressed closer against him, and her hardened nipples grazed his skin. He pulled her top up, and she lifted her arms in perfect unison. The scrap of silky material fell to the floor.

"Amazing," he uttered on a whisper, trailing his fingers over her curves and between her exquisite breasts. When her breath caught, he cupped them. Firm, yet soft, a perfect fit.

She tilted her head back, which pushed her breasts more fully into his hands. Suddenly feeling her wasn't enough. He needed to taste her, and so he kissed her, sucking on her tongue, exploring her mouth. Then he tasted every inch of her from her chin down her throat, tracing the edges of the hollow at the base. She tasted of clean female and the faint tang of soap. He wanted to taste more of her.

She exhaled in pleasure, her fingers moving through his hair, tugging it like she couldn't pull him close enough. His cock throbbed with wanting her, making his jeans uncomfortably tight. He wanted—needed—to be buried inside her. Tendrils of magick crackled over his skin and through his body. What the hell? He'd never felt anything like that before.

There was a lot that he'd never experienced before meeting Violet.

Her Dragon was heating up, too, all around her waist where he now held her. Its essence was now in him. He felt it connect to his own magick, twisting together the way magick vines could wrap all around you. She must have felt it, too, because her hand went to her tattoo. Her Dragon stretched sensually, its eyes afire like sparkling amethysts.

"It's not supposed to want a Deuce," she whispered, surprise in her voice.

"Does it want a Deuce?"

"Very much."

He traced his finger lightly over her tattoo, feeling the energy it exuded. He knew enough about Dragon essence to gain an advantage in battle. He knew nothing about how it *felt* to be Dragon. "Do *you* want a Deuce?"

Her gaze held his. "Very, very much."

He pressed his forehead against hers. He was disciplined. Strong. But not with Violet. "Something about you pulls at me, tears away my resistance." His voice was raw. "You tug at my wild side, the part of me I buried long ago."

"Is that the part you forgot was inside you, the ache that never went away?"

He brushed her hair from her face, his thumb grazing her cheek. "I forgot until you. Every time I'm close to you, that side of me takes over. And right now, more than ever, I need to keep my head straight. We shouldn't do this." The mist in his eyes swirled something fierce, belying his directive.

Violet felt his words in her body. The ache in them, the wanting. "You're trying to be Vega-like, and I get that. Honor. Discipline," she said. "And there are sound, logical reasons for not going further. But right now, I need your arms wrapped around me so I feel safe for the first time since Arlo's death. I need your body pressed up against mine so I can pull your heat and strength into me. And what I need, really need, is the hot kind of comfort that only a man can give me. Only you."

He hesitated for a moment, and then reached for her on a groan. His mouth found hers, his hands cradling her face. "Why are you making it so hard for me to be good?"

He *was* hard. He wanted her. She didn't want to think about all the differences between them, didn't want to think about tomorrow or what consequences it might bring. She wanted him, too, and she wasn't going to let him suffer another unresolved hard-on. Remembering how Kade had told her his fantasies, how he'd responded to her when he'd been blindfolded, made her shed her own inhibitions. She gave a tug on his pants. "Take these off, Kade. That's an order."

Surprise sparked in his eyes, and he lifted his face to the ceiling. "Oh, no. You're really killing me here, Violet."

"No backtalk."

He pulled his gaze back to hers, both agony and arousal on his expression. "Yes, ma'am."

"Faster."

"Anything you say, ma'am." Now it was only arousal burning in his eyes. He unbuttoned and unzipped his pants, pushing them down to the floor and stepping out of them.

She hooked her finger over the waistband of his boxer briefs. "Now these." She pulled it and let it snap back against his erection. He blinked at the sensation, then complied.

"You looked good on my bed. I want you on it again."

He grabbed a crinkly package out of his pants pocket and marched to her room. When he tossed it onto the nightstand and turned around, he was at full attention...in every way.

She stepped up close to him. "Make love to me. We'll sort out everything else later."

She slid her hands over his chest, the contours of his muscles and smooth discs around his nipples. The feeling of being alive rushed through her, her blood pulsing, her heartbeat pounding. And a strong man crushing her against him as though he couldn't get enough of her. Oh, yes, hot comfort.

His tongue moved through her mouth, exploring, devouring. His hands skimmed down her back and beneath the waistband of her panties. He cupped her cheeks and let the tips of his thumbs trail up the seam of her behind as he drew his hands back up. She pressed her hips closer, rocking her pelvis against his erection. He let out a soft growl, drawing his hands low enough to touch her wetness. She'd never been wet without the guy having to work at it. Kade had gotten her that way and hadn't even touched her intimately. Now she growled, echoing the roar of her Dragon. She'd never made that sound before. The primal nature of it stirred her deep inside.

"Vee," he whispered, lowering her to the bed and nuzzling her neck as he came down with her.

She remembered the way she'd told him not to call her that. Now the word trickled through her blood on her soft exhale. He braced himself over her, his mouth working its magic across her skin, her breasts. He sucked just hard enough to make her squirm without hurting her. She clutched at him, tracing her nails across his scalp.

His fingers hooked on the waistband of her pajamas and shoved them down her hips. She wiggled the rest of the way out of them and kicked them off the bed. His fingers and thumb drew a line to the delicate skin of her inner thighs, and then he cupped her pubic area. A tantalizing vibration pulsed deep into her core, so wild, so crazy, she shuddered.

"What was *that*?" she managed between gasps as waves of an electrical thrumming sensation shot pleasure through her body.

His chuckle was low and throaty. "Sex magick. It's a nonlethal way to use our magick."

"Nonlethal, my ass. You're killing me."

The sensual spiral wound through her entire body, making her pull his thick hair as her body arched.

His sexy chuckle was just as stimulating. "Oh, you'll live, babe, and then you'll be begging me for it again and again."

She shot him a look at his arrogance, but his devilish smile extinguished any spark of ire. Then he sent another wave of magick that knocked her flat on the bed again. She clutched at the sheets, feeling like she might lift right off the bed.

She was on the edge of a mind-bending orgasm when his mouth came down on her, and his tongue slowly moved around her folds. Her breath came in short pants now. Her hips writhed, seemingly of their own accord. She opened herself to him and fully spread her legs. Her hands tangled in her sheets in an attempt to anchor herself. She screamed, long and guttural, as the climax swept her mind and body away. Her Dragon's essence rolled over her, heating her skin as it pressed close to the surface. It reveled in the sensuality and danced in pleasure.

More, more, more...

"More," she echoed on a halted breath.

Yeah, she was begging. That's how good it felt. She didn't even care that she was begging.

He ran his right hand down her inner thigh and slid a finger into her vagina, while his thumb circled her already sensitive clit. Another wave of sex magick flowed from it, convulsing her body and loosing another orgasm. Along with another primal scream. She thought she might have ripped the thousand-thread-count sheets she'd paid a for-tune for, but who cared? This time he let his tongue alone take her to yet another orgasm, and damn, it was good that way, too.

When she could breathe and think again, she realized he was kissing his way back up her body. The tip of his pe-nis left a wet trail as it glided along the path his mouth had just made. It felt like velvet and steel against her heated skin. He kissed along her jawline and murmured, "You even taste good, like a summer wine."

Violet pushed him back to the bed and straddled him, leaning down so that her hair grazed his chest. She ran her tongue down his neck and across his pecs. Her body was low enough to skim his as she moved. Her nipples tingled as they glided over the hard planes of his chest. She felt his thick erection beneath her stomach, and then in the hollow between her breasts. He let out a low exhale as she sank lower against him.

He ran his hands along her back, his fingers flexing whenever she put extra pressure on his penis. She felt the faint sprinkling of hairs that grew soft and even more sparse as she moved down the center of his stomach. She took the thick length of him into her mouth, though he was too long to take him wholly in.

She laved the smooth head with her tongue, the length of his shaft with her mouth. Her teeth brushed softly against his skin, and he panted. When he arched, his fingers curling into her shoulders, she moved to his inner thighs. She wanted him to come inside her, hungered for it. He didn't wait for her leisurely ascent, pulling her level to his face and kissing her so hard and deep, she lost herself in it.

"I'll get the condom," she said on a gasping breath a few

moments later. She crawled to the nightstand and grabbed it with trembling fingers. Sex had never been a need like this, a desperate need to have him inside her.

While she was still on all fours, his hands slid around her waist, and he pulled her ass against his pelvis. He leaned close behind her, his body over hers, and kissed the back of her neck. She glanced up and caught the shadowy reflection of them in the mirror above the dresser. The sight of him draped over her, predatory, animalistic, rocketed through her.

Her Dragon purred and made her arch into him even more. She handed him the package and heard him tear it open. He moved away for a second, then braced his hands on her behind and positioned himself to enter. She pushed against him, wanting to feel all of him.

He braced his weight with one hand, the other slid beneath her stomach, and he filled her in exactly the way she needed. Like that unnamed ache he'd spoken of, she had yearned for this but never knew what it was. No, it wasn't just a man inside her, or sexual release, but something more.

Something Kade.

He leaned down over her, as he'd done before, his mouth near her ear. She loved the sound of his breathing growing ragged and the way his fingers tightened on her stomach when she moved into the thrust. When her own breathing grew labored and her insides felt as though they were about to burst, he touched her clit again and sent another blast of sex magick.

Sparks caught her eye. In the mirror, she saw a flash of blue light shimmer over his skin. It tickled all along her back.

"You're sparking!" she said between breaths.

"Yeah...I know." He sounded as surprised as she did. And then he sent another surge of magick.

The orgasm tore through her, ripping her apart. Kade thrust hard into her, and his body shuddered. He held her tight, more of those sparks tripping over her as their orgasms swept over them.

"Holy dragonfire," she said, trying to catch her breath.

"Yeah," he managed on his own sawed breathing.

They rode the sensations, moving in a slow rhythm inside her. Several seconds later, he gently pulled out and wrapped his arms around her, falling to his side with her in his embrace. He looked beautiful, his face flushed and dewy, his eyes bright. She hoped she looked half as good.

She ran her fingers along his arm. "You had electricity—magick running all over you," she said, watching the last of the glimmers fade from his skin.

He lifted his arm, flexing his hand. "I've never had that happen before. That was wild." He brushed his fingers down her face. "Everything about it was wild."

She nodded, moving her mouth to kiss the tip of those fingers. "Thanks for...well, the hot comfort."

"It was a lot more than that." He pinned her with his gaze. "Wasn't it?"

"Yeah." What were they going to do about it? She couldn't quite nudge that question past her lips. Too many things were already zinging around in her mind, her body. Like how right it felt to be in his arms, how everything about him felt so right, which didn't make any sense at all.

He glanced toward the window, where dawn was beginning to lighten the sky. "It's almost morning."

"Does that mean you have to go?" She was kidding, yet the thought tightened her chest.

"I'm not going anywhere, babe."

The words washed over her, spoken in his low, intimate voice. Especially *babe*. No one had ever called her that other than Kade's pretend usage. Maybe a whispered "oh, baby," but nothing meaningful. "Good." She snuggled closer, her face next to his. She wouldn't ask him about the future, wouldn't extract any promises. She wasn't ready to make any herself.

She would always be a Dragon, a Fringer. And Kade was a Deuce, a Vega to the core. But in the quiet afterglow of the most incredible sex of her entire life—hell, she'd never even imagined that it could be *that* good—Violet didn't care about their differences or the inevitable end to their arrangement. She wanted to sink into this moment. She stroked his dagger tattoo. "Does your tattoo have a consciousness? Does it make demands?"

"No. The tattoo is probably like your Dragon in the way it changes my cellular structure, but mine is just a weapon. The Guard commissions a magick inker to make them."

Her finger traced the V on the dagger's hilt. "Tell me what it's like to be you. To be respected, perhaps feared."

He laughed, shaking his head. "The people whom I want to fear me—my opponents—aren't usually afraid of me. They think they're better, faster. They're usually wrong."

"Oh, and tell me what it's like to be so humble, too, while you're at it."

Another laugh, as rich as chocolate. "Who needs to be humble when you're great?"

She nudged him.

His smile faded. "People respect me because I'm a Vega, not because I'm Kade Kavanaugh. Probably like they disrespect you for being a Castanega. It's not personal."

"I wish I could see it that way."

He kept staring at the ceiling, absently stroking her arm with his finger. "I know how it feels to have people look at you like you're dirt."

She propped herself up on her elbow. "I would have guessed you had a charmed life."

"I did until twenty years ago, when my father tried to release a prisoner."

He told her the sketchy details, pain and humiliation etching into his voice. "It drives me crazy not knowing exactly what happened. Did he fall madly in love with this delusional woman? Seems unlikely. Everything for him was about his reputation."

"But why did people look at *you* like you were dirt? Your father was the one who supposedly went against the law. Ah, people judging you for your family's sins."

"Yes, but that was only part of it. There were some who were jealous of my fast rise to Vega, especially since I flouted the rules. When they called my ascent into question, the Guard backed down and demoted me." He met her gaze. "The way you probably felt walking in there was how I felt every day. For five years, sacrificing who I was, toeing the line and ignoring my instincts just to prove myself. And now..." His expression tightened. He obviously wasn't used to sharing, which made this even more special. "My sister is an Argus. If I screw up, she's going to pay for it."

Violet remembered the woman with the green eyes like

Kade's. "You mean screw up as in investigating this on your own?"

"Yeah."

"I'm glad you did."

He pressed his forehead against hers. "Me too." His sincerity saturated those words . . . and her heart.

"It's odd how much we have in common," she said. And how perfectly natural lying there sharing their bodies and souls felt. "My father also died under mysterious circumstances. We'll never know why he ended up on Garza land, and why they felt compelled to shoot him."

His expression darkened. "Did you ever doubt your father? Ever think he was up to something he shouldn't have been?"

She shook her head emphatically. "My people have flaws, no doubt, but my dad wouldn't have been up to no good."

"I thought my father had fallen prey to human emotions. I didn't know him, not on any deep level. I believed the rumors. I bought into the corruption of a man but never considered the corruption of the Guard." Kade looked torn. "My father was a regimented, cold hard-ass, but he always backed me up. When I got into trouble for breaking the rules, he reminded my commanding officer that I went with my gut, just like he'd taught me. That I usually succeeded."

"And you regret not believing in your father," she said, reading his pained expression.

"Yes."

She sighed, looking at her closet door. "My biggest regret is not wearing the dress my father bought me when I was nine. I was a tomboy, because that's how I was raised.

I knew Dad suspected that I wanted to be girly, at least at times. It meant a lot to me, but the only time I wore the dress, my brothers teased me and called me 'baby doll.' I put the dress away. Dad never even saw me wear it."

Kade pulled her closer against him. "Regrets suck. But I don't regret this."

Chapter 13

Even in deep sleep, Kade heard his phone vibrate. Morning light spilled onto the bed, where he had made the most amazing love with a woman he was supposed to kill. He had no doubt that he'd made the right decision, but the consequences were going to be tricky as hell. Because keeping Violet alive was now the most important thing in his life.

Her dark hair spilled across her pillow, eyelashes fanning her cheeks as she slept. Her mouth curved in a slight smile, and her fingers twitched where they lay on the bed between them. He wanted to wake her and lose himself in her again. They had connected in a way he'd never done with anyone. And he had no idea what to do about it either.

He rolled out of bed and grabbed his pants, then went into the bathroom. When he came out a few minutes later, she was still asleep. He stepped outside and squinted in the bright sunshine. Chumley followed him and wandered out to the yard, though the dog kept an eye on Kade. Maybe he wasn't used to seeing strange men at Violet's house. Kade liked that idea way too much.

Birds called to one another in the trees, and in the distance, he heard an engine. Kade couldn't put off reading the text he'd heard come in earlier, assuming it was from Ferro. Kade had to buy time with some valid excuse. But it wasn't a text from his boss; it was from Mia: CALL ME ASAP!

She never bothered him when she knew he was on a mission. Kade walked beyond the trees that bordered the house and called her.

She answered with, "Thank the gods. Kade, are you all right?"

"Yeah, why?"

"Good, because I'm going to *kill* you. Ferro called me into his office this morning. I was freaking that something had happened to you, because why would he want to talk to *me*?"

Uh-oh. "What did he want?" *And please get to the point.*

"First it was about Dad. Tell me, Kade, did he get involved with some woman in the prison and die trying to break her out?"

Hell. "He told you that?" He smacked the trunk of a pine tree.

"Yes, and I wanted to tell him he was full of shit, but he's a superior officer, so I had to sit there and stuff my shock and disgust. Which you know is very hard for me. So now I'm asking you: who's the one full of shit?"

Damn, it wasn't Ferro's place to tell her that. "I fudged the truth."

"*Fudged*!" She took a deep breath, and he knew her pain because he'd felt it, too.

"You were seven at the time and didn't need to know all that. Later...I wanted you to consider him someone to look up to."

"That's why Mom killed herself, isn't it? The scandal? The betrayal."

"I've always thought so. But I don't know the whole story about our father. We can't be sure that he was romantically involved with this woman. I'm beginning to wonder—"

"And now you! That's why Ferro told me, because he thinks you're doing the same thing with this Violet. Are you in love with her?"

A flash of his hands on her body, the taste of her...

"You are!" Mia hissed. "Otherwise you would have denied it immediately."

"I'm not in love with her," he whispered, though the images, and the way they made him feel, mocked his words. He couldn't have Mia believing he was. "How could I be? I didn't really know her until this assignment."

"And your assignment was to kill her."

"Yeah."

"But you know her now? You took time to get to know her when you were supposed to just go in and terminate her?"

Cripes, his little sister was questioning him. He couldn't say how he'd come up on Violet crying, how her vulnerability had touched him in a way he couldn't explain. How her strength, smile, and sass touched him, too.

Mia went on. "You're the one who told me to do what I'm told, that the Guard has a reason for everything."

"That's what I thought. But nothing about this assignment makes sense. A good friend and former Vega recently told me to trust my gut when something didn't feel right. That's what I'm doing. You should, too."

"By going against the Guard and losing everything you've worked for? What are you thinking?"

"That's just it, Mia. I'm thinking that this assignment isn't right." He pinched the bridge of his nose. "Why does Ferro suspect I'm involved with Violet?"

"He didn't say. He told me to talk sense into you before he sent someone else to ... remedy the situation. I don't know what that means, but I don't like the sound of it."

Kade kicked the dirt. Why had Ferro dragged Mia into this? Because ... Ferro must know the Carnelian Dragon. It all fit together, the way the pieces of teak he'd installed on his old boat had. The Carnelian had reported to Ferro that Kade was fighting beside Violet. And now he was going to send someone else out. Kade didn't like the sound of that either.

"Mia, I'm not going rogue because I've lost my head over a woman. Tell Ferro I'm deep undercover, unraveling a bigger conspiracy. Buy me time but stay out of this. Tell him I'm making perfect sense."

"Why can't you tell him?"

"Because if I talk to that son of a bitch right now, I'll spew." He broke off a branch, crushing it and getting sap on his hand. The pungent scent of pine filled his nose. "Did he tell you anything specific about the woman our father tried to release?"

"No, just the overall story. Why?"

"I never heard the details either. They were confidential. You don't remember much about our father, but he lived for the Guard and then the Concilium. He also trusted his instincts and taught me to do so as well. Even if he caught hell for it. After he died, I shoved his advice into a deep well inside me. I lost respect for everything he was and said. Now I'm wondering, what if his saving that woman was part of something else? What if she was telling the truth?" There had been evidence pointing to multiple kidnappings, all involving children. His father had worked the case. What if it had been one of the Concilium members his father had trusted?

"Now you're sounding paranoid."

"Maybe. But right now I've got to take care of Violet." *Take care of her.* His chest ached at the thought of keeping her safe, in his arms, in his bed.

"Kade, are you sure about this?"

He could hear the strain in her voice, strain he'd caused. "I'm sure, Mia. I'm sorry you got dragged in." Not only was his own career crumbling around him, but hers might be, too. She would be associated with the Vega who went rogue. He knew the taint of that.

The hairs on the back of his neck stood in the same moment he heard a whisper of sound nearby. "I have to go." He turned to find two murderous-looking men coming toward him: Violet's brothers.

Violet heard the front door close and more than one set of footsteps clomping down her hallway. Her eyes flew open, and she lurched upright. Kade was gone.

Jessup's voice shouted, "Vee! Get out here."

She scrambled out of bed, her mind searching for reasons they could be summoning her like this. "Hold on a damned minute." She threw on clothing and pulled open the door.

Jaime Rush

Where was Kade? Not in the bathroom.

Jessup's expression was grim. Behind him, Ryan didn't look any happier. And both looked as though they'd just been in a scuffle, hair mussed, Jessup's face bruised.

"What happened?" Her heart lodged in her throat like a clump of mud.

"No, nobody's dead. Yet." Jessup's mouth tightened. He was pissed. "I overheard your boyfriend out there on the phone talking to a woman."

She had to backtrack her harrowing thoughts. This was about Kade being a cheater? "Yeah, so what? I told you I wasn't serious about him." Still, her heart tightened even more.

"He's not serious about you either. He told the woman he wasn't in love with you, and how could he be when he didn't know you until this assignment? Want to know what that *assignment* is?" He waited a beat. "Killing you."

"What? That's crazy."

"He said he's undercover. What he's doing is pretending to be in love with you so he can strike when you're not expecting it. You think there's a conspiracy, that someone's targeting the Fringers. Well, guess what? Your boyfriend is targeting *you*." He jabbed his finger within an inch of her nose. "You can say all you want, but you've got a thing for him. Your bad judgment where men is concerned brought an enemy right into our camp."

"Wait." She shook her head, unable to even fathom what Jessup was insinuating. "What exactly did you overhear?"

"Someone named Mia was all pissed."

"Mia is his sister."

"Well, that makes sense. She was all over him about not

telling her the truth. Because the guy lies." He nodded to punctuate that.

Kade wasn't in love with her. Why those words hit her hardest, she didn't know. And of course, they'd only recently gotten to know one another, so it wasn't *love*. But it felt like...in love.

"You're sure he said he was supposed to kill me?"

"The woman said his assignment was to kill you, kind of a question. Even with my Dragon hearing, I couldn't tell the context. But he said yes."

She processed that. It explained why Kade had come here, why he'd sneaked up on her instead of calling like any normal person would. If she hadn't sensed him, she'd be dead. But she had, so he'd had to concoct a story. Her blood felt as though it were thickening by the second, slowing her heartbeat. Seducing her must have come easy for him. She tangled her fingers in the fabric of her shirt. Even worse, she'd been the one to invite him—no, order him—to her bedroom. She'd responded to his touch, his magick, so easily.

I'm a bad, bad man, Vee.

She turned her focus from the ache in her chest to her brothers. "What were you doing out there anyway?"

Jessup tapped his chest. "I'm keeping an eye on things, a good idea right now. I never trusted that guy. I heard the part of the conversation about his assignment and went to get Ryan. Your boy was telling her he was going to 'take care of you' when I came back. Take care...as in kill you. What I don't understand is why the hell would the Guard want you dead?"

"I went to them." The words dropped out like stones.

Both her brothers stared as though she'd grown a second

nose. Finally Jessup spoke. "I *know* I didn't hear you say you went to the Guard."

"I was desperate. I went to report Arlo's murder. I wanted them to look into it, hoping their investigation would prevent any more bloodshed." She told them about Ferro's map and the pins. "They know what's going on, yet Kade's boss dismissed me. Soon after, Kade showed up here." To kill her. "He gave me some story about coming on his own to investigate because it didn't feel right. And I believed him. He went back to Headquarters to get more information, but his boss blew him off, too."

Jessup sneered. "That's what he told you."

She pushed on, filling them in on everything that happened. "Kade and I fought her together. She would have killed him, and Kade would have killed her, too, if either had the chance. That was real." But what about everything else?

"And you don't think we would have helped you?" Jessup said, a growl in his voice.

"You'd help all right, going off and killing the wrong people and starting another war. Kade is levelheaded, not emotionally involved with the clans. He could find out things on the Guard end, so I accepted his help. If he were planning to take me out, he's had plenty of opportunities." She held on to that truth. How many times had they been alone, including earlier that morning?

Jessup shook his head. "Who knows what he's up to?"

"Except the barn wall," Ryan said with a laugh.

Jessup gave her one of his satisfied smirks. "I grabbed the cuff off the barn wall. He wasn't easy to take down, least 'til I got the cuff on him." He gave Ryan a nod. "Let's go *take care of* him."

The two turned to the front door. She ran after them, knowing what that meant. But was it the same way Kade had meant it? "I'm coming, too. Let me talk to him."

"No way, little sis. He'll give you some story, and you'll be all, 'Oh, please, don't kill him.'"

She grabbed Jessup's arm, halting him. "I brought him into this, and I'll deal with him. I'm not going to be swayed by anything but the truth." If she could tell the difference.

They both gave her a skeptical look, and a grunt that meant they weren't agreeing but they weren't disagreeing. For now.

"Have you talked to him yet?" she asked as they continued through the woods.

"No, he was out cold. Dragon foot connecting with human head equals a KO. It always amazes me how heavy dead weight is."

"But . . . he's alive?"

Again, why should she care, when he'd come here to kill her? *I only want answers.*

"At the moment."

This time Kade wasn't stripped down. He wore jeans and a blindfold. He turned to them as they approached.

"What, you decided to spare him the underwear humiliation?" she asked Jessup.

"Didn't have any on." He gave her a derisive look. "Do I want to know what happened to 'em?"

Kade said, "Look, we don't have time to discuss my underwear. We—"

"You sure damned don't," Jessup said.

Violet slapped his arm and mouthed, *I'm handling this.*

She stepped up onto the stool so she was face-to-face with him. "Kade, I told them the truth about how we met."

She lifted his blindfold, looking into his green eyes, thinking of how he'd shared his ambitions and how he'd sold his soul for the Guard. Was he that good an actor? "Now it's time for you to tell me the truth about why you came here."

A red mark marred the side of his face. He released a breath of surrender. "After you left Headquarters, Ferro ordered me to take you out."

"To kill me?" Her voice quivered.

"Yes."

"That's why you came here. To carry out that order. Then I caught you, and you had to come up with a story. Is that what everything you've said has been about? Maneuvering me into being...comfortable with you." She wouldn't say in love. Not here, not ever.

"No." He held her gaze, dark mist swirling in his eyes, then shifted his gaze beyond her. "Didn't you hear the part about the assignment not feeling right from the beginning? That I was going with my gut?"

Jessup crossed his arms over his chest. "Nope."

"Convenient," Kade muttered. To her he said, "I questioned the order, even though we're not supposed to. I was told that you were connected to the murders."

She nearly choked at that. "*Me*? Behind the murders?"

"Now that I know you, it's preposterous. Until yesterday, I only knew you as a Fringe hellcat. So I came here to complete my assignment. You were sobbing, and my gut screamed that you weren't responsible. I've never hesitated on a mission, never second-guessed my superior. So I stood there like an idiot, and you reared up and kicked my ass."

She glanced back at her brothers, who were listening to every word. About the sobbing. But at least about the kicking ass part, too. She turned to Kade again. "You're as dedicated a Vega as they come. So I'm supposed to believe that the sight of me crying made you disobey a command?"

"No, that made me see you as more than a crazy-assed Fringer. You were human...and vulnerable. The only thing I lied about was why I'd come in the first place. The more we talked, the more things sounded wrong about this whole situation, which corroborated my instinct. I've been putting off my boss with excuses while trying to figure this out. Now Ferro's dragged my sister into it."

"You never told her about your father?"

Kade shook his head. "I tried to protect her from that whole mess. Ferro is insinuating to Mia that I'm losing my head over a woman the same way he did."

"But you're not." Thank gods it hadn't come out as a question.

"Vee—"

"Violet. You don't get to call me Vee."

He released another breath. "Violet, I've never lost my head over a woman. But you...you—"

"All right, that's enough," Jessup said, yanking her off the stepstool.

She pulled her arm away from him. "Let him finish."

"What, so he can tell you how special you are, beautiful, or whatever other line he's got in his arsenal? I can already see the flames flickering in your eyes. The man was going to execute you."

"I do not have flickers in my eyes over him." She blinked just in case.

Kade said, "Vee—Violet, you can hate me all you want, but right now we're in big trouble. The Carnelian must have reported to Ferro that we were fighting together. Mia is going to have to tell Ferro that I still haven't completed my mission. Ferro is going to send someone else to, as Mia quoted him, 'remedy the situation.' That means finishing you. I don't know how high this goes, so I can't risk going over his head. What I can do is make sure you're safe."

Jessup asked, "Is that what 'taking care of her' was supposed to mean?"

Kade seemed to run his conversation through his mind. "Yeah, exactly."

Jessup stepped in front of Violet. "We'll take care of her. After all, sounds like we'll be protecting her from a trained killer like you. If someone's coming for her, we'll take him out at first sight. Or her, if they send your sister."

Fear tightened Kade's face. "If she comes here, it'll be to try to talk sense into me. She's not a killer. Don't hurt her."

She could tell Kade was not a man used to asking for mercy. He leaned back against the wall, closing his eyes for a moment. His voice was low when he said, "When my replacement comes, his assignment will be to kill me, too. Ferro can't afford to have me investigating and questioning him. If you leave me here like this, I'll die." He looked at all of them. "I can help keep Violet safe." He met her gaze. "You figured out there was something going on, and you unfortunately brought your suspicions right to the man behind it."

"Why would some Guard dude want to start a war in the Fringe?" Ryan asked. "It doesn't make sense."

"No, it doesn't," Kade said. "It's a lot easier for me to believe that Violet is some crazed psycho bitch than to suspect my superior is setting up a war. It goes against everything I believe in, everything I've worked most of my life for." She saw the truth in that, at least. Unless he was a consummate actor, this was tearing him apart.

Vegas are trained to be spies and go undercover. Everything he's told you could be part of a plan. And if you believe him, you could not only put yourself at risk but also everyone you love.

She turned away, doubt tearing at her. There was the Kade who'd shared his ache at not believing in his father. Who had made sexy and tender love to her. Then there was the Vega Kade. Her brothers were right, damn it. She couldn't trust her judgment where Kade was concerned.

Behind her, Jessup said, "When your Vega buddy comes, we'll see what he does. If he tries to kill you, we may intervene. If he's here to rescue you, we'll take care of you both."

Chapter 14

Ferro watched Mia in the parking lot beneath the sodium lights. Judging by her anxious pacing, he suspected the conversation had not gone well with her brother. He still couldn't believe Kade fell for a target, after everything he'd been through with his father. And a Castanega, no less.

Mia lowered her hand, her face full of tension, and slowly walked into the building. He waited for her knock.

"Come."

She shored her shoulders as she came in, brimming with confidence. "My brother isn't romantically involved with the target."

"And you know this how?"

"He told me. I believe him, considering how much he disdains the Fringers, especially that family. Sir, my brother hasn't been emotionally involved with any woman for as long as I've known him. He told me that being a Vega means sacrificing long-term relationships. He asked me to tell you that he's undercover, working on something big. He'll report to you when he can."

Ferro nodded, putting on the same kind of mask she was. "Very well. Thank you, Kavanaugh. If you hear anything else, you'll let me know?"

"Of course."

"You may go now."

Relief crossed her features. "Thank you, sir." She spun on her heel and left.

He picked up his phone and scrolled down the list of Vegas. His finger pressed on a name he knew well. "It's Ferro," he said, though he was sure his name appeared on the screen. "Report to me immediately."

"On my way."

Vegas were always on call.

Ferro pulled the map from the drawer where he now kept it out of sight. If the Castanega woman hadn't seen this, things might have gone differently. If she hadn't busted into his office like a crazed animal. Dispatching *her* was no big deal.

He now had marked the map rather than using the pins. There should be enough deaths to start the clans fighting. Why was it taking so long for them to retaliate in a bigger way? Not just a revenge kill here or there but full-out war?

Ferro felt the presence of his sire. What was he doing, coming here to his workplace? Ferro knelt as the Dragon god materialized in the usual way, opening a window to Ferro's dimension. Drakos was all Dragon, truly every bit the beast. His scales were the darkest of dark, his head as large as Ferro's desk. Whiskers trailed from his lips, and fangs speared down below his chin.

"Sire," Ferro said.

"Stand. I grow weaker by the day and need your reassurance that things are progressing on schedule."

The gods didn't reveal their secrets or their weaknesses, but Drakos had come to him in confidence. He was dying.

Ferro stood. "They are, my sire. I have Breathed a Dragon nearly every day these past three months. Some strong, some weak, but I'm gathering power all the same. My dear Onyx is gaining power as well, and when the war in the Fringe erupts, we'll swoop in and take the most powerful. That should be enough to sustain you. I have, however, encountered a small complication—"

"Complication?" The word was like a gavel pounding on the table.

"Nothing worrisome. I am in the process of remedying it now."

Ferro had enjoyed the rare relationship he had with his sire. Most of the gods who'd created progeny disdained them. Crescents were, after all, an inferior mix of human and god. Drakos had been one of those gods, too, back in the days of Lucifera.

"We don't have much time," Drakos said. "The death of a god is like that of a star. We flicker for some time, and then . . . poof."

His chest tightened at the thought. "We'll be ready."

Drakos smiled, though it was weak. "I am putting my life in your hands."

"We are your honored servants. We will be ready to Breathe our accumulated power into you. You're certain this will work?"

"Very. Just as I am certain about your reward."

True immortality. Crescents lived long lives, but they

weren't immune to death and injury. Unless they had the help of a god. It was a secret Ferro kept with great pride.

Drakos started to say something else, but he flickered and disappeared. Ferro held back the fearful call of Drako's name. No, he wouldn't believe the god was dead, not when they were so close.

A knock on his door jarred him from his thoughts. "Come."

Dune walked in, his muscular body holding the posture of a soldier reporting for duty. "You have need of me, sir?"

"I do. I have a matter of a sensitive nature. When I tell you about it, you'll understand why I chose you."

His chest puffed. "I appreciate your confidence, sir."

Dune was an overachiever who enjoyed his job a little too much. As he'd never overstepped his bounds, that was fine with Ferro.

He came around his desk. "Yesterday I sent Kavanaugh on a kill mission. He was to take out the woman who came here demanding we investigate her brother's death."

"The Fringer that Kavanaugh allowed to walk into your office? If I'd been closer—"

"Never mind that. It appears that he cannot complete his mission. That, in fact, he is refusing to. As you know, insubordination cannot be tolerated in the Guard."

Behind the swirling mist, Dune's eyes were as dark as his skin. He already understood. "Of course not."

"Kavanaugh has apparently reverted to his wild days. That in itself would only be grounds for firing. However, I believe he has allied with the target, and that makes him dangerous. I know there is no love lost between you two, so you will not falter in eliminating both him and Violet

Castanega. And anyone else who might become involved in the altercation."

Dune's mouth cracked into a grin that revealed his white teeth. "Consider it done." Before he closed the door behind him, he said, "I'll report as soon as I'm finished."

Ferro allowed himself to feel a moment's regret at wiping out one of his better Vegas. Even in his undisciplined days, Kavanaugh was skilled and efficient.

Ferro pushed aside his regrets and called Onyx. "How are you feeling?"

"Better." Her voice, though, sounded frail. "I should be ready to continue today."

"Take time to heal. I've sent another Vega to eliminate the problem. It's best if you regain your strength today. Then, tomorrow, you'll be ready."

"We're running out of time. The full effect of the solar storm hits us tomorrow. We've got to have enough power by then."

Ferro felt the urgency as much as she did. "We are very close, my dear. Perhaps close enough. But no, we'll not take any chances. For my hunt, I have a lead on an old Dragon who's hiding out in a church. Acting as a priest, after two hundred years of preying on the innocent. Preying, and now praying." He allowed himself a laugh.

"Be careful."

He heard the old fear in her voice, the one that paralyzed her in her weak moments. She had lost so much in her life. He was all she had now. It was a position he rather liked, just as he liked the way she looked up at him as though *he* were a god.

"I'll be fine. I've been hunting right along with you. No one has defeated me yet."

Her laughter was tremulous. "And soon...soon no one will defeat us."

"Tomorrow we step things up. So far our actions haven't incited the war. Curious, considering the brutal nature of the Fringers."

"I think it's Violet. So far she's kept her own family from acting on Arlo's murder. I saw her going to the Augusts after I took out Butch. She also met with the head of the Peregrine clan. She must be persuasive, desperate to keep peace. I know how to push them over the edge. I need to kill a child, an innocent. Fringers hate when the children are targeted. Then things should finally heat up."

They'd left the blindfold off. That was the good thing. The only good thing. Kade tried to summon his magick, flexing his fingers until they cramped. No deal. He figured they had some Lucifer's Gold in the cuffs, but knowing that didn't help.

In the distance, he heard the sounds of people calling out to each other, engines starting. Business as usual. But he could see no one. Jessup had threatened to watch him, but if he was, he was well hidden.

There were plenty of places to hide, but here Kade was, in full sight of the Vega sent to kill him. He struggled again to free himself. Maybe Violet's brothers would be able to protect her. Maybe not. Idiots thought just because they could swing through the trees that they were invincible. If Kade weren't distracted, weren't caught up in dealing with Mia or emotions that were tying him in knots, no one would have caught him off guard.

"Violet, if you're out there, talk to me. Someone's going to come kill me. Then he's going to go after you. Maybe you can live with me dying in a defenseless position, but think about yourself, your people."

Nothing. He'd seen her break, just a little, when she stood in front of him. Then doubt clouded her face. She'd walked away, leaving him to die. Fucking irony. The real irony was how her distrust cut into him. Her turning away hurt him in a way no woman had before.

He heard the footsteps first. The crackle of pine needles beneath a boot. Kade zeroed in on the sound, staring into the woods. Waiting like a lame duck. *Hell.*

He saw the tall figure, nearly camouflaged by the tight-knit pines. Then the distinct shape of a man, tall, dark, with broad shoulders.

Double hell. Dune. Yeah, Ferro wanted Kade out. Permanently.

Dune checked the surroundings as he advanced, but mostly his eyes were on Kade. He wore the smile of a man about to cut into an aged filet mignon. That smile widened as he approached, taking in Kade's predicament.

"Kavanaugh," Dune said in what might have passed as a greeting in any other situation.

"Dune."

"Ferro thinks you've gone rogue over a woman." He surveyed the situation. "Looks like you're into some kinky stuff."

Kade forced a laugh. "Not hardly. I was ambushed. If you'll cut me down—"

"Why haven't you Changed? Used your magick to cut yourself free?" Dune reached out to touch the cuffs, then drew his fingers back as though he'd been burned. "Lucifer's Gold. Interesting that Fringers would have such a thing. I'll have to take these with me." Dune stepped back and jerked his arm. It took Kade a second to realize he was slamming his fist into Kade's stomach.

Kade couldn't physically double over, but he coughed and sucked in a breath. "What the hell was that for?" he managed.

"Where should I start? Being a hotheaded asshole who skipped past me up the ranks because of his daddy, even as he broke all the rules." Dune hit him again, but this time Kade was ready and tightened his stomach muscles. It still hurt but didn't take his breath away.

"Wasn't it enough that I got demoted?" Dune had sure rubbed it in enough.

"No, it wasn't. But you know what was enough? Being the one who terminated your daddy."

Rage burned through Kade, but he gritted his teeth and swallowed it back. "You were only following orders." The hardest words he'd ever had to utter, and yet, that was a Vega's job. Didn't matter who it was.

Now the target was Kade.

All these years, Dune had never once hinted that he'd been the one to take out his father and the prisoner. It carved him into pieces, but Kade held it in. Dune was playing with him first. Kade was not going to play back.

"Some jobs I enjoy a lot more than others." Dune grinned, the smug smile Kade hated. "Like that one. And this one. I like taking down the high and mighty." He took in Kade again, his derisive gaze sweeping over him, and laughed. "Well, the once high and mighty. This is almost too easy."

Kade knew better than to appeal to Dune. He'd been given an opportunity to wipe Kade, and he wasn't going to be talked out of it. It was no use appealing for Violet's life either, not when she was the original target.

"You can hate me all you want," Kade said, "but you have to admit I'm good. Look what Violet and her clan did to me despite my skills. They're tough and clever and fast. And there are a lot more of them than you. They'll flatten you."

Dune summoned his dagger from his arm, running his long fingers along the edge. Sparks of blue arced between them, reflecting off the blade. "Thank you for the warning. If that's what it was. I can manage. See, *I'm* not distracted. I saw the way you were looking at the Castanega girl at Headquarters. I hope you enjoyed your piece of trashy Fringe ass, since you threw your life away to get it. Just like your father."

Kade fought back the words that wanted to charge out. *Don't let him get to you.*

Dune lifted the blade and held it inches from Kade's face. He drew it down, making the magick crackle from it. Every shard cut and burned across his skin like tiny razor blades. Dune paused at the waistline of his pants. "Is it a genetic thing? Are you Kavanaughs just stupid for women? Maybe I should have a taste of her, see what it is that's got you upside down. Before I wipe her."

"Bastard. Leave her out of this. She doesn't deserve to be a target. Ferro's got an agenda, and Violet was smart enough to figure it out. I stopped being a Guard pawn and started thinking for myself. Wanna give it a try?"

Dune chuckled. "And end up where you are? I don't think so. No, I'm going to do my job and report in, get my nice, fat paycheck, and move on to the next assignment. The girl, I won't think twice about. You...I'll have fond memories of you for a long time."

Chapter 15

Violet had watched the jerk she'd seen at Guard headquarters approach Kade, taunting him the way he'd done then. She flinched when Dune punched him in the stomach. Jessup's hand gripped her shoulder as she started to Catalyze. He shook his head. The man who'd come here, just as Kade said he would, might notice three Dragons sitting up in the trees. Especially when the branches broke under their weight.

The second time the big black guy hit Kade, it didn't seem to hurt as much but she still cringed at the abuse. Everything Dune said corroborated what Kade had told her. She watched him swallow back any reaction when the man admitted he'd terminated Kade's father. Gods.

When Kade talked about how her clan had gotten the best of him, had she heard pride in his voice? What was he trying to do, dissuade Dune? That's how it sounded. Then Dune called her trashy Fringe ass.

She felt her brothers bristle. Hell, she bristled. Especially when Dune talked about tasting her. She shuddered with revulsion. The man was nasty, mean, and...wait a minute. *Kade had thrown his life away for her?*

Everything Kade said made it harder to hate him. And only when he defended her did he reveal any kind of emotion. She glanced at Jessup, who mouthed, *Acting*.

Dune waved his knife around, and then he turned the sharp point toward Kade. Not acting. The man wanted Kade dead, hated him the same way the Carnelian hated Violet.

She Catalyzed and flew down at an angle that put her feet first, the hard part of her heels aimed at the target. He looked up a second before she made contact. *Smash.* The man went flying through the air. She Catalyzed back to human so she could release Kade, needing the dexterity of human hands to work the cuffs.

"Violet—"

"Shut up." She released his legs last, spinning to face the man coming at them.

Ryan and Jessup landed a few feet away in Dragon form.

Dune took them in, not looking the least bit worried. "Thought you might have reinforcements, so I brought a few of my own." He snapped his fingers as Kade released his dagger.

Two demons materialized from the nearby woods. She knew nothing about the horrid creatures, other than stories handed down from earlier generations. They were vile things, vaguely human in shape with mottled brown skin and pointed ears. They smiled with evil glee and launched themselves at her brothers.

Dune slashed at Kade, sending a long arc of lightning at

him. Kade dodged it, cutting down at an angle with his own bolt. Violet Catalyzed again and shot a breath of darts at Dune. He threw out a shield of dark gray, deflecting them so they fell harmlessly to the ground and disintegrated. He dropped the shield and threw something round and blue at her. She moved out of the way, but it hit her anyway, leaving a searing pain across her side.

Before she could even see what it had done, one of the demons grabbed for her, yanking out a scale. Sharp pain lanced her. Ryan slammed into it, sending it to the ground. She spun around to find Kade and Dune fighting dagger to dagger. That sexy electricity sparked over Kade's skin. Dune's sparks were brass colored and not as bright.

"Glad you could bring your little honey into this," Dune said, thrusting.

Kade sent a long bolt that circled around Dune, making him spin around to defend against it. Kade sliced at an angle, shredding the back of Dune's shirt and cutting into his dark skin. Dune shouted in pain and disappeared in a burst of smoke.

"What—" She hardly had the word out of her mouth when she felt his presence behind her.

Kade turned to face her and threw his dagger. It whistled past, with an inch to spare, and sank into Dune as he was about to grab her throat. He howled in pain and pulled at it. Amazingly, the dagger flew back past her, spinning around so it landed in Kade's hand handle first.

She knew so little about Deuces. Right now that was dangerous. She spun around and whacked Dune with her tail before he could stagger out of the way, holding his shoulder as blood poured out between his fingers. He raised his good hand in her direction, and a yellow orb soared out of his palm. Kade knocked into her, taking the brunt of the orb as it hit him in the chest. They both fell to the ground, Kade groaning and clutching at the scorch mark on his skin. The orb, a blob the size of a basketball, flew at her now. She sent a shower of spikes at it, spearing it like a pincushion. The orb shook, dipping in midair, and then shattered.

She heard her brothers battling the demons, catching a glimpse of red eyes and sharp teeth as one pounced on Jessup. A sizzling sound made her turn around. Another orb flew at her. She saw Kade throw an orb to intercept it, but the yellow orb dodged it and hit her anyway. Heat seared right through her scales as it exploded.

Dune, still favoring his shoulder, created another orb and sent it their way. Kade morphed into a creature with a huge black maw, catching the orb as though it were a gumball. It disappeared into the blackness and fizzled out.

Just as quickly he morphed back to human, visibly drawing in his strength. She pulled her gaze away and faced Dune again. He was coming at her with his dagger, holding it with his good hand. Kade leaped through the air, spinning before landing beside Dune. As Dune brought the dagger down at her with its arc of lightning, Kade brought his up to stop him. Their forks of wicked light intersected, crackling and shooting sparks as each man fought to gain control. Kade's effort bulged the veins on his arms. His jaw tightened, and he let out an ungodly sound as the lightning bolt grew brighter and stronger. Indigo sparks flickered across his skin. The strain of using his power tore at Dune, too, as a guttural sound emitted from him and his muscles quivered. Violet moved away from them, intending to circle behind Dune.

"Creston!" Dune shouted, a word she'd never heard.

Not a word but a name. A demon rammed into Kade from behind, throwing him forward enough to free Dune's bolt. Kade was propelled forward, and his bolt cut right through Dune, from left shoulder to right hip. For a moment his eyes widened, and then his face went slack. He fell to the ground in two pieces, both making a wet *thump* as they landed.

Creston launched onto Kade's back, talons scratching his shoulders. Kade swung his dagger back and forth, unable to do more then whip the demon with the shards of magick. Violet came up behind its corded, muscular back. It whipped its tail at her, stinging her across her cheek. She snapped at it, biting it in two. Before the demon even had a chance to react to that, she sank her fangs into its back. Its spine cracked between her teeth, and it made a guttural sound before it disintegrated.

Behind her, something squealed in pain right before what sounded like a huge bug being squashed beneath an even larger shoe. Another demon evaporated at Jessup's feet. She turned to Kade, finding him staring at the ground where Dune lay. Kade's chest rose and fell as he caught his breath, blood dripping from superficial scratches. She followed his gaze to Dune's body, the bizarre grotesqueness of it beyond anything she had ever seen.

"I've hated that son of a bitch for seventy years." Kade's voice sounded hollow. Not victorious. Not satisfied. Definitely in shock. Surely he'd seen violence like this. But by killing one of his fellow officers, he'd officially severed his connection with the Guard. Gone rogue, in their eyes.

Kade stepped toward the corpse, rifling through the

pocket and extracting a cell phone. He pressed the buttons, looked at the screen, then threw the phone down again. She could see him burying whatever he was feeling. The mist in his eyes swirled, though, giving away his pain. He turned, wiping his hand down his face. Blood was smeared down his arm.

She limped forward, picking up the phone. Her hand was shaking, and she had to hold it with both hands to read the last text exchange between Dune and Ferro:

AT THE TARGETS' LOCATION NOW.

ADVISE WHEN DONE.

Targets. Two or more. Kade had been telling the truth. The Guard had sent someone else, and he had also been a target. She wanted to see him as an emotionless killer, but she couldn't get Dune's taunts out of her mind. Or the way Kade had tried to dissuade him from killing her. His expression was raw. He'd just lost everything and probably destroyed his sister's career in the bargain. He cared about Mia. Maybe he cared about Violet, too.

He threw himself between you and an orb. He cares.

Her brothers came up beside her, both breathing heavily as well. "He wasn't acting," Jessup said, looking at Dune's remains.

"Nope," Ryan said with a long slow shake of his head.

Kade turned to them. "We have a small window of time before they realize Dune's not coming back and send someone else. Or worse, more than one. Probably that Carnelian bitch, too. First I have to warn my sister, try to keep her out of this. The only way to do that is to make her believe what they're going to tell her."

He pulled out his phone and dialed. "Mia, it's Kade. Go somewhere you can talk in private." He waited a few seconds, pacing, but Violet could see his mind working. "Listen. I want you to hear it from me first. What I said before about not being in love with Violet." He met Violet's gaze. "I lied. You saw it before I did, at Headquarters. When I got here, I couldn't do it. There's something between us I can't describe, can't even believe. I'm wild crazy in love with her, and I'm going to do everything I can to protect her. Things are going to get ugly."

So Mia had seen that weird spark between them at the station. She was talking in a high-pitched voice but Violet couldn't quite discern the words. She wasn't happy, that was for sure.

"He's acting," Jessup whispered.

"Nope, I think he's telling the truth," Ryan said.

"Wanna bet?"

"Loser cleans out the alligator pens for two weeks by himself."

Violet tuned them out, focusing only on Kade. She swore her heartbeat slowed as she studied his face. He was telling the truth now. It was in his voice, his eyes.

"Yeah, just like our father," he said. "Crazy must run in our genes." He waited while Mia screamed something else. "No, I'm not thinking with my dick. This goes way beyond that . . . Violet Castanega is innocent, and she doesn't deserve to die. I don't care who I take down with me—"

"Even me?" Mia asked, her voice so shrill Violet could hear it.

Kade's jaw ticked, his mouth stretching into a frown as he stared into the woods. "Yeah, even you. So when the shit hits the fan, tell Ferro and whoever else about this conversation. But only after it comes out. Promise me, Mia.

My life depends on it...Yes, they're trying to have me killed...and yes, she's worth it. I have to go." He disconnected, his fingers tight on the phone.

Violet stalked to him. She would have grabbed his shirt and shaken him if he'd had one. "*You turned her against you?*" The words nearly shrieked out of her.

"It was my only choice."

Now he'd really lost everything because of her.

Something shimmered all around him, and suddenly she was staring up into Dune's face. Dune, in one piece. She screamed and stumbled back. The image flickered, and it was Kade again.

"Illusion," he said, fatigue in his voice. "Just like my life, like everything I've believed in up to now. Everything I've been. Now I'm going to sink fully into illusion and report in to Ferro about my mission."

"As...Dune?"

"I can hold the illusion for short periods of time. Enough to get into the building." Kade looked at his watch. "For the last three months, Ferro has gone out to lunch every day at two o'clock sharp. I'll show up just past two, when he's gone. All I have to do is get into his office and find something that proves what he's up to. At the least, figure it out so we know how to fight back. What I want to do is choke answers out of him, but I know better. The man's a First Gen. Even if I survive long enough to get my hands around his throat, he won't give up a word."

"First Gen?" she asked. "First generation Crescent?" She remembered the painting in his office. "Drakos is his sire."

Kade nodded. "And Ferro's proud of it. Yeah, even Drakos does belong to the Tryah."

"So you're going to sneak into his office and look for evidence. But what if he's still at the building when you get there?"

"Then I'll report in as Dune, personally tell him you and I are dead."

She glanced back at Dune's body and shuddered. They almost had been. "How reliable is your illusion?"

"For a few minutes at a time, perfect."

"But..."

He pulled Dune's wallet out of his pocket and picked up the cell phone. "I've never used it like this. It's one of those unspoken rules: never impersonate anyone. It's akin to the Mundanes impersonating an officer. Except that penalty will be nothing compared to my punishment in this case. But either way I'm a dead man, so I'll make it work." He met her gaze, and she saw dedication in his eyes. "I'm highly motivated."

To protect her. She placed her hand on her chest, trying to calm her erratic heartbeat. "I don't like it. You're walking into enemy territory."

He gave her a soft smile. "Someone else I know did that recently. If she can do it, I can."

"Kade, this is different. They weren't going to kill me on sight." She tunneled her fingers through her hair. "The biggest risk I thought I was taking was being disdained, which I was." She glanced at her brothers. "And having my family find out."

Kade's smile was long gone. "But they didn't disown you. They didn't hurt you or kill you, even when they thought you'd taken up with me. Family sticks together. They're loyal." Unlike the Guard, Kade's "family." "I'm going to get answers. I'm already a rogue agent as far as they're concerned. Going after Ferro isn't going to make it any worse."

"I'm coming with you," she said, the words out before she could even consider them.

Her brothers started to object, but Kade beat them to it. "No way. You're a target. Now it's possible that they will take you out as soon as you walk in. Stay here." He met Jessup's and Ryan's gazes. "Be ready, in case I don't come back. Once the Guard targets you, they don't change their mind. And they won't care if you or any of your clan gets in the crossfire." He looked at Dune, then waved his hand. The mangled body disappeared. Kade reached in his pocket for his phone, then stopped and rocked his head back. "It's such a habit to put on the cover illusion and call for cleanup." The illusion fell.

"We'll take care of the body," Jessup said. "Feed it to the gators."

Kade searched for his shoes and put them on. She felt frozen, perhaps as he had when he'd come upon her crying.

He paused in front of her, lifting his hand to her face but dropping it before making contact. "Give me your cell number. I'll let you know what's going on." He programmed it into his phone under the name Astrid. "In case they get hold of my phone. It won't be an obvious link to you." He called the number and disconnected. "Now you'll have mine, in case something comes up." He started walking away.

She leaned forward, but Jessup closed his hand over her shoulder. "You're not going with him. Dumb idea."

The dappled shadows played over his shoulders and back as he walked into the woods. He paused, turned around. She waited for him to say something—anything. But he turned and continued on.

"They'll kill him if they know it's him," she whispered. Her heart twisted at the thought. She didn't know what she felt for Kade. She didn't want to feel anything for him. He was magick and illusion. Deuces were, after all, named for their two-facedness. How much was real?

Well, she'd known him for one full day, had fought him, fought *with* him, and made glorious love with him. No one had ever felt so right and so wrong all at once. No one had made her hot and aroused and angry and afraid and...no one had made her feel so much. He was a cold killer and a man willing to throw it all away to do the right thing.

And now he was out of sight. What if she never saw him again? She started to move, but Jessup's grip tightened.

"She's in love with him," Ryan said behind her.

"She's not stupid enough to fall for someone like him," Jessup said, ever the skeptic. "Not after what Bren did to her."

She spun around. "Hullo, I'm right here, listening to every word you're saying. And Bren didn't *do* anything to me."

Ryan continued to ignore her, talking to Jessup. "She melted when Kade was talking about how crazy he was about her."

"That was all a lie, to push his sister away," Jessup said. "Which was admirable, I have to admit."

"I wasn't melting," she said. "I was devastated that he was going to cut ties to her like that. To save her." But her heart had responded to the words.

Jessup leaned closer to Ryan. "Our Vee isn't going to let a guy break her heart again. And a man whose whole life has been dedicated to fighting and killing isn't the right one for her. Besides, he's probably going to die today."

Chapter 16

In a way, Violet knowing the truth was much better than having that heavy rock of a secret in his chest. Kade popped his trunk and pulled out a clean shirt. He did a quick cleanup, treated the cuts, and shrugged into it. Now he could let go of any illusions that he could have her. And he had to face it: after giving in and making love with her, he'd been doing just that, building the illusion of a future. He had to focus on finding out what the hell was going on and making sure she was safe. Later he could pull himself out of the rubble that would be his life and figure out what he was going to do.

Without Violet.

Who'd ignited his magick.

All those beautiful, adventurous Deuce women he'd been with and not one had done that. Not one had reached in and wrapped her long, capable fingers around his heart.

He got in the car and texted Ferro a simple message: DONE.

A few seconds later: EXCELLENT. REPORT IN IMMEDI-
ATELY.

Facing the man would be difficult. Maintaining his cool
when all he wanted to do was kill him even harder.

YES, SIR. ON MY WAY BACK.

Sometime later, he pulled past the employee parking lot
and left his car in a busy restaurant's lot. When no one
was around, he summoned Dune's visage and stepped out
of the car. He could easily take on the arrogant swagger,
the square shoulders... because Kade had those, too. *When
you're the best of the badasses, you absorb it into your
body, your personality.*

Kade was no longer one of them. He felt the glimmer
of the man he used to be, the one who didn't fit into the
Vega mold, or the Kavanaugh mold. He didn't know that
guy anymore, though. For twenty years, he'd been stuffed
away, chastised and humbled.

He used Dune's card to enter through the employee
entrance. A long time ago, they'd used magick to prove
their identity. In the way Dragons could no longer fly because of population and technology issues, Deuces had
to limit their use of magick in public. Now it was a card.
A sorry exchange, though it worked well for Kade at the
moment.

He nodded at another Vega and ignored the Arguses,
like Dune did. Holding on to the illusion this long took all
of his effort. The magick pinched every muscle and organ
in his body. Dune was an easier illusion to pull off than,
say, a Dragon, but it was still work all the same. Could he
sell it to Ferro?

Taking a deep breath, he knocked on Ferro's door. After
his customary "Come," Kade stepped inside and closed the

door behind him. If Ferro made him, Kade would fight. Ferro might be more powerful but he was out of practice as far as combat went. Another reason Kade eschewed the higher positions.

Ferro took him in, his eyes shrewd. He scanned Kade's body. *He knew*. Already, in the first seconds, he knew. Damn it.

Kade prepared for him to Catalyze, but Ferro kept his cool. Even the flames in his eyes weren't wildly flickering. He'd seen enough Dragons gearing up to fight to know the signs. Maybe he didn't suspect after all. Yet.

Ferro stepped around from behind his desk. "Not one scratch or cut? Not even a bruise? Kavanaugh's good. I find it hard to believe you could kill him and the woman and not sustain any injury."

Kade gave him Dune's most arrogant smile. "Because I'm better." He ducked his head. "But I have to confess, it was far easier than I thought. Kavanaugh was trussed up. As he was trying to convince me to release him, he told me that the woman's brothers ambushed him. I took him out right there, and then went after the woman. If that's all, sir—"

"What else did he say?"

Psychological stress made the illusion even harder to hold on to. Kade's muscles were cramping now. "He spouted some nonsense about a conspiracy." He laughed. "Even accused you of being in on it. Once his head was no longer attached to his body, he had nothing more to say about it." He took a step back toward the door.

"How did the woman die?"

Kade had prepared for all of this, but Ferro was usually content to hear the end result. Why was he so curious now?

Because he has a personal stake in it. "She must have heard Kavanaugh's screams. I punched a hole through her chest the moment she came around the corner."

That's what Dune would have done. The thought of that weakened Kade and made it even harder to hold the illusion. He waited impatiently for Ferro to dismiss him. He'd get suspicious if Dune was in too much of a hurry to leave. Dune enjoyed his kills and loved to regale anyone who would listen with every nuance of his fight.

"Good job," Ferro said, turning toward the desk.

Kade fought a sigh of relief as he gripped the doorknob. "Wait."

Kade had to pry his fingers off the knob and hide his grimace as he turned his pain-wracked body back to Ferro.

"You said Kavanaugh was trussed up. But he was conscious. Why wasn't he using his power?"

Hell, he didn't want to go there. "I touched the rope they used to hold him. I think it had Lucifer's Gold threaded in it."

"And you didn't take it? I don't like the idea of Fringers possessing something like that."

"I could hear others coming, having heard the screams as well. I decided it was best to retreat than engage an unknown number of enemies."

Ferro held his gaze, then gave a quick nod. "Understood. Retrieve it at your earliest convenience but tell no one. Give it to me."

"Yes, sir." He barely held on, praying that Ferro wouldn't stop him again as he reached for the doorknob. His fingers were stiff, fumbling. He stepped out and closed the door just as his illusion flickered. He shot a look at the pit, people going about their business. Did they know that one of their own had gone rogue? Would he be detained on sight? Or worse, shot? Mia sat, staring off into space, her expression bereft.

Hold on for one more minute.

Kade walked awkwardly to Dune's office, happy that Guard policy dictated no locked doors. He collapsed to the floor the second the door closed behind him. The illusion pulled out of his cells the same way a needle pulled out of the body. The dark skin vanished, his body went from the bigger, bulkier physique back to Kade's lean state.

He lay there for several minutes, blocking the door with his body. Illusions like Changing were one of the most intense and laborious of the Deuce magick abilities. For Dragons, it was natural to Catalyze, or so he'd been told. Not so, Deuces.

He watched the minute hand of the clock tick away, until five minutes had passed. His head throbbed with each tick of the second hand, no doubt the effects of being knocked in the head. It was two fifteen. Ferro should be gone now. Kade had to use the desk to help him to his feet. Once more he'd have to conjure the illusion.

He pulled Dune in again, repulsed at the reflection in the mirror—vain bastard—hanging on the wall. It flickered.

Hold on. Your life depends on it.

He walked out and headed to Ferro's door. In the event that Ferro had changed his plans, Kade came up with some other tidbit to give him about the assignment. He knocked. No answer. He opened the door and walked in, closing it behind him.

Seeing no one inside, he released the illusion, this time pushing past the exhaustion. No time for that. He started looking through the desk drawers. He found the map, with a yellow dot in August territory, next to the red one. Written beside it was the name Kaitlyn. Beneath that was a calendar with names written in each box of the last three months. The same time frame as his daily two o'clock sojourns. Sometimes it wasn't a name but a note like *Unk dragon in Opa Locka* and a number. Most of the numbers ranged from three to the thirties. And on the next day's square, the letters *SS* were written in thick black marker and circled several times. Solar storm, had to be. That was the only thing on here that made sense.

He called Violet, feeling something surge inside him at the sound of her voice. She had every reason to hate him, and she probably did. But she was going to work civilly because she was levelheaded. "Are you where you can write down some names?"

"Hold on." He heard a scuffling noise. "How's it going?"

"I'm in Ferro's office. So far so good."

"I'm ready."

He listed off several of the names on the calendar. "Dragons, I think. See what you can find out. The solar storm plays into whatever they're up to. And there's a target—in August territory. Kaitlyn."

"Kaitlyn! She's a child! Nine, maybe ten."

"Then do what you can to protect her. As long as Ferro thinks Dune has done his job, you're safe. I'm going to stake out his home. Dune will go missing, but that shouldn't be connected to his previous assignment since I'm dead."

"Don't say that," she said in a rush of words.

He wanted to say more, but it wasn't the time. Especially when he heard the doorknob turn. In those seconds, he pressed the phone power button at the same time as he conjured the illusion. He didn't have time to put the map and calendar away before Ferro walked into his office. Kade dropped the phone into the trash as he pushed the chair in.

"He was right," Ferro said, closing the door. His gaze shifted to what Kade had been looking at.

"Who was right?" Kade stepped away from the desk.

"That doesn't matter. He told me someone was in my office. You know, something didn't feel right about Dune's report. He takes too much enjoyment from his kills. This time he was in a hurry. You can drop the illusion, Kavanaugh."

He did, feeling the drain on his already taxed body. "Tell me what's going on. That's all I wanted."

"I think you know enough."

Kade's dagger slid automatically into his hand. He would have to kill Ferro if he had any chance to get out of this alive. Ferro wouldn't be able to maneuver as Dragon in the small space, but as a First Gen, he didn't have to Catalyze to use some of his powers. Ferro's face shimmered, both man and Dragon.

Kade ducked the dark rope of smoke that whipped out like a snake, the signature of an Obsidian Dragon. He sent an arc of magick slicing across Ferro's shoulder that cut through shirt and skin. Blood bloomed through the torn material. Why hadn't he tried to avoid it? The man hadn't even moved.

Ferro spun toward the door and opened it. "Code Red!" *Come immediately, be ready to fight.*

And they did, Arguses and Vegas rushing toward the door to find Kade with his dagger at the ready, Ferro's shoulder bleeding. Ah, that's why he hadn't evaded the swipe.

"Get him!" Ferro shouted, pointing to Kade. "He's gone Red!"

Not the same as a Dragon going Red Lust, but it meant the same thing—magick psychosis.

Kade brought his dagger in, raising his arms. "Ferro's having innocent people killed. He's—"

A flash of magick hit him, knocking him against the desk. He gained his footing just as four of his fellow Vegas tackled him. A cuff snapped over his wrist before he could use his magick to throw them back, these containing a larger dose of Lucifer's Gold. His magick died. The Vegas shoved him against the wall and jerked his hands behind his back before snapping on the other cuff, these meant to restrain physically as well.

"Sorry, buddy," one of them said in a low voice.

As he was pushed out into the pit and down toward the prison entrance, the last thing he heard was Mia's terrified scream.

Violet stared at the phone every few minutes as she re-searched the names Kade had given her—all Dragons, all dead. She didn't like that he'd hung up so abruptly and hadn't called back. *It's only been twelve minutes. He'll call back soon.*

When her phone rang, she lunged for it. Not Kade but Ernie. She frowned. Why would he be calling her?

"What's up?" she asked. *Please don't let my clan be there causing trouble.*

His voice was low as he said, "You'd better come on down here. A few of the clans are having a meeting. Didn't start out that way, but they're talking. And that would be a good thing, but they're talking about your clan and the murders in the same conversation. You didn't hear it from me." He hung up.

She thought about bringing her brothers but decided against it. They would cause more trouble, and, really, she had enough right now.

There were only a few vehicles in the lot when she pulled in a short time later. At the door, she took a deep breath, smoothed her shirt, and walked in all casual-like. A group of men and women clustered at the low tables inside Ernie's bar. Peregrines along with the Augusts and a few Murphys, the people who had likely killed Arlo. Rage rippled through her and burned where her Dragon resided. She put her hand at her waist and sauntered over.

"Well, lookee who's here. Fancy that." One of the Murphys shot a glare at Ernie, who was wiping glasses.

"I came in for a beer. Been a helluva last few days." She took them all in, anger simmering in their eyes. "Fancy *you* all sitting here playing nice."

Toth August came to his full, lanky height. "That's more than your clan is doing."

Danger prickled over her skin. "What are you talking about?"

Bob Murphy stood, too, and held up a key ring. "One of yours came onto our land and killed Dan. Left this for us to find."

Bren said, "My cousin saw you pick up something over at our place, after Butch got killed. You came over, pretending to be all concerned, but I think you were hiding evidence. I know you're trying to protect your brothers, but someone's gotta pay."

They started moving in on her, fists at their sides.

"Stop!" She held out her hand, standing firm. "We're not murdering people. The Guard is."

They paused and looked at each other. Then burst out laughing.

"The Guard snuck onto our land and planted your key ring, did they?" Bob said.

Well, when he put it like that. "Look, I know it sounds unbelievable. I haven't had a chance to figure out the why of it. Marshall," she said to the Peregrine patriarch she'd spoken with, "you said there were footprints leading to the Wolfrums. And you," she said to the Augusts, "you found a handkerchief that likely belonged to the Spears boy. Think about it. Suddenly members of three clans independently decide to murder someone and leave evidence, to boot. Blatant evidence."

"Why not? Everyone's getting restless, with the solar storm coming. But that doesn't mean we're going to put up with it."

The solar storm. How did the power of the storm factor in? It made the *Deus Vis* fluctuate, affected weaker Crescents and made others loopy, like the effect of the full moon.

She turned to Toth. "You've got to call your people, tell them to watch out for Kaitlyn."

"Is that a threat?" Bren's eyes narrowed.

"No, it's a warning. Someone in the Guard has a map of all our territories, and he's methodically targeting us. We caught a female Carnelian about to Breathe Paul

Slade...after she murdered him." She met their gazes.
"Everyone who's been killed so far has been Breathed.
She's doing it for the power, but we stopped her from
Breathing Paul."

"Who's 'we'?" Bren asked.

"The guy I was with." She wanted to check her phone
again and see if he'd called. She had a bad feeling about
him going back to Headquarters. "He's Guard, but he's
been helping me investigate this on his own time."

"The Guard?" Bren said. "You brought the Guard into
our business!"

"The very Guard you're saying is trying to get us to
kill each other," Bob said, crossing his arms in front of his
chest.

"He left the Guard over this, because he suspects corruption." She wasn't going to get into all that. "I want
peace here. I don't want to have to bury my family, and I
know you don't want to bury yours either."

Toth at least seemed to be listening to her. "Why would
someone target Kaitlyn? She hasn't been Awakened yet, so
it's not for her power."

"If someone wanted to incite war among the clans,
killing a child would do it."

Bren blew out a skeptical breath. "I think someone in
your clan has gone haywire, and you're trying to cover his
tracks." He glanced at the others. "I say we make her tell
us who it is."

Several men grabbed for her. She Catalyzed and blew
out a swath of darts. Two hit targets, sending them to the
floor. Several Catalyzed, too, knocking tables and chairs
across the room.

"Enough!" A shot rang out, and they all turned to see

Ernie holding the gun aimed at the ceiling. His own Dragon eyes flickered fiercely. "You know the rules. No Catalyzing except in the Conference Room."

"Fine, we'll take it in there," Bren said with a nod.

She went cold as she Catalyzed back to human and grabbed up her shredded clothes. If they all got her in there...

Ernie shook the gun. "No ganging up on one person, ignats. What kinda place you think I'm running here? She's not the one killing your folk."

"No, but she knows who is," Toth said.

She shot Ernie a grateful look. He wasn't Switzerland when it counted. Then she turned to the group. "Yes, I do. Lieutenant Alec Ferro of the Guard and his Carnelian cohort. Ferro's a First Gen, by the way, whose sire is Drakos."

More disbelief moved across their expressions. Clearly most of them knew Drakos was one of the Tryah.

She continued before they could start arguing with her again. "I've seen Ferro's map of our territories, and he's got yellow pins for potential targets. There was one in the Slade territory right before Paul was murdered. And another one in your territory, Bren. With Kaitlyn's name written next to it." She felt her phone vibrate in her pocket, but now wasn't the time to answer it. "Damn it, call your people, you...ignat." She gave Ernie a look of solidarity, using his particular word for the Fringe favorite *idjit*.

Bren obviously wanted to give her a piece of his mind, but he yanked out his phone and called. "Where's Kaitlyn?" After a pause, he said, "Go find' her. Violet Castanega has some cockeyed idea that she's in danger." He aimed his narrow-eyed gaze at her. "Among other cockeyed ideas."

They all waited for Bren to find out that Kaitlyn hadn't been seen since that morning. A minute later, Bren said, "Well, go find her. I know she runs all over the place."

Violet recalled the Carnelian's hungry, vicious smile when the Slade girl had come running to Paul's side. She slid her phone from her pocket and looked at the missed call information. Not a number she recognized. "I have to go." She took them all in again, putting every bit of emotion in her eyes. "Please don't be rash. Give me time to figure this out."

Violet walked out, calling the number and watching her back at the same time. "It's Violet. Someone from this number—"

"This is your fault!" a woman screamed, tears thickening her voice.

"Who is this?"

"Mia Kavanaugh. I don't know what you're up to, but you got what you wanted."

"Whoa, what happened?" Her chest was already tight, because it wasn't good, not if Mia was calling like this.

"You made him crazy. He doesn't care about his career, me, or his life. He threw it all away for you! And now they have him, and I can't even see him, and—"

"Slow down. The Guard has him?"

"He tried to kill his boss, just...snapped. That's what Ferro said. Snapped. But he was fine when he left here to..."

"Kill me," Violet said quietly, hardly able to push the words out. She leaned against her car, her body sagging.

"For whatever you've done. Then he spends time with you and throws everything away. I can see how dangerous you are, why they want you dead, you manipulative, evil—"

"No, you don't see at all. Kade didn't throw you away. He just didn't want to involve you." She needed to get Mia on her side, and to do that she had to calm her down. "Listen to me, Mia. He realized Ferro was involved in something devious, and that the order to kill me was only because I had figured it out. Once he killed Dune—"

"He *killed* Dune! Oh, my gods, oh, my gods."

"Dune was sent here to execute him. Kade had no choice. And once that happened, he knew he couldn't go back." She swallowed hard, because everything she said rang true. "He told you he'd fallen for me to push you away, so you wouldn't be dragged down like he was when your father tried to break that woman out of prison."

"You know about that? He told *you*?" Mia's outrage rocked the airwaves. "He didn't tell me, but he told you. No, he's crazy."

"Mia, everything he did was to protect you. He was devastated by his father's supposed betrayal. I could see it in his face, hear it in his voice. He was only trying to spare you the fallout by turning you against him. I was mad at him when he did that, but I understand it now. My brothers would probably do the same for me."

A moment of silence. "He *is* in love with you," she said quietly. "He's never shared his feelings with me about anything. Not our father's death, not about everything he'd gone through."

Violet let those words sink in. Was he in love with her? She was so turned around as far as Kade went. "Ferro is going to kill Kade because he knows too much. Did they hurt him?"

"Ten officers dragged him out of here, and now he's in the psych ward. Ferro promised I could see him later, when they had him . . . sedated."

Violet didn't like the sound of that, though the promise meant he would be alive for her to see. "Mia, I need your help. You have to get me the layout for the Headquarters building. I'm going to break in and get him out of there."

"You're going to do *what*?"

That came from behind her. Violet spun to find Jessup and Ryan approaching.

"I'm breaking Kade out of prison. They will kill him in there, just like his father was killed. They'll make it look like Kade snapped, and it'll be shoved under the official carpet."

"I'll meet you," Mia said, her voice stronger now. "And sketch out the floor plan."

"Where's a safe place to talk?"

"Kade's boat." Mia gave her directions and disconnected.

"No way," Jessup said.

"She's going to do it," Ryan said. "She's got that fire in her eyes, like she used to get right before she drove off with the swamp buggy when Dad said she couldn't."

"'Cause she was only eleven." Jessup studied her. "You were such a spitfire. Then you got so practical."

"Someone had to be the levelheaded one," she said.

"You're not being levelheaded now. Breaking into Headquarters." Jessup shook his head, making a hank of his hair swing with the movement. "You gotta be crazy to even think it."

"I'm not letting him die in there." She put her hands on their backs and pushed them to the truck. "You stay out of this. I don't need you badgering me or trying to talk me out of it."

Jessup stopped and turned to face her. "Uh-uh, little sister. We're going with you."

Chapter 17

———

Onyx watched the girl wander through the woods, so innocent and curious. Kaitlyn bent down to pick up a bug, lifting it to the light that streamed down through the Australian pines. Its wings beat a staccato rhythm, and then Kaitlyn let it go.

Jealousy consumed her at the girl's guileless smile. Onyx remembered when she was young and naïve. Before she'd witnessed her first murder—her younger sister when Onyx was just ten.

Soon no one would ever hurt Onyx again. She would have immortality. That was almost as important to her as saving a god. Well, maybe more. The whole I'm-almost-a-god-because-I-consort-with-one thing was Ferro's. Not that he would say it outright, but she knew he relished having a relationship with his sire. He didn't seem bothered that Drakos never showed affection or any real kinship.

Ferro would be displeased that she'd disobeyed him by taking care of the girl now, but that was nothing new. They were running out of time, and the Fringers weren't erupting into a blood war as she had thought they would. Killing this girl would do it. Onyx would gain no power, so she hadn't Catalyzed. No need; the kid wouldn't fight. She would be surprised by the pleasant woman who'd gotten lost in the woods. This girl didn't grow up in the era of fear and blood. She wouldn't have reason to suspect a thing until Onyx drew the knife across her throat.

"Kaitlyn!"

Panicked voices called from the near distance, feet stomping across the dirt. Dragon feet. In broad daylight. Shrill and urgent whistles pierced the air.

The girl lifted her head and whistled in response. Onyx stepped way back into the shadows as five Dragons raced into view. Two women and three men Catalyzed back to human as they reached her.

"What's wrong, Mama, Daddy?" she asked, as insipid and clueless as Snow White.

A woman pulled her into her arms, making Onyx ache at the sight. Her own mother, gone. Her daddy, dead.

"We didn't know where you were," the mother said, relief saturating her voice.

"But I always wander the woods, and you never got worried before."

"Violet was pulling our leg," one man said.

"Maybe she was trying to get us away from the house. Let's go."

Three of them Catalyzed and raced back. The other two walked with the girl, who wasn't Awakened yet and so couldn't become Dragon.

Violet had warned them. How the hell had she known? But wait. Violet was dead. Had she warned them before

Ferro's trusty Vega had offed her and her boyfriend? Onyx slipped through the forest to her car.

She drove toward the vacant land next to the Castanegas, intending to spy on Violet's house. She didn't have to go far. Violet pulled out of Ernie's just ahead of her. Her two brothers followed in their truck.

Onyx fumbled for her phone and called Ferro. He answered on the third ring. "I can't talk right now—"

"Violet's alive. I'm driving right behind her."

"You're supposed to be home recuperating."

She ignored his chastisement. "Didn't you hear me?"

"I suspected as much. I'm in the middle of a situation. One of my officers came in and tried to kill me. I'll have to call you back."

That officer had to be Kade Kavanaugh. Ferro was with others and couldn't talk candidly; she recognized that formal tone in his voice.

She focused on Violet again, could almost feel her blood oozing through her hands. Could taste it. Red Lust licked at her, breathing down her neck with its seductive heat.

Kill, her Dragon whispered. She put her hand to her stomach, where its energy resided. "Soon. Very soon."

Both vehicles turned into the Castanega entrance. Onyx continued on and made her way down the weed-overgrown driveway, past the abandoned buildings, and parked. And waited. But Violet never made it to her home. Onyx waited at the edge of the property. The bitch would come home sometime.

Jessup parked his truck at the main house, and he and Ryan got into Violet's car. They drove into the congested city and followed the directions Mia had given to the marina. Violet spotted her waiting at the end of Dock C, the breeze tossing her dark hair. Worry darkened the mist in her eyes and curved her mouth into a frown. She came forward when she saw Violet, though her expression grew wary at seeing her brothers following close behind. Jessup and Ryan flanked Violet when she stopped in front of Mia, looking thorny as always in the presence of authority.

Mia shored her shoulders. "Who are you?"

Violet made quick introductions. "They're coming in with me."

Jessup said, "We don't like your brother, but Violet's got it in her head that she owes him."

Ryan rolled his eyes at Jessup. "You think she's doing this because she *owes* him? Dude, get a reality check. She's in love with the guy."

Violet gave them both a quelling look and turned back to Mia. "Let's go where we can talk."

Mia searched Violet's face. "Are you? In love with Kade?"

Several answers crashed into Violet's mind at once, but she didn't allow herself time to sort through them. "I don't know what I feel for him. He was sent to kill me, after all. But he didn't. I do know I'm scared for him. And I'm scared not to see him again."

Mia nodded, then gestured for them to follow her down the dock. She'd said "Kade's boat." Violet didn't even know he had a boat, but then again, she knew so little about him.

The boat Mia led them to was vintage, about thirty-six

feet long, and in beautiful condition. Mia stepped onto the flat railing agilely, though Ryan put his hand out to steady her. She ignored it, jumping down and lifting her hand to Violet.

There were two retro-looking chairs beneath a blue tarp, along with a small table. She could clearly imagine Kade sitting there, a beer in hand, talking about the designer who'd come up with the chair. The image tweaked her heart.

Her brothers showed off, launching themselves over the railing and landing with a *thump* on the deck. Mia waved them down into the cabin. The place was neat, with cups and plates stored in tilt-proof bins above the counter in a miniature kitchen. This was where Kade was more himself. She could see that, with curtains so tropically garish they had to be a joke. One shelf held empty beer bottles from different places. On the sofa sat a banged-up guitar.

Mia followed Violet's gaze to it, hers heavy and sad. "Kade told me he was jamming to 'Wild Thing' on his guitar. Naked. Someone called the cops on him, and he went up on deck with nothing but that guitar. They threatened to haul him in for indecent exposure. I can't even imagine him doing that."

"That was the part he gave up for the Guard."

And the part that called to Violet, that pulled and twisted.

They crammed in at the table, and Violet opened her folder. "I'm going to give you a quick rundown of what Kade and I have been investigating, so you'll understand why he did what he did."

"He said he was thinking. Trusting his gut." Mia put her hand on her stomach. "And that I should do the same.

When you told me what he'd told you...it hurt. Hurt that he told you things he never told me. But once I got past that, and what he was doing, I realized my gut is saying my brother's not crazy."

Kade had shared things, intimate things, about himself. If he were putting on a show to gain her trust, he would have focused on seducing her. But when they'd been kissing in her living room, it was Kade who had stopped. At least he'd tried to. Violet had seduced him, as it turned out.

I'm a bad, bad man, Vee.

Now she knew why he'd said that. He had tried to keep them from getting too close. Because he was a good man.

Violet told Mia about the territory map she saw in Ferro's office and what Kade had reported. "Have you heard about the Dragon deaths lately? A lot of them. I looked up some of the names Kade gave me. The ones I could find—dead. I don't know whether they were Breathed or not, but given what's been happening here, I'd assume so."

Mia gave her an odd look. "You're different than I thought you'd be."

Jessup leaned closer to her, making Mia shift away. "Thought we were all idjits, din't ya?"

Ryan smacked his arm. "Don't mind him. He can be a butthead."

"Boys," Violet admonished.

Mia gave Ryan a softer look before laying out two pieces of paper she'd taped together. On it was a rough outline of a building. "Here are the exits, and over here is where the prisoners are kept. Over here is the psych ward, where...well, that's where Kade will probably be. I had prison duty a few years back so I know how it works." Her mouth tightened when she met Violet's eyes. "And I'm going with you."

"Are you sure? You can stay out of this, preserve your career."

"My career with an agency that would kill innocent people? Who put my brother in prison for doing the right thing?"

"We don't know if the Guard is wholly corrupt or if it's just Ferro."

"Either way, I'm in."

Drakos met with his two...well, he wouldn't consider them *friends* by any means. Cohorts, he supposed. Once the gods existed in a magnificent plane, privy to all of the humans' doings, receptive to their adulation and prayers. Then the humans turned their backs on them, more concerned with the physical world.

Alas, he was among the many gods who pooled their power to become physical, falling to the pleasures of physicality and even to the thrill of creating progeny. He and his cohorts, collectively known as the Tryah, were the first to see what a mistake that was as each "bundle of joy" sucked out a little more of their power. Inciting the war was a brilliant idea, reducing the numbers of both humans and Crescents.

Too bad it had resulted in the sinking of the island, condemning the fallen gods to a featureless plane and tethering them to earth and the Crescents they bore. But some of those Crescents had proven useful, tempted into service with their dreams, their weaknesses. Or for the rewards promised them.

"Things are not going well with your plan," Drakos said to the Deuce god.

Fallon's long, dour countenance soured even more. "My minions are being bedeviled by a Dragon duo. Worry not. It will be remedied by Purcell, my dedicated Crescent."

Each god had their own way to see the plan through. Each thought his part of the plan was the best. Time would tell.

Drakos said, "My progeny, too, has run into trouble with a Deuce and Dragon. Amazing what one or two mere Crescents can do when they set their minds on something."

Fallon made a growling sound. "They have become attached to one another. I suppose not unlike the lust we felt for the humans of Lucifera. But we would not sacrifice ourselves for their safety and well-being as some Crescents are willing to do for each other. It confounds me."

"Love, they call it," Drakos said, lifting his upper lip in a snarl.

Demis pulled his wings close around him. "Put your fangs away," the fallen angel said. "They are unsightly."

Demis was as stuck here as the rest of them. He thought he was better than a god. When he got too invested in his superiority, Drakos liked to remind him of his gaffe during their physicality. Demis had unknowingly mated with Dragon gods in human form, producing unstable, powerful hybrids.

Fallon lifted his hands. "Fight not. Once our plan succeeds, we can go back to hating one another. For now, we must work together. It helped us to succeed before and will do so again." He turned to Drakos. "Remember, that dedication you so disdain is the same that they give to us. Those few who still do, anyway. Our minions are invaluable to our plan, after all."

Drakos would not admit that he was right. "But they have weaknesses. My descendant has not been able to dispatch the troublesome Crescents." Drakos filled them in on the circumstances regarding Violet and Kade.

Fallon nodded. "I can help where the Vega is concerned. Tell your minion that I will send my servant to him. Purcell will bring him something useful."

"Thank you." The words were always hard to push out. Gods rarely asked for help, rarely needed it, back in the— as the humans called it—"good old days." It pained him, but the end of this torment was near.

From their plane, Drakos could see the energy of the solar storm approaching like a fiery tsunami. Small waves and flares already reached the physical plane. He took in the beauty of the coming storm. Freedom . . . at last.

Kade knew he'd played right into Ferro's hands. Everyone in the building had seen evidence that he'd attacked his superior officer without provocation. His rants about conspiracies only lent credence to Ferro's assertion that Kade had gone off the rails. It happened to Vegas sometimes. The pressures of the job, nightmares, and lack of a personal life all contributed.

The worst part was not being able to complete a mission that mattered more than any other Guard mission he'd ever taken.

No, the worst was not seeing Violet again, not helping her. Keeping her safe.

He could hardly do that sitting in the sterile white room, bound in a straightjacket reinforced with Lucifer's Gold. They weren't going to keep him in there for long. Ferro would dispatch him at the earliest convenience.

Kade thought of his father, who must have come here to visit the prisoner. Now Kade knew in the depths of his gut that his father hadn't gone crazy. He had suspected truth in whatever the woman told him. Someone with a corrupt plan had wanted her out of the picture. Just like Ferro wanted Violet out of the picture.

Stewart Kavanaugh had put everything on the line in that most important mission—and failed. For the first time in twenty years, Kade felt pride in his father's actions. He knew him in a much deeper way. At least he had that. But now Kade was going to fail in the same way.

The door opened and an orderly came in, eyeing him warily. Kade had seen the guy around but couldn't bring a name to mind. No nametag in sight. The Argus jail staff rarely mingled with Vegas or even Arguses. By design, for this very reason.

The man closed the door and assessed Kade's jacket. Then he approached, testing the straps. "Got to be too much, eh?" he said, opening a metal case mounted on the wall and pulling out a clipboard. "You guys think you're so tough and important, but when you fall, you fall hard." But he wasn't really talking to Kade as he filled out something, just making lame conversation.

"How many Vegas go nuts?" Kade asked, and he could tell the man was surprised at how sane he sounded.

"I've been working the psych ward for thirty years,

seen..." He looked up and counted off with his fingers. "Twelve, maybe, go completely insane. Others just need some downtime."

Kade latched onto the first number. "You were here when my father tried to break out the prisoner twenty years ago. Stewart Kavanaugh."

"Yeah, heard you're his son. You think crazy runs in the genes?"

"I'm not crazy."

He chuckled. "Heard that before."

"Is that what the woman my father tried to break out said?"

He shook his head. "She had an elaborate story, that one of the Concilium members was kidnapping kids and sucking out their essence. Said her name was...Willow, I think, though she didn't remember her last name. She claimed she'd been kidnapped as a young child and the Concilium member had kept her all those years."

"Who was the member?"

"Can't repeat that kind of hearsay."

"Did anyone ever check into her story? Just to make sure?"

He shrugged, hanging up the clipboard. "I heard she was homeless, a wreck of a Crescent. She was better off dead. You shoulda seen her, banging herself against the walls, screaming. Thing was, she started out just telling her story over and over again, but she went downhill fast." He tilted his head. "What's your story?"

Kade laughed, shaking his head. He would sound just as crazy. "Ferro's trying to incite clan wars down in the Fringe. He's going to kill me in here."

"Well, you did try to kill him. Those guys don't like

that, you know." The orderly was used to dealing with insane people. He spoke softly and evenly.

"He tried to have me killed first. I didn't like it either. He wants me out of the picture to shut me up."

The man gave a slow shake of his head. "You people concoct the nuttiest stories..."

"What if the stories are true? You think the Guard is immune to corruption? What happens if someone figures it out? They get brought here. Labeled insane. Dispatched."

The man met his gaze dead-on. "I follow orders. I don't question. I do what I'm told and then go home at the end of the day. I spend time with my kids and wife. And I stay alive." He left, making sure the door locked properly. After one last glance through the large window, he left.

Hell.

Ferro appeared in the window a few minutes later, unlocking the door. The man with him was an old Deuce. Kade couldn't place his name.

Ferro gestured for the man to precede him into the room, following and locking the door behind him. The stranger held an ornate box—a spell box. This couldn't be good. Kade had heard of them, possessed by those who practiced Shadow Magick. The man handed the box to Ferro and waved his hand over the window. He produced an illusion spell so anyone walking past would see only what the conjurer wanted him to see. Which would not be Kade getting whatever was in that box.

The man took the box back. Something was moving inside it, bumping against the sides.

Triple hell. He skipped right past double.

Ferro approached Kade, kneeling down to his level. "This is a harsh lesson in the evils of insubordination. I do not enjoy this. Despite your reckless past, you've been a good officer. You chose the wrong mission to abort, I'm afraid. And for that, you must go away."

"That's a nice way of putting being executed."

"I'm not executing you. There would be questions. Procedures. Paperwork." He shook his head. "Messy. You've already created quite the spectacle, but you've managed to offer a solution as well." He stood. "You won't die, not right away. You will simply go insane. Everyone already thinks you've snapped, so if they come to visit—someone like your sister, perhaps—they will see for themselves that you are truly out of your mind."

The mention of Mia spiked even more fear into him. "She has nothing to do with this. She already thinks I'm mad, so you don't need to bring her here."

Ferro smiled. "As long as she accepts the story and leaves well enough alone, she'll be fine."

"And Violet?"

His smile mingled with an expression of disbelief. He shook his head. "All this over a woman."

"She has nothing to do with whatever plan you've got cooked up. Leave her out of this."

"Can't do that. Like you, she's trouble. You'll have to be satisfied with your sister's safety."

The thought of Violet dying crushed Kade's heart. All he could hope for was that she was clever and strong enough to evade them.

The man—Purcell, he thought his name was—opened the box and grabbed a black thing the size of a cockroach that tried to jump out. It wriggled in his hand where he held it tight.

"No doubt you've heard of the Black Bore Orb," the man said, as though they were having polite conversation.

Every cell in Kade's body froze. "Stories about them. I've never seen one."

"Well, you are about to get to know one very well. It bores into a person's memories, fracturing them like a mirror being hit over and over, until all the pieces are so fragmented, they make no sense at all."

Ferro stared at the orb with gruesome fascination. "Will it hurt?"

"I don't think it's terribly painful, per se, if their hands are bound and they can't scratch at their heads or eyes to tear the thing out. It's hard to tell. The recipient always screams, but I believe that to be the result of the chaos of distorted memories that's going on in their minds." The man turned back to Kade. "Soon it won't matter because your mind will be gone."

Was that supposed to comfort him? Kade couldn't take his eyes from the squirming orb, so eager to do its job.

Ferro asked, "How long will it take?"

"In three hours' time, his mind will give up trying to make sense of what doesn't make sense."

Ferro's expression turned grim. "Do it."

The man stepped forward. Kade tried to evade him, jerking his head away. But he felt it drive into his ear with a suction sound, muffling everything but the horrid scrabbling sound as it pushed its way into his brain. He hit his head against the wall, trying to dislodge it. Pain washed through him, but it didn't stop the orb.

Memories tumbled through his mind, like a deck of cards thrown up into the air. Mentally he grabbed for them, as though he could keep them safe. He latched onto one: making love to Violet. He saw her beautiful face as he touched her, kissed her... and then she fractured.

Chapter 18

Mia walked into Headquarters, passing through the secure side door with her identity card and walking into the pit area. Violet walked in right behind her, so close she could smell the woman's shampoo.

Several officers who were clustered together looked up, and their conversation came to an abrupt halt. They stared at Mia, some with pity, some with derision.

Nobody saw Violet. She was surrounded by a glass orb, similar to the illusion orb Kade had created on the Slade property. Mia said it made whatever it contained invisible and was better suited for well-lighted areas than the mirror orb. It looked as fragile as a bubble, the same way the mirror orb had. Violet kept her hands at her sides, afraid to accidentally poke it and have it burst.

Ferro came out of the unmarked door leading to the prison area. Violet knew the layout, had imprinted it during the short drive from the marina. The prison was on the third floor, up a dedicated passage.

Ferro's face was pale and drawn, but he recovered his cool expression when he saw Mia approaching.

"I want to see him," she said, her voice filled with emotion Violet knew was genuine.

"I'm not sure that's a good idea. He had a reaction to the anti-psychotic meds. I'd rather you wait until he calms down."

"No, I want to see him now." Her voice was raised, shrill enough for anyone in the pit area to hear. And they did, turning their way.

"Very well, but it's not pretty."

This is probably the first time Kade has been called unpretty, Violet thought with an edge of hysteria.

Everywhere signs warned RESTRICTED ACCESS. Ferro led the way past the double doors that housed the morgue. Violet shivered.

He's not in there.

But Ryan and Jessup would be waiting on the other side of the rear exit. Mia said there were usually only one or two employees in there at any given time. Violet took note of where the fire stairs came out, almost across from the morgue. Good.

Squeezing into the elevator scared the hell out of Violet, who held her breath as the door slid soundlessly closed. The lurch of her stomach had nothing to do with the quick lift of the car to the third floor. The door opened to a security station armed with a guard. Violet bet the wall separating the small foyer and the prison consisted of bulletproof glass. Maybe even magick-proof glass, if there was such a thing.

Ferro signed in for both himself and Mia. The guard on the other side of the glass punched in a code that Violet memorized. Once the door slid open, he gave a respectful nod to Ferro, but his eyes narrowed as he assessed Mia. Could he sense Violet? The door closed with a loud clang, snapping against the bubble.

Please hold, please, please, pretty please.

Mia glanced back, her expression tight. They followed Ferro down a hall lined with cells, two guards monitoring the area. One greeted Mia with a nod that indicated recognition. When Violet had hoped Mia could use her connections, she explained that once she'd chosen not to remain in the prison, the staff cut ties to her. A necessary prejudice, she said, as the prison and psych ward staff didn't mix with the other Guard staff.

Several prisoners sat or stood around in their cells, coming to attention when they caught sight of Mia. Violet had seen movies where the convicts hooted and hollered when a woman entered their domain, but these did not. Mostly men, one woman, and more empty cells than filled ones. No Kade.

They turned the corner, finding another security checkpoint. This man wore a white uniform, and his shaved head reflected the harsh fluorescent lights above.

"Back already?" he said to Ferro, then took note of Mia.

"Beckett, this is Kavanaugh's sister. She wants to see him."

Something in his eyes softened with pity. "I would say 'good to see you again,' but it doesn't seem quite appropriate, does it?" His mouth tightened when he looked at Ferro as he stood and pulled out the keys.

Violet sized him up. He was big, muscular, but she could take the Deuce. Mia had described the cuff that the orderly would use to restrain an out-of-control inmate. It hung from his belt and gleamed with Lucifer's Gold.

There were no other prisoners—or were they considered patients here? No other staff either. That would make things easier. Violet took note of the emergency exit door that led to the fire stairs.

Three cells down, Ferro stopped and faced a window reinforced with wire mesh. Mia gasped, throwing her hands against the glass. The bubble shimmered as she lost her focus on it.

"Mia," Violet whispered. The bubble started to disintegrate.

Mia jerked her head to Violet, who stood beside Ferro. The bubble snapped together again. Only then could Violet turn to look at what had upset Mia so badly.

She couldn't gasp, couldn't breathe. Kade, bound in a straightjacket, banged his head against the wall and uttered words that made no sense. They funneled out through a speaker.

"Bore...bore." He let out a groan. "Don't leave, no. No!"

Ferro pressed the button, which muted it. "He's been muttering nonsense since we brought him here."

"This is from a reaction to a drug?" Mia nearly shouted to Beckett, her hands curled at her sides.

"We had to get him under control quickly," he said in an unconvincing tone.

"What drug? What did you give him?" Mia asked in the same high-pitched tone.

"Just a standard pharmaceutical. I've never seen a reaction like this before." He consulted a chart. "It's—"

Kade threw himself at the window, hitting his forehead

so hard that it cut the skin and left a bloody smear across the glass. His eyes were wide, but they flickered with recognition at Mia. Violet saw the stark fear in those eyes and...something else. She blinked and focused on them. Not the mist, but something dark moving across his irises. Mia saw it, too. And from the horrified expression on her face, she knew what it meant.

"That's enough," Ferro said. "It's hard for me to watch him. I imagine it's much more painful for—"

The bubble disintegrated at the same moment Mia sent a wall of hot, sharp magick at Ferro. He stumbled and fell, taken off guard. Violet Catalyzed and rammed him before he could even begin to get to his feet. He skidded down the hall, arms and legs flailing.

"Open one of the empty cells, Beckett!" Mia ordered, pinning him against the wall with a magick "net." She grabbed the cuff, unsnapping it the way she might have many times in her stint here, and tossed it to Violet.

Beckett nodded and pulled out a card like the one Mia had used. He swiped it in the lock of the cell beside Kade's, and the door opened.

Ferro vibrated, about to Catalyze as Violet approached. He was a First Gen, and from the scales she saw shimmer at his skin's surface, an Obsidian Dragon. She launched at him and slapped the cuff on his wrist. He yanked her, sending her crashing to the floor with him.

He got a good look at her. "How in the hell..."

She shoved him into the cell and opened her mouth to tear out his throat. A force, hot and heavy, pushed her back out into the hallway and slammed the door shut. The lock clicked all by itself.

How in the hell right back at you.

"Violet, I need help!"

Mia was struggling with Kade, who was now out of his cell and dashing himself against the walls.

Beckett was still held in the net, though he didn't seem to be doing much to break free and stop them. He only gave them a sympathetic look as they pulled Kade down the hall to the fire exit. They weren't going to risk the elevator, navigating the stairs instead. Not easy with a thrashing Kade.

They burst out of the fire exit door, and Violet whistled the *Get ready!* signal the moment she opened the door. Jessup's presence inside the room surprised her, but only a little. The plan had been for her brothers to wait outside, but Jessup had never been one to follow directions. He helped them get Kade through the morgue. Ryan held the other door, and Violet barely noticed the man tied up on one of the exam tables, a terrified look on his face.

"How'd you get in?" Violet asked once they exited.

"Guy came out for a cig break. We were ready; we saw the butts all over the ground."

They pulled Kade toward Violet's SUV. Ryan opened the back door, pushed Kade in, then followed him, having to fight him the whole way. Even with his arms immobile. Mia climbed in with them. Jessup and Violet jumped into the front seats, and she sped off.

Ryan sat on Kade, holding down his shoulders. "What the hell did they do to him?"

"Bore!" Mia cried, her wide eyes going to Violet. "That's what he said, wasn't it?"

"Yes, but I have no idea—"

"Bore orb! Oh, gods." She gasped, covering her mouth. "I see it in his eyes."

"Mia, what's a bore orb?"

"It's an orb. Oh, gods, oh, gods..."

"Yeah, I got that." Violet was about to explode. "I saw something dark moving in the mist of his eyes. What does it do?"

"I've never seen one, only heard about them. They come from Shadow Magick. Black magick," she clarified. "It bores into a person's mind, makes them insane."

Violet shot a quick look at Kade, who was moving the only thing he could beneath Ryan's weight: his head.

"Dad...," he uttered, pain in his voice.

"How do we get it out of him?" Violet asked.

"I...don't know." The first bit of hope lit Mia's face. "I can call my professor in the Guard Academy. She knows about Shadow Magick."

"Try not to sound too freaked out. You don't want to raise suspicion."

Mia's hands were shaking as she went through her contact list on her phone. "Professor Double, it's Mia Kavanaugh...good, thanks." Mia grimaced at the lie. "I need your help on...a case. Someone was given a Black Bore Orb...yeah, it's awful." Her voice broke. "We need to know how to get it out.... No, we aren't in a position to bring the patient to you. Can you talk me through it?"

Mia nodded as she listened. "Uh-huh...oh. I don't know how long ago he got it, but—"

"He called me two hours ago," Violet whispered. "I think that's when he was caught."

"Two hours, probably less." Mia's face fell again. "We have to try. All right, I'll call if I need you."

"Should we take Kade to this person?" Violet asked.

"No, she's bound by duty to report it."

Violet searched for a place to pull over. "Do you want me to stop?"

"Keep going. Where *are* we going, anyway?"

"To the Fringe. It's our territory... when they come for us." She knew they would. "We need to bring Kade back around before then. What did she say?"

Mia straddled Kade, but he continued to buck and refused to calm down. "It's not good, not good at all. It's going to, oh, gods..."

Ryan shook her shoulders. "Calm down and speak, woman!"

Mia's eyes blinked, and she took a breath. "The Bore splinters a person's memories. Three hours after getting it, Kade will be insane."

"What if we stop it before then?" Violet asked.

"I don't know. The outcome sounds iffy."

Jessup said, "Do you want me to drive? You're looking back there more than you're watching the road. And all of your blood just left your head. You're as pale as a swamp lily."

"I'm fine."

"I'll watch to make sure we aren't being followed. You watch the road. Ryan and Mia can handle Kade."

Violet wanted to be back there with them, but there was nothing she could do. The glow of Mia's magick in the rearview mirror caught Violet's eye. Mia created a clear, glassy orb like the one she'd made to camouflage Violet, only smaller. She leaned forward, her eyes pinched shut as she concentrated. "Come on, come out of there, damn you," she said, her voice grinding with her effort.

Minutes dragged by as Violet tried to keep her focus on the road. It sounded as though Mia were wrestling with a demon back there.

"You're getting it!" Ryan said. "It looks like a black bug coming out of his ear."

Mia screamed.

"Damn, it went back in. Mia, get hold of yourself and try again," Ryan said.

Violet gripped the wheel, frustration at Mia growing.

"Okay, I will," she said, her voice resolute. She formed the bubble again, grunting with the effort. A thousand minutes passed, it seemed.

"It's coming out again." Ryan braced his hands on her shoulders, leaning over her to watch. "Stay with it, Mia. Don't freak out."

With a gasp, Mia fell backward against Ryan. The orb floated, containing a disgusting-looking bug thing crawling inside.

"Kill it!" Violet screamed. Bugs she didn't care about, but that thing terrified her.

Mia straightened and, with her hands, sent a dark orb that swallowed up the clear one. With a loud *smack* both orbs disappeared.

"Kade!" Mia leaned forward, out of Violet's view. "Kade, can you hear me?"

"Is he conscious?" Violet asked, her heart teetering between fear and hope. She could hear him murmuring, but it sounded like nonsense.

"No. He's not in pain anymore, not making that horrible grimace anyway. Kade!"

More murmurings, no actual response.

"Is he still fighting?" Violet asked.

"He's struggling to get out of the straightjacket. I'm afraid to release him."

Violet shook her head. "No, leave it on, as awful as it is.

We need to keep him constrained while we're on the road."

The bore wasn't in there destroying his mind anymore. Violet took comfort in that as it took friggin' forever to get home. But how much was gone, destroyed, altered?

Once they reached the less congested roads of the Fringe, Violet sped. They drove past her ma, who was pulling weeds in the flower beds. She stood, giving her a curious look at the sight of Ryan and a strange woman crouched in the backseat. Violet gave her a wave and bright smile but didn't pause to talk. Gods, if she only knew...

Her brothers carried Kade into her home. His legs were stable enough to stand, but his eyes... hardly any mist, no sign of recognition now as he twisted in his constraints.

Violet stepped forward, trying to figure out how to free him. Mia helped as they unbuckled the straps.

Jessup said, "Are you sure that's a good idea?"

Violet gritted her teeth at the effort. "Yes. I can't stand him in this thing for another second."

It took several seconds, but she and Mia finally unraveled the thing. Kade fought them, pushed them back, and flung the jacket.

"Kade," Violet said, standing a foot in front of him. "Kade, look at me."

He did, his eyes wild. Suddenly he swung his hands out, and Jessup pulled her out of the way as magick shot out and shattered her ceiling light. He blew Ryan back against the table with another blast.

"Die, you son of a bitch!" Kade shouted, manifesting his dagger. He saw something, but it wasn't them.

"He's caught in a memory fragment," Violet said. "Not fighting you but someone in his past."

Ryan picked himself up as Kade swung the dagger in arcs. "That doesn't help keep my ass in one piece." He slapped his hand against his chest. "My Dragon wants out bad."

"No, your Dragon will kill him." She turned to Kade. "Kade!"

He stopped, looking past her, as though he'd heard a distant sound.

"Stop, Kade." She walked closer to him. "It's Vee. Do you remember me?"

He took her in, narrowing his eyes. Yes, she was reaching him.

"Kade, please stop fighting. You're safe now." She put her hand to his cheek. "Please."

He said something unintelligible and raised his dagger again. Jessup knocked him back, sending him rolling over her coffee table and onto the couch where they'd...

He was up, his dagger now a tattoo again, and raced out of the house. Jessup shook his head and went after him, Violet and the others close behind. They came to an abrupt halt at the sight of Kade standing in the yard, looking down, hands fisted at his sides.

"My father wouldn't do something like that." He shook his head.

"He's slipped into another memory," Violet whispered, her heart breaking for him. In the memory of, perhaps, hearing about his father's death and supposed betrayal.

Jessup leaned closer. "We have to contain him, Violet. He's dangerous, to us and to himself. We have to pin him to the wall, just until..."

Until what? He died? Went fully crazy? Jessup gave her a soft look, rare for him. He was right.

"You're going to do *what*?" Mia nearly shouted.

Ryan put his hand over her mouth and leaned close. "Damn, woman, calm down and hush up. We've got to keep him in this memory right now, the one where he's not trying to kill us." He explained what the wall of shame was.

Violet shook her head. "Go get the cuffs from the wall. We'll contain him here, at my house. He needs to feel safe and comfortable."

She could tell Jessup was going to argue, but he nodded instead. "I'll be right back. Ryan, stay close."

"He didn't do this," Kade said, his voice hoarse.

Violet approached Kade, touching his arm. "You're right. He would never break out a prisoner without good reason."

Jessup was back within a few minutes, and Violet distracted him while her brother cuffed Kade's wrists. "Would you like to see your father?"

Kade let her lead him into the house, her brothers flanking her in case he slipped to another memory. She kept her hand on his arm. He was alive, with her, and yet...not with her at all. He stared ahead, pain clear on his face.

Violet was able to lead him to the bed, but he shifted into another memory and spun around, back in fight mode.

"Kade!" Violet said, taking his face in her hands and making him look at her. "You must get on the bed. It's safe."

His body trembled, with fear or rage, she wasn't sure.

"Get on the bed, Kade. That's an order."

He did listen to her, though a part of him warred with her command. She could see that in his eyes and his stiff movements as he lay down. Jessup and Ryan fastened the cuffs to the bedposts while she continued to distract Kade. The moment he realized he was immobile, he struggled, bucking against the mattress. If she could bring him back to the memory of being here, maybe she could bring him back to her.

She walked up to him, looking at his beautiful face now filled with rage. "Kade, you remember being here, don't you? You remember me."

He looked at her, and she saw a glimmer of recognition. His mouth curved up in a smile.

Yes. He remembers!

"You're the bitch who went on a rampage at the preschool. Who killed four children with your orbs," he snarled. His fingers stretched, itching to use his deadly magick on her.

She stumbled back at the rage burning in his eyes. "No, Kade. I'm Violet. I'm..." Her voice broke.

Mia braved his rage, coming close to him. "You *have* to remember me, Kade. I'm your sister, damn it. You're my hero, that knight on a white steed I looked up to when I had no one else. You lied to me about our father's death, but I know you did it to protect me, and it's all right. It's..."

He looked right at Mia. "Mother, how could you leave your daughter alone? *Now*? You cowardly bitch."

Mia let out a small cry and moved back. "He's never going to come back," she said, her voice full of tears. "This is what he's going to be like, skipping from one memory to another, and maybe he'll stop on one of me, or you, but then he'll be gone again, and—"

She burst into tears, and Ryan pulled her into his arms, awkwardly patting her back. Violet was too caught up in the possibility of what Mia had said to be bothered by the fact that Ryan had never comforted her like that.

She turned back to Kade. The cut on his forehead had crusted blood on it. "The memories are there."

"Some of them," Mia said through her sobs. "We don't even know if the ones that matter are still in there!"

Gods, the woman was melodramatic. Violet tuned her out, watching Kade struggle to free himself. If the memories were there...was there a way to knit them back together? She wasn't going to give up on him.

She sat on the edge of the bed, leaning close to his face. "Kade, you had orders to kill me, but you didn't. I attacked you, and we wrestled in the mud. And...you liked it." She laughed, though it sounded hollow. "And later, we kissed. That was the best kiss I'd ever experienced, and..." Her voice broke.

She wouldn't talk about their lovemaking with everyone standing around. Her fingers trailed down the dip in his chin. "Remember that kiss, Kade." She put her mouth on his, closed her eyes, and prayed. His mouth moved against hers. She felt the sharp bite of his teeth and jerked back so hard she nearly fell off the bed.

"You can't keep me here forever," he said to her, his upper lip lifted in a snarl. "They'll send other Vegas. They know I'm here."

He was in another memory, living in a fragment of a life full of danger, of death and killing people. She put her fingers to her lip and looked. Blood.

"That's enough, Vee," Jessup said. "This is beyond what we can deal with. Maybe we can find someone who—"

"No." She turned to the group. "Nobody can reach him like someone he knows."

"He thinks I'm our mother!" Mia said, clutching her stomach. "How am I going to reach him when he obviously hates her?"

"He thought I was someone else, too." Violet checked her lip. Still bleeding. "But we're in there, Mia. All of us. And how he feels about us is in there as well."

Mia tugged on her hair. "You have the best chance of reaching him, Violet. He obviously has deep feelings toward you, opening up like he did, and he bit you!"

Her hopelessness seeped into Violet. *Be levelheaded.*

"He listens to me." She turned back to him. "Kade!"

He turned to her, confusion in his eyes. It hit her then. His deeply rooted fantasy about a woman ordering him around. Not a memory that could be shattered because it wasn't a memory, other than a little teasing, but a fantasy. And he'd felt enough of a connection with her to tell her. Tears filled her eyes. Hope. "I can reach him."

"How?" Mia asked, clearly not feeling it.

Violet took all of them in. "You have to leave me alone with him."

"No way," Jessup said. "I know you, Vee. You'll soften up and release him. And he'll kill you. He won't mean to, but he will."

She glanced at Kade. "Last time he felt in his gut that killing me was wrong. And I feel in my gut that this is the only way I can reach him, pull him back."

Ryan said, "She's got the look again—"

"Yeah, I see it." Jessup furrowed his brows at her. When she thought he would argue further, he said, "Whistle if you need help."

She smiled, full of gratitude that he trusted her. "I will."

Mia turned her heavy gaze to Kade. Tears glazed her

cheeks, and her mouth turned down in a frown. She had lost her mother and her father at such a young age. She looked like that young girl again. "Please save my brother."

"I will," Violet said again. Then words floated into her mind: *Or I'll die trying.*

Chapter 19

Ferro knew Drakos had saved his life by shoving Violet out of the cell and locking him inside. As much as he hated to admit it, Violet had been a threat. He'd seen the murderous rage in her eyes. His salvation was small comfort. The woman had bested him. *Two* women, including one of his own Arguses. First Kade had joined forces with Violet, and now Mia had.

But what did they have? Kade, who would be mental mush, and Violet's suspicions, with no way to prove them.

Still, he wanted her dead.

He sat in his office while other officers investigated how the jailbreak had happened. Officially, it looked like a desperate sister broke in to save her mentally ill brother. Clearly psychosis ran in the family. Once Mia was captured, she, too, would be treated with the Black Bore Orb.

He called Onyx. "Violet and Kade Kavanaugh's sister broke Kade out of the psych ward. I imagine they'll be returning to Castanega land to try to nurse him back to health. Fortunately for us, that will never happen. Not mentally, anyway, and he may be more dangerous to them than to us."

"Why?"

He told her about the Black Bore Orb. He had bristled at the idea of having Purcell, whom he knew only as a member of the Concilium, coming in and taking care of his problems. But Ferro had to admit that the orb had been a brilliant idea. Kade went crazy within sight of witnesses, and even with him out there, he was harmless. To Ferro, anyway.

"The idea of it gives me the creepy chills," she said. "Remind me never to piss off a Deuce of his order. Can I finally take out Violet? You know I so want to."

He crossed his ankles on his desk. "We're too close to have anything happen to us. We're Drakos's lifeline. But we do need to ignite the clan wars. They're already on alert, ready for attack. One more murder, clearly committed by the Castanegas, and they'll be out of the picture. Then you can swoop in and take those who have killed and Breathed the others, thus gaining more power than you would taking one at a time."

"But I want to kill Violet," she whined.

"If she survives, take her after we've fed Drakos our power. We can't afford to risk your safety when we're this close. Remember what's at stake. You'll never again have to fear for your life. When you come for Violet after Friday, no one will defeat you."

Violet waited for everyone to completely vacate the premises. Her chest was so tight she could hardly breathe. She had an idea—if things worked out well—and ran outside to turn on the hose by her workshop, laying the end in the soggy area where they had fought. She returned to Kade and sat on the bed again, putting herself only an inch from his face. He stared past her with a fierce intensity.

What scared her most was that he had no mist in his eyes. Just moss green, normal as a Mundane's. And blank.

"Kade, look at me."

He slowly shifted his gaze to her. "You." Clearly he wasn't seeing *her*, not by the vicious tone in his voice.

"Kade, I want you to kiss me."

He frowned, both disgusted and puzzled. "What?"

"Kiss me," she ordered. She straddled him and leaned forward, only a hairsbreadth away from him. "Now."

He closed the distance and complied. To feel his mouth on hers . . . she closed her eyes and put her hand against his jaw.

"Kiss me like you did this morning," she said. "You opened your mouth, touched my tongue with yours." She ran her hands over the front of his chest. "Do it again."

"Last month," he said. "I . . . we . . ."

"No, this morning, with me. Violet Castanega." Even if he was remembering a fragment with someone else, at least he wasn't being hostile. She could live with that. "You made love to me this morning, touched me, pleasured me, made me come over and over." She opened her mouth and sucked his lower lip into hers. Her lip ached, but the pain was nothing compared to the joy of feeling him again. "Remember, Kade."

"I touched you," he said, and desire heated his eyes.

He joined the kiss, sliding his tongue inside her mouth, tilting his head for a better angle. She closed her eyes and pressed her body into his. He grew hard, and she moved against his erection and made him groan.

"We made amazing love," she said between kisses.

Suddenly he lifted his head, knocking his forehead into hers. "The boat just rocked. Someone came onboard."

"No, Kade, it was just the wake. You're safe. We're safe here."

She ran her hands over his shoulders, along his arms. She laced her fingers with his. His fingers remained stiff and straight. *Tap into the fantasy, keep him there and away from memories.*

"Squeeze my hands," she ordered.

He complied, clamping his fingers over hers. Panic fluttered through her. She was as secured there as he was.

"Release me," she said.

He held her, an intense look on his face. The pressure squeezed the blood from her fingers.

"Release me, Kade."

His grip loosened, and she slid her hands free.

"Why am I cuffed to the bed?" He looked at his hands. "You're keeping me captive?"

"We're playing a game." She nuzzled the curve of his neck, kissing the warm skin there, feeling his hair tickling her cheek. "I'm your master; you are my slave. You do as I say. Call me master."

"A sex game?"

"Exactly."

He nodded in understanding, a smile slowly spreading across his face. "Master."

"Tell me you're my slave."

"I'm your slave."

She ran her hands up beneath his shirt, her fingers bumping over the ridges of his stomach. She kissed his chin, traced her tongue along that superhero indent, nibbled on his lower lip. This time he dipped his head and kissed her without being ordered to. Reflex? Or another memory. No, she had to keep him out of his memories.

"You love me," she said, pinning him with her gaze.

He met her gaze. "I love you."

Though the words weren't genuine, they washed over her anyway. *Silly girl.* "I love you, too." She braced her hands on either side of his face. "We've loved each other from that first time we met. Our gazes met across the crowded dance floor. Do you remember?"

His eyebrows furrowed as he searched for the memory. Of course, he would find none, exactly what she wanted. He shook his head.

"It's okay, because *I* remember. I remember for both of us. We danced to 'Take My Breath Away,' and you told me how much you loved the group Berlin. And I told you I did, too, because the lead singer sounds so strong and sure of herself. You said you liked her cool half black and half blond hair in the old music videos."

"I don't—"

"And we kissed on the dance floor, at the end of the song, and we kept kissing right into the next one, which was Mon A Q's 'Stay in Love,' and we laughed because when we came out of it everyone was watching us. Kiss me like that again."

He did, fully and thoroughly.

It was the last test, and she reached up and released the cuffs. "I'm your master."

"I'm your slave."

She rubbed his cheek. "Good boy. Come with me." She pulled him up and led him outside to the muddy pit. The smell of moist earth reminded her of hot summer days rolling through the marsh in a swamp buggy. He was still barefoot. "Feel the mud between your toes."

He looked down, as though he'd never seen mud squishing around his feet before. She had to keep him in the place between his memories.

"You like making love in the mud, love the way it looks over my skin, my bare breasts. Take my shirt off."

As long as he kept obeying her, she'd be safe. If she lost him, he could kill her. He pulled her shirt over her head, dropping it to the damp ground.

"Take off your shirt. And your pants."

He complied, standing in all his naked glory. The muscles in his body tensed, rippled.

"Take off my pants. Stay here with me. Think of nothing but my body."

He stepped closer and worked the button on her pants, unzipping them. He hooked his fingers over her waistband and pushed them down, using his foot to dislodge them completely.

"And now my panties. Very slowly. Very, very slowly."

His focus was now on her belly button as he knelt in front of her on one knee.

"This is how you proposed to me. You offered me this ring." She held out her hand, the wrong one, and showed him a ring she had made.

She could see him try to pull the memory. He gave up and continued with his assigned task. He wrapped his index fingers around the thin strap at her hips and slid them down. Slowly. His movements were deliberate, studied. His face was even with her pelvis. At any moment, she had to be ready for him to shift to a violent memory where she was the villain. "You've touched this body. Made love to this body. Do you remember?"

There! She saw the mist in his eyes swirl. For the first time, he seemed to remember something she wanted him to.

She took his hands and ran them down her legs. "You traced circles in the spots behind my knees, and we were both surprised how erotic it felt."

He took over the motion, staring at his fingers as though they were moving of their own volition. The memory was there, at the edge of his mind. She could see it. Dare she let him slide into it rather than keeping him in the fantasy?

Yes.

His thumbs rubbed down the front of her thighs, his fingers skimming the sensitive skin behind her knees. He moved his hands up now, his thumbs grazing her inner thighs.

"You made me wet without even touching me," she said, sliding one hand up to the apex of her thighs. "You used your tongue in remarkable ways. Do you remember, Kade? Please, please remember."

She saw him shift into another memory a moment before he punched her in the stomach, sending her backward into the mud puddle. The breath gushed out of her, from the impact and the shock. Her Dragon heated, but she restrained it, scrambling back as he approached.

"Where should I start? Being a hotheaded asshole who skipped past me up the ranks because of his daddy, even as he broke all the rules?"

He was Dune! Somehow so affected by those vile words, he'd assimilated them.

She held out her hand as the dagger materialized in his hand. "Back, Kade!"

Magick crackled along the blade's edge; his fingers tightened on the handle. He stared at her and saw himself.

"We made love in this mud puddle, Kade. Get down here, on your knees. Down, now!" She jabbed to the place in front of her.

He was caught between the warped memory and that sensual place she'd reached.

"You love me, Kade. You want to feel the mud over my breasts." She grabbed a handful and rubbed it over them.

He stood frozen, his body reacting as his mind warred with his memory.

"Touch me, Kade. I need you to touch me." Her hand moved over her breasts, fingers sliding between them as she held his gaze.

His dagger slid back to a tattoo, and he took three stiff steps toward her and dropped to his knees. His hands slid over the places her own hands had just been, their mouths colliding. She let go and slathered mud over him. He kept stroking her, kissing her fiercely. She ran her hands down his back, down to his firm ass, slippery with mud. He gripped her around the waist and pulled her pelvis against his.

He made sounds of pleasure as he plundered her mouth like a man starving. He squeezed her ass as he ground her into his erection. He was so hard it actually hurt, but she'd take that kind of pain any day.

He kissed to her jawline, her neck. Her Dragon instincts, already on alert, reared up as his mouth moved across that vulnerable area. He had her in his grip, his strong hands splayed on her back. She wouldn't be able to move if he shifted to a violent memory and attacked her.

Hold on.

He arched her back as he kissed down her collarbone. His teeth grazed the inside curve of her breast. She could barely move within the confines of his grip. She couldn't swallow past the fear in her throat. "Kade, stop kissing me. Now."

He didn't. His mouth moved over her nipple. His fingers dug into her back as he held her tight. She'd lost control of him.

"Kade, you will obey me now!"

He took her mouth so abruptly they both fell into the mud with a splash. Beneath him, trapped, not good. The hose was right by her head, pouring water over her hair, gurgling softly. She could reach for it if she could get her hand free and use it as a weapon. But he was still ravaging her mouth. She tasted the mud, felt the grit of it as their tongues slid together in a mad rush.

"I can't...can't stop kissing you, Vee. I..."

She clutched at his hair. "You have to— What did you call me?"

"Need...," he said, breathless, talking and kissing her at the same time. "Need...you, Vee. Burning through me." He'd called her Vee.

Hope rushed through her, as hot as desire. "I'm here, babe. I need you, too, need you inside me."

His body pressed hers into the soft earth. He cantilevered his weight, mindful of not crushing her. When he pulled back, he looked down at her with affection, running his hand over her face and painting her with even more mud. The smile on his face, the mist swirling in his eyes...

The mist was fully back.

"You're my master?" he asked.

He was still in the fantasy. "Yes."

"And we're married."

She nodded. "And trying to have a baby."

He kept looking at her, his mind working to make sense of it, she guessed. She held her breath.

He slid his finger across her chin. "I don't remember marrying you or seeing you in a wedding dress."

"It was a lovely wedding. Five bridesmaids and grooms-men, on the beach."

Panic flitted across his expression. "Why can't I remember?"

"It's okay. You have holes in your memory. Let's not talk about that right now."

"I do remember making love to you." He slid his hand down over her breast. "And touching you like this. In the mud. In bed. Bits and pieces of heaven."

She could hardly breathe. "Who am I?" She wanted to make sure.

He sputtered a laugh. "My wife. That's what you just said."

She felt like she was balancing a gem on a wire. Tug the wrong way, it would fall and shatter. "What's my name?"

"Vee. Violet when you're mad at me."

She laughed, though it came out as more of a sob. "Who are you?"

His eyebrows furrowed again, just for a second. "Kade. Every time you said my name, it tugged me out of some dark place. I was in a shadowy alley, and then I was dancing with you. I was fighting a demon and then I was touching you."

He looked down at her, letting his gaze move over her slowly. "I remember being in the mud with you. How beautiful and sexy you looked." He got to his feet, then extended his hand and helped her up. He took the hose and poured the water over her, watching it wash away the mud. "How much more beautiful you look without it."

He held it over her head, and she closed her eyes. She was afraid, so afraid, to hope he was coming back to her permanently. But that was all she had, hope and Kade there with her, right now. She took the hose and sprayed him down, then dropped it.

He pulled her into him, kissing her with such ferocity that they staggered back until they hit the workshop's wall. He dug his fingers into her wet hair, then dragged them down her sides. "I need you. The need...it's like a fire inside me...devouring me," he said on staggered breaths. She felt the truth of his need in the desperate growl of his voice.

Because I brought you back, reached deep into you. She touched his face. "I need you, too. Because I'm madly, crazy in love with you." The words slipped out. She was. Oh, she so was.

His mouth crashed into hers. He grabbed her ass and hoisted her up, bracing her back against the wall. She wrapped her legs around his waist and felt him drive into her. A sound between a gasp and a groan came from deep within as she clutched him. She tilted her head back, and he moved his mouth down her throat.

He held her securely, moaning as he thrust in and out. He felt so damned good filling her, loving her, squeezing her behind and murmuring, "I'm madly, crazy in love with you, too, Vee." Her name. Her.

She lost herself to him, to their lovemaking. He buried his face in the crook of her neck, softly biting her skin. Those nips only ramped up the coil of pressure building and swirling inside her. Her Dragon loved them, urging her to nip back. She dug her nails into his back, drawing them down to the curve of his ass. The orgasm claimed her, shook her, and tightened every muscle in her body.

He kept moving, her spasms causing him to growl like a lion, and then his body jerked as he came in one final thrust. He held on tight, shuddering in his pleasure. She watched him come back to himself, catching her breath as his chest rose and fell in sync with his breathing. She waited for his eyes to open, for him to see her. Her and not an enemy or some other woman.

He smiled as he took her in. "I'm taking you to the house and properly loving you on our bed." He blinked, relief coloring his expression. "I remember the Series 7 chair. Have we utilized that chair in sinful ways?"

A whistle pierced the air, rising high, low, and high again. *Are you all right?*

She stuck her pinky in her mouth and answered. "My brothers are coming to the house. We'll have to wait on the chair and the bed."

"The couch, the kitchen counter..." He set her down, then picked up the hose and gently washed her thighs and then himself. "It's like I can't get enough of you, babe."

Babe. She stifled a sigh.

They turned off the hose, retrieved their clothing, and walked to the house. He laced his fingers with hers, just as she'd ordered him to do earlier. He gave her a devilish smile. "Playing master and slave is a huge turn-on."

She gave him the same kind of smile. "I like ordering you around."

Once they reached the house, they dried off and got dressed. She heard the three approach. "Wait for me inside, slave."

He raised an eyebrow at her command, which was so much better than the robotic way he'd obeyed before. He was in there.

"Say 'yes, master,'" she whispered.

He bowed. "Yes, master."

Her heart clutched at the sight. She didn't want to lose him. "I have to talk to my brothers alone for a few minutes." She kissed him, a quick peck. "Start dinner."

He went inside, and she met them halfway across the yard. She had to prepare them. Mia looked as though she'd been crying, which made Violet feel vaguely guilty for having incredible sex at the same time.

Jessup said, "Where is he? And why is your hair wet?"

She touched her damp strands. "Long story." No way was she getting into how she'd reached Kade's mind. "He's inside, getting dinner ready."

"Does that mean—"

"He's back. Mostly," she added, before Mia could get too excited. "I had to put memories in his head that didn't happen. It was the only way to draw him out of the real memories. I had to make up things as I went. So he thinks we're married. He doesn't seem to remember anything about the bore or being captured. I'm afraid to trigger something, so we have to play along with what he thinks is real."

Mia nodded. "Whatever we have to do. Does he remember me?"

"I don't know. We'll find out." She nodded for them to follow.

"Meanwhile, we still have these sons of bitches to deal with," Jessup said.

"And a Kade who doesn't know who our enemies are," Violet added.

They walked inside and to the kitchen, where Kade had every cabinet door open. He turned as they came in and smiled. "Oh, hey, Mia. Did I forget that you were coming for dinner?" His expression shadowed. "I can't remember much of anything. Like where anything is in our kitchen." He gave Violet a pained look. "How long have we been married?"

"Just eight months."

He seemed to search for that memory. "I have pieces of memories. Like...like a broken mirror. There are a bunch of shards that reflect something back to me, but there are a lot of empty spots where the shards have fallen to the floor." Fear flickered across his face, but he gave her a heart-clenching smile. "I have bits and pieces of you."

She hoped it wasn't the one where he was going to kill her. His memories were a house of cards. She put her hand to his cheek. "It's okay, sweetheart. They'll come back. Don't push it."

He took her hand in his. "Was I in an accident?"

She wrestled with when to tell him the truth. "Ferro..." She let the word hang, checking his reaction.

"My boss?" No, he recalled nothing about his betrayal by the mildly curious expression on his face. "What about him?"

"He's a bad, bad man," she said, exactly how Kade had once referred to himself.

Kade blinked, like he'd heard that phrase before. She saw the wobble, felt his hand tighten on hers.

Quickly she said, "The doctor said to let the memories come back on their own." Amazing how easy the lies flowed. It hit her then, that her and Kade's whole relationship was built on lies.

He brushed a strand of hair from her forehead. "This has been hard on you. I see the strain in your eyes." She tightened her mouth, nodding. He pulled her into his arms, his body strong and warm and real. "I love you, Vee. I may not remember everything, but I feel that."

She had to choke back a sob. She held on tight to him, glancing over at their audience. Mia, particularly, watched with surprised wonder. Her eyes were teary, and in them Violet saw the same mixture of both hope and fear.

Kade backed up, and he seemed to only then become aware of the others and gave them a sheepish grin. "Sorry, the world falls away when I look at Vee."

Jessup couldn't hide his sharp grin. "Yeah, it's been like that since you two first met."

"You're Vee's brothers." Kade pointed at him, snapping his fingers as he obviously tried to recall his name. "Jessie? No, Jessup. And Ryan."

Relief passed over their features, until Kade frowned. "We were fighting. Why?" That blank darkness crept across his eyes.

Violet shook his arm. "Like brothers do," she said brightly. "Wrestling."

He blinked, coming back. "But I saw—"

"Don't worry about that. I'm starved."

Kade took the three in. "Do you want to join us?"

Out of Kade's sight, she gestured for them to go. "They have to keep an eye on the property. We've had some trouble here lately."

Kade's eyebrows furrowed. "I should be out there, too." He turned his arm so that his dagger showed. His fingers traced the V, and for a moment he was lost in the sight of it.

"Kade?"

"I fight for a living. I can help." He remembered his identity as a Vega. Because it was so ingrained in him probably.

She patted his arm. "You have to recuperate. You can fight soon."

The mist in his eyes swirled at the prospect. He liked fighting for the right and just.

"First we eat," she said.

He leaned close, nuzzling her neck. "And then we work more on making babies."

She couldn't help but look at her brothers at that one. Their shocked expressions almost made her choke. Why, oh why, had she uttered that particular embellishment?

Kade straightened. "Guess I shouldn't talk about that kind of thing in front of your brothers. We'll see you around then. Be careful. And, Ryan, if you put the moves on my sister and break her heart, I'll cut off your appendages one by one. Got it?"

Violet only then noticed Ryan's proximity to Mia, how closely he'd been watching her reactions to Kade. How he cared what she felt.

Ryan looked surprised and embarrassed, but he swallowed back words of denial. "I won't hurt her, I promise."

Those words stilled Kade. He had said similar words to her mother. The blankness moved across his eyes as the memory tried to come.

Violet gripped his arm. "Kade, let's work on dinner. I'll show you where everything is again."

She needed him to remember his past, and she was terrified that when he did, she would lose him forever.

Chapter 20

Ferro paced his living room. Onyx would kill another Fringer, start the war, and then they would move forward on the last phase of the plan. He couldn't stand losing. His ego railed and raged. Ferro glanced at his watch. Kade would be insane by now. Violet would not have him as her ally.

She would have her people, of course, and Mia. He wanted Violet dead. *He* wanted to kill her. Onyx had her own reasons for wanting to tear Violet limb from limb, but hadn't Ferro done enough for her? He'd taken her in, taught her skills, and now gave her the opportunity to live forever. He would take this one thing for himself.

He stopped, feeling the shimmering presence of Drakos. His image appeared, a fierce Dragon who did not look pleased.

"I know what you are thinking," Drakos said. "Do not do it. I grow closer to dying each day. You and Onyx have nearly enough power between you to Breathe into me and save me. If one of you dies, so do I. We are too close to risk it."

Ferro had said the same thing to Onyx. "I know, I know. I just can't stand losing. They are all inferior to me, and yet they have won. Violet has won."

"Calm your ego. Do not let it rule you. Onyx is ready to make the final kill in the Fringe?"

"Yes. She has chosen a target that will ensure maximum outrage. The evidence will point directly to the Castanegas, which will no doubt push the clans over the edge." And someone else would kill Violet. Not his fangs tearing into her scales, not his claw sinking into her kill zone. Not his satisfaction to watch her die while she stared into the face of her killer.

"So she will die, and you will get what you want."

Ferro ran his hand down his face, nodding. "Yes. I will go Breathe another Dragon to sate my restlessness. More power for you."

"Very well. Make sure you continue to choose the once-powerful but now weak. The addicts who should not be out there anyway."

"Yes, sire."

Drakos faded away. Ferro grabbed his keys and headed to the door leading into his garage. He texted Onyx as soon as he was on his way.

"I'm in position," she whispered several minutes later. "I'm waiting for it to get darker. I can't afford for them to see me. The Murphys are already discussing how to wreak revenge on whoever's behind the murders. I've seen members of the Peregrine clan here, too. They're still not completely sure it's the Castanegas. I have Jessup's jeans and Gatorland employee shirt, properly shredded. It's a shame he won't be able to grab them up when he Catalyzes back to human and retreats after murdering the child."

"That should push them all over the edge, and the whole clan will die." He glanced at the clock. Her plan would give him time to steal the prize right out from under her selfish snout.

Kade stirred spaghetti sauce and tried to figure out what the hell was going on. Beside him, Violet poured pasta into the pot of boiling water. She caught him looking at her. Her hesitant smile was filled with worry and fear and love, everything a wife would probably feel if her husband didn't remember much of his life.

Except he didn't think she was his wife. He had feelings for her, yes. When he woke from what felt like a nightmare-addled sleep and was making love with her, it felt good. Her body felt familiar, her mouth tasted like home, and burying himself deep inside her...completely right.

He glanced down at his hand. No wedding ring. She wore a ring but not a band. Maybe they weren't traditional people. He glanced into the living room. He remembered the Jacobsen chair. Knew their bedroom was down the hall. But he didn't know what she did for a living. He only had pieces of his own career. His head hurt whenever he thought about the missing bits, like a drill tunneling into his brain. He rubbed his forehead, wincing at a sore spot on his forehead.

"You all right?" she asked, giving him her divided attention while she separated the strands of spaghetti with a big fork.

"No." Might as well be honest. He *was* an honest person. Wasn't he?

She moved closer, placing her hands on his chest. He could see indecision on her face, her mouth slightly open, wanting to say something. She had a cut on her lip, and it was a little swollen. A memory tugged at him, and he brushed his finger gently over it. "Did I *hit* you?" The thought horrified him.

She shook her head. "I tripped and hit the side of the door."

He knew that was a lie, too. "Tell me what's going on, Vee. You don't want me to remember my past. Every time I try, you dissuade me." He brushed his finger over her lip again. "I feel like I did something terrible. Like I was a bad person."

"You weren't. Aren't. Things are complicated right now, and it's dangerous for you to remember. You described your memories being like a broken mirror, and that's probably accurate. I'm afraid that if you try to remember, you might go into those blank spots and not come out. Or that maybe the rest of the shards will fall out." Her hands flattened, pressing gently against him. "I'm scared to lose you completely. So right now I want you to stay in this reality."

"You're in danger." The words came out before he could consider them. He grazed her cheek with the back of his hand. "Someone's trying to kill you."

He saw the flash of a memory, a man sneaking up on Violet while she was crying, lifting his dagger. It rocked through his head, making him jerk back. He heard her calling his name from far away. The memory was a tiny slice of mirror in which he could see the fight. He felt her shaking his body, bringing him back.

"Kade, you can't go there!" she was saying, studying his eyes as though they might pop out of his head.

He blinked, wobbling on his feet. "Me. It was me sneaking up on you. *With a knife!*" He held out his arm. "*My* dagger. What the hell, Vee?" He gestured to his head. "This happened because I was trying to hurt you, didn't it? I tried to attack you, your brothers beat me..." Nothing more came.

"You're trying to make sense of things that aren't going to make sense to you right now. Listen to me. We play...games. Sexy games. Like the mud wrestling. Sneak attacks. That's all it was."

She was lying to him. He knew it, felt it. She wouldn't have been crying if they were playing sex games.

He pulled her hand closer, looking at a delicate gold wire and stone ring that wasn't a wedding ring, and then released it and went into the living area. "No pictures of us or our wedding." He went down the hall to "their" bedroom and snapped the light on in the closet. "No men's clothing." A dress. He remembered the little girl's dress though. Confusion pounded in his head. She'd followed him in, now gripping the doorframe, her eyes wide. "We're not married, are we? It was a lie to...what?"

"Keep you sane, Kade. It was a lie to keep you sane." She choked on a sob, clutching at her upper chest. "If you go to the real memories, you will go insane. You might hurt yourself. Or me. I broke into the Guard prison to save you. Me, Mia, my brothers. We took a huge risk, but we did it." Her voice was thick with emotion. "I will not lose you now."

"She's still lying to you, Kavanaugh."

They both spun to find Ferro standing behind Violet. She screamed and stumbled away, Catalyzing instantly.

Ferro kept an eye on her as he faced Kade. "You're right. You are not married to her. As a Vega, marriage is frowned upon. You were assigned to terminate her. Then you lost your memory, and she's playing you. She's a very dangerous person. You have to take her out."

The shard that contained the memory of him sneaking up behind her trembled, reverberating in his brain, and fell with a shattering crash. He clutched his head, groaning in pain as he sank to his knees. He got a glimmer of another shard, of Ferro...

"Kade!" Violet screamed.

He bounded to his feet, watching Ferro's Dragon smash her bed and shove Violet through the window.

Ferro followed through the broken opening, his claws gripping her throat. "You will die," he gritted out as they landed on the ground.

Kade launched himself out the window, too, cutting his hand on the broken glass. Shards, like his memories. He instinctively started to jump into the fight...except he didn't know what side to fight on. Violet, who lied? Who was a Guard target? His target. He must follow through on his orders.

Violet used her strong legs to shove Ferro off her. He rolled but instantly got to his feet. Violet was on hers, too. Blood dripped down her deep amethyst scales. Her wing was crumpled, probably enough to render her flightless. Ferro sent a stream of black mist at her, and it wrapped around her throat and dragged her toward him. She clawed at it, digging her feet into the ground and leaning her weight back.

Kade started to move up behind her but froze. He knew this feeling. He focused on the shard that had fallen, and it felt as though it were cutting right into his brain with its sharp edges. He could see all of them now, thousands of shards with a sliver of a memory in them. His boat. Mia as a child bawling over their father's death. How Kade thought he should cry, too, but couldn't. So many to search through.

"Kavanaugh, get her!" Ferro commanded.

The command brought him back to the present, to Violet running away. Kade jerked into motion, tackling her. As a human, his size was nowhere near enough to stop her. He felt his dagger fill his hand, crackling with magick. Yes, that felt right.

She turned as he lifted his dagger, the point aimed at the kill spot just beneath her chin. All he had to do was drive it up into her brain.

"No, Kade, please!" She shook him off as the point touched the tender area, and he hit the ground and rolled. His body knew what to do, at least, using the momentum to get him back on his feet.

Ferro barreled toward a tree, but Kade couldn't see Violet. His gaze went higher, and there she was, naked and human, climbing a large oak tree like a damned Fire Elemental. He saw the rope, and another memory flickered through his mind: Jessup swinging from one of those ropes and knocking him into unconsciousness. Another memory that corroborated what Ferro had told him and contradicted her version.

She clutched the rope, ready to either assault Ferro or get away. Kade sent a bolt of magick at the rope, severing it the moment she started to swing down. She screamed as she fell, hitting the ground hard.

Finally, this was almost over. So why didn't he feel triumphant? Ferro raced over, throwing a "nice job" his way.

Violet Catalyzed and struggled to get up, but Ferro pinned her with his body. His tail swished in the dirt, something Kade had seen Dragons do when they were about to go for the kill. Like a cat when it was ready to pounce. His dark wings stretched out on either side of him, the sign of an ecstatic or triumphant Dragon.

He remembered that.

"Kade, go," she said, her eyes pleading with him. "He's going to kill you, too."

He's a bad, bad man.

He saw a shard of a white room, of Ferro standing nearby. He tried to hold on to it, but it fell away. All he had was what he knew. Violet had lied, Ferro was his commander, and he was Vega. He followed commands. He killed when necessary.

"She's trying to play you," Ferro said. "Just like she's been playing you since you got here." Ferro turned back to Violet, leaning close to her face. "You have caused me a lot of trouble. Cost me a lot." He flicked a glance at Kade. "And now I am going to have the pleasure of killing you while I look in your eyes and taste your fear and sorrow." Ferro extended one curved claw, nearly three inches long, and aimed for her kill zone. He brought it down slowly, torturously.

Everything Kade knew fled, leaving only what he felt for that Dragon on the ground. The woman she was. Shards reflected memories of holding her in bed. Her Breathing into him, healing him. His need for her, so raw and real. And even now, after he'd attacked her, she was warning him to get away.

He felt...love. Like his heart was going to burst, like he would die with her. That unleashed a flurry of shards in his mind, smashing into each other as though they were caught in a whirlwind, singing like wind chimes.

"Ferro!"

The Dragon jerked toward Kade, who was approaching. "She has caused me a lot of trouble, too. I want to kill her."

Violet let out an agonized sound, garbled beneath Ferro's weight.

"No. She is mine. But you can cut off her head when I'm done if that makes you feel better."

The dagger filled Kade's hand as he stepped close, planting his bare foot on her hand. "I suppose that will have to do." He lowered the dagger as though in deference--and rammed it up into Ferro's kill zone, twisting it.

Ferro gasped, and his eyes rolled back. Kade kicked him so that he wouldn't fall on Violet. She spun and moved away.

Something in the air changed, electric and angry. He swiveled around to face the ethereal image of a Dragon deity. Only his head was visible, looking into their dimension through a window of sorts. Kade readied his dagger and his magick, though he'd heard fighting a god was useless. He moved in front of Violet, blocking her as much as a man could for a Dragon. She stood mesmerized; he couldn't blame her. He'd never seen one of the gods either.

The god moved to Ferro, who was gasping, his lifeblood pouring out of the wound. He lifted his hand to him, claws curled inward. "Drakos, save me."

"I warned you not to go after her."

"I know. I'm...sorry. Save me, and we can kill both of them and be done with this."

Both of them?

"Your rage and ego have become a liability. I believe I'll take your power now, before someone else does."

"But why?" Ferro screamed. "I can gather more power. We need as much as we can get if we're going to keep you from dying."

"I was going to kill you and your Carnelian woman anyway." The words seemed to strike a physical blow on Ferro. "I omitted one detail: gods can't Breathe in healing power like Crescents can. We take it at your peril. But only when you offer. And both you and Onyx have offered."

Violet lunged forward, knocking Kade aside and crouching over Ferro. He saw her inhale a fine black mist as she held Ferro down. Her scales glowed, luminescent.

"No!" the god shouted, and Kade readied himself to protect Violet from her impulsive act. Drakos Breathed fiery spikes that petered out once they passed the opening of the window. His Dragon face was contorted with anger and frustration. The window slammed shut so violently that the ground shook.

Kade turned to Violet, who collapsed on the ground, naked and human. The tattoo wrapped around her waist glowed, flashing brilliant colors. Ferro also Catalyzed back to human, something Dragons did upon their deaths. He no longer had his black dragon tattoo on his chest.

Kade dropped down beside Violet, who was taking such

deep, gasping breaths that he was afraid she'd pass out. She clutched at his hand, staring into his eyes. "Red...Lust."

She'd taken too much power at once. It could overwhelm Dragons, sending them over the edge of their humanity. They became engorged with bloodlust. Kade only knew one way to stop it—killing the crazed Dragon. No, damn it. He would not kill her now.

"Whistle," she whispered, her body trembling now. Sweat covered her skin, glistening in the dying light. "Help."

He closed his eyes and searched his fractured memories for what that meant. Whistle. The Fringers whistled, their second language. But he didn't know how...

He did. She'd taught him. He shot to his feet and made the sound the way she'd shown him. The night they'd fought the Carnelian. Another memory clicked into place, pulling at his brain like having his fingernails yanked out. He whistled again and again, searching the woods for signs of her brothers. Anyone.

She arched, clutching her stomach and groaning.

"Will Catalyzing help?" he asked.

"Have to hold on to human."

He sat beside her, pulling her into his arms and holding her so tight he could feel her trembling right to his bone. She was so hot, her skin damp with perspiration. His nose touched hers.

She had kept him here, sane and whole; he would do the same for her. "You're an amazing woman, Vee. Watching you fight Ferro, taking the power intended for Drakos, hell, you're as strong and brave as any Vega I've ever known." She nearly smiled at that, but pain seized her again.

He heard footsteps, saw a flash out of the corner of his

eye. Before that could register, two Dragons flew through wide swaths between the trees. They landed and became two naked men in a split second. Ryan and Jessup raced over, their worried gazes on her.

"She Breathed Ferro, to keep the Dragon god from taking his power. It was too much. Ferro has killed a lot of Dragons, one every day for three months." Kade wasn't sure how he knew that, but he had a vague memory of seeing a calendar.

Jessup gestured for Kade to step away. He didn't want to, but he relinquished control. While they Catalyzed and worked on healing Violet, Kade watched and paced. Damn, he was so tense, he saw light flashing out of the corner of his eye.

Flashes. He focused on their origin. Smitty. Hell. The man was perched on a lower branch snapping away with his camera. He'd seen it all, Ferro and Violet and maybe even Drakos.

Smitty climbed down from the tree and took off. Kade raced through the woods after him, catching up quickly. Smitty was terrified, looking behind him, tripping on roots the way people did in horror films. He fell, sprawling out on the ground, and Kade crouched over him.

Smitty rolled to his side and screamed. "Who are you people? *What* are you people?"

Kade grabbed hold of him by his bony shoulders and waved his hands over Smitty's bulging eyes. Green light emanated from his palms, washing over the man's face.

"You don't want to come back to this property anymore," Kade said in a calm, low voice. He wanted to throttle the guy for taking him away from Violet. "There are no Dragons here, no gator apes, nothing."

Smitty nodded, his eyes blank. Deuces couldn't implant memories the way Caidos could, but he could suggest things.

"You will go directly home and give up your quest. Understand?"

"Yes."

"You saw nothing out of the ordinary, other than a lightning strike that came out of the blue and hit you." Kade took his camera, sending enough magick to short out the circuitry and fry the memory chip. Then he handed it back. "Go now."

The man walked casually, as though he hadn't just seen Dragons fighting. Kade ran back to Violet.

Mia was there now. How had he missed her? She searched his face. "Kade?"

He passed her, though, focusing on Violet, who was still on the ground, flanked by her brothers. They were all in Dragon form now, her brothers Breathing into her. He felt so damned helpless. He looked up to the tree where he'd shot down her rope. The seared end swung in a breeze; the rest of it lay coiled on the ground. Gods, he'd almost killed her. He clutched his head as more pieces came together.

"Kade, are you all right?" Mia asked.

"Stop bugging me, sis. I'm going to be fine. I'm worried about Vee right now."

She smiled. "You kinda sounded like the real Kade just then."

The real Kade. Who was he, anyway? More memories came together. The one who slid down banisters and flouted the rules? The one who lived to be a Vega?

Violet mumbled something, though her eyes were closed. Jessup and Ryan stood, Catalyzing to human again.

"We need to get her inside." Jessup leaned down to Violet. "Catalyze back to human, Vee."

She mumbled again, shaking her head.

Kade knelt beside her and gently shook her arm. "Come back to human, babe. That's an order."

She became a naked and dirt-smudged woman, hard scales becoming soft skin. Her brothers moved in, but Kade scooped her up in his arms. "I've got her." He had her, and he'd never let her go.

He could scarcely keep his eyes off her as he walked into the house and laid her on the couch. The bedroom was a mess. The whole place smelled like marinara sauce.

"Turn off the stove burners," he said to Mia.

He pulled the blanket down from the back of the couch and laid it over Violet. She wasn't trembling anymore. Her brothers' healing Breath had erased the cuts on her face and body.

He sank down beside her. Memories twisted around each other. He held her hand, stroking her fingers, and let them come. The recent past was the clearest. Why the hell they were in the mud naked and making love, that he'd like to know.

She opened her eyes, but it seemed to take a few moments to get her focus. She smiled, soft and sweet. Her eyes were hazy, like she'd woken from a long, deep sleep.

"Kade?"

"Yeah, babe."

That made her smile even more. "Are you really back?"

"I can feel the memories weaving together. I think it's going to take time to make sense of what I'm seeing." He brushed his hand down her cheek. "The important parts are intact. Close your eyes and rest. I'll be right here."

When Violet's eyes drifted shut, he turned to Mia. "The orderly in the psych ward worked there when our father broke out that prisoner. He told me her name." He tried to pull it out of his memories. "Wither. Widow. No, Willow. I want to find out more about her."

Jessup stepped closer. "Did you say 'Willow'?"

"Yeah. She claimed she'd been kidnapped as a child by a member of the Concilium."

Jessup looked over at Ryan. "Remember the Murphy girl who went missing, what, thirty years ago?"

"Yeah, Willow. I always thought the name was silly since we don't have willow trees around here."

Kade traded a look with Mia. "So she was telling the truth about being kidnapped. Our father trusted his instinct and had the guts to try to break her out of prison, just like you all did with me." He heard the relief in his voice. "He died doing the right thing."

"Maybe they put the Black Bore Orb in her mind, too," Mia said.

Kade frowned. "Black Bore Orb?"

"It's what Ferro put in your head that fractured your memories."

His head hurt just hearing about it. He was in no hurry to remember that. Kade watched Violet sleep while he told the others that Ferro and Onyx had been killing people to save Drakos. He rolled that name around in his head. It resonated. And it wasn't good. He remembered a painting in Ferro's office. "Drakos is a member of the Tryah."

Jessup wrinkled his nose. "Tryah? I vaguely remember them being the gods who started the war. If it weren't for them, we could have been living on a tropical island eating coconuts and watching beautiful naked women all day."

Ryan punched his arm. "Focus. We're not out of the woods yet."

Kade looked at Violet, sleeping so peacefully. "Onyx is still out there. And she wants Violet dead even more than Ferro did."

Chapter 21

Onyx couldn't find a child to kill. Ever since word got out about the August girl being threatened, the clans had tightened their hold on their children. So she killed a teenage boy instead, an August who was patrolling the property. She let him scream long enough to draw others before dropping Jessup's shredded clothes.

It was dawn before she'd finally made the kill, and she was exhausted. Ferro wasn't answering her texts. She knew he was upset about the jailbreak. Maybe he'd been hurt more than he'd let on. She worried about him, but she knew he'd want her to move forward. The effects of the solar storm would hit sometime that day. Wouldn't Drakos be pleased if she was the one who brought the most power to him?

She was already on her way to Violet's house before the first August arrived.

When Violet woke, Kade was sitting nearby watching over her. He smiled. "Feel better?"

She took note of how she felt. Not wretched, no trace of wanting to kill anyone in a mindless frenzy. "Yes, I think so."

He helped her sit up. "I hope the hammering didn't interrupt your rest. Your brothers and I patched up the bedroom wall. A temporary fix, but it'll keep the weather and animals out anyway."

"You and my brothers worked together? And they were nice to you?" She liked that idea.

"They were civil. Though they did make fun of my hammering technique. I'm much handier with a sword than a hammer." He showed her his thumb, which bore testament to that with a bruise.

"Aw, poor baby." She pulled it to her mouth and planted a soft kiss on it. Which fired up the mist in his eyes. She opened his hand and moved her mouth over his palm, her gaze on his.

"I have this memory of us making love in the mud. Just bits and pieces, but I do remember it was incredible."

"I had to keep you from slipping into your real memories." She wouldn't tell him how he'd tried to kill her.

"You said something about lying to keep me sane."

She nodded. "You kept falling into memories of fighting, being in danger. So I kept you in a fantasy world, which included us being married. And since making love in the mud was one of your fantasies..." She shrugged.

He grinned. "It was a nice fantasy, all of it."

What was he saying? That he liked being married to her?

Before she could delve into that, a series of long whistles pierced the air, like an alarmed bird call. Violet turned to Kade. "There's trouble. Big trouble." She ran outside and strained to hear more. There was shouting in the distance, angry calls. "Clan wars," she said. "They're here."

She ran back inside and called Jessup. "What's going on?"

"There's a lynch mob moving in from the borders of our land. They think we're the ones behind the murders. I heard Bren say I killed Sam August. Get out of here while you can."

Sam. Another teenager. Violet clutched the phone. "Jessup, we can't just hide while—"

"You're still weak, and Kade's memories are unstable. You've both been through hell. Stay out of it. We can beat them, Vee." She could hear the smile in his voice, his eagerness to fight. "We'll annihilate them the way we did the Garzas. They're on our land, and they're here to kill us. We have every right."

"But you know they only *think* we've killed their people."

"Doesn't change the fact that they're here to kill us."

Kade leaned close to the phone, his cheek brushing hers. "Where's Mia?"

"With Ryan," Jessup said. "She's been practicing with her dagger, and she's not half bad."

"But she's inexperienced when it comes to fighting."

"Ryan's going to keep an eye on her. Smitten son of a bitch." Jessup's disgust lanced his words. "Whistle if you need us. Use the speaker system if necessary. Look, I gotta go. Be careful."

Kade's face sharpened in warrior mode. "We can't let them fight alone."

"Well, they're hardly alone." She could see that his own hunger to fight was still alive and well.

Another call came in. She didn't recognize the number. "Hello?"

"Violet?" A woman's voice.

"Yes, who's this?"

"I hear you're having a bit of trouble with the neighbors. A shame. I know your mother always runs to the gator house to secure it at the first sign of danger. Gods forbid something should happen to the family's livelihood." She chuckled, while Violet's blood turned to ice.

"What do you want?"

"You, darling. Alone. Leave your brain-addled lover there. Not that he'd be of much use anyway."

Violet met Kade's eyes. Ferro's accomplice. "Who are you? I obviously know you."

"I'll tell you when you get here. We can catch up on old times. If I see anyone else, your mother will be alligator stew." She disconnected.

Violet turned to Kade. "She's got my mother! In the gator pens." She had to take deep breaths or she'd be as hysterical as Mia usually was. "She wants me to come alone. If she sees you or anyone, she'll kill her."

Kade shuddered. "With the alligators? Hate those things," he muttered. "I'm coming with you, but don't worry. She won't see me."

Yes, the orb that camouflaged. "She thinks you're brain damaged. She won't be expecting you to help me. Are you sure you're ready to fight?"

He stretched his arm, the dagger shimmering. "It's what I am. If I can't fight for the Guard anymore, I'll fight for you." Those moss green eyes shimmered with his conviction and devotion.

Her heart melted, but she tucked the feeling away for

later. She dialed Jessup again, hoping he would be able to answer. He was breathless when he did three rings later. "What's up?"

"I need you to get those men near the speakers." She wasn't going to tell him about their mother. That would set him into a rampage, and Violet needed to play this cool.

"What, you gonna serenade us with some soothing music?"

"Just do it, Jessup." She hung up, driving her fingers through her hair as she headed to the front door. "I can't lose my ma." The thought of it pounded through her, raising the old Violet who would also fly into an emotion-driven frenzy. "She's been through so much. I'm going to tear that Carnelian bitch to shreds when I get my hands on her. I'm going to—"

Kade took her arms and turned her to face him. "You're the strongest woman I know, and you're more than a capable fighter. Hell, you broke me out of the Guard's prison. If you can do that, you can save her, Vee, but you have to keep your head."

His confidence in her meant a lot, coming from a soldier like Kade. She only nodded, unable to say anything as she drew in his strength, his composure.

He gave her a quick kiss and said, "Let's get your ma."

They plunged into the woods, following the path that led toward the gator house.

When they saw a building up ahead, he whispered, "Is that it?"

"No, that's the barn where you—" She didn't want to get into those unfortunate hours he'd spent there. "There's something I want to get." She detoured to the wall of shame and stopped short. "The cuffs are gone."

Kade stared at the weathered boards, and she saw him struggling with his memories. *Please don't go blank on me.*

"The cuffs with the Lucifer's Gold," he said. "I think it's my fault that they're gone. When I was reporting in as Dune, I had to tell Ferro about the cuffs to explain why Kade wasn't using his magick to escape. He must have told the Carnelian."

"I was going to use them on the Carnelian. But she's...damn it, she beat me to it. She's obviously using them on my ma to keep her from Catalyzing." Violet slapped her hand to her chest, which felt like it was caving in. "She's helpless."

He took her hand and gave it a squeeze, giving her strength and calm. "We'll save her. Together we have enough power." He lifted their joined hands and kissed the back of hers.

She took a deep breath. "Thank you."

The crack of a tree falling broke through the sound of her heavy breathing. The mob was drawing closer. The Carnelian might kill her mother if she heard others approaching, thinking that it was Violet's clan. She had to get there first.

In unison, they released their handhold and continued their sprint down the path. Each minute that passed felt like an hour. This trek had never felt so long. So arduous. Her legs ached and her lungs burned. She spotted the gnarled cypress tree that meant they were nearly there and signaled Kade. He pulled the orb around him and disappeared. Violet felt eyes on her as she approached the long gator house. Her heart felt as though it weighed a hundred pounds as it thudded heavily in her chest. After unlocking the back door, she walked through the office. She flipped the switch

for the speakers just before stepping into the steamy area
where the gators lived.

She walked in, breathing shallowly. A long boardwalk
split the building in half, with pens on either side filled
with gators of varying sizes. It wasn't their regular feeding
time, so they weren't as active. But if someone fell in,
they'd react instantly.

Her heart stopped at the sight of the woman holding her
ma with her arm across her throat. A cuff circled one of
Ma's hands, but she was calm and very still, her mouth
in a tight line. Stoic as always, but her eyes gave away
her terror...especially at seeing Violet. She gave a subtle
shake of her head. *Go.*

Violet shook her head, too. *I'm not leaving you, Ma.*

She shifted her focus to the woman who was holding
her, eager to figure out who this hateful adversary was. But
she didn't look familiar. Violet remained close to the wall
and the switch that would turn on the intercom. Several
stations were put in place as a way to alert others if someone was injured or fell into the pens. It was a rule that the
speaker system always got turned on when someone was in
the gator house. Violet's finger touched the smooth metal
lever and tried to push it up. It wasn't budging.

"Remember me now, Violet?" the woman said. She had
a smug smile, beautiful as she was, with dark hair and glit-
tering eyes.

Violet pushed harder, and the lever finally moved with a
rusty sound. "No, I don't."

The smile vanished. "Pilar Garza. Oh, you probably
thought I'd died when your family massacred mine. I was
gone that day. Lucky me." Her smile returned, brittle this
time.

Violet's gaze kept shifting to her mother as she took one step at a time, drawing closer. She thought she saw the outline of Kade's bubble behind Pilar and her mother. She couldn't afford to look too hard and draw Pilar's attention to him. "You seem to forget that someone in your family killed my father. We did not attack you unprovoked. But this isn't about our families, is it?"

"Of course it is. And how much I hate you. Have always hated you."

"Because I was better at wrestling than you were when we were, what, fourteen? Because when you tried to distract me I didn't get my arm torn off? Because you were shunned and banned due to your bad behavior?"

"Your father killed mine!"

"That was your doing. You pouted and sulked so much that your father challenged mine to the Conference Room. Your father wasn't supposed to die in there." Mostly the Conference Room was about brute force, releasing aggression, not duels to the death. "Your father tried to kill mine. He had to protect himself."

Pilar gave her a cruel smile. "Do you want to know why your father was on our property? I saw him at the edge, calling for one of your pigs. I pretended to be hurt, and he came over to help me. I stabbed him. And while he bled out, I remembered seeing you two at the store laughing together. He put his arm around your shoulders, and you leaned into him. And I thought about how I didn't have my father anymore, and now you wouldn't either."

Her father had been tricked. He'd been trying to help her and was killed for it. Violet saw the shock register on her ma's face, too. She focused on Pilar. "*You* caused the deaths of your whole family," Violet said. "You started a war."

Pilar pointed, jerking Violet's ma off-balance. "You started it!"

Violet knew there was no point in reasoning with a woman who could only rationalize her own actions. She buried her shock and anger. "Let my mother go. You said we were making a deal. Me for her."

"Vee, no, damn it!" her ma said. "I've lived a long life. You are not giving yours for mine."

But Violet didn't intend to give her life. "I'm a big girl, Ma. I make my own decisions. And I already made the deal. You and Daddy taught me to live up to my word, after all." She focused on Pilar again. "Since you've been so forthcoming, I have a revelation for you as well. Ferro's dead."

Pilar stumbled, which shoved Violet's mother into the railing along the boardwalk. "You didn't kill Ferro. He's in Miami."

"He's lying in the woods. He came to kill me. Seems the two of you don't like me much. I'll try not to take it to heart. Someone I care about very much recently gave me that advice, not to take things too personally."

Pilar lifted her chin. "You couldn't kill Ferro. He's much more powerful than you will ever be."

"I got lucky." Violet wasn't going to mention Kade's part. Let her continue thinking he was insane. She approached Pilar slowly, her hands out at her sides. "He took you in, didn't he? That's how you came together with this plan of yours to save Drakos."

Her eyes widened. "How..."

"Because Drakos came to Ferro as we fought. And funny, I thought he'd save Ferro as he lay dying and begging for help. Instead he chastised him for not waiting. He was going to finish him, Breathe him. That's the only way he can take the power you've been accumulating. So do you really want to throw everything away for a god who's betrayed you?"

"You're lying! Drakos is going to make me immortal."

Violet thought about that girl Pilar had intended to kill. "You hate us all in the Fringe so much that you'd set us up to kill each other? Leave more children without parents when you know how painful that is?" She hoped Jessup had pushed aside his bloodlust and gotten the others to listen. "You were going to kill Kaitlyn. A child! That's against the rules. My clan never killed any Garza children."

"Only because there were none at the time. Saving a god is more important than any child's life. Certainly more important than any of you Fringers. All they'll be good for is the power I Breathe from those who survive the clan wars. They will be the most powerful and worthy of my time and effort."

Violet hoped they heard that. She now stood directly in front of Pilar. She had to fight not to look when she saw Kade appear as the orb evaporated.

"Let her go." Violet held out her hand. "And put the other cuff on me."

Pilar pushed her mother away and reached the open cuff toward Violet's wrist. As the metal touched her skin, Pilar gasped and looked down at the tip of Kade's blade protruding from her chest. Blue shards of magick came off the bloody blade and pulsed through her body. She snapped the cuff closed and Catalyzed. With all of her power, she'd heal fast in Dragon form. She flicked her tail at Kade, who didn't move quite fast enough because his focus was on that cuff around Violet's wrist. He was thrown to the edge of the walkway, the railing stopping him from falling over the edge. Pilar inhaled, ready to incinerate him.

Violet unlatched one of the gates and pushed Pilar through the opening and into the gator pit. She landed with a splash, and then Violet heard several other splashes as the gators moved toward her. Pilar sent a torrent of flames at the creatures to keep them at bay. She turned and smashed into the walkway that led through the center of the building, sending Violet stumbling down the slanted boards and into the water.

Oh, crap. The sight of her usually signaled the arrival of food to the gators. If she didn't have gator chow to offer them, they'd take her instead. She couldn't Catalyze with the damned cuff on. Vigorous pushing at it couldn't nudge it past her wrist bone. Some of the gators swished through the water toward her, their mouths partially open.

Kade Changed into the largest gator she'd ever seen and threw himself into the muddy melee of tails and teeth and fangs and fire. He charged toward her, stepping on other gators and pushing them beneath the water.

Pilar, blood still gushing from the wound in her chest, tried to climb up the broken walkway. Gators pulled at her tail. She was too big for any one gator to tussle with, but the beasts didn't care. Several of them were fighting over her. She kept them at bay with her periodic bursts of flame, but one managed to take a chunk out of her tail. She howled in pain, screaming obscenities.

Violet tried to climb out of the water, barely clinging to one of the boards. Her feet kept slipping on the wet wood.

"Oh, no you don't." Pilar reached out and knocked her off, sending Violet face-first into the water. One gator clamped its mouth around her arm, its teeth puncturing her skin. It would do the death roll with her, spinning her around and pinning her to the bottom of the pen. Her scream was drowned out by the water in her mouth. Suddenly the gator released her, and then another one took her into its massive jaws. With teeth as soft as pillows.

Kade.

He set her on the intact portion of the walkway and then turned to Pilar, precariously balanced on the broken boards. She kicked at the encroaching gators, which were even more fueled by the blood in the water. Kade lunged at her from one of the narrow catwalks that ran perpendicular to the main walkway. Pilar sent a blast of Obsidian Dragon magick at him. A black oily cloud smothered the huge gator. Kade dropped the illusion, becoming man and slipping out of the cloud's grasp. Pilar shot a plume of fiery spikes at him. He dropped to a crouch as they flew over his head and singed his hair. He staggered back upright, fatigue clear in his expression.

Pilar moved slower, too. But she seemed as determined as Kade to win. While the two fought, Violet climbed over the broken parts of the walkway behind Pilar. The shards of wood bit into her skin as she used them for handholds. Kade drew his dagger and sent an arc of lightning at Pilar's throat. Pilar blocked it with her black cloud, now using it as a shield. Kade's bolts shredded the shield, but he wielded his magick dagger as though it weighed fifty pounds.

Violet was only inches from Pilar when she lost her footing as one of the boards shifted with her movements. Before Violet could get a solid grip on the boards, she spotted an insidious black stream snaking its way over the thrashing water toward Kade's feet. It started to wrap around his ankles. If it knocked him off-balance, he'd fall into the bay on the other side, where the largest alligators lived.

Violet reached out with her cuffed hand and grabbed Pilar's wing, the only thing she could reach. Pilar's magick evaporated because of the Lucifer's Gold, and she became a naked human holding on to the top of the slanted walkway. The gash on her tail translated to a deep cut at her tailbone. Violet gripped her upper arm to keep her from falling.

"Drakos, save me!" Pilar screamed, looking up.

"Don't be stupid," Violet said. "I told you what happened to Ferro."

The air shimmered, and Drakos's image appeared a few feet from them. A pissed-off Drakos, given the sour expression on his Dragon face. "You have both failed me. Though you carry the essence of gods, you are but weak humans."

"Weak? I am strong! I hold the power of many."

"You are weak of spirit and mind. You would do anything, believe anything, to get your fondest desire. But it was your fear of dying that gave me the most power over you...and made you gullible."

Pilar's expression contorted in a pain much harsher than the physical. "Are you saying you lied about giving me immortality?"

His chilling smile was her answer. "And now I shall take what you have been gathering for me." His image moved closer.

Violet wasn't about to let him take Pilar's power. Nor was she going to take it. As Drakos began to suck in Pilar's life essence, Violet pushed her into the water. The gators were faster than Pilar, tearing her apart before she could

Catalyze. Drakos tried to finish pulling in her essence, but Pilar's death was too quick. The gators had waited long enough, teased by the blood and food.

A hand on her shoulder made her jerk, nearly dislodging her from her position. Kade gripped her, barely keeping his own balance. "You okay?" he asked.

She nodded, unable to get any words out to describe everything she felt. Horrified. Shocked. Relieved. Together they made their way back to the solid portion of the walkway.

Violet's mother raced forward and clutched her. "Vee, you were foolish to put yourself in danger for your old ma."

Violet held her tight. "My old ma means a lot to me."

It was the first time she'd seen her mother express any kind of emotion. Tears streamed down her face when she pulled back and whispered, "Thank you."

Sounds from the doorway drew her attention to Jessup, Ryan, and Mia. Behind them several members of the other clans pressed close, rage on their faces.

"We heard a woman talking about killing our Kaitlyn," Bren said.

"Pilar Garza," one of the Murphys said.

Violet merely pointed to the pit where gators were still fighting. Several of the men raced forward and looked where Violet could not. After a few moments, they backed up with expressions of grim satisfaction. They all walked out into the fresh air. Violet helped her ma outside. Those gathered peppered Violet with questions, and she tried to answer them the best she could.

"Never heard of a dying god before," one said.

Kade took the keys from Jessup and unlocked Violet's

cuff. "He lied to Ferro and Pilar about their just rewards. He was probably lying about that, too."

No one apologized for the murders. One by one the other clans trailed off, their anger and bloodlust still simmering. When the last of them were gone, Jessup turned back to her. "You did good, thinking of the speakers."

"And you did good getting them to listen."

He shook his head. "Wasn't easy. I wanted to kill 'em. But sometimes...sometimes peace is better." He gave her a begrudging smile.

She'd take full credit for bringing her brothers around to that reasoning. It was nothing shy of a miracle. "I want to live my life not being afraid. I want to raise kids who can run free without fear."

"Kids?" Jessup and her mother said at the same time.

"In the future." Far in the future, she hoped. She resisted the urge to put her hand to her belly. *Not ready for that yet.*

Jessup pointed to Kade, but his gaze was on her. "Now that this is over, is he going?"

She turned to Kade, who stood so close beside her she could feel his body heat. *Are you?*

His hands squeezed her shoulders. "I'm her husband. I'm not going anywhere."

Had he slipped into his pseudomemories again? He had that content expression he'd worn when they nuzzled and cooked together as husband and wife.

"He doesn't remember..." Jessup let his words trail off meaningfully, the question clear.

Violet wasn't sure, and she wasn't going to risk losing Kade by telling him. She moved into his embrace. If he wanted to stay, she wouldn't kowtow to her clan's prejudices. "I love who I want."

Jessup rolled his eyes, then shifted them to Mia and Ryan. "What about her?"

Ryan ran his fingers down her arm. "Hey, if Vee gets to keep him"—he gestured to Kade—"I can keep her."

Mia swung around, looking both indignant and intrigued.

Ryan lifted his hands. "Kidding. How 'bout we have lunch and see what's what?"

Well, what d'ya know?

"Hell, no," Jessup said, but Ryan wasn't paying him any attention. He and Mia were already wandering away. He gave them a look of disgust and turned back to Violet. "Want to grab a bite at the house? I'm starved."

Violet did put her hand to her stomach this time. "I can't even think about food right now. We'll come up later and check on everyone."

Jessup looked like he wanted to force her to go with him, but he merely gave her a nod. "Ryan and I will come back later and get your wrecked wall fixed proper."

"Thanks."

She and Kade started back toward her house, coming up on the barn. He was taking in their surroundings. Not in a worried way, ready for attack, but almost in an admiring way. "I thought it was marsh and bugs and snakes, but it's beautiful here." His gaze moved to her. "Really beautiful." He brushed the back of his hand against her cheek.

Her heart twisted. He *was* once again caught in that fake memory, still living the lie she'd fabricated. She took his hand, stopping him. "You know we're not really married. Right?"

He gave her a pulse-pounding smile. "I know. I was just

tweaking your brother." He looked up toward the tops of the trees. "Teach me how to swing on those ropes. I have this bit of memory where your brother swings down at me from up there."

She remembered when he talked about how she tugged at his wild side. "You don't remember everything, do you?"

Kade rubbed his head. "It feels like rubber bands snapping inside my brain. With every snap, something else fills in. But there are still a lot of blank spots."

"Let's swing on the rope."

They kicked off their shoes, and she led the way to the tall live oak. She showed him the crevices for footholds and mounds that were once branches and now served as handles. He kept up easily, and soon they were stepping across the thick branch to where the ropes hung. She pulled one up and handed it to Kade, then brought the other one up for her.

His fingers wrapped around the rope, but he was looking at everything around him. She could see that wild side he'd talked about; it sparked in his eyes, shone in the way he seemed so natural up there.

She felt as precariously balanced inside as she did standing on that branch, her toes curled over the rough bark. She tightened her lips, but the words needed to be said. "Kade, we've been wrapped in a bundle of lies since you came here. You're investigating, you're in love with me, you're not in love with me, we're married." *Trying to have a baby.* She pinched the bridge of her nose. She would tell him about that later. "I feel things for you that don't make sense at all. And the thought of losing you made them even stronger."

He released a soft breath. "But you didn't lose me. I'm here."

"But do you even know who you are? What you feel? What's real, Kade?" She let out a breath of exasperation. She was about to get herself all tangled up in her words and emotions. Instead, she grasped the rope with both hands, jumped, and swung down. Speed tickled her tummy as she flew through the air. All too soon, her feet touched down on the earth.

He clapped, the rope shaking in his hold. "Nicely done." He mirrored her moves and flew down. She stepped out of his trajectory, but he came in at a slightly different angle. She put her hands out to slow him, he tried to shift, and they both ended up in a pile of limbs on the ground.

He hovered over her. "You okay? Sorry about that."

"You've been knocking me on my ass since that moment our eyes met across the pit at Headquarters. Figuratively and literally."

"Ditto." He lowered his mouth to hers. The kiss was soft and sweet, and he studied her for a moment afterward. "You're afraid I'm going to hurt you...break your heart. Because someone else did." He narrowed his eyes, trying to recall something obviously. "Bren."

"No, I never loved him. I never felt like this with him."

"Like what?"

Crazy, madly in love. "Like I'd break into the Guard prison to save him."

"Which astounds me that you did it. And succeeded." He brushed her hair from her face. "But he hurt you anyway."

She shook her head, but the truth prickled through her. No more lies between her and Kade. "I guess he did. I *thought* I was in love with him, that he wanted me for who I was. I *know* I'm in love with you, and I'm scared that you don't feel the same way."

He sat back, pulling her hands up so they faced each other, their knees touching. He didn't let go. "Vee, when I shot you down—gods, I'm sorry I did that—I knew you'd been lying about us being married. I started getting pieces of memories, a flash of me coming up behind you, about to terminate you—"

He shook his head. "It was damned confusing because I remembered loving you. It was like I was two different people. Then Ferro appeared, and I slipped into that Vega role I've been in for most of my life. That felt more familiar than being a husband, further confirming that you were lying to me. But as Ferro was about to finish you, it was the devastation I felt at the thought of you dying that started snapping everything together. You reached into my dark shattered mind because of what I meant to you. And I pulled the shards back together because of what you meant to me."

He braced his hand against her cheek. "So no matter the lies and illusions, what we feel for each other is real." He planted another of those devastatingly tender kisses on her mouth. "*That's* real, Violet Castanega."

The Tryah closed the window between their dimension and the Earthly plane. Drakos sagged into the chair. He had been so close to escaping this place of gray hopelessness.

"Don't give up yet," Demis said, looking smug. "My Caido minions are powerful and dedicated, and they have been working on gathering power in their own way. They'll have enough to see our plan through."

Fallon huffed out an impatient breath. "But they're using *children*. How much power can they really gain from them?"

"They may not possess the power of a Breathed Dragon, but they hold the purity of their emotions: love, hate, fear. My minions have been harnessing and storing these emotions for just this time."

"And they, too, have hit snags before," Drakos said, taking some gratification in that. "When the two young Caidos escaped many years ago, nearly exposing the whole operation."

"And the woman who escaped and accused your minion of kidnapping her," Fallon reminded him. "I've had to intervene twice to save your godly asses, giving Purcell Black Bore Orbs."

Demis raised his eyebrow at the usage of Earth plane language. "We work toward a common goal. Let us not nitpick. In the end, I will be the one to carry the plan to fruition. Then you will both give me the respect I deserve."

Drakos would never respect one of the fallen angels. But he would play along, if it meant their freedom at long last.

Violet lay cradled in Kade's arms. They'd figured out how much was real, like the way their bodies fit each other's so perfectly and how right it felt making love now that they were in a place of truth. She lay next to him, her leg slung over his thighs, tracing her fingers over his stomach.

"Purcell!" he said, sitting up abruptly.

"Well, I'm glad you didn't call out someone else's name while we were making love."

He chuckled. "Silly girl, Purcell is a man."

She furrowed her eyebrows. "Even more so."

He shook his head, but his smile faded as he obviously returned to whatever thought had made him spoil the mood. "Purcell is the son of a bitch who put the Black Bore Orb in my head."

"And you're thinking of him now . . . why?" But now that she was thinking of him, she wanted to sink her talons into his throat.

Kade's Crescent mist darkened in his eyes. "Right before you went to the Guard, an old Vega buddy called me out of the blue, asking who could create a star orb. That's an orb like an intelligent missile, remote controlled by the Deuce who created it. And only a very powerful, very old Deuce can create such an orb. Someone who could also create a Black Bore Orb. Cyntag and a woman brought me a book to decipher, and they were obviously involved in something."

He leaned down to the floor and fished his phone out of his pants pocket, affording her with an exquisite view of his bare ass. But she could hardly enjoy it, as Kade sat right back and dialed, putting the phone on speaker. "Hey, Cyntag, it's Kade. I think I know who's behind that star orb. A Deuce named Purcell—"

"Way ahead of you, bro. Purcell is dead, as of this morning. He was involved in a plot to manipulate the *Deus Vis* and starve us of the energy we need. But according to Brom, there's more to it than that."

"A hell of a lot more. Like the Tryah."

"The Tryah? But they've been dormant for centuries."

"Not anymore. Drakos was working with my boss. He and a female were killing Dragons and stockpiling their power. I thought that's all there was to it until I realized Purcell was powerful enough to produce your star orb."

"The Tryah," Cyntag said, as though absorbing the implications. "The three-headed monster Brom saw in his prophetic vision. We fought and defeated one head, and Brom said there were others fighting the remaining two heads. You're one of those others, obviously. Need help?"

"We stopped Drakos's plan. Ferro and his cohort are dead. How do we find the third head?"

"Unfortunately, Brom doesn't know, though he assures me that the ones fighting are capable. I felt one of the gods trying to help Purcell. Probably the Deuce god. Can't remember his name. So the third is Demis, the angel who was supposed to watch over Lucifera. Whatever it is that they're trying to do involves the solar storm and how it'll affect the *Deus Vis*. And I have a bad feeling it involves a lot of Crescents dying."

Kade put his arm around Violet. "We have to find a way to help. Standing by doing nothing is unacceptable." His Vega was talking now. "Going to the Concilium or the Guard is too risky. There's obviously corruption in the system."

"Let's get together and see what we can figure out."

"Sounds good. I've got a lot to fill you in on. Will I finally find out why you left the Guard?"

"Yeah, but I can tell you now that it has everything to do with the woman I brought to your boat."

"I thought so." He squeezed Violet closer. "I have a feeling I'm going to understand your motives a lot more than you think."

Get set for dragons,
angels, and dark magic—

in the next sexy Hidden novel!

Please turn this page for a preview of

Angel Seduced.

Chapter 1

Kye Rivers bypassed the velvet rope that corralled the line of people waiting to get into the Witch's Brew. Too bad the handful of Mundane humans didn't know that this exclusive Miami nightclub only allowed in Deuces like her. Of course, they knew nothing at all about Crescents, humans who carried the DNA of a fallen angel, a Dragon, or sorcerer god.

Kye traded a greeting with the bouncer and went into the jam-packed cave of a building. One guy was clearly using a little sex magick to get the girl across the table into a nearly orgasmic state. A woman was casting an attraction spell on the guy she was talking to. Kye snapped her finger as she passed them and broke it. *Get him to like you on your own terms, chickie.*

Sarai raced over, her serving tray tucked under her arm. "Kye, wait 'til you see the new bartender! His name is Kasabian. He's totally hot. And"—she gave her the *wait for it* grin—"he's Caido."

"No way. Maybe it's a Deuce illusion, like his gimmick."

"He couldn't hold it for two whole shifts. Plus, he's healed a couple of people."

All three classes of Crescents traced their ancestry to a mysterious island in the Bermuda Triangle, where humans had procreated with gods, but none intermingled much. Caidos, half fallen angels, were downright reclusive.

Sarai snapped her gum. "There was quite a stir at first, as you can imagine. The women were all gaga and the guys were all 'why's the pretty boy Caido working here?' But people are starting to warm to him. He's nice. Not snotty like Tad or slutty like Donnie was."

Kye's gaze went right to the new face behind the bar. The gorgeous new face. Red lights within the thick glass counter cast a glow over the angles of his cheeks and the gloss of his dark-blond hair. Kasabian might be new to the Brew, but he was clearly not new to tending. He flipped bottles, poured, and returned them to their places with the speed and grace of a juggler. By the relaxed smile on his face, she could tell he was enjoying it. So were the people watching him in rapt awe. Of course, that could be the Thrall, the way Caidos could hypnotize with their preternatural beauty. Because of what Kye did for a living, she'd learned to shut out that allure.

But damn, fascination stirred deep in her chest.

Whoa, cut that shit out.

Kye shrugged. "Just another pretty Caido." She pushed her long blond hair back over her shoulder. "Think I'll order a drink now."

"I totally know you're checking him out—" Sarai's teasing smile disappeared. She gripped her arm, the mist in her eyes stirring like storm-tossed clouds. "Don't do it!"

"You're freaking over me ordering a drink from the guy?"

Sarai shook her head. "I'm feeling a lot more than a drink. First, I sensed that there could be something good and hot and sexy between the two of you. Then I got a really bad feeling."

Kye splayed her hand on her chest. "Uh, remember who you're talking to. The girl you're always giving a hard time because I never date."

"Remember who's doing the talking. I had a feeling about that guy Katie was dating, and he ended up being a drug dealer. I warned Rhea that her brakes were going to give out, and the mechanic said they wouldn't have lasted another day."

"I don't doubt your forecasts. Maybe something good and bad would come from getting involved, but I'd never get romantic with a Brew employee anyway." She patted Sarai's hand. "I need to meet him. He's in my world, after all." The Brew was her second home, the employees a sort of family.

Kasabian looked up, zoning right in on her as she approached. His green eyes held the Caido glitter, like sun on early morning frost. Each of the three types of Crescents held their unique magick in their eyes, visible only to other Crescents.

He watched her, even as he shoved limes into two Coronas and pushed them across the counter to the men waiting for them. "What can I get you, love?" he asked when she reached him. *"Love"? What kind of Caido was this guy?*

The smooth edge of the counter pressed into her palms as she leaned forward. "Know how to make the Whis-

Kye?" she called out over the pounding beat of Katy Perry's "E.T."

His mouth curved into a heart-stopping smile as his gaze lingered on the patch on her black leather jacket that read NO DOES NOT MEAN CONVINCE ME. "You must be Kye. Before he left, Donnie filled me in on the special customers. From what I've heard, you're quite special." He held out his hand. "I'm Kasabian."

A strange twist of anticipation and fear overtook her, but she slid her hand into his—and instantly knew why. A jolt like a low-level electrical surge went through her. She pulled her hand back, heat flushing over her. He was watching her as though he expected her to react, so she did her best not to.

He turned and pulled down the bottle of Johnnie Walker Black whiskey with one hand, a highball glass in another. There were no available stools, but the couple beside her shifted so she could settle in more comfortably. Which she shouldn't do. Which she did.

Kasabian mixed the drink Mike, the club's owner, had concocted for her years ago. Whiskey, Mountain Dew, and a splash of orange juice, just enough liquor for a tiny buzz. He snuggled a wedge of orange on the rim and slid the glass in front of her. Someone farther down the bar flagged Kasabian down.

"Don't go," he said, moving away to take an order. He made three different drinks and pulled one draft. His tight yellow shirt showed off a physique he got doing more than tossing bottles. Not bodybuilder thick, but lean and well defined. He returned to her. "Mike told me you're a Zensu Deuce, that you pick up people's sensual pathos and fix them. He thinks you're a goddess."

Embarrassment stung her cheeks but warmed her heart. That was a lot more appreciation than she'd ever gotten from her own family over her gift. She couldn't go into how she'd helped Mike with his sexual dysfunction, discovering it stemmed from an impotency spell cast by an ex.

"I'm a certified sex therapist," she felt compelled to say. "With a doctorate in clinical sexology."

"Plus a dash of magick."

"To be honest, it's mostly the magick."

Kasabian regarded her with a curious expression. "You pick up people's feelings?"

"It can work that way, if someone asks me to open the door. I don't make a habit of eavesdropping. In fact, I keep the psychic door closed most of the time."

He gestured for her to lean closer, then did the same. She had the bizarre notion that he was going to kiss her. Even more bizarre, she involuntarily licked her lips in anticipation. His mouth moved close to her ear, brushing the shell of it ever so slightly as he said, "So, what do you get from me?"

She tried to stifle her shiver at his touch. He leaned back, and she saw that his question was a challenge, maybe a test. She opened the door and ...holy Zensu, a wave of desire, pain, and heat washed over her. Desire for her. *He's Caido. This can't be right.* It spiraled inside her like a vine, a dark hunger twining through her until she slammed the door shut.

She worked to mask her surprise, along with the flush on her face. She had to lean close to him now. "Caidos don't have sexual pathos ...or sexual anything. You're all shut down." She grabbed her drink.

Kasabian's raised eyebrow and smile said, *I don't believe you.* He gave her a wink and tipped his chin toward the dance floor. "Go dance, give me something to watch."

Was he serious? His playful smile could go both ways.

A woman tugged her sleeve. "Are you Kye? I was told you could help me with...a problem."

"Yes, yes, I can." Kye gratefully led her to her usual table, a RESERVED sign sitting on the shiny black top. Mike let her conduct business in the club, and she insisted on giving him a cut. Some people felt more comfortable talking about their sexual issues in loud, smoky surroundings. The club had become her second office.

It was damn annoying how Kye's attention kept straying to Kasabian through the night, how her mind kept replaying their conversation. Women gawked and flirted, but he didn't flirt back. He was friendly with everyone, but Kye didn't see the kind of intense attention he'd shown her. She was glad to see him leave while she finished up with a client session after closing time.

Her relief evaporated when she stepped into the well-lit parking lot and spotted him leaning against a deep yellow sports car. As though he were waiting for her. The thought fluttered in her chest. Not helping, the Lotus's license plate read NOANGEL, and black angel wings spread across the hood. Caidos in particular were drawn to fancy, fast cars, funded by the good investments many had made in real estate before the boom.

But the man himself was far sexier than his car. His legs were stretched out in front of him, ankles crossed casually. His arms were loosely crossed in front of his chest, which made his biceps bulge nicely. She told herself it was enough to enjoy the view. Men who took care of their bodies, working out enough to build muscle without looking too jacked up, were eye candy. No calories in looking.

The thick black heels of her short boots clunked on the asphalt. She felt such an odd pull toward him that she forced herself to give him a brief smile and bypass him.

"Aren't you hot in that?" he asked, gesturing as though he were wearing a jacket.

She slowed to a stop in front of him. "Only when I dance." No matter how warm she got, she never took off the black leather jacket with her patches and studs.

"And you didn't dance." He tilted his head, giving her an oh-my-gods-stop-my-heart pout. "Pity."

"Are you flirting with me?"

He arched an eyebrow. "You make it sound like a crime."

"What you're hearing is surprise. I know it's painful for Caidos to feel desire, punishment you unfairly suffer because your angel forefathers fell to human temptation. Don't worry. As a therapist, I'm sworn to secrecy," she added. "Caido clients tell me it's easier to shut down their desire. Yet you do … feel desire."

"Ah, so you did sense it."

"You threw me off back at the bar. First that you were flirting, then that you asked me outright to feel you. I mean, to sense your feelings. You're different."

"Very. I don't usually flirt." He let his gaze drift down over her black leather skirt and fishnet stockings. His eyes met hers again, jumpstarting her heart. "You have a strange effect on me."

Ditto, buddy. Which made her all too aware that they were outside alone together.

His chuckle rolled across her skin. "Don't worry, I'm not waiting out here to pounce on you."

She'd forgotten how Caidos could pick up others' emotions. "But you are waiting for me."

"Yes, I am."

"You're not going to ask me out or anything, are you? Because I don't date." He didn't say anything, which made for a really awkward few seconds. "It's a general rule, nothing personal. If...that's what you were going to ask." She would have *thwapped* herself on the forehead if it wouldn't look stupid.

And, of course, as a Caido, he picked up everything she was feeling, which put an incredibly sexy smile on his face. "As much as I'd love to hook up with you, it's not feasible. Or wise."

He'd love to hook up with her. She tried to stanch her reaction to those words.

He gave her a sympathetic smile. "The love guru doesn't date? That's sad."

She debated being obtuse but decided it was better that he know she wasn't just playing hard to get. "Being involved with someone interferes with my abilities. The drama and distraction, even if things are going well, takes over my mind. All I get is noise when I read someone."

"And that terrifies you. Why?"

She really hated that he could read her. "Helping people is important to me."

"Which leads beautifully to the reason I'm waiting for you. The Caido/Deuce couple who came in and greeted you like you were their best friend, who danced together, and kissed...you helped them, didn't you?"

Kye had watched them snuggling together on the dance

floor with just a tiny bit of longing. "Sorry, client confidentiality."

He rubbed his chin. "So you did help them. The only way they could be together is by doing the Essex. I assume you know what that is."

She had been horrified and saddened to learn that the emotions Caidos picked up from others cut through them like a knife. It was a secret they held very closely, for their own well-being. Kasabian was testing her. She knew he wouldn't volunteer the information to just anyone. "That's when a Caido facilitates the exchange of his magick essence with a Dragon's or Deuce's. It's how a Caido heals other Crescents' emotional or physical pain. Unbeknownst to those Crescents, their essence has a balancing effect on him so he's not as sensitive to others' emotions. Or desires." She almost wanted to give him a *Did I get it right?* smile.

He nodded. "But it only temporarily eases his pain. So a long-term relationship would eventually deplete her essence, because he would have to do it with her every day. No self-respecting Caido would endanger someone he cares about. So how is it that they're together?"

"I can only give you a general answer. Not one specific to any couple in particular. I've come up with a way to make the Essex permanent."

He pushed away from the car, interest crackling off him as he came closer. "Tell me more."

She fought the instinct to back up a step. "I've had a few mixed-Caido couples approach me about circumventing the pain. They hadn't meant to fall in love, but now they wanted to be together. I tried several different spells and magick devices, but nothing worked."

He crossed his arms in front of him and rocked back on his heels. "And you take it very hard when you can't fix someone."

"You get that from me, too?"

"I suppose we both bear a similar burden in picking up feelings we have no business sensing. How does it work?"

She laid one of her hands on top of the other and let her fingers barely settle between each other. "With the Essex, you're limited to how much essence you can exchange, kind of the way my fingers can't slide together. That's why it's temporary. The Cobra, which I named for the tantric position, allows both essences to reach fully toward each other, like this." She laced her hands together, fingers straight so that they formed an X. "This starts the bonding process. The last step is when both parties actually pull each other's essence into their souls, permanently locking them together." Her fingers wrapped over her hands as though in prayer. "At least, I think it's permanent. The first couple did it four months ago, and it's still holding strong."

"Why haven't I heard about this magick of yours? The Caido community should be buzzing."

"I haven't made it public yet. There are some side effects I'm still working out. The Caido is bombarded by every emotion he's ever repressed. It can be intense. One Caido had to, as he put it, get deprogrammed. Another effect: the couple is emotionally bonded, perhaps permanently. And one Caido experienced a resurgence of buried memories."

Kasabian's eyes shimmered. "Buried memories?"

"It apparently caused some big problems, but he couldn't give me any details beyond that. He just wanted me to know that it happened."

He went silent for a few moments, rubbing his fingers across his mouth. "Can you do it so a Caido can simply experience desire?"

"Only if you have a committed partner who wants to be permanently bonded to you."

"That would not be a good thing. For any woman."

"Why?" The mystery of him pulled at her, the dark desire she'd sensed.

"Oh, love, there you go, needing to help even though you know you should run the other way." He lowered his chin, the streetlight reflecting off his razor-sharp jawline. "And you should. I'm forty ways fucked-up."

She swallowed. No one had ever made her this off-balance. "I do want to help. Too many messed up people are not only suffering but also inflicting their misery on others."

"I assure you that I'm not inflicting my anything on anyone." He reached out with the back of his hand and brushed it down her cheek. "As much as I'd like to."

She stumbled back, his touch curling throughout her body. "I should go."

Hunger flashed in his eyes. "Yes, you should."

Go, run, and never look back.

Chapter 2

ᐸᐧ

One more game, Mr. Grey?" one of the Youth Haven kids called out as he ran the basketball down the court.

Kasabian dropped down on the bleachers, catching his breath. "I'm done."

"Getting old, Kasabian?" one of the older kids chided.

"Yeah, thirty-two and over the hill." Of course, that was to these kids. They couldn't yet comprehend how long Crescents lived, how those years would drag on. "Five hours straight, and I can't take a break without getting harassed?" Had he been this relentless when he lived here at Youth Haven? Yeah, probably, in his eagerness for a grown-up's attention.

Most of the Haven kids were Caidos, but some were Dragon or Deuce orphans.

"I'm done, too." Daniel Portofino, another volunteer, flopped down beside him, panting. "Man, I can't believe you do this and then work until three in the morning."

"Helping out here is recreation for me." He liked giving

back to the place that had taken him in after his mother's murder when he was twelve. "Actually, so is bartending."

"I don't know how you do that either. All those emotions, people getting hot for each other, jealousy...that's got to kill you."

Even joy felt like a thousand razor blades across their souls. "I'd rather suffer than shut myself off from humanity." Kasabian wasn't about to tell anyone he craved emotions. He leaned back on the bleacher behind him. "Ever been in love, Daniel?" At his surprised look, Kasabian added, "Not seriously in love but crushing on someone even though you knew it wouldn't work? Because we're Caido."

Daniel stared at him for a long second, some odd emotion flashing behind his dark blue eyes. "Once. Long time ago. You?"

Kasabian chuckled, shaking his head. "There's this Deuce chick who hangs out at the Witch's Brew, and she's freakin' amazing."

"A *Deuce*?"

Caidos couldn't pick up each other's emotions, but Kasabian didn't need supernatural ability to see that the idea annoyed Daniel. Who cared? It felt good to talk about her. "Long blond hair, the creamiest skin I've ever seen, dresses all biker-chick in black leather and fishnets. Last night she finally danced for me, within sight of my bar. She kept checking to see if I was watching." And he was, every spare second. It had been a long time since he'd desired a woman, and then only fleetingly. With Kye, he couldn't seem to stop.

"Sounds painful. You going to act on it?"

"I have to do the Essex twice a night to dull the pain.

But wanting her is as far as it's going to go." The only thing he and Kye could ever do was exchange furtive glances.

"Smart. That kind of thing never works."

"Actually, it could." For normal Caidos, anyway. "She's a Zensu Deuce, and she's come up with a permanent Essex so the Caido is immune to his lover's emotions."

"Caidos should stick with their own."

It was easier for Caidos to get together. Desire still hurt, but with their dampened emotions, it wasn't as painful. "Yeah, and if there were plenty of Caido females, it wouldn't be a problem." Part of the curse their forbearers passed on was a lack of females in their Crescent class. At least that was the theory.

Daniel's mouth tightened, like he was preparing some kind of lecture, but his sulk turned into a speculative look. "I know a couple who might be interested in her services. What's her name?"

"Kye Rivers." Damn but he liked the way her name rolled off his tongue. "But remember, she's not offering this magick to just anyone. In fact, I probably shouldn't have mentioned it, so keep it to yourself."

"Kasabian!"

Hayden Masters approached from the end of the bleachers. He acknowledged Daniel with a nod but focused on Kasabian. "Can I talk to you for a sec?"

Kasabian pushed up, excusing himself. He bumped knuckles with the big Caido, and they headed out of the gym.

Hayden lowered his voice. "Something came up at work that you need to know about. Even though you're not supposed to know about it."

"Gotcha."

Hayden was a Vega in the Guard, the Crescent's police force. He'd shared some of his cases, mostly hunting down Crescents who broke the laws of the Hidden. Rule Number One was to never reveal the magick of the Hidden to Mundanes. Other rules focused on not using fangs, orbs, or other magick weapons on either Mundanes or Crescents. Not that everyone obeyed.

They stepped out into the humid air, the afternoon sun cooking them until they stepped beneath a tree by the tennis courts. Two Haven residents were batting a ball half-heartedly back and forth.

Hayden braced his hand against the trunk of the tree. "A five-year-old Caido boy was picked up this morning, just wandering the streets. The kid was weak, disoriented, and mute. Whatever he'd gone through traumatized him pretty bad. And he had this." He yanked up his shirt to reveal a faint gray starburst over his diaphragm.

Kasabian felt a squeeze where his own scar was. "Hell. Whoever kidnapped us more than twenty years ago is still doing it."

Kasabian remembered the group of kids who'd escaped with him, none with any memory of their captivity. Once sexual abuse had been eliminated, all they had were questions. Four years of his life, all of his captivity, were shut away in some part of his brain that no magick could touch.

Kye's voice echoed in his mind: *One Caido experienced a resurgence of buried memories.*

Buried or locked?

"Did you talk to the kid?" Kasabian asked.

"Yeah, for about three minutes. My sergeant called me in because he knows about our ordeal and recognized the scar. He thought if I showed the kid my scar, maybe he'd open up. And I think he would have, only my sergeant pulled me out of the room. He said the Concilium was taking over the investigation. Sensitive matters and some such bullshit." Hayden smacked the tree, making leaves float down. "Within minutes, the kid's gone, lost in the system."

"Who gave the order?"

"My boss didn't say a name, but I could tell he wasn't happy about it. You know how it is with the Guard. There's a lot of stuff we aren't privy to. We don't always know the Guard's motives, and the Concilium is even murkier."

"Hell, we don't even know who's on the Concilium, and they're supposed to be representing us." The United Nations of magick beings was headed by old Crescents, meeting in covert locations and more concerned about keeping the Hidden secret than anything else.

"My guess is that someone knows what these marks mean. Wouldn't be the first time something was covered up *to protect society*," Hayden added with finger quotes.

"Five years old. So damned young for being used like...well, however the hell they were using us." Kasabian shook his head in disgust. "Younger than when we were taken." Kasabian spotted Daniel coming outside and turned away, making it obvious that he and Hayden were in the middle of a private discussion. The guy was always following him around.

"If it's like last time, the bastards are taking kids from hookers or drugged-out mothers who either are taking a payoff or are too scared to report their kid missing." A shadow passed over Hayden's features.

When they were able to track down the mothers, they

got a story about how some government official had offered to send the boy to a camp and get him away from the situation while the mother cleaned her life up. Pressure had a way of cracking people with magick. Crescents worried about being incinerated by Dragons, stalked by demons, hurt by spells.

Living in solitude often got to Caidos, and some lost their way, falling to the lure of a drug called Abyss. It was a highly addictive mix of heroin and magick that blocked the pain of emotions. Like addicts in the Mundane world, they'd do anything for another hit, including selling their bodies. And their babies. Kasabian and Hayden spent a lot of their free time getting those kids into Haven.

Hayden pushed away from the tree. "I'm going to see if the sketch artist can draw the boy; then I'll see if anyone knows him. I'll let you know what I find."

"I'll check around, too." Kasabian bypassed the courts to avoid Daniel and get inside.

Cory, one of the guys who ran Haven, was going over some details for the middle school kids' overnight trip to the Everglades. Cory looked up. "I keep expecting the headmaster of the Deuce Academy, who's coordinating things on their end, to postpone the trip, what with all the talk of the solar storm effects hitting as early as Thursday. Even the Mundane news is reporting on possible GPS distortion and electronic outages. We'll feel it in deeper ways. Some of the younger Caidos are already experiencing headaches and 'bad feelings.'"

"We've weathered them in the past. We'll get through this one." The solar storm was the least of Kasabian's concerns. "Have you heard about kids going missing recently?"

"I hear things here and there, but nothing definitive. Rumors. You know Lyle?"

"Skinny Caido with the choppy hair? Came here, what, a year ago? Keeps to himself."

Cory nodded. "He's barely hanging on to his required grades. I've suspected him of running drugs, maybe Abyss. I hate to even think it, a twelve-year-old doing that. Caught him sneaking out a few times, though I couldn't find anything on him but a bunch of pictures of the same kid. His missing brother, he said. I wasn't sure if he was telling the truth or using it as a cover."

Kasabian found Lyle at a computer in the library. The kid quickly closed the browser screen, a suspicious move. Kasabian decided not to call him on it, turning a chair at the next computer around and sitting down backward. Despite that it was obvious that Kasabian was there to talk to him, Lyle opened a new screen and pulled up one of the curriculum programs, studiously ignoring him. His eyes were bloodshot, face gaunt.

"You came from the Vale, didn't you?" Kasabian asked, finally getting the kid's attention. The Vale was a run-down area populated by all the addicts.

"Yeah." Lyle kept his gaze on the computer screen, but he was working really hard to do it.

"I'm investigating some disappearances. Have you heard anything about kids going missing from there?"

Lyle turned to him, his mouth working. He pulled back whatever words he was going to say and affected a nonchalant shrug. "Kids disappeared, yeah. Went to some kind of camp but never came back. Not that it mattered, because the mothers moved."

That surprised Kasabian. "The mothers left the area?"

"It was some kind of government assistance thing. Crescent government. We were *told* that the kids went to their family's new residence."

Kasabian rubbed his mouth and considered what angle to use. "But they lied." Not a question. "How do you know?"

The kid was clearly in a war with himself: tell the nosy guy the truth or distrust him as he did everyone else.

Kasabian knew how he felt. Sharing didn't come easy for him either, but he needed to if he was going to get anywhere. "I was kidnapped when I was eight. I was lucky. I escaped. The people who took me, I think they're still taking kids. I want to stop them."

Lyle's expression slowly revealed his pain. "My brother went to a camp a year ago. They said I was too old to go with him."

"How old was your brother?"

"Four."

"And you never saw him again."

Lyle chewed his lip, his eyes staring at nothing. Finally he shook his head. "We moved to the Bend soon after."

The Bend. Kasabian had heard about the gated community that housed middle- and low-income Crescent families, especially single mothers. It was touted as being safe and claimed to educate those mothers so they could support their families. And get off drugs.

"They never returned your brother," Kasabian said gently.

"They said three months. Then it was six months. I told Mom we shouldn't have left the Vale. What if they brought him back there? She said they knew where we were. She didn't even…"

"Seem concerned?" Kasabian finished, guessing.

Lyle's mouth tightened as he held back the outrage and grief. He merely shook his head.

Because she knew the kid wasn't coming back.

"She kept talking about how nice our apartment, our life, was," Lyle whispered. "Finally she admitted that Jonathan had been adopted by another family." Lyle met Kasabian's gaze with a fierce expression. "I accused her of selling him, and I could tell I was right. I ran away and came here."

The pieces were coming together. "You sneak out to the Vale to search for him."

Lyle searched Kasabian's face, sensing whether he could trust him. Finally he nodded.

"Can I help you?"

"No. But thanks. I can do it on my own."

Just like Kasabian, not wanting to involve anyone else. The poor kid had been dealing with this alone, driving himself to exhaustion.

"I understand. No one cares about your situation like you do. But sometimes you need help, even when you don't want it. Or trust it. Sometimes what you're after is more important than doing it on your own. I'm going to look into this. If I run across your brother, it would be helpful if I had a picture of him."

Lyle pulled out his worn nylon wallet and extracted one of many color copies. On the back was the boy's name, age, height, and weight, along with the date he'd gone missing. The boys looked nothing alike, Jonathan with straight brown hair while Lyle's was dark blond. Lyle's face was lean and sharp, Jonathan's round, his eyes soulful.

Kasabian ran his thumb along the edge of the photographic copy paper. "Thanks."

"I should be thanking you."

"Don't thank me yet."

Kasabian left Lyle in the library, feeling the unease his sympathy caused in his body. He let it come as he gathered information from both the kids and the counselors. Nothing conclusive, just tidbits here and there that added up. One kid was thought to have drowned in a canal. No body was ever recovered. One kid wandered off and was never seen again.

Kasabian found Cory on the worn-out chair in front of his desk. "Lyle's not running drugs. He's trying to find his little brother. Give him space, okay?"

Kasabian saw Cory's reaction in a quick-fire burst: surprise, guilt, and then a nod. He didn't stick around to feel or say more. Cory would have questions—shit, so did he—but answers, well, he was painfully short on those.

You have the answers...

Right. Buried deep in the recesses of his mind. He rubbed the scar on his chest.

Years of counseling and interrogations had failed to unlock the part of his mind that imprisoned the memories of his childhood abduction. A burning jolt spiraled from the pit of his stomach. Kasabian was no stranger to pain. His Caido heritage was as much a part of him as his jacked-up childhood was. Oh, he knew he'd never be "right." It was too late to save himself, but he could help these kids. Get to the bottom of the abductions and put a stop to them once and for all.

Good thing for him he knew a chick from a bar with just the kind of magick he needed.

Kye's sexy, empathic magick was too dangerous for someone with his...personality. But she possessed the magick he needed to unleash the repressed memories in his mind.

He'd vowed to stay away from her. But now he needed to get close. Very, very close.

Chapter 3

Y ou want me to do *what*?"

Kye stared across her table at Kasabian, where he'd sat after closing his bar. She was sure that the echo of the night's pounding music was distorting his words.

"It's not a want. I need to do the Cobra with you."

His words catapulted through her body. "Just so you can lust without pain? No way."

No longer in the tight shirt encouraged by Mike for the purposes of being eye candy, Kasabian wore one of those urban shirts with angel wings on the back. He smelled like limes, clean and citrusy. "My request isn't about lust. You said one Caido recovered buried memories."

"Yeah." She drew the word out, now completely unsure where he was going.

"When I was eight, I was kidnapped and spent four years in captivity. I escaped, along with four other children. Three of them were Deuce or Dragon, and they were so weak they were nearly dead. I heard they survived, but I never saw them again. There were two of us Caidos."

He unbuttoned his shirt and pulled it apart to reveal what looked like a gray starburst tattoo at his solar plexus. "Whatever they did to us left these scars...and made us crave feelings. What they did to the other kids nearly depleted their essences. The problem is, we don't know anything because they memory-locked us. That's a Caido ability to lock away memories of a specific period of time or event. So when you mentioned that the Caido's buried memories returned, you got my attention." He buttoned his shirt again.

This was not at all what Kye expected. A proposal, a desperate and selfish plea, but not children in danger. She saw the pain of what he'd gone through and his fear for those kids. "I'm sorry that happened to you, but doing the Cobra just to revive those memories, well, I can't even guarantee it will work. And if we bond, I have no idea how to unbond."

"I dismissed approaching you for those reasons. But now there's more at stake. The Caido who escaped with me works for the Guard. Hayden told me a boy was found with the same mark." Kasabian touched the starburst through his shirt. "He may have escaped from the same people who had us. Before Hayden could get the traumatized kid to talk, he was whisked away by someone connected to the Concilium. Whatever the people who took us all those years ago were doing...they're doing it again. There are secondhand stories about Crescent social workers taking kids to camps so the mothers can get back on track. No one ever hears from either again."

Kids taken from their homes and nearly starved to

death? Kye shuddered. Who knew what other horrors those young children were exposed to? She looked at Kasabian, really looked at him. For a moment, she was tempted to pry, to delve deep, to glimpse the pain he'd endured.

He raked a hand through his hair. "Because of the Concilium's involvement, we don't know whom to trust. We have to figure it out on our own. Hayden's working on finding the boy. If I can remember anything from our captivity, it might help us figure out who's behind this. Will you do the Cobra with me? I've done the Essex enough to know how to control it. Once you set your magick in place, we touch, back off, and hope it's enough to trigger the return of my memories. I promise not to take in your essence."

She thought of the boy, of children in danger, and found herself saying, "Okay."

"Tonight. Now."

Her fingers curled in the fabric of her skirt. "I always perform it at the Caido's residence so he'll be comfortable. The bombardment is pretty intense. I always monitor that part. His girlfriend stays with him through the night in case anything happens. Is there someone who can stay with you?"

Kasabian shook his head. "I'll handle it."

"You don't know what there is to handle."

Kye followed his yellow Lotus all the way to SoBe— South Beach.

Why am I doing this? Her fingers tightened on the steering wheel as she pulled into the parking lot of an old Florida-style apartment complex. *Children. I'm doing this for the children.*

Kasabian gestured to a parking spot, then pulled his Lotus into one farther down. She slid out of her jacket, folded it, and laid it in the trunk of her BMW coupe. The black and red patch with vampire fangs was on top, an ominous portent. She quickly shed her fishnets and black boots, changing into black and red flip-flops.

Kasabian rested his hand on her shoulder as he guided her through a gated entrance into a lush courtyard. The pool was lit, and a few people lounged around. They all greeted Kasabian and gave her a curious look. One couple was getting all kissy-face in the corner of the pool. The woman's nervousness glowed a pale yellow and made Kye's stomach churn a little as it reached for her. It was not dissimilar to her mother's gift of mediumship, as she described it, the way spirits sensed and migrated to a receptive soul. In Kye's case, those emotions sought her out as a willing receptacle. She closed the psychic door.

They took the stairs to the second level. Kasabian unlocked the door and gestured for her to precede him. He flicked a switch, and three corner torchieres threw soft light over the living area. Nice place, with dark wood floors and moss green walls and plants all over in dark wicker baskets.

He waved toward a dry bar in the corner. "Want a Whis-Kye?"

"Maybe just a splash of whiskey straight up."

Her gaze went to a picture of a little boy clipped by an alligator magnet to his stainless steel fridge. He had haunted eyes and a smile he was obviously forcing for the photographer's sake. She walked closer to it. "Is this the boy who was found?"

Kasabian stepped up behind her, his presence nearly overwhelming. "No. This is a boy who's been missing for a year. He's the younger brother of one of the kids at the youth home where I volunteer. I want to find him." He stared at the picture, anger and pain in eyes that were now more hazel than green. The shade of whiskey. "I need to find him in a way I can't explain. Like it's eating at my soul." He tapped the photograph. "Maybe it's because I imagine my mother looking at my picture the way Lyle, this boy's brother, looks at his."

He handed her a glass of amber liquid, dark gold in the ambient light. She took it, inhaling the smoky scent. He started making an absinthe, pouring water over a melting sugar cube into a glass of opaque green liquid. The menthol aroma filled her nose and made her eyes water.

She leaned against the black granite counter and watched him. "Every Caido who's done the Cobra had one of those first."

He lifted his glass up, and when she touched hers to it, he said, "Here's to liquid courage."

Kye felt no speck of courage as she threw back her splash and a half. *You have control over this.*

He finished his drink and came to stand in front of her. "Tell me what to do."

He was at her mercy. It gave her a weird sense of power she'd never felt before. "The Caidos dropped fast once the process was complete, so you want to be on carpet. The bombardment lasts anywhere from one to two hours and then you pretty much pass out for the night. The Caido who recovered his memories woke with them the next morning."

"Hopefully it won't be as bad for me. I haven't stuffed back my emotions as much. In fact, I crave them: joy, heartache, jealousy, anything. That's why I work in a club, so I can soak them all in."

"But don't they hurt you?"

"I have to do the Essex once a night to manage the pain. It's a fair trade. My essence temporarily eases a Crescent's heartache, and theirs eases mine."

Now she understood that strange twist of emotions she'd picked up from him that first time.

He gave her a soft smile. "And you want to know why."

She started to say no, that it was none of her business. Might as well be honest. "Of course."

"I think it has something to do with what they were doing to me while I was being held captive. Hayden feels the same."

"So that's why you're different." Finally, she had an answer.

His smile darkened. "Part of it."

Great. *Part* of an answer.

"Get comfortable," she said.

He raised an eyebrow. "That usually means being naked."

The mental picture of him standing naked in front of her sent an odd tingling right down to the core of her belly. She blinked, pushing it away. "Stop that," she said to both him and her wild imagination.

"Just saying." He stripped out of his shirt, which made his pecs and biceps move in all kinds of interesting ways, and tossed it on the couch. His torso was golden tanned, caramel male perfection. He undid the top button of his jeans, kicked off his shoes, and stood in the middle of the rug. "You going to catch me when I fall?"

Her gaze, which had centered on the faint hairline that went down to those undone jeans, snapped to eyes with a smile in them. She almost said, *I could ask the same of you.* Whoa, where had that thought come from?

"I'll try." With a hard swallow, Kye stepped up in front of him. "How does the Essex work on your end? Can you see the exchange?"

"No, I feel it like a blind man pulling taffy, pulling their essence toward me, sending mine into them." He demonstrated, weaving his long fingers through the air that reminded her more of an orchestra leader. Watching, with his words wrapping around her mind, sent a shiver through her body.

She cleared her throat. "You'll send your essence out to me. Then I'll take over. Close your eyes and get into the same state you get into just before you do the Essex."

He held out his hands. "We need to connect physically."

His hands slid against hers, his fingers locking around her wrists. Why did his touch always jolt her deep inside? He blinked, obviously feeling it, too.

"Close your eyes," she ordered, completely unnerved and unable to tear her gaze from his. When he complied, she studied him for a moment, the planes of his cheeks, the thickness of his lashes. Friggin' gorgeous. It seemed surreal, him standing in front of her like this, them about to do this.

She closed her eyes and summoned her magick. It manifested as a beautiful column of dark pink. Then she pulled her own deep yellow essence toward the column. "Send your essence to me." In her mind's eye, cool, silvery smoke floated toward hers, and she directed it toward the column as well. "We're going to start with the Essex, our essences just touching."

When they did, even that mere brush took her breath away. She focused on the pink column, sending it to wrap around their essences. It required a part of her, that small extension of her essence, but nothing too intense. Here was that sought-after addictive state where a Caido could feel without pain.

But Kye was beginning to "feel" something, too.

Kasabian's essence was powerful, his magick strong and compelling and...sexy. It spiraled in languid, sensuous circles, and her essence began to wind around his of its own volition.

A slow smile spread across his handsome face. "Damn, I wish we were doing this for different reasons." His eyes opened for a moment, glowing brightly with such blatant hunger, it made parts of her ache. "This feels incredible with you."

Better than with anyone else? she wanted to ask. *No, don't ask.*

"Like a sensual dance," she heard herself saying. She was a Zensu Deuce, versed in sexual pathos and magick. She knew the chemistry between them was rare. But that was a path she could *not* tread. She caught herself physically leaning closer to him, too, and pulled back her body and her essence with a soft inhalation. "Which it shouldn't. Close your eyes and focus."

"Don't worry, Kye. I know it's not about that." He tightened his hold on her. "I won't do that to us."

This wasn't about sex, wasn't about *them*. She recalled the photo on Kasabian's refrigerator.

"Do you remember when I showed you how the Cobra worked using my hands? Right now our essences are resting against each other, the way my fingers laid on top of each other. We're going to the next step now. Our essences are going to slide together like my fingers did, but remaining straight like an X." She felt the sensuality of the two colors sliding against each other throughout her body. Lord, but she wanted to let them intertwine, the way her body wanted to intertwine with "We can't go to the final step. Let's stay here for a few seconds and see if that will trigger the bombardment."

Mmm, it felt good in a way that it shouldn't. Like lying naked in bed with an achingly beautiful man and not being able to make love to him. Heat began to generate wherever their essences touched, slowly filling her entire essence.

"I think it's beginning," she said on a soft breath. "I don't know exactly how it feels, since I haven't done it myself, but my subjects reported heat right before things got going."

His fingers tightened on hers. "Yeah, I feel it, too, heat and pressure building inside me. And..." His voice dropped to both a puzzled and concerned tone. "Something else."

Like a sudden storm, his essence darkened and whipped into a fury. Its tendrils grabbed on to hers. She tried to pull back, but he pulled harder. *No!* His hold tightened, surrounding her completely. In the same moment it felt seductively powerful and suffocating. Heat exploded between them, and she lost all sense of where he ended and where she began. *No!* She struggled, both psychically and physically, to free herself. She stumbled back, landing bottom-first on the coffee table. She was free of him. Except...no, she wasn't. She felt him inside her.

He'd bonded them.

Her eyes snapped open. He dropped to the floor, caught up in his trauma. She wanted to grab his shirt and demand that he release her, but he was lost to her now. But she wasn't helpless. She slapped her hand on his chest and summoned her magick again. *Come on, come on.* The pink column formed in her mind's eye, but her yellow was twisted with dark silver and then it vanished. She psychically groped for it, but she couldn't muster the power to pull it back.

He had broken his promise!

As much as she wanted to run, she couldn't leave him alone. She watched him arch in pain, fingers digging into the carpet. So many emotions roared through him like a freight train that she couldn't single any one out. She sank down beside him, her hand on his shoulder for support even as she wanted to scratch his eyes out.

She had never seen that darkness in a Caido's essence before. It scared her, even more so because a mystifying wanting pulsed through her. Part of what made him very different, and no doubt forty ways fucked-up—the part he hadn't told her about—was now bonded with her.

THE DISH

Where Authors Give You the Inside Scoop

♥ ♥ ♥ ♥ ♥ ♥ ♥ ♥ ♥ ♥ ♥ ♥ ♥ ♥ ♥ ♥

From the desk of Jaime Rush

Dear Reader,

Enemies to lovers is a concept I've always loved. Yes, it's a challenge, and maybe that's what I like most. It's a given that the couple is going to have instant chemistry—it is a romance, after all! But they're going to fight it harder because they have history and a good reason. Each person believes they're in the right.

That's how Kade Kavanaugh feels. Being a member of the Guard, my supernatural world's police force, he has had plenty of run-ins with Violet Castanega's family. They live in the Fringe, a wild and uncivilized community of Dragon shifters who think they are on the fringe of the law as well. And mostly they are, except when their illegal activities threaten to catch the attention of the Muds, the Mundane human police. Because Rule Number One is simple: Never reveal the existence of the Hidden community that has existed amid the glitter and glamour of Miami for over three hundred years. Mundanes would panic if they knew that Crescents—humans who hold the essence of Dragons, sorcerers (like Kade), and fallen angels—lived among them.

Violet is fiercely loyal to her Dragon clan, even if it does sometimes flout the law. But when one of her brothers is murdered by a Dragon bent on firing up the clan wars, she has no choice but to go to the Guard for help. There she encounters Kade, whom she attacked the last time he tried to arrest her brother.

My job as a writer is to throw these two unsuspecting people together in ways that will test their loyalties and their integrity. And definitely test their resolve to resist getting involved with not only a member of another class of Crescent, but a sworn enemy to boot. Juicy conflict, hot passion, and supernatural action—a combination that truly tested my hero and heroine. But their biggest lesson is never to judge someone by their name, their heritage, or their actions. I think that's a good lesson for all of us.

We all have magic in our imaginations. Mine has always contained murder, mayhem, and romance. Feel free to wander through the madness of my mind any time. A good place to start is my website www.jaimerush.com, or that of my romantic suspense alter-ego, www.tinawainscott.com.

Jaime Rush

♥ ♥ ♥ ♥ ♥ ♥ ♥ ♥ ♥ ♥ ♥ ♥ ♥ ♥ ♥

From the desk of Kristen Ashley

Dear Reader,

While writing MOTORCYCLE MAN I was in a very dark time of my life. An *extended* dark time, which is very rare. Indeed, it's only ever happened that once.

In fact, I wrote nearly an entirely different book for my hero, Tack. He had a different heroine. And it had a different plot. Completely. But it didn't work for me and it has never seen the light of day. I abandoned it totally (something I've never done), gave it time, and started anew.

I had thought it was rubbish. Of course, on going back and reading it later, I realize it wasn't. I actually think it's great. It just wasn't Tack. And the heroine was not right for him. But never fear, I like it enough; when I have time (whenever that is in this decade), I intend to rework it and release it, because that hero and heroine's story really should be told.

Nevertheless, when I finally found the dream woman who would belong to Kane "Tack" Allen in MOTOR-CYCLE MAN, I was still questioning my work because things in life weren't going so great.

You see, sometimes I battle my characters. Sometimes they urge me to take risks I feel I'm not ready to take. Sometimes they encourage me to glide along an edge that's a little scary even as it is thrilling. And when life is also scary, your confidence gets shaken in a way it's tough to bounce back from.

But Kane "Tack" Allen is an edgy, risky guy, so he was pretty adamant (as he can be) that he wanted me to just let go and ride it with him. Not only that, but lift up my hands and enjoy the hell out of that ride.

But as I was writing it, I still fought him. Particularly the scene in Tyra's office early on in the book, where they have a misunderstanding and Tack decides to make his feelings perfectly clear and in order to do that, he gets Tyra's attention in a way that's utterly unacceptable.

I fretted about this scene, but Tack refused to let me soften it. I even sent it to my girl, a girl who knows me and my writing inside and out. If I remember correctly, her response was that it was indeed shocking, but I should go with it.

Ride it out.

In releasing MOTORCYCLE MAN, I was very afraid that my life had negatively affected my writing and the risks Tack urged me to take would not be well received.

As you can imagine, I was absolutely *elated* when I found I'd done the right thing. When Tack and Tyra swiftly became one of my most popular couples. That Tack had rightly encouraged me to trust in myself, my instincts, my writing, and give myself to my characters to let them be precisely what they were, let them shine, not water them down, and last, give my readers the honesty. They could take it. Because it was genuine. It came from the soul.

It was real.

And because of all this, MOTORCYCLE MAN will always hold a firm place in my heart. Because that novel and Kane "Tack" Allen gave me the freedom I was searching for. The freedom to ride this wave. Ride it wild. Ride it free.

Lift up my hands and ride it being nothing but me.

Kristen Ashley

❤ ❤ ❤ ❤ ❤ ❤ ❤ ❤ ❤ ❤ ❤ ❤ ❤ ❤ ❤

From the desk of Christie Craig

Dear Reader,

Here are two things about love I took from my own life and used in TEXAS HOLD 'EM:

1. Love can make us stupid.

   Sexy PI Austin Brook is a smooth-talking good ol' boy Texan. Where women are concerned, he wings it. Why not? He's got charm to spare. But one glance at Leah Reece and he's a stumbling, bumbling idiot. First he accidentally blows his horn as she's passing in front of his truck, causing her to toss up her arms and drop her groceries. Wanting to help, he snatches up a plastic bag containing a broken bottle of wine and manages to douse Leah with Cabernet from the waist up. And since he likes wine and wet T-shirt contests, it only makes her more appealing and him more nervous.

   For myself? On a first date with a good ol' Texan, we were both jittery. I'd dressed up in a short skirt. The guy, thinking he should be a gentleman, pulled my chair out in the crowded restaurant. I had my bottom almost in the seat when he moved it out. *Way out.* *He* might've looked like a gentleman, but there was nothing ladylike about how I went down. All the way to the floor, legs sprawled out, skirt up to my yin-yang. Laughter filled the room. Snickering in spite of his apologetic look, he added, "Nice legs."

Later when he dropped me off at my apartment, I struggled to get the door of his sports car open. Forever the gentlemen—hey, that's Texans for you—he rushed to open my door, and then shut it. Standing close, he heard my moan, and completely misunderstood. He dipped in for a kiss.

I stopped him. "Can you open the car door?"

"Why?" he asked.

I moaned again. "Because my hand's still in the door."

With a bruised butt, and three busted fingernails, I eventually did let him score a kiss. It's amazing I married that man.

2. Love is scary.

Divorced, and a single mother, I wasn't looking for love when I met Mr. Craig. Life had taught me that love can hurt. And I'm not talking about a sore backside or fingernails. I'm talking about the heart.

Neither Austin nor Leah is open to love. Isn't that what makes it so perfect and yet still so dad-blasted frightening? We don't find love; love finds us. And like me, Leah's and Austin's pasts have left them leery.

At age six, Leah realized her daddy had another family, one he obviously loved better because they had his name and he called that home. Oh, when older, she still gave love a shot, got married, expected the happily-ever-after, and instead got a divorce and a credit card bill for all his phone sex. It's not that Leah doesn't believe in love; she just doesn't trust herself to know the real thing.

Austin, abandoned by his mother at age three, passed from one foster home to another, and learned caring about people gave them power to hurt you. His last and final (he swears) heartache happened when his fiancé dumped him after he got convicted of a murder he didn't commit.

As scary as love is, Leah and Austin give it another shot. Not to give away any spoilers, but I think it'll work out fine for them. I know it has for me. I'll soon be celebrating my thirtieth wedding anniversary. So here's to laughter, good books, and getting knocked on your butt by love.

Happy reading!

Christie Craig

♥ ♥ ♥ ♥ ♥ ♥ ♥ ♥ ♥ ♥ ♥ ♥ ♥ ♥ ♥ ♥

From the desk of Laura Drake

Dear Reader,

There's just something about the soft side of a hard man that I've never been able to resist—how about you?

Max Jameson looks like a modern-day Marlboro Man. He's a western cattleman, meaning he's stubborn, hard-working, and an eternal optimist. But given his current problems, there's not enough duct tape in all of Colorado to fix them.

To introduce you to the heroine of NOTHING

SWEETER, Aubrey Madison (aka Bree Tanner), I thought I'd share with you her list of life lessons:

1. Nothing is sweeter than freedom.
2. It is impossible to outrun your own conscience.
3. "When you're going through hell, keep going." —Winston Churchill
4. There are more kinds of family than blood kin.
5. A stuck-up socialite can make a pretty good friend when the chips are on the table.
6. Real men (and bulls) wear pink.
7. "To forgive is to set a prisoner free, and discover that the prisoner is you." —Louis B. Smede

I hope you'll enjoy NOTHING SWEETER. Keep your eyes open for a cameo of JB and Charla from *The Sweet Spot*, and watch for them all to turn up in *Sweet on You*, the last book in the series!

♥ ♥ ♥ ♥ ♥ ♥ ♥ ♥ ♥ ♥ ♥ ♥ ♥ ♥ ♥ ♥

From the desk of Rebecca Zanetti

Dear Reader,

I met my husband camping when we were about eight years old, and he taught me how to play Red Rover so he could hold my hand. He was a sweet, chubby, brown-eyed boy. We lost touch, and years later, I walked into a bar (yeah, a bar), and there he was. Except this time, he was six-foot-five, muscled, with dark hair, a tattoo, a leather jacket, and held a motorcycle helmet under one hand. To put it simply, I was intrigued. He's still the sweet guy but has a bit of an edge. Now we're married and have two kids, two dogs, and a crazy cat.

People change...and often we don't know them as well as we think we do. In fact, I've always been fascinated by the idea that we never truly know what's in the minds or even the pasts of the people around us. What if your best friend worked for the CIA years ago? Or the mild-mannered janitor at your child's elementary school is a retired Marine sniper who didn't like retirement and has found a good way to fill his life with joy? What if your baby sister was a criminal informant in college?

What if the calm and always-in-control man you married is one of the deadliest men alive?

And what if you're now being threatened by an outside source? What happens to that calm control now? That was the main premise for FORGOTTEN SINS. Josie Dean, a woman with a lonely past, married Shane Dean in a whirlwind of passion and energy. Then he disappeared two years ago. The story starts with him back in her life, with danger surrounding him, and with the edge he'd always partially hidden finally exposed.

Of course, Shane has amnesia, and in his discovery of finding himself, he reveals himself to the one woman he ever truly loved. He'd always held back, always treated her with kid gloves.

Now, not knowing his deadly training, there's no holding back. The primal, arousing man she'd believed existed has to take the forefront as he protects them from the danger stalking him from his past. Yeah, he'd always been fun and sexy...with hints of dominance in the bedroom. Now the hints disappear to unveil the true Shane Dean—the man Josie hoped she'd married.

I hope you truly enjoy Shane and Josie's story.

Best,

Rebecca Zanetti

RebeccaZanetti.com
Twitter, @RebeccaZanetti
Facebook.com/RebeccaZanetti.Author.FanPage

♥ ♥ ♥ ♥ ♥ ♥ ♥ ♥ ♥ ♥ ♥ ♥ ♥ ♥

From the desk of Kate Meader

Dear Reader,

FEEL THE HEAT is the first in my smokin' Hot in the Kitchen series, about an Italian restaurant–owning family and the sexy, sizzling chefs who love them. And don't we all want a hotter-than-Hades, caring, alpha chef like Jack Kilroy in our lives? A man who cooks, defends his lady, and knows how to treat her right both in the kitchen *and* in the bedroom is worth his weight in focaccia (and the British accent doesn't hurt). But sometimes we've got to work with what the gods have given us. So if you have a husband/boyfriend/sex slave who believes guy cooking = grilling, but outside of the summer months, you won't catch him dead in an apron, read on.

"But he just makes a mess" or "I'm a better cook," I

hear you whine. Who cares? The benefits to encouraging your man to cook are multifold.

1. Guys who cook know how to multitask. If he can watch a couple of bubbling pots, chop those herbs, and pour you a glass of wine, all while *you* put your feet up, it'll eventually translate to other areas. Childcare, taking out the trash, maybe even doing the dishes as he whips up that *coq au vin*.

    Guys who cook know how to get creative. You might ask your man: "Is this made with sour cream, babe?"

    Cue worry crease on guy's brow that looks so adorable. "No, I didn't have any so I used Greek yogurt instead. Does it taste okay?"

    Hold praise for a beat "That's so creative, babe, and less fattening."

    (Positive reinforcement is key during the early training phase.)

2. Guys who cook have a direct correlation to a woman's TBR list. He's brought you that glass of Pinot and he's back in the kitchen where he belongs. Now you can get down to the important stuff—making a dent in your stories about fictional boyfriends who probably cook better than your guy. (In the case of Jack Kilroy, Shane Doyle, and Tad DeLuca, the sexy heroes of the Hot in the Kitchen series, this conclusion is a given.)

3. Guys who cook will evolve into guys who shop for groceries. Nuff said.

4. Guys who cook make better lovers. Chefs have very skillful hands, often callused and scarred from years

of kitchen abuse. Those fast-moving, rough hands are going to take your sexytimes to the next level! As long as your guy is burning himself while he learns, it can only be beneficial to you further down the road.

So get your guy in an apron and let the good times roll. Remember, chefs do it better...

Happy cooking, eating, and reading!

Kate Meader

www.katemeader.com

Find out more about Forever Romance!

Visit us at
www.hachettebookgroup.com/publishing_forever.aspx

Find us on Facebook
http://www.facebook.com/ForeverRomance

Follow us on Twitter
http://twitter.com/ForeverRomance

NEW AND UPCOMING TITLES

Each month we feature our new titles
and reader favorites.

CONTESTS AND GIVEAWAYS

We give away galleys, autographed copies,
and all kinds of exclusive items.

AUTHOR INFO

You'll find bios, articles, and links to personal websites
for all your favorite authors—and so much more.

GET SOCIAL

Connect with your favorite authors, editors, and
other Forever fans, and share what's important to you.

THE BUZZ

Sign up for our monthly romance newsletter,
and be the first to read all about it.